⟲ S0-ACQ-090

THE
YOUNG
SAVAGES

Fred Mustard Stewart

TOR®

A TOM DOHERTY ASSOCIATES BOOK
NEW YORK

As always, for my wife, Joan.

This is a work of fiction. All the characters and events portrayed in this book are either products of the author's imagination or are used fictitiously.

THE YOUNG SAVAGES

A Tor Book
Published by Tom Doherty Associates, Inc.
175 Fifth Avenue
New York, NY 10010

Tor Books on the World Wide Web:
http://www.tor.com

Tor® is a registered trademark of Tom Doherty Associates, Inc.

ISBN: 0-812-57194-0
Library of Congress Card Catalog Number: 97-40423

First edition: February 1998
First mass market edition: April 1999

Printed in the United States of America

0 9 8 7 6 5 4 3 2 1

My thanks to my agent, Peter Lampack, and my editor, Claire Eddy, for their excellent suggestions. I would also like to thank Mitch Krevat for his advice on Judaism, and Chris O'Loughlin, captain of the fencing team of the New York Athletic Club, for his expertise on fencing.

PART ONE

THE WILD WEST

1. Julie Savage was beautiful, wildly in love, and, at the age of twenty-seven, rather desperate to get married.

"Oh, Momma," she exclaimed as she examined her reflection in the full-length mirror in her second-floor bedroom of her father's Fifth Avenue mansion, "I think Norman is going to propose to me tonight! I feel it in my bones! And of course I'm going to say 'yes'—I'm not going to be one bit coy. At my age, one can't afford to be coy."

"Dear Julie, you worry far too much about your age," said Fiammetta, who was standing beside her stepdaughter. Fiammetta could speak bravely about age, but she consistently fudged about her own, clinging to the fiction that she was only thirty-nine. "You're a lovely, cultivated girl who most men would be lucky to marry."

"Then why haven't any of them asked? And you know as well as I. But Norman doesn't seem to care. Isn't he the most beautiful man in the world, as well as the most intelligent and charming and . . ."

"Yes, yes," Fiammetta interrupted, examining the gorgeous white ball gown she had bought for Julie at A. T. Stewart and Company, the largest department store in the country. "Norman is a paragon, a very bright young man with a great future. But Julie, dear, don't count your rabbits before they hatch."

"Chickens," Julie corrected, giggling. After twenty years living, on and off, in New York, the Italian-born Fiammetta still sometimes butchered her English. The fact that her son, Johnny Savage, had an Italian mother had made him something of an exotic at Harvard, where his class of 1880 had been mostly Protestant. But the fact that Fiammetta was a countess had softened the blow. Fiammetta had wanted Johnny to go to college in Europe—either the University of Bologna, or Oxford or Cambridge. But her husband, Justin Savage, had insisted on an American college, so the compromise had been Harvard. But the fight had increased the tensions in the marriage between Justin and Fiammetta, a marriage that had once been one of the great love stories of nineteenth-century New York.

"Chickens," Fiammetta said with a shrug. "Norman may not propose tonight, so don't count on it."

Julie turned on her stepmother, her fascinating amber eyes flashing with anger.

"Why would you say that? I know he loves me! He's always trying to touch me, hold my hand, kiss me . . . and I love him! I'm crazy about him! Why are you always so cynical about everything?"

Fiammetta put her hand on Julie's shoulder, which she had allowed her to expose with the ball gown's daring décolletage.

"Julie," she said, "I'm only trying to save you from being disappointed. I'm sure Norman is in love with you, but his parents are very . . ." She searched for the diplomatic word. Norman Prescott's father, a wealthy stockbroker on Wall Street, was a notorious snob. ". . . conservative, and Walter Prescott has a strong influence over his son."

"It's because I'm half-Chinese!" Julie blurted out. "You think because of that they'd object to me! Isn't that right?"

"We have to be realistic . . ."

"Norman's not like that! I swear it! All the other awful, snobby men in New York may stay away from me because my eyes are different from theirs, but Norman won't. You'll see! He loves me and I love him, and love will win in the end."

"I hope you're right . . ."

The door to the large bedroom opened, and Justin Savage came in. It was an icy December night in 1882. Unlike Fiammetta, Justin admitted to being forty-four, but Julie still thought he was the most handsome man in the world—aside from Norman. Justin, who was wearing white tie and tails, smiled at the daughter he had sired with the exotic Chinese pirate, Chang-mei, and whose freedom from the rascally Dowager Empress of China he had bought at such great expense.

"Julie," he said, "you look beautiful. Except . . ." he looked at Fiammetta, "don't you think that dress is a little low?"

"Papa, it's what all the girls are wearing, so don't you try and ruin my night for me too."

"Who's trying to ruin your night?" Justin asked, coming across the flowered Axminster carpet to kiss his daughter's forehead.

"Momma. She says Norman won't propose to me tonight, and I know he will."

"I didn't say he won't," Fiammetta said, with some annoyance. "I just said one never knows about young men. And with this ghastly weather, it will be a miracle if anyone comes tonight at all. By the way," she said to her husband, "young Teddy Roosevelt and his wife are coming after all. He thought he might have to be in Albany—though what in God's name anyone in his right mind would be doing in Albany in this weather!—but the meeting of the Assembly was canceled."

"I'm glad of that. Teddy's interesting, and his wife is charming."

"And Lord and Lady Churchill are coming, also. He had some sort of mysterious attack yesterday, but Jennie sent word around that he was better today. He's rather peculiar, that Lord Randolph. Always taking ill! Jenny said she misses young Winston, and will be glad to get back to England, particularly with this dreadful weather."

"I've had the servants light fires outside for the coachmen," Justin said. "And the sidewalks have been salted to melt the ice."

"It's going to be a beautiful evening!" Julie exclaimed, clasping her hands together, her face lighting up with a dreamy smile. "A night of beauty and romance! And Norman is going to propose to me."

She shot her stepmother a meaningful glance.

Her father gave her a kiss. Justin, who adored his daughter, knew only too well that this beautiful, exotic girl had been turned into a sort of pariah by the hidebound world of New York Society with its fierce prejudices. Anti-Semitism was rampant; a few summers before, Joseph Seligman, the country's leading German-Jewish banker, had been refused entry to the exclusive Grand Union Hotel at Saratoga, then the queen of resorts, because the hotel did not accept "Israelites." Blacks might have been emancipated by President Lincoln two decades before, but only a hopeless optimist could say that their lot had been much improved. The thousands of Chinese laborers who had been imported to build the transcontinental railroad after the Civil War might have provided the muscle that linked the nation, but the Chinese were still widely considered to be opium-puffing heathens who had bizarre sexual practices. Justin knew that his daughter had not escaped this prejudice, despite the fact that she had received a far better education than most women of her generation and had traveled with her parents all over Europe. Over the years, Justin had hopelessly spoiled his daughter, taking her to countless plays, operas, and concerts. Julie Savage had had an enchanted youth, as had her half brother, Johnny. Breathtakingly beautiful, heiress to a great fortune, she should have been besieged by suitors. But though her parents' social position assured that she would be invited to the city's balls and cotillions, Julie would sit through these affairs a veritable wallflower, shunned by the young men. Only Norman Prescott seemed to have overcome the general prejudice, and Justin prayed Julie was right and Norman would propose to her that night, which was one of the reasons he had decided to hold the ball. But Justin knew ever-practical Fiammetta might have gauged the situation correctly.

Sometimes Justin wondered if he had been right taking his child away from the Forbidden City in Peking and bringing her to New York. But then he told himself again that he had had no alternative: leaving Julie at the mercy of the wily Dowager Empress of China was out of the question. All New York had been fascinated for years by Justin's story, his shipping out as a boy on one of his father's clipper ships only to narrowly escape being murdered at sea, a murder arranged by his villainous half brother, Sylvaner; his capture by Chinese pirates, his wild adventures with Julie's mother, his later adventures in Italy with Garibaldi, where he met and fell in love with Fiammetta, the enormously wealthy and lusty Countess of Mondragone; and his final return to New York, where he squared accounts with Sylvaner and emerged as head of the family and one of New York's richest and most influential bankers.

Now, Justin's red-gold hair was beginning to tinge with gray, but he had lost none of his energy, ability, or wits. He would need them all if Norman Prescott didn't propose to Julie that night.

Justin was determined to make his daughter happy, but time was running out.

Two blocks farther north on Fifth Avenue, another beautiful girl was examining herself before a mirror in her bedroom.

"I've seen Julie's dress, and it's much prettier than this one," Rachel Lieberman said to her mother, Hildegarde, who was standing beside her eighteen-year-old daughter.

"Nonsense, that's a beautiful dress. And you look lovely."

Rachel turned around, looking over her shoulder at the reflection of her back. The bodice of the white dress was a series of ruffles that went up to her neck, while the very big skirt was swathed with white organdy. A belt of artificial flowers trailed down one side of the skirt.

"But it's so prissy. And I hate the flowers. Julie's dress goes way off her shoulders. It's very sophisticated."

"Julie's older than you," said her mother, who was wearing an elegant sea-green silk dress with an enormous bustle in the back. Around her neck was a spectacular necklace of diamonds and pearls, a gift from her adoring husband, Ben, who had shared so many adventures with Justin Savage back in China.

"Johnny likes sophisticated women," Rachel went on, pinching her cheeks to bring out the color. Her skin was alabaster white. "He told me."

"You know what I think of Johnny Savage," her mother said, pursing her lips. "As fond as I am of his father, Johnny is a wild young man with a dissolute reputation who drinks too much for his own good."

Rachel shot her mother a sly look.

"He's also the best-looking man in New York."

"Looks aren't everything. I suppose it's kind of him to ask to be your escort . . ."

" 'Kind'? He's crazy for me! He told me so."

"He's crazy for any half-attractive woman. His morals are extremely lax. Don't get any ideas in your head about any serious relationship with Johnny Savage. There are plenty of eligible young men in this town—like the young Rosen boy, for example."

"Oh, Nicky's all right, but he's so serious. He's boring. Momma, why don't you admit that the reason you don't like Johnny is that he's not Jewish."

"That's not true."

"I think it is. What if I did what Uncle August did and married a gentile?"

Uncle August was actually Rachel's great-uncle, August Belmont, one of the most influential men in New York. Born August Schönberg in western Germany, he was the son of a poor merchant. Eschewing a university education—he needed to make money—he went to Frankfurt in his teens and took a nonpaying job with the Rothschilds, the leading Jewish banking house in Europe. He started by sweeping floors; but his quick wits so impressed the Rothschilds that in a few years he was sitting in on discussions in the partners' room. The Rothschilds, impressed as much by his charm as his intelligence, sent him to the Naples branch of the family bank, where he picked up a smattering of Italian, polished his manners, and changed his name to Belmont (which, like Schönberg, meant "beautiful mountain"). He handled financial dealings with the Papal court so well that, at the age of twenty-one, he was sent by the Rothschilds to Havana, where, sniffing profits to be made in America after the Panic of 1837, he moved on to New York. Financed by the Rothschilds, he made a fortune and later on actually upheld the credit of the Federal government during a series of bank failures. Known as a ladies' man (he limped from a wound in his thigh suffered during a duel over a woman's honor), he surprised everyone by marrying the beautiful Caroline Slidell Perry, the daughter of Commodore Matthew Perry, who later

was credited with opening Japan to the west. Rachel knew
that her mother, who was proud of her Jewishness, had never
quite swallowed Uncle August's marrying a gentile.

Her mother opened the bedroom door, glaring at her
daughter.

"Uncle August's marrying Caroline Perry," she said, "is
something he must square with his own conscience. But I pray
to God you would never be so foolish as to do the same thing."

And she slammed out of the room. Rachel smiled
slightly—sometimes it was fun annoying her mother—then
looked at her reflection again. Her jet-black hair hung down
her back in a roll, padded with a velvet "rat," and her violet
eyes, she knew, were perhaps her best feature. Satisfied that
she looked smashing, she started to leave, when she stopped
and took another look at her reflection.

Taking a nail scissor off her dresser, she cut off the belt of
artificial flowers and tossed it in a wastebasket.

2.　　"I HEAR LORD AND LADY RANDOLPH CHURCHILL
are going to be at the party tonight," said Alice Lee Roosevelt as she and her husband of two years, Teddy Roosevelt, rode uptown in a hansom cab en route to the Savage
mansion.

"That's right," Teddy Roosevelt replied. "Johnny told me
his father invited them."

"Isn't Lady Randolph a New Yorker?"

"Yes. Her name was Jennie Jerome," Teddy said. He was
sitting beside her. It was extremely cold, and they both wore a
blanket over their laps as the cab rattled up Fifth Avenue. "My
father knew her father, whose name was Leonard Jerome. He
was August Belmont's best friend and a high-living stock ma-
nipulator. Father considered him a bit of a bounder—ladies'
man, fast horses, that sort of thing. He made a fortune on Wall
Street, then lost most of it in the Crash of '73."

In fact, Winston Churchill's American grandfather was

well-known in the fast-paced New York of the day. The tabloids of the era reveled in gory crime, loving nothing more than dismembered bodies, "Vampire Killers," "Human Fiends Seeking Bloodlust Thrills," etc. But they also featured Leonard Jerome's polo matches and horse races at the racetrack he built, Jerome Park. They also loved his "sponsorship" of such famous singers as Jenny Lind and Adelina Patti, the truth being that Jerome made them his mistresses. New Yorkers ogled the five-story mansion he built on Madison Square, just around the corner from the theater district he loved so much, Broadway up to Forty-Second Street, which was known as the Rialto.

"Isn't Jennie Jerome a great beauty?" Alice Roosevelt went on. "Or should I say Lady Randolph?"

"Oh yes. She and Lord Randolph fell in love at first sight—" He reached over and squeezed Alice's gloved hand. "Just as we did."

"Teddy, dear, you're an incurable romantic."

"Well, we *did* fall in love at first sight," Teddy said in his squeaky voice that, when he got excited, which was often, could scramble up the scale to a near falsetto. "I took one look at you, and said to myself, 'Roosevelt, old chap, this beautiful creature is going to be your wife!' And you are."

Alice, whose Boston father was a partner in the brokerage firm of Lee, Higginson, was indeed beautiful, with honey blond hair she wore in fashionable water curls about her temples and intense blue eyes. While she had not exactly fallen in love at first sight of Teddy—in fact, her first impression of him was that he was as strange as his friends had said—by the time she came to appreciate his many extraordinary qualities and his enormous vitality she was as deeply in love with him as he was with her. It was at her suggestion that he had shaved off his Dundreary side whiskers and grown a mustache instead, which, with his thick pince-nez eyeglasses, were already becoming well-known as his trademark in New York politics.

"Is the Savage house quite grand?" she went on, looking out the cab window at the passing gaslights.

"Oh yes. Richard Morris Hunt was the architect—he's the

fellow doing all the big palaces going up on 'Millionaire's Row.' Johnny's mother being Italian, she wanted a palazzo, and Hunt gave it to her. Cost millions, I hear. A bit showy for my taste, but nice if you like that sort of thing."

"You mean, Italian? I adore Italian. Is Johnny Savage as racy as his reputation?"

Teddy chuckled.

"More so. You'd die if you knew what we called him at Harvard."

"What?"

"It's unrepeatable."

"You must tell me!"

"Never."

"Is he romantically entangled with any girl in particular?"

"Well, he told me he's escorting Rachel Lieberman tonight, but I doubt that much will come of that. But you never know with Johnny. I've got a business proposition for him tonight."

"Not the cowboy thing?"

"Yes, the cowboy thing."

"I think it's very risky."

"A chance to make a fortune! And the West, Alice! It's the most beautiful country in the world."

"You Harvard cowboys are like a bunch of children."

"Johnny's as crazy about the West as I am. Besides, he tells me he's bored silly working at his father's bank. He wants an adventure, just as I do. Life's got to be an adventure, Alice! A great, big, wonderful adventure! Otherwise, one might as well be dead."

Teddy Roosevelt and Johnny Savage had known each other their entire lives, being almost exact contemporaries. As children, they had been close neighbors, the Roosevelts inhabiting a luxurious mansion at 6 West Fifty-seventh Street in Manhattan and the Savages living around the corner at Fifth Avenue and Fifty-fourth Street. Johnny and Teddy had attended the same Monday night dancing classes with Mr. Dodsworth as children, and they had many mutual friends. The Roosevelts were more patrician in what was known as the Knickerbocker society of old New York: the first Roosevelt had arrived in New Amsterdam in 1649. The Savages, on the other hand, could date their prominence in New York only from the early decades of the century when Johnny's grandfather, Nathaniel Savage, had founded the family fortune with his line of extremely profitable clipper ships involved in the China trade.

Both Johnny and Teddy loved the novels of a certain Captain Mayne Reid, the most popular writer of fiction for young men of the day, whose books, with titles like *The Boy Hunters*, *The Hunter's Feast*, and *The Scalp Hunters*, were fast-paced adventures of life in the Wild West, extolling the glories of nature in that great, still mostly uncharted out-of-doors paradise beyond the Mississippi.

Johnny and Teddy had spent many hours at Harvard talking about someday going out West. It was a dream that finally was about to come true.

Because Justin Savage had been born a bastard and had endured such incredible hardships at the hands of his murderous half brother, Justin escaped many of the prejudices of the more conventional members of his generation. Thus it had never occurred to him that forming a business partnership with Ben Lieberman, a Jew, was anything out of the ordinary, although Jews and gentiles almost never formed partnerships at the time. The two "worlds" of gentile and Jewish society lived almost completely separately. One of the few places the two worlds overlapped socially was in Justin's house on Fifth Avenue and Fifty-fourth Street.

The house was inspired by the Farnese Palace at Caprarola northwest of Rome, which had been designed by a student of Michelangelo. The building took over two years, and the tabloids had fun speculating as to the cost of the five-story house. When it was completed, it was generally agreed to be a handsome addition to the architecture of Fifth Avenue, which was becoming known as "Millionaire's Row" despite the fact that the city's leading abortionist, Madame Restell, owned a large town house at the northeast

corner of Fifty-second Street and Fifth Avenue. Madame
Restell conveniently slit her throat in a bathtub after being
arrested by that scourge of vice, Anthony Comstock, so the
moral tone of the avenue was brightened, relieving such
well-heeled neighbors as the Rockefellers and Huntingtons.

Justin and Fiammetta's palazzo, built of soft reddish brick
with a red tile roof and an almost severe Renaissance facade,
had the look of a sunny villa on the Mediterranean.

On the night of the ball, however, the weather was anything but Mediterranean. As the coaches and carriages pulled
up to the Fifth Avenue entrance of the brightly lighted mansion, the temperature hovered at zero, and an icy wind was
blowing in from the north. Justin's servants had placed four
large steel drums on the sidewalk and lighted fires in them
for the comfort of the coachmen, and a red carpet had been
laid on the sidewalk for the comfort of the guests. As steam
issued from the nostrils of the horses and a crowd of curious
onlookers watched from across the street, New York's gilded
plutocracy piled out of their expensive carriages and walked
the red carpet to the wrought-iron front doors of the house.

Julie was standing at one of the windows overlooking Fifth
Avenue in the front drawing room of the house, her face so
close to the window glass, her breath frosted it. She was tense,
watching the carriages pull up in front of the house. She knew
that Norman's parents had not accepted the invitation to the
ball, their feeble excuse being that the senior Mr. Prescott had
a cold. But she was certain Norman would come on his own.
Her certainty was part bravado. It was possible her stepmother might be correct, and Norman might not come.

She saw Teddy and Alice Roosevelt get out of their cab
and come to the front door. Shortly afterward, her brother,
Johnny, helped Rachel Lieberman out of her father's carriage, followed by Rachel's parents, Hildegarde looking
somewhat forbidding in her sables and diamonds.

Then her heart jumped. A cab had arrived, and Norman
was stepping out.

"He's here!" she whispered to herself, smiling. "He came!
Oh, and look at him!"

As the tall Yaleman in the top hat hurried up the red carpet to the front door, Julie almost ran across the furniture-cluttered drawing room to the front entrance hall, where her parents were receiving the guests. Justin and Fiammetta's architect might have designed a fine Italian palazzo, but the interior was thoroughly contemporary, filled with heavy furniture, Japanese and Chinese vases, numerous potted palms, statues, bibelots, ottomans, and rugs in all the Victorian love of clutter.

However, the entrance hall was something of an exception. Here, the architect had insisted on a more classic simplicity, and aside from a small circular fountain in the middle of the room and a number of palms under the curving stairway, there was no bric-a-brac to interrupt the beauty of the white marble floor and walls. Justin and Fiammetta were standing by the fountain greeting the guests, Fiammetta looking spectacular in a maroon silk ball gown with her famous diamond-and-ruby necklace, earrings, and matching tiara. But Julie had no eyes for either her parents or the line of guests passing by them, then up the stair to the second-floor ballroom.

Julie's eyes were only for Norman. He had come in the house and was giving his coat and hat to one of the footmen. Then he spotted Julie. A smile came over his face as he started toward her. A radiant smile on her face, Julie held out her white-gloved hands, which he took.

"You look beautiful," he whispered.

"So do you," she whispered back as Fiammetta watched the young couple from the fountain. She was anything but immune to the attractions of male good looks, and she could see why Julie had fallen head over heels for the tall young man with the curly yellow hair.

But Fiammetta felt in her bones her stepdaughter was heading for trouble. She was fond of Julie, although she felt none of the fierce love she had for her own flesh and blood, Johnny. A disastrous romance with Norman Prescott could make the Savage family the laughingstock of the town, the last thing Fiammetta wanted. But so far, she hadn't brought the subject up with Justin. She knew that when it came to Julie, Justin was intensely defensive.

In the light of future events, it was somewhat curious that Lady Randolph Churchill, the mother of eight-year-old Winston, should be at the same party with Teddy Roosevelt, the uncle-to-be of Eleanor Roosevelt, who had been born that year. But the two families shared a somewhat more ominous connection. Eleanor's father, Teddy's younger brother, was already displaying signs of the alcoholism that would kill him at the age of thirty-four. And Lord Randolph Churchill, the younger son of the Duke of Marlborough, had learned something only the day before that had seriously shaken his composure.

He had told his wife, who had feared the worst, but Jennie had the charm and assurance needed never to show in public her anxieties. As Johnny looked at her as she waltzed around the ballroom with her husband, he was dazzled by her beauty.

"Lady Randolph is a real stunner," he said to Rachel as he danced with her. "Her husband's rather odd-looking, though, with those bulging eyes."

"Yes, and he's a bit chilly," Rachel said, "but I suppose one could say that about a lot of English lords. He's supposed to be quite brilliant. He's in Parliament, you know. Jennie's asked Momma and me to stay at Blenheim Palace with them when we go to Europe next summer, which should be interesting."

"Yes, it should."

"Do you have any summer plans, Johnny?"

"As a matter of fact, Teddy Roosevelt just asked me to go out West with him next summer and do a bit of hunting. I'm hoping my father will give me the time off to go. I've always wanted to see the Badlands."

"That sounds rather grim."

"No, Teddy says it's beautiful out there. In the Dakota Territory, you know."

"Aren't you afraid of the Indians?"

"Well, a little. But I guess they won't scalp us. Did I tell you I like your dress?"

"Thank you. Momma is furious with me because I altered it behind her back."

"Yes, she doesn't look to be in a very good mood. I have the odd feeling she doesn't much like me."

"Oh no, that's just her way. Who couldn't like you, Johnny? You're a very nice fellow."

She gave him her prettiest smile. Johnny smiled back at her.

Johnny was thinking: She certainly is a beauty and she has such spunk! But one false move with her and she'll tell her father, who'll tell my father, who'll give me hell.

Lord Randolph Churchill was thinking: It's back! Just as I feared . . . that damned doctor yesterday gave me the news . . . I'm a doomed man. . . . But by God, I won't show it!

"Do you love me?" Julie was asking as Norman twirled her around the floor of the white-and-gold ballroom overlooking Fifth Avenue.

"Haven't I told you a dozen times?" he replied with a smile.

"Yes, but I want to hear it again."

"Very well, I love you. I adore you, in fact. I dream about you all the time."

"And I adore you, Norman."

The eight-piece orchestra was playing "The Artist's Life," one of Mr. Strauss's latest hits, and several dozen couples were swinging around the dance floor.

"Julie?"

Dum-dee-dum-dee-dum-dee-dum. . . .

"Yes?"

"Is there some place we could talk for a moment in private?"

This is it! she thought.

"Oh, I think we could find a place somewhere," she laughed, trying to keep her intense excitement from showing. "There are only about fifty rooms in this house. Let's go downstairs to the library."

He took her hand and led her off the dance floor. From the

other side of the room, Fiammetta watched them, a nervous look in her eyes.

The library was an extravaganza of elaborately carved walnut with shelf after shelf of leather-bound tomes, many of them reference works on Chinese history, reflecting Justin's intense interest in the subject. When Julie led Norman into the room, he closed the door and took her in his arms, kissing her passionately.

"Julie," he said, softly, "I haven't talked to your father, but . . . will you marry me?"

She almost yipped with delight.

"Yes!" She kissed him again and again. "Oh, Norman, yes—with all my heart! I love you so much!" She hesitated. "Have you spoken to your father?"

"No, but I will. First thing in the morning." He kissed her again. "It's all going to be all right, darling," he whispered. "And we're going to be very, very happy."

At three-thirty the next morning, a half hour after the last guest had left the ball, Johnny was tiptoeing down the upstairs hall for the servants' stair when his sister peeped out of her bedroom.

"Johnny," she whispered, "where are you going?"

He put his finger to his lips and hurried over to her door.

"Some of my friends are going out for a little party," he whispered. "The old man doesn't know."

"Did you hear the news?"

"What?"

"Norman Prescott proposed to me, and I accepted! Give me a kiss."

"Hey, congratulations!" Johnny kissed her cheek. He was well aware of how anxious his sister was about getting a husband. "Norman's a fine fellow."

"I'm so happy I could bust!"

"Well, don't. Now I really have to get going."

"You've got whiskey on your breath."

"It's just champagne. Good night, Julie."

Blowing her a kiss, he started down the hall again.

Julie went back into her room and closed the door. She leaned against it and smiled dreamily.

"Norman," she whispered to herself. "How I love you!"

Forty-five minutes later, Johnny finished another glass of champagne. Totally naked, he climbed in bed with Irene, one of the prettiest girls at Josie Wood's "Establishment" on Mercer Street, one of the most popular bordellos in New York and in the heart of what was known as the "red-light district," whorehouses advertising their wares by putting red lights over their doors.

"Johnny, honey," the pretty girl from Alabama said, "you're hung like a hound dog. Mah goodness, you could win a contest!"

Johnny laughed.

"I'm not sure being compared to a hound dog is a compliment," he said as he squeezed her ample breasts, "but I'll take it as one."

Johnny shared many things in common with his good friend, Teddy Roosevelt, but in some ways they were quite different. Although Teddy had fallen passionately in love with Alice Lee, he was a bit of a prude and would never have gone to a whorehouse. Johnny, on the other hand, loved whores, and at Harvard had been a leader of the more raffish young men in his class, who had given him the bawdy nickname Teddy had referred to in the hansom cab. Physically, the two young men were quite different. Teddy was slight, only five-foot-eight and weighing in at 130 pounds when he boxed at Harvard. He had bulging teeth, oversize blue-gray myopic eyes, and his laugh had been described by his beautiful Southern mother as an "ungreased squeak." When he talked, he spewed words with a force that surprised people. Many of his friends considered him strange, particularly since his fascination with natural history had spread rumors that he kept live birds, rats, mice, and snakes in his off-campus rooms at Cambridge. But much of his peculiarities could be attributed to the fact that, from the age of three onward, he had been subject to violent attacks of bronchial asthma, attacks that often brought him close to death. At the time, there was no sure remedy to the disease, so Teddy grew up in the constant shadow of a painful, choking death.

Johnny Savage, on the other hand, was a young god. Six-foot-two, with thick blond hair, sparkling blue eyes, and a face that combined the best features of his parents, Justin and Fiammetta, he was an Adonis who was also a superb athlete. At Harvard, he had been star quarterback of the football team (which had just, two years before, reduced its size from fifteen members to eleven—the game was just beginning to catch on), an ace swimmer, boxer, and tennis player. While Teddy was something of a recluse, socially, Johnny loved to drink the night away on champagne, endless quantities of beer and ale and shandygaff, a mixture of beer and ginger ale. At Harvard, the favorite pub was Carl's below sidewalk level on Brighton Street. *Scribner's Magazine* had written that "there were at Harvard lads of good morals and lads with an inclination toward unwholesome experiment." Johnny Savage was definitely included in the latter category.

His extreme good looks, his father's vast wealth, and his incredible success with women led his classmates to give him the nickname "Goldenballs."

3.   THE LETTER WAS DELIVERED TO THE SAVAGE mansion the next morning at eight-thirty by the Prescotts' coachman. Oswald, the Savages' butler, put the envelope on a silver tray and took it to the breakfast room, where Justin and Fiammetta were having their coffee, talking about the ball the previous night.

"This was just delivered, madame," the butler said, bringing the tray to Fiammetta.

"Thank you."

She took the letter and looked at it.

"Oswald, is my son up yet?" Justin asked.

"I believe, sir, that he is not in the house."

"Not in—? Where is he?"

"I have no idea, sir."

Oswald left for the pantry as Justin wiped his mouth with his napkin.

"That young scamp," he said. "He must have sneaked out last night. This means trouble."

"This is going to mean more trouble," Fiammetta said, opening the envelope. She took out the contents and read the note quickly. "It's from Walter Prescott. 'Dear Mrs. Savage,' it reads. 'My son, Norman, will be going abroad for a year to improve his French. Will you be so kind as to inform your daughter, Julie, that any arrangements Norman might have made as to their future have by necessity been canceled. I am, yours most sincerely . . .' et cetera." She put the letter beside her coffee cup and looked across the table at her husband. Justin looked sad.

"I tried to warn her," Fiammetta said.

"Yes, I know." Justin sighed and put down his napkin as he stood up. "I'll tell her," he said. "But it's going to break her heart."

He took the letter and left the room.

Upstairs, he knocked on her door.

"Julie," he called, "are you awake?"

"Yes. Come in, Papa. I have something wonderful to tell you."

Justin opened the door and went in. Julie was sitting up in her bed, her face radiant with happiness. Justin closed the door and went over to her, kissing her forehead then sitting on the edge of the bed.

"I was about to get dressed and come down to tell you and

Mother," she said. "But I was so excited, I didn't get to sleep until almost five o'clock, and then I overslept. Anyway, the most wonderful thing has happened. Norman proposed to me, and I accepted. Oh Papa"—she threw her arms around him and hugged him—"I'm so happy! So wonderfully, wonderfully happy! Tell me you're happy for me."

Justin smiled and ran his hand over her thick black hair.

"Yes, darling," he said.

She sat back in her pillows.

"And we're going to have the most beautiful wedding! And my wedding dress is going to be so beautiful! I can hardly wait to start planning everything. Of course, Norman and I haven't picked a date yet, but I think it must be in the spring, don't you? Perhaps in April. April's such a lovely month."

"Julie."

"Yes?"

"You know I love you very much."

"Of course. And I adore you! You're the best father in the world."

He smiled. "I've tried to be a good father. You've been happy here, haven't you?"

"Yes. Well, I wasn't so happy lately, the way all the eligible men in New York were treating me. But I don't care now! I have the handsomest fiancé and everybody is going to be pea green with envy."

"I know you're a very strong girl. Nothing could ever really defeat you."

She looked confused.

"What do you mean, 'defeat'? You make it sound like a war or something."

"Life can be a war. Believe me, I know from my own experience." He reached in his jacket pocket and pulled out the letter. "This was delivered a few minutes ago."

He held it out. Julie, concerned, took it. She looked at the envelope, then pulled out the letter and read it. Then she looked at her father, and his heart broke for the hurt on her face.

"I don't believe this," she said. "Norman loves me, and he wouldn't let his father get away with this. I don't believe it."

She leaned her face against his shoulder a moment. Then she released him. "Papa, I have to get dressed. I'm going to see Norman."

"Julie, maybe you'd be better off waiting . . ."

"No! I have to talk to Norman. I know this can't be true." Justin stood up.

"Do you want me to go with you?"

"No, I have to go by myself. Will you have Jake bring around the carriage for me?"

Justin walked across the room and opened the door. He looked back at his beloved daughter, who was already hurrying to her bathroom. He was not surprised she hadn't cried. He knew how strong this daughter of a Chinese pirate was.

But he was afraid the tears would come later.

Fifteen minutes later, Julie put on the beautiful dark blue, sable-lined cloak and hood her father had given her and hurried downstairs, where Oswald opened the door. She hurried out into the icy cold.

I'm not going to lose him! she told herself as she crossed the snow-swept sidewalk to one of her father's carriages. I'm not!

"And where have you been, young man?" Justin asked a half hour later as Johnny came in the front door of the house.

"I spent the night with Teddy and Alice Roosevelt," Johnny said, removing his overcoat. "We got to talking about next summer and didn't realize how late it had gotten, so I stayed over. Could I talk with you a moment, Father? It's rather important."

Justin leaned down to pick up a small matchbox that had dropped out of his son's overcoat pocket. He looked at it. On it was printed "Josie Wood's." He looked at Johnny.

"You know, I don't try to pry into your private life, Johnny. I often think I'm much too lenient with you. But I damned well hate being lied to."

He handed the matches back. Johnny looked at them and had the grace to look sheepish.

"Sorry, Father," he said. "The truth is, I had a bit too much to drink, and, well"—he shrugged and grinned—"those primal urges got the better of me. I trust you're not going to give me a sermon about my morals?"

"As I've said to you on several occasions, I'm in no position to sermonize to anyone about morals. It's no secret, God knows, that I led a fairly wild youth. But I never lied to my father, I never drank too much, and I never went to brothels. I love you, Johnny, but I sometimes worry about what you're going to turn out to be."

"Yes, sir, I have the same worries myself. Which is what I wanted to talk to you about."

"Then let's go into the library."

He started toward the room. Johnny followed him.

"By the way, Julie told me last night she's engaged," Johnny said. "That's wonderful news, isn't it?"

"I'm afraid it's not all that wonderful. The fact is, the engagement is off."

Johnny frowned as he followed his father into the library.

"Off? What happened?"

"I fear Norman's father doesn't want a half-Chinese daughter-in-law."

"Poor Julie."

"Yes, poor Julie."

Justin sat down and motioned to Johnny to sit beside him.

"Now," he said, "what did you want to see me about, Johnny?"

"Teddy Roosevelt has asked me to go to the Dakota Territory with him next summer. He's very interested in getting in the cattle business out there, and . . ."

"You mean, Teddy is abandoning politics?"

"No, sir, but he loves the West, as I do, and he feels it's important that he spend some time out there while he's still young. He also hopes to make some money from cattle. I mean, Teddy's well-off, but he has a lot of expenses, and being in the State Assembly doesn't pay much. As far as that goes, I don't get paid much at the bank . . ."

"Are you asking for a raise?"

Johnny smiled.

"No, sir. But I am asking for time off next summer to go with Teddy. You see, Teddy feels that life is a great adventure, and that most people never really get that adventure until they're too old, and I agree with him. I mean, you had a great adventure when you were young—perhaps the greatest! Going to China, becoming a pirate, being with Garibaldi—I mean, that was exciting stuff! I'd like to have some of that in my life. Is that asking too much?"

Justin scratched his cheek.

"No, I suppose not," he finally said. "I was planning to give you a promotion next year, but . . . how long do you think this adventure will take?"

"Three months."

"Well, things are slower here in the summer. I suppose it will be all right."

Johnny smiled as he jumped up.

"Gosh, Father, that's capital! Really capital! Thanks a lot!"

"I don't begrudge you good adventure, son. But I hate it when you lie to me."

"I'm truly sorry about that."

"You see, Johnny, you were born with everything. I was born with nothing. I'm probably too easy on you because I realize what an enormous advantage I had over you."

Johnny stared at his father. He was stunned.

"Father, that's the most extraordinary thing you've ever said to me, and I think it's probably true."

An hour later, Julie's carriage returned. Justin went to the entrance hall as Oswald opened the front door. Julie came in. She ran across the hall toward the stairs.

"So?" Justin asked.

"They wouldn't let me see him," she cried. "They wouldn't even let me in the house. Mr. Prescott called me a 'half-breed.' "

She ran up the stairs. Moments later, Justin heard her slam her bedroom door.

And then, the sobs.

Justin climbed the stairs to do his best to console her. But when he knocked on her door, she said, "Go away."

"Julie, it's me," he said, trying the door. But it was locked.

"I don't want to see you or anyone! You should have left me in China!"

Justin closed his eyes. His heart was breaking for her.

4. **"I'M TERRIBLY WORRIED ABOUT JULIE,"** JUSTIN SAID a week later as he lunched with his business partner, Ben Lieberman, at Delmonico's, New York's best restaurant on Madison Square (not far from New York's best brothel, known as The Louvre). Ben's relationship, through his wife, Hildegarde, with August Belmont had led him to an appreciation of fine food, wines, and cigars. Belmont had introduced New York to the fattening delights of European cuisine (New Yorkers before then had been mostly meat and potato eaters); Belmont's personal chef had trained with the legendary Câreme; and it was said that when a prominent New Yorker was told the huge amount of money that Belmont spent each month on wine, he dropped dead of a heart attack.

"I think Walter Prescott is a stuffy old fart," Ben said, digging into his mutton chop. "A girl as beautiful as Julie is a rare prize, and who gives a damn if she's half-Chinese?"

"Apparently quite a lot of people. Julie's holed herself up in her bedroom for a week now, crying. And she blames a lot of this on me."

"You? Come on, Justin: you practically killed yourself getting her out of China! Not to mention the money you had to pay that old bitch, the Dowager Empress, to spring her from the Forbidden City."

"But I didn't think about how she would be received here in New York. I guess because I've always been such a prime misfit myself, I didn't realize how hard it would be for her. I'm afraid she's going to do something . . . well, drastic."

"You don't mean suicide?" Ben said in an alarmed tone.

The waiter refilled their glasses with the Lafite-Rothschild that was Uncle August's favorite.

"I don't know," Justin said. "I certainly hope not that. But her heart is broken, and she's devastated. I wish to God I could think of something to help her, but she doesn't want to talk to me or anyone."

"She's young," Ben said, lighting one of his beloved cigars. "She'll recover. Maybe you should send her to Europe next summer with Hildegarde and Rachel. They're taking the Churchills up on their offer to stay at Blenheim Palace."

"That's a wonderful idea. I'll try it on Julie."

The next morning at ten o'clock, an hour after Justin had left the house to go downtown to his office, Julie let herself out of her bedroom. She was wearing her sable-lined cape and hood, for the weather continued to be bitter cold, and was carrying one of her purses. She came down the stairs to the entrance hall, where she encountered the butler.

"Oswald, I'm going shopping," she said.

"Very well, Miss Julie."

Oswald opened the front door. Julie went outside. She walked down Fifth Avenue, pausing by a mailbox. She took a letter from her purse and put it in the slot. Then she hailed a cab, climbed in, and started downtown.

At three that afternoon, Justin was sitting at his partner's desk opposite Ben going over some papers dealing with a large loan the bank was considering making to a real estate developer when Nelson Evans, his secretary, knocked and came into the office. "Excuse me, Mr. Savage," he said, "but a messenger just brought this note from Mrs. Savage."

He crossed the Oriental rug and handed the envelope to Justin, who tore it open and read:

"Darling: Julie has vanished. Come home at once. Fiammetta."

Justin stood up.

"Ben, I have to go home. Something's happened to Julie."

His partner looked concerned as Justin hurried out of the office.

A half hour later, Oswald let him into the Fifth Avenue house.

"Oswald, what happened?" he asked.

"Miss Julie left this morning shortly after ten. She told me she was going shopping. She hasn't come back since."

"Where's my wife?"

"In the drawing room, sir."

Justin went through the double doors into the drawing room, where Fiammetta was working on her latest petit point, a pastime that was becoming a passion.

"Where do you think she's gone?" he asked.

"She's run away."

"How do you know?"

"I just know."

"But where? She has no money . . . I'll hire detectives . . . She's a young girl who knows nothing of the world, God knows what may happen to her!"

"Julie's much tougher than you think. Anyone who could survive growing up in that nest of vipers, the Forbidden City, can handle New York—or wherever she's gone."

Justin turned on her.

"You don't love her like I do!" he shouted. "You never did!"

"Well it's true she's not my child."

"You think if Julie's gone, Johnny will inherit everything!"

"Justin, that's beneath you," Fiammetta said, giving him an icy glare. "I'll pretend you never said that."

Justin frowned.

"I'm sorry," he said, more softly. "I didn't mean that. It's just that I'm . . ."

He shook his head helplessly.

"I'd suggest you don't do anything until you've heard from her. I'm sure she'll write."

Justin sighed.

"Perhaps you're right."

He left the room. Fiammetta went back to her petit point. She was beginning to realize that the great passion she had felt for Justin had cooled over the years, worn down by dozens of quarrels and strains. How happy they had been in Italy. She was thinking of Rome. Rome, so warm and sensual. So different from stuffy New York.

So full of passion.

When Justin came home from the office the next afternoon, Fiammetta met him in the entrance hall and handed him a letter.

"This came this morning," she said. "It's from Julie."

Justin took it and hurried into the library, where he opened the envelope and took out the letter. He sat down at his desk to read it.

"Dear Father," it began, "by the time you receive this, I will be well on my way to San Francisco. Please don't try to come after me or stop me: I know what I'm doing. I've been terribly unfair to you these past few days, blaming my unhappiness on you. It was only in my misery that I could make such an absurd accusation. You've been the best father in the world, and I'll always love you.

"But I now know that I can never be accepted in your world, dear as you are to me. I will always be the 'halfbreed.' I must try and find happiness in another world.

"I have taken the beautiful pearls you gave me and sold them. I will use the money to pay for my journey back to China . . ."

"China?" Justin muttered to himself. "She can't be so foolish . . ." He continued reading:

"It's strange, but my memories of the Forbidden City, where I grew up, are dear to me. Even the Dowager Empress, who frightened me, still was kind to me in her way. I will go back to her and ask her help in trying to build a life for me in the land of my mother.

"I will miss you, dearest Father, and Johnny and Fiammetta. I will not miss New York . . . which has broken my heart.

"Your loving daughter,

"Julie."

"Where has she gone?" Fiammetta asked, standing in the doorway to the library.

"It's worse than I thought," he said. "She's trying to go to China."

"China! Dear God."

"She's forgotten she'll be a half-breed there, as well. After all I did to get her out of there twenty years ago, now she's going back in!" He stood up and started for the door. "If this isn't the damnedest mess—!"

"Darling, where are you going?"

"To Chicago, to see Mr. Pinkerton. I don't have any choice: Julie has to be stopped."

"Your father's gone to Chicago," Fiammetta said that evening as Johnny joined her at the dining room table. "To try and stop Julie from going to China."

Johnny gawked.

"China? Is she crazy? Why would she want to go back to that terrible place?"

"She thinks of it as her home."

Johnny unfolded his napkin.

"Well, I hope Father can stop her."

"Yes, of course. But it's you I want to talk about . . ."

She paused as Oswald brought in the soup course. The dining room was a magnificent Renaissance-style room with intricately carved gilt pilasters, tall windows overlooking Fifty-fourth Street, and several old master paintings hanging on the red walls. The long table was laden with heavy silver candlesticks. In the center, a tall Georgian silver epergne blossomed with hothouse flowers and fresh fruit, no minor expenditure in snowy December.

"Your father tells me you're going out West this summer with Teddy Roosevelt. Do you think that's wise?"

"I don't know if it's wise, but I'm looking forward to it."

"You could come to Italy with me."

"You know I love Italy, but I want to see the West."

"Your father and I have fought over you for years. First it was your name: I wanted you to be called 'Gianfranco,' but he insisted we Americanize you to Johnny. I wanted you to be educated in Europe, but he insisted on Harvard. Well, he's won so far—at a considerable strain to our marriage, I might add. You're sowing your wild oats now, which is understandable, but soon you'll be looking for a wife. And I want you to have an Italian wife. Someday you'll inherit a large fortune from me—an Italian fortune. I want you to come with me to Italy this summer, instead of running off on some foolish adventure in the Badlands, wherever they are. I have several girls in mind for you in Italy. One's a countess, and there are two princesses. They're all from the finest families in Italy— you couldn't do better! Think about it, my darling son. Why waste your youth on this strange new world out West, when there is so much waiting for you in the old world?"

"There's plenty of time, Mother."

"You're wrong. Youth goes in a wink of the eye."

"I'll make a bargain with you: I'll go West with Teddy this summer, and the next vacation I get, I'll spend it in Italy with you. Is it a deal?"

Fiammetta gave him a cool look.

"It's not a very good one for me, but I suppose it's the best I can get out of you. But remember: just as Julie is half-Chinese, you're half-Italian. And I'll never let you forget it. Never."

Julie's run away, trouble between my father and mother, Mother trying to pull me away with her to Italy . . . Johnny thought with a mounting sense of panic . . . My family's starting to come apart at the seams!

Allan Pinkerton was born in Glasgow and emigrated to the United States in the 1840s. He became sheriff of Chicago, and in 1850 he founded the first detective agency in America.

While solving a series of train robberies, he got to know Abraham Lincoln, who was the attorney for the railroad company in question. It was Pinkerton who warned Lincoln that there was a plot to assassinate him when he arrived in Washington to become president in 1861, and it was Pinkerton who slipped him into Washington on another, unscheduled train. During the Civil War, Pinkerton became head of intelligence for the Union side; after the war, his agency gained national fame when Pinkerton men rounded up the notorious Reno Brothers, a gang of bank robbers, and, later, almost took Jesse James in a bloody shootout at a farm in Missouri. By the time Justin came into his Chicago office, Allan Pinkerton was the most famous detective on earth, even though his rough-and-tumble methods were causing many people to question his ethics.

"Ah, Mr. Savage," the bearded Pinkerton said, shaking Justin's hand. "When I received your cable, I took the liberty of sending one of my agents to San Francisco. His name is Leroy Seymour, a veteran of the war—on the Union side, I hasten to add—and I have no finer man in my employ. We should have word of your daughter within the week."

"That's good news to my ears, Mr. Pinkerton," Justin said. "My daughter is very precious to me, needless to say. I will spare no expense to stop her from this folly."

"Pray sit down, sir, and fill me in on the details. The more I know, the better equipped I will be to apprehend her."

5.   THE TRIP THAT WAS TO CHANGE JULIE SAVAGE'S LIFE was in many ways a journey into the unknown; for although the transcontinental railroad was in its twelfth year of operation, transporting almost a million passengers a year on its daily four-day trips between Omaha, Nebraska, and Sacramento, California, the western half of the United States was still considered "wild," filled with perils like murderous Indians, train robbers, cardsharps, and such natural disasters as plains fires, avalanches, and floods. While the Indians were still feared by most Americans—it had been only a few years since the great Indian Chief Crazy Horse had killed Custer and his men at the Battle of the Little Bighorn—their days of freedom were tragically numbered: the West was filling up with a speed that surprised most Americans. Still, in 1882 it took a certain amount of guts to ride the Pacific Express.

Julie was luckier than most. She had sold her pearl necklace for $2500, a considerable sum at the time. This enabled her to travel first-class on one of Mr. Pullman's Palace Cars for the sum of $100. For an extra $4 a day, she had bought a ticket on the weekly Pacific Hotel Express, a special train that had the luxury of a dining car—all passengers on other trains, including first-class, were forced to get off the trains and bolt down their food at railroad restaurants. Compared to the second-class passengers, not to mention the miserable third-class passengers who were mostly immigrants, lured from the backwaters of Europe by the extravagant claims of the railroad companies' advertisements, Julie was traveling deluxe. But even so, train travel had its discomforts. Julie had bought a new wardrobe in Chicago, and forewarned by travel pieces she had read in popular magazines, she bought drab dresses in brown or black because one of the curses of train travel shared by all classes was the dust from the countryside and the soot from the engine's smokestack. After a few days, one simply gave up trying to shake the dirt and dust out and resigned oneself to a certain amount of filth.

The Palace Cars had upper and lower berths—the invention of George Pullman, which was to make him a fortune. By day, Julie could sit in a comfortable benchlike seat upholstered in green velvet and heavily fringed, from which she could watch the passing countryside through the window. By night, the porter converted it into a curtained bed.

As the train pulled out of the Omaha station at eight in the morning, a tall, lanky young man in a knee-length buffalo-skin coat came down the aisle of "The Platte," which was the name of the car, and stopped by Julie, looking at her with interest. He had thick, curly brown hair that hung almost to his shoulders. Beneath the leather coat, she saw he was dressed in a tweed suit that gave him the look of a bit of the dude. He carried in his left hand a carpetbag.

"This seat available, ma'am?" he asked, speaking with a Western drawl.

"Yes," Julie said.

He stowed his carpetbag under the fringed seat, hung his coat on a hook by the window, then sat down opposite her. As the train picked up speed passing by the Omaha stockyards, the man stared at her in a manner that made her a bit uncomfortable. She felt he was undressing her with his cornflower blue eyes. Finally, he said:

"Your first trip West, ma'am?"

"That's right."

"Going all the way to Sacramento?"

"Yes, and then to San Francisco."

"That's my hometown, San Francisco. Beautiful place, except it keeps burning down, like Chicago. Where are you from, if I may be so bold?"

"New York."

"Ah, New York. Never been there, but I'd love to go one day. You have relatives in San Francisco?"

Julie didn't like being questioned. On the other hand, his manner was so pleasant, she couldn't very well not answer him without being rude. And, faced with four days of proximity to the man, she couldn't ignore him.

"No," she said. "I'm traveling to China."

He looked surprised.

"China? That's a far piece for a young lady to go alone. You got relatives in China?"

"Yes. My family are missionaries in China," she lied. "I've spent the past four years at a ladies' seminary outside New York."

"I see." He smiled, rather insolently, she thought, and his eyes wandered lazily down her body, from her hat to her high-button traveling shoes. Then back up again. Lazily. Sensuously.

Then he leaned forward and extended his hand.

"My name's Lance Morrow. Shall we become friends?

Since we're going to be so close for the next four days. Sleeping on top of each other, so to speak." His eyes indicated the folded-up berth above their heads.

Julie hesitated, then reached out her gloved hand and shook his.

"My name is Julie," she said. "Julie Savage."

"Miss Julie Savage?"

"That's right."

He squeezed her hand slightly and smiled. His clean-shaven face really was quite extraordinary, she thought. The idea of sleeping for the next four nights only a few feet below him was somehow . . . unnerving.

"Interested in breakfast?" he said as the chimes of the porter were heard at the end of the car. "Let's see what kind of grub Mr. Pullman is offering these days."

He released her hand and stood up. Caution told her to decline the invitation, but her stomach was howling for food.

Wondering what her father would think if he knew she was eating breakfast with a total stranger, she stood up.

"The dining car's this way," Lance said, gesturing toward the front of the train that was now barreling along the tracks through snowbanked fields at the breathtaking speed of fifty-five miles an hour.

Julie thought, as she walked down the aisle of the swaying Pullman car, that if nothing else, the forced intimacy of train travel was going to rewrite the hidebound rules of her society.

And she decided that might not be a bad thing after all.

The dining car was a frenzy of overdecoration, not one inch of its walls or ceiling left unadorned. Polished mahogany panels and elaborate brass sconces competed with mirrors and gaudy paintings of cherubs to dazzle the passengers, while fringed draw-back curtains framed the windows. A porter seated them at the end of the car and presented them with menus which featured three different breakfasts at fifty cents, seventy-five cents, and a dollar. The car was half-full as a waiter poured strong, hot coffee into china cups.

"I'm gonna splurge," Lance said. "The dollar breakfast, eggs sunny-side up."

"Yessir," said the waiter. "And you, miss?"

"The same, please."

As the waiter headed for the galley, Lance said, "So you're a missionary's daughter?"

"That's right. And what do you do, Mr. Morrow?"

"I'm a salesman."

"What do you sell?"

"Bibles."

She stared at him.

"You don't look like a particularly pious person."

He grinned.

"What's piety got to do with selling Bibles? I just came from a convention in Chicago. They're putting out some really beautiful Bibles, illustrated with spectacular pictures, and all of Jesus' sayings are printed in red ink so you can get right to the meat, if you know what I mean."

" 'Meat' is an odd way to describe Christ's teachings."

"No offense meant. Course, you being a missionary's daughter I should have phrased it more politely. Are both your parents Chinese?"

"My father's American."

"And where do your parents live?"

"New York."

"I thought you said they were in China?"

Julie looked a bit uncomfortable.

"Yes, they are. In Shanghai. I meant they come from New York."

She's lying, Lance thought. Interesting. She is absolutely gorgeous!

As the train roared across the great Nebraska plain, its engine's huge stack belching smoke, the sky began to darken, and by three that afternoon snow began to fall. Julie, who had been watching the passing landscape with a sort of fascination, said to Lance, "What happens if snow covers the track?"

"They send a snowplow. In the winter of '66, they had forty-four blizzards. One storm lasted thirteen days without letup, and the snowplow needed twelve locomotives to get through the drifts. I hope I'll have the pleasure of your company at dinner?"

She looked at him.

"Surely there's someone else more interesting than I?" she said.

"There's no one half as interesting as you, Miss Savage."

"After four days, we'll run out of conversation."

"Let me worry about that. May I call you Julie?"

She hesitated, then looked out the window. The snow was becoming heavier, almost a white blur as the flakes sped past the glass. She saw something perhaps fifty feet away from the train.

"Look," she said. "Buffalo! A whole herd of them! Aren't they magnificent creatures?"

"Yes, they are. They taste good, too. You didn't answer me. May I call you Julie?"

She looked at him uncertainly.

"Yes," she finally said.

"And I hope you'll call me Lance."

For all her being raised in the Forbidden City in Peking, surrounded by conniving concubines and hundreds of malicious eunuchs, Julie remained very much a Victorian in matters of sex. She had seen her brother, Johnny, naked several times and was aware that men's anatomies were in several respects quite different from women's, but she was unsure about the actual mechanics of lovemaking. The subject of childbirth was kept a well-guarded secret from children, and Julie was under the impression that if a man touched her anywhere above the knee, she would become pregnant. She was also extremely modest and had already,

on the trip from New York to Chicago, experienced the tor-
turous difficulties of dressing and undressing in the Pullman
bunks without accidentally exposing herself through the
curtains that concealed the bed from the aisle.

But this night, with Lance only a few feet above her, undressing seemed even more risky. She kept looking at the
upper berth, half-expecting Lance's head to appear through
the curtains, ogling her. When she finally got under the covers and turned off her lamp, she felt greatly relieved. She
closed her eyes for a few moments, thinking of her family,
her home, and her past, all of which she was leaving behind
in this desperate search to find happiness. Not for the first
time, she shuddered as she considered the enormity of the
gamble she was taking.

But she was determined to continue.

Opening her eyes, she parted the window curtain and
looked out. The snow had stopped now, and a gibbous moon
revealed the immense plains of America, stretching end-
lessly under their blanket of virgin snow. It was an awe-
some, beautiful sight, and Julie marveled at the miracle of
engineering that enabled her to barrel through the night in
the relative comfort of her berth.

It was then she spotted a horse perhaps a quarter mile
from the train. An Indian was on the horse, watching the
train as it sped by. Her first impulse was fright, for stories of
Indians attacking trains, or removing parts of the rail to stop
them, were rife in the Eastern tabloids. But as the Indian disappeared from sight and she saw no others, she relaxed. She
wondered what he thought of this iron monster of steam and
speed that was so swiftly bringing "civilization" to the land
that had belonged to his people since time immemorial.

She was awakened by Lance climbing into her berth.

"What are you doing?" she whispered, sitting up. "Get
out of here!"

"Shh." He held a finger to his mouth. He was wearing a
flannel nightgown and was barefoot. He rebuttoned the cur-

tain, then sat cross-legged beside her. "I won't harm you,"
he whispered. "It's just that I can't get to sleep for thinking
about you. I've fallen in love with you, Julie. I honestly
mean that, it's not just a line. I had to tell you."

"You might have waited till breakfast."

"I couldn't wait." He took her hand and raised it to his
mouth, kissing it tenderly. She stared at him, amazed by his
behavior. And yet, she was also fascinated.

He put her hand against his chest.

"Feel my heart beating," he whispered. "Each beat is saying, 'Julie, Julie, Julie.' Can you feel it?"

"Yes . . ." His chest was hard. She was amazed at the excitement flooding through her body.

"Do you love me?" he whispered.

"Of course not . . . I hardly know you . . . Please go before
someone finds you here . . ."

He released her hand.

"All right, I'll go. But at least, now you know how I feel
about you. Someday, you're going to be my wife."

He unbuttoned the curtain and slipped out, leaving Julie
speechless. And terribly excited.

His wife? she thought. Can he be serious?

But it occurred to her that as she knew hardly anything
about him, he knew hardly anything about her except what
he saw. Apparently, the fact that she was a "half-breed"
didn't bother him.

6.   WHEN JULIE AWOKE THE NEXT MORNING, THE
first thing she realized was that the train was going much
more slowly than when she had fallen asleep. Parting the
curtain, she saw that the snow had started again, coming
down in even greater quantities than the day before. In fact,
it looked like a first-class blizzard. But then, they were in the
very depths of winter, that day being Christmas Eve day.

Wrapping herself in a peignoir, she unbuttoned the curtains

and got out of her berth to make her way to what was euphem-
ized as the "Ladies' Dressing Room," a reminder of how uncomfortable the Victorians were with bodily functions. After
washing up, she returned to her berth to struggle into her traveling clothes. When she was dressed, she got out of her berth
and went to the front of the train. The dining car was almost
full, but a smiling Lance waved to her: he had saved her a seat.
Feeling a pang of pleasure at seeing him, she made her way to
his table and sat opposite him as the waiter poured coffee.

"Did you sleep well?" he asked.

"Yes."

"I didn't. I was up all night, thinking of you."

"Lance, I'm flattered by your attentions, but . . ."

"You don't like me."

"I didn't say that. But . . ." she lowered her voice ". . . your
crawling into my berth last night was really inexcusable."

"I'm disappointed in you."

"Why?"

"I thought you had the fire and fun of romance in you. Instead, you're just another proper young lady . . ."

The train jolted to a halt. They both looked out the window.

"What's wrong?" Julie asked.

"Maybe it's the snow."

After a moment, a conductor came into the dining car and
announced, "Ladies and gentlemen, there's no cause for
alarm. The snow has drifted over the tracks, and there may
be a delay until the snowplow can be brought and attached.
Meanwhile, enjoy your breakfast."

Lance picked up his coffee cup.

"Life is full of surprises," he said. "By the way, tonight's
Christmas Eve, and the waiter tells me they put on a real
feast. You'll feast with me?"

"You really are persistent, aren't you?"

"Like a dog with a bone. Will you?"

She smiled. He really was rather irresistible.

"Yes, I'd be delighted to."

Two hours later, the train was still not moving. Julie and Lance had returned to their seats when they heard gunshots and screams. Lance stood up. To Julie's surprise, he pulled a gun from inside his jacket.

"You wait here," he said, softly. "I'll see what's happening."

As the other passengers in the car began talking excitedly, Lance ran down the aisle to the forward door, opened it, and vanished. By now, Julie could see masked men on horseback outside the train. There were at least a half dozen on her side, aiming their guns at the train windows. She nervously stared at them as more gunfire was heard from the direction of the dining car.

A few minutes later, Lance came running back into the car. Hurrying down the aisle, he stopped beside her.

"How much money do you have on you?" he whispered.

"A little under eighteen hundred dollars."

"Hide it if you can. The conductor told me it's the Horton Gang. They've robbed several trains over the past few months . . . They've shot two guards on the mail car and wounded a conductor. They're going through the train taking everything they can get."

Alarmed, Julie pulled her suitcase from beneath her seat, opened it, and then her purse. As Lance watched, more than a little surprised that a young woman would be carrying so much cash, Julie pulled from her purse an envelope stuffed with greenbacks. She started to put the envelope into a pile of her lingerie in the suitcase, but Lance whispered, "Keep some money in your purse to give them." Realizing the wisdom of this advice, Julie took out a hundred dollars and put it in her purse. Then she closed the suitcase and pushed it back under the seat, as Lance ran to the end of the car again. She looked out the window to see a number of terrified-looking passengers of both sexes leaving the front of the train. Their hands were in the air, and a number of the bandits were guarding them with guns.

Lance reappeared and hurried down the aisle to her.

"I was wrong," he whispered. "Give them the money in your suitcase."

"I will not! It's all the money I have in the world."

"They're threatening to shoot anybody who holds out on them. That's why those passengers outside are guarded."

Julie looked back through the window at the passengers standing in the snow. Just then, four men with bandannas tied over the lower part of their faces came into the car. Two of them held guns, the other two carried wicker baskets.

"No one will be hurt," one of them announced, "if you all cooperate. You"—he aimed his gun at Lance—"throw down your gun."

Lance hesitated.

"Don't be a fool," Julie whispered. "Do it!"

He tossed the gun on the floor of the car.

"Kick it to me," the masked man ordered.

Lance obeyed. The gun slid down the car. One of the men picked it up.

"Now," the first man said, "give us all your valuables. We'll pass down the car with the baskets. Think of it as a church offering, except we want everything: cash, watches, jewelry. If anyone holds out on us, you'll be shot, so I advise all of you not to be cute. All right, let's go."

The men started down the car as the terrified-looking passengers pulled out their wallets and opened their purses.

"Those gold earbobs, ma'am," the leader said to an elderly woman. "They're mighty pretty."

"Oh please, my late husband gave them to me," the woman implored.

"Mustn't be too sentimental, ma'am. It's a tough world. Toss them in the basket."

With a little sob, the woman obeyed, dropping them in the basket that was already half-full with cash, gold, and jewelry. The robbers moved down the aisle, collecting from both sides. As they approached Lance and Julie, the former whispered, "Remember, give them the money in the suitcase."

"But I'll be left with nothing!"

"I'll take care of you. Better broke than dead."

"No! I won't do it! It's all the money I have in the world! It's my passage money to China!"

"What's the pretty little lady saying?" the leader asked, coming up to them and eyeing Julie.

"She says she has most of her money in her suitcase," Lance said, calmly. "It's under her seat."

"Damn you!" Julie burst out, causing several of the ladies in the car to gasp.

The masked man looked at Lance, then back to Julie.

"It's lucky for you you came clean," he said, "because the next thing we do is check the luggage."

Five male passengers and three women started yelling, "We have things in our valises!"

The robbers grinned as the passengers hastily pulled out their suitcases and opened them, Julie among them. Shooting Lance dirty looks, she opened her bag and pulled out the envelope, handing it to the masked man. Then she took the money from her purse and gave that to him also as Lance emptied his wallet. The robber took the money without saying anything. Then he whispered to Julie, "You're lucky, honey. You're mighty pretty, and I'd hate to have had to shoot you." Then he turned to the others, and shouted, "Take the cheaters outside!"

The persons involved began sobbing and screaming as the robbers pushed them to the rear door of the car. "Please have mercy!" one woman cried. "I have two children at home!"

"You can't be serious," Lance said to the leader. "You've got the money, what more do you want?"

"Gotta teach the next ones not to hold out," he said. "And if you don't shut up, you'll join them dead ones."

Then he and the other bandits left the car. Julie, Lance, and the other passengers hurried to the right-hand windows to watch. Outside, the passengers were herded with passengers from the other cars into a circle in the snow ten feet from the train. They were sobbing and screaming hysterically.

"I can't believe they're going to kill them," Julie said to Lance. "It's inhuman!"

"Charlie Horton's killed passengers before—lots of them. And don't worry about your money. I'll pay you back in San Francisco. I'm sorry. . . ."

He was interrupted by a volley of shots. The people in the car groaned as the passengers outside were riddled with bullets. They fell on the snow, which quickly became stained with blood.

Julie turned to look at Lance beside her at the window. Her face was pale.

"You have nothing to be sorry for," she said. "You saved my life. I'll never forget."

Lance looked at her and said nothing.

"It's a wire from Allan Pinkerton," Justin said to Fiammetta and Johnny. The family was in the drawing room of the Fifth Avenue house, where a beautiful Christmas tree had been put up in one corner. It was Christmas Eve and snowing heavily in Manhattan. Oswald had just delivered the telegram. "Pinkerton's agent is on the train behind Julie," Justin went on, a look of concern on his face. "Julie's train was held up this morning by the Horton Gang, who murdered twenty-three of the passengers."

"Why?" exclaimed Fiammetta.

"Is Julie safe?" Johnny asked.

"Yes, thank God," Justin said. "Her train was stopped by snowdrifts, which is how the Horton Gang got on board. A snowplow has freed the train, which is now on its way to San Francisco."

"What a fool she is to undertake this mad adventure," Fiammetta said. "The West is a barbaric place, certainly no place for a young girl—unchaperoned, I might add."

"According to the telegram, she's found a chaperone, of sorts. A man named Lance Morrow. One of the conductors on Julie's train waited for the second train, and he told Pinkerton's agent that Morrow saved Julie from being shot."

"Thank heavens for that," Johnny said.

"It's not an unmixed blessing," Justin said. "According to Pinkerton, this Lance Morrow has a criminal record."

"You see?" Fiammetta said to Johnny. "Robbers, murderers, criminals—this is the West you're so eager to go to next summer! You'd better start rethinking your priorities."

"Mother," Johnny said, "there won't be any danger . . ."

"No danger? Are you mad? Look what's happened to your sister, and she's on a train! Justin, talk to him. Put some sense into his head."

"Your mother may be right," Justin said. "I've come close to losing Julie. I don't want to take any chances losing you."

"Father, you promised! And Teddy Roosevelt tells me there's nothing in the Badlands except buffalo and cattle. I'll be safe!"

"Teddy Roosevelt? That puny little man with the squeaky voice?" Fiammetta snorted. "What does he know about danger, or the West for that matter? The whole idea of you and your Harvard friends going out West to play cowboy is as mad as . . . as mad as Julie trying to go to China! And look at the trouble and anxiety she's caused your father! You're being selfish and thoughtless, Johnny. If you go anywhere this summer, you should come with me to Rome. There are properties there you've never even seen, properties that one day will be yours. It's time for you to grow up."

"Your mother's right," Justin said.

"Father, all she wants is to get me to Rome so she can find me an Italian wife," Johnny said, bitterly.

"And what's wrong with an Italian wife?" Fiammetta exclaimed. "*I'm* an Italian wife!"

"But I want to go West!" Johnny shouted. "I want an adventure!"

"Will you two stop it?" Justin was also shouting. "I'm worried sick about Julie, and you two are fighting over next summer! It's Christmas Eve, dammit!"

Oswald appeared in the doorway, looking a bit nervous from the shouting.

"Excuse me," he said. "Dinner is served."

7. AFTER THE HORTON GANG MASSACRE, THE ARMY
assigned twelve soldiers to guard the train for the rest of its
journey west, and officials of the railroad came aboard to re-
assure the devastated passengers that their stolen money
would be refunded by the railroad's insurance company, and
that for the rest of the trip to San Francisco everything on the
train would be free. While Lance was skeptical about the insurance "adjustment," at least Julie felt somewhat relieved
with the presence of the soldiers. And when Lance again offered to loan her any amount of money once they reached
San Francisco, she said, "That's very kind of you, Lance,
and I appreciate your offer. But how could I repay you? I
don't know how long I'll be in China."

"Did you ever think of changing your mind and staying in
San Francisco with me?"

"I couldn't do that."

"Why not?"

"Well, I . . . I just couldn't."

He smiled slightly at her.

"But you're thinking about it, aren't you?" he said. "Now,
why don't you admit you're falling in love with me?"

"Lance, you're a brave man, and I owe you my life. But
you're also conceited."

He laughed.

"That's probably true," he said. "But still and all . . ." he
lowered his voice to a whisper ". . . you're falling in love."
And he winked at her.

The porter rang the chimes for Christmas Eve dinner.

"Come on, let's eat. I'm starved, and it's on the house. Or
should I say, the train?"

When the train reached Promontory, in northern Utah, the
passengers switched from the Union Pacific's Pullman Palace
cars into the Silver Palace cars of the Central Pacific line.
Julie was curious to see Promontory, because it was here that

the two competing railroad lines had met thirteen years before, and the famous golden spike was driven to mark the completion of the transcontinental railroad (the golden spike was symbolic; it was removed moments later to be replaced by a more practical steel spike). But however historic Promontory might be, Julie thought it certainly didn't amount to much. It consisted of a railroad depot and express office on one side of the track and a few one-story, canvas-topped structures, occupied by various businesses, on the other.

"There's a floating crap game going on over there," Lance said as he accompanied Julie through the snow to the other train. "Plus three-card monte and *vingt-et-un.* Three tourists from Cincinnati lost a hundred and thirty dollars in thirty minutes here last week."

"How do you know that?" Julie asked. She was wearing the sable-lined cloak her father had given her.

"Oh, I hear gossip."

"At a Bible convention?"

He laughed.

"Nothing in the Bible about shooting craps. That's a beautiful cloak you're wearing. What's the fur?"

"Beaver," she lied. After the train robbery, she was somewhat nervous about wearing such an expensive fur.

"I know furs. That's not beaver, it's sable."

"Then why did you ask me?"

"To see what you'd say."

"Then you think I'm a liar?"

He smiled.

"You've been lying to me ever since we met."

She looked at him as the Central Pacific porter helped her to climb aboard the Silver Palace car from the ankle-deep snow.

Ten minutes later, after they were seated and the train started to pull out of Promontory, heading for the Nevada border, Lance said, "In the first place, your parents aren't missionaries in China."

"How do you know that?"

"You told me your parents were in New York, which is a long way from China. Besides, there's a very famous banker in New York named Justin Savage who spent many years in China and was married to a famous Chinese pirate . . ."

"Madame Ching. She was my mother."

"Then you admit it?"

"There's nothing to admit. My father led an unusual youth, but he committed no crimes."

"Then why are you running away from him?"

"What makes you think I'm running away?"

"Because you've lied to me." He leaned forward. "I've told you I love you, which is the truth. Why can't you level with me?"

"What do you want me to say?"

"The truth."

She looked out the window, fighting back the tears.

"All right," she sighed, "I'll tell you the truth. The truth is that in New York I'm an outcast because I'm half-Chinese and have slanted eyes. I'm going back to China to try and find a world I can fit into."

"I can offer you a world you can fit into. And San Francisco is a lot closer than China."

"What are you talking about?"

"What do you think? I'm proposing to you."

"Lance, how can you even think about romance after the horrible thing that happened to those poor passengers?"

"Out here in the West you get used to violence and death."

"Perhaps you're used to it, but I'm not . . ."

"Marry me and you won't have to worry about anything. I'm a very rich man."

"How can anyone get rich selling Bibles?"

"I don't sell Bibles. I lied to you, just as you lied to me."

"Then what do you do?"

"When we get to San Francisco, I'll show you. I don't mean to brag, but wait till you see my house. It's a mansion, one of the grandest houses in San Francisco, right on Nob Hill with a beautiful view of the Pacific Ocean. You'll love it. And I'll make you Queen of San Francisco!"

What in the world does he do? she thought. He must be ashamed of it since he lied about it. He saved my life, and he has the face of an angel even if he's got a bit of the devil in him. Am I falling in love with him?

A few days later, the train entered the Summit Tunnel, the easternmost and longest of the six tunnels that had been bored through the Sierra Nevada Mountains by the Central Pacific construction crews, drilling and blasting a twenty-foot-high hole through solid granite at the maximum rate of eight inches a day. As the car plunged into darkness, Julie felt Lance sit beside her and put his arm around her. Then he pulled her to him and put his mouth on hers, kissing her hungrily. She put up no resistance, enjoying the feel of his body.

"I love you," he whispered. "Tell me you love me."

"I think . . . perhaps . . ."

"Perhaps? Can't you do better than that?"

"Oh Lance, I'm so confused . . ."

"Let me make the decisions for both of us. That way, you'll no longer be confused."

"You make it sound so simple, but it can't be."

"Just leave everything to me."

He kissed her again. Suddenly, the train came out of the tunnel. Embarrassed, Julie gave him a little shove, indicating he should go back to his seat.

But he didn't.

Now the train was creeping along the dizzying shelf of Cape Horn, almost two thousand feet above the thin, faraway thread of the American River.

"Some view, isn't it?" Lance said, nodding toward the window. "We'll be in Sacramento soon, then it's a short hop to San Francisco. You'd better start making up your mind."

"I know. I'm thinking about what you said."

"I won't take 'no' for an answer."

She looked at him and sighed.

After all, she thought, isn't this what I want? A man to love me?

"There's a street in San Francisco named Liedesdorff Street," Lance said a few minutes later, "that has a rather interesting story. Would you like to hear it?"

"Yes, why not?"

"The story is about a handsome young man named William Liedesdorff. This happened fifty years ago in New Orleans. Liedesdorff was the son of an itinerant Dane and a West Indian native girl. An English planter had taken a paternal interest in him, and sent him to New Orleans to work in the office of the planter's brother, who was a wealthy cotton merchant. Of course, this was slave days, so the planter cautioned Liedesdorff not to disclose his mixed parentage, and apparently the young man was sufficiently white not to cause comment." Lance pulled a cigar from his coat pocket and lit it as Julie watched him, wondering what he was getting at. After exhaling a cloud of smoke, he went on: "Liedesdorff was a heartbreaker, very popular with the ladies of New Orleans, but he finally met a beautiful blonde who broke his heart. Her name was Hortense, and her family traced its forefathers to aristocrats of Louis XIV's France.

"The planter and his brother both died and left their estates to Liedesdorff, so he was now a rich man. Being very much in love with Hortense, he wanted to make her his wife. But according to the strict codes of those days, if he told her the truth about his mother's blood, he would be automatically exiled—possibly even forced into slavery. Still, he was an honest man, and he wanted her to know.

"But he proposed before he told her. Hortense was thrilled, as she was very much in love with William. Her father approved the marriage, thinking William an exceptionally promising potential son-in-law. Liedesdorff gave Hortense a beautiful diamond engagement ring, and everything seemed rosy.

"But Liedesdorff's secret tormented him. He walked the streets of New Orleans trying to get up the courage to tell Hortense the truth about himself. Finally, a few nights before the wedding, he threw himself on his knees and told her.

"Weeping bitterly, Hortense said her father would never

agree to the wedding now, and they must never see each other again. Nevertheless, she told him, she would love him until she died.

"The next morning, Liedesdorff received a package from Hortense's father containing every gift he had given her. With it was a note from the father, severing all relations between his family and the young man. Liedesdorff, fed up with New Orleans, sold everything he owned, bought a schooner, and stocked it with merchandise for a trading voyage to the Pacific: he was never coming back. The day before he sailed, he was walking on Canal Street when he saw a funeral procession. There were white plumes on the horses, which meant the death of someone young. Then Liedesdorff saw Hortense's father, mother, and little sister. Shocked, he asked someone whose funeral it was. 'A young society girl,' the man said. 'She almost married a mulatto. She died yesterday—from a broken heart, they say. Her name was Hortense . . .' That night, the priest who had administered the last rites to the dying girl brought Liedesdorff a tiny gold crucifix. It had been hers, and the priest said she sent it to tell William that she had loved him to the end."

There were tears streaming down Julie's cheeks.

"Why are you telling me this?" she whispered.

"Because I think something like this may have happened to you."

She pulled a handkerchief from her purse and wiped her eyes.

"Yes," she said. "It did. In reverse."

"Did you love him?"

"Very much. But the morning after he proposed to me, his father sent a note . . . just like Hortense's father . . ."

She stopped, starting to sob again. Lance leaned over and took her hand.

"But you see, the end of Liedesdorff's story is happy. He moved to San Francisco and became so successful they named a street after him. My point is, just because you had a tragic thing happen to you because of your blood, it doesn't mean that you can't have a happy ending, just like William Liedesdorff."

With tears swimming in her eyes, Julie squeezed his hand.

"That's very kind of you," she said, softly. "And I hope you're right."

"I could be your happy ending."

He has a good heart, she thought.

The San Francisco that Julie arrived at on that late-December day wasn't even a half century old, yet the city on the magnificent bay was already a booming metropolis, the unrivaled Queen of the Pacific. The millions from the Gold Rush that had turned the port into a boomtown thirty years before had been succeeded by hundreds of millions more after some prospectors discovered silver on land owned by an old prospector named Pancake Comstock, who chuckled gleefully when he sold out his shares for $11,000. The others, not realizing the enormity of their find, also sold out. All the discoverers of the fabled Comstock Lode died either broke, insane, or working as a short-order cook. Poor old Pancake Comstock, who had given his name to the legendary bonanza, spent the rest of his life trying to strike it rich again. Finally tiring of failing, he sat down beside the Bozeman Trail in Montana and blew his brains out.

Whatever moral might be derived from these sorry tales, the millions kept pouring into San Francisco, and the panhandling prospectors kept searching for new El Dorados, fired by what was called "Comstock madness." Some of them succeeded. New gold and silver mines, such as the Ophir, the Yellow Jacket, the Kentuck, the Gould, the Eclipse, the Hale and Norcross, and richest of all, Virginia City, poured a stream of wealth into the new banks on California Street. The San Francisco Stock Exchange was a nonstop frenzy of speculative madness. Of course, not everyone got rich. But enough did to make San Francisco a city of millionaires, and they lost no time erecting their palaces on what became known as Nob Hill, acquiring mistresses, swilling champagne at such fabled restaurants as the Poodle Dog, Marchand's, and the Maison Dorée, and selling off their daughters to titled Europeans—in short, doing exactly the same as their fellow millionaires back East.

But what first struck Julie as she got off the train at Oakland was the weather. Accustomed to the icy winters and boiling summers of both Peking and New York, she was amazed to find the temperature at a balmy 65 degrees. "It's like spring!" she exclaimed to Lance, who was signaling to a baggageman.

"We've got the finest weather in America," he said, "and if that makes me sound like a booster, well, I am. I even like the rain and fog."

Seven minutes later, they got on board the Bay ferry which took them across the Bay to the opposite side, where it docked at the foot of Market Street.

"There's Hop Sing," Lance said, pointing to a young Chinese in a smart green-and-brown livery, with a shiny top hat on his head. "He'll take us home."

"Lance, I've told you I can't stay at your place . . ."

"None of that nonsense. You're staying with me till we work something out."

As nervous as she was at the prospect of staying with him without a proper chaperone, since she didn't have a penny, she decided she really didn't have much choice. Besides, she was dying of curiosity to see his house and find out what exactly it was he did. Hop Sing, a fine-looking young man, took both their luggage as he stared at Julie.

"Who pretty lady, Boss Man?" he asked Lance.

"This is Miss Julie, a friend of mine. She's going to be staying with us for a while."

"Miss Julie, you speak Chinese?" he asked.

"Mandarin, but no Cantonese."

Hop Sing looked disappointed. But saying nothing further, he picked up the bags and led them through the crowd to a handsome open-air carriage on Market Street. He placed the bags on a rear rack, tying them with leather straps, as Lance held the door for Julie.

But before she could climb in, she saw a group of a half dozen men hurrying toward them.

"Lance!" one of them yelled. "You was on the train that the Horton Gang robbed!"

"Were you an eyewitness to the massacre?" another said, as they swarmed around the carriage.

"Julie, get inside," Lance said. "I'll deal with these guys."

"Who are they?"

"Reporters."

Julie climbed in as the reporters gawked at her.

"Hey, Lance," said the first man, "you got a new singsong girl for the saloon?"

"She's a real looker!" said another, grinning at her.

To everyone's surprise, Lance slugged the man on the jaw so hard, he fell back against the carriage, then slumped to the street.

"This lady, you stupid bastards," Lance shouted, "is my fiancée, Miss Julie Savage from New York City, so you'll mind your goddamned manners!"

Julie didn't know which word surprised her more: fiancée, bastards, or saloon.

"Welcome to Nob Hill," Lance said a while later as his carriage strained up the steep street. "Three of the Big Four who built the Central Pacific live up here. See that monstrosity of a house?" He pointed to a strange, turreted mansion with a huge greenhouse on one side. The style of the house was something Julie had never seen, like a huge fairy-tale castle done in hideous taste. "That was built by Mark Hopkins, who used to sell beans and bacons to the gold miners. Charlie Crocker—that's his place over there—started out selling hairnets and shirts in a Sacramento dry goods store, and Leland Stanford began in the grocery business. Now they're all rich as God. My neighbor, Jim Flood, was a bartender down on Washington Street until he bought a lot of stock in the Comstock Lode. Now he owns that big, dark stone mansion over there. And right across the street from Jim Flood is your humble self."

The carriage had pulled up in front of a big, vaguely French Renaissance mansion that also sported a turret.

"You live in there all by yourself?" Julie said, wonderingly.

"Well, I have a lot of company. And if you move in with me, we could fill the place up with babies."

As Hop Sing opened the carriage door for Julie to get out, she looked at Lance, who was smiling mischievously at her. She said nothing, getting out to stare up at the bizarre house looming over her.

"The point is," Lance said, taking her by the elbow and gently guiding her up the walk, "in San Francisco, everybody started out a nobody, just as I did."

"How *did* you start out?" she asked.

"As soon as we get ensconced and in some clean clothes, I'll tell you the whole sordid story, my beautiful Julie. And you'll discover that I am irresistibly wicked and immoral, someone no decent girl like you should have anything to do with at all."

She was burning with curiosity.

"You intrigue me," she said.

"I know."

And he winked.

"Do you know what a crimp is?" he asked an hour later as he lit a cigar in his paneled library on the first floor. The paneling was beautiful, but the bookshelves were almost empty, holding only a few cheap editions of Wild West novels and Horatio Alger stories. They had bathed—the house was equipped with the most modern plumbing fixtures—and Julie, who had been given an enormous guest room overlooking the Flood Mansion across the street (and, rather ominously, she noted, next door to Lance's bedroom), had changed into clean clothes.

"No, what's a crimp?"

"Good. I'd have been shocked if you had known. A crimp is a low-life fellow who shanghais sailors, gets them drunk at the Barbary Coast dives, then sells them to the captains of ships going to the Orient. I, my sweet Julie, started out life as a crimp."

He blew out a cloud of cigar smoke as she stared at him.

"Then you went from that into selling Bibles?" she said. "I mean, to become respectable."

He chuckled.

"I made a lot of money crimping—by the way, things here in San Francisco aren't quite as wild as they were in those days—and I bought myself a saloon. I own several saloons now, including the Golden Nugget on Portsmouth Square, the biggest in town. And to expose all my sores, I also own what I call 'entertaining rooms'—which are really bordellos—and I have a prison record. Now, what do you say to that?"

"Lance, why are you telling me all this?"

He threw the cigar into the roaring fire and came to her, taking her hands and raising her to her feet.

"Because I'm crazy about you," he whispered, kissing her, hard. "I took one look at you in the train and it was as if a thunderbolt had hit me. I want you to love me, and I figure you'll find out the truth about me sooner or later, so it's better if I tell you the whole ugly picture sooner. Have I made a mistake? Do you look down your nose at me?"

She squeezed him, passionately.

"God, no," she whispered. "I love your honesty. And who am I to judge anyone, when I've been judged all my life because of my eyes being different?"

"To me, your eyes are the most beautiful thing about you." He kissed her again. "No," he corrected himself. "It's your lips. No, wait a minute: your nose. Or is it your hair? Or maybe . . . just maybe . . ." She felt his hands on her breasts. "It's your beautiful breasts, which I'm dying to kiss and lick. In fact, I'm dying to kiss and lick you all over."

"You're a shocking man, Lance Morrow."

"Not for a former crimp."

They both laughed.

Shortly after, he left the house to go downtown to "check on the business," as he told her. Julie, left alone, wandered around the tall-ceilinged rooms of the big house, wondering about Lance and his "business." Even in a vulgar age, the house was decorated in vulgar taste. In fact, it looked rather like a high-class saloon, an effect heightened by the presence of innumerable paintings and statues of nude women, including one enormous painting of a nude "Venus" hanging on the stairway wall which made Julie blush slightly.

And yet, despite everything, she found herself infatuated with Lance, who was like no other man she had ever met. She could hardly wait for him to get home.

Home? she thought, looking around the big drawing room cluttered with ugly, if expensive, furniture. Could this be home for me? Could I really be in love with this disreputable man? But good Lord, he's charming! All right, Julie: grow up. You have to make a decision. And something tells me you're going to have to make it soon.

She saw from her bedroom window the wagons pull up in front of the house at sunset that afternoon. The wagons were marked "The Golden Nugget, Portsmouth Square." Fascinated, she watched men climbing out of the wagons—three in all—and beginning to carry large copper containers around the house to the servants' entrance in back, as well as big boxes. She wondered what in the world was going on.

She found out at seven when Hop Sing knocked on her door.

"Mister Lance is downstairs, waiting for you," he informed her as she opened the door.

"Thank you. I'll be right down."

Having assumed that something special was in the wind, she had put on her best dress—a stunning violet creation trimmed with feathers. Now she checked her reflection in the mirror. Satisfied she looked her best, she left her bedroom and went down the upstairs hall to the staircase. As she started down, she saw Lance at the bottom of the stair, looking up at her, a roguish smile on his face. He had put on a formal tailcoat, and with his shoulder-length hair, she thought he looked rather like a young Buffalo Bill.

"You look wonderful," he said as she joined him. She looked around the entrance hall, which was banked with huge bouquets of flowers in wicker baskets.

"What's the occasion?" she asked.

"You're the occasion. This is 'Welcome to San Francisco, Julie Savage.' "

"Lance!" she exclaimed. "You must have bought every flower in the city!"

"I tried." He took her arm. "Come: I had my chef at the Golden Nugget make us the finest dinner in town—and by the way, he's a damned good cook, the best in the West, as I say. We're going to drink champagne and have a wonderful dinner, and then . . ."

He kissed her cheek.

"I feel," she said, "that my virtue is in mortal danger."

"You're absolutely right. Do you mind?"

She smiled at him.

"Lance, you crazy man, you've woven a spell. I'm ashamed to admit it, but I don't mind at all. In fact—I'm looking forward to it. But I *will* resist you."

"Good. I love a fight."

He had hired a violinist, who played romantic melodies from behind a standing screen as they ate in the candlelit dining room. Julie, a bit giddy from the champagne and wine, said to Lance, "It's not fair."

"What's not fair?"

"How can I possibly resist anyone who's gone to all this trouble to welcome me?"

He smiled as he raised his glass.

"You can't," he said. "But keep trying. It makes it much more romantic."

"You terrible man. Ever since I met you, I've kept telling myself to watch out, but I can't! So what can I do?"

"Relax and enjoy."

He signaled Hop Sing to refill her glass.

A half hour later, he picked her up in his arms and carried her up the stairway to her bedroom. She put her arms around his neck and purred with pleasure as he pushed the door open with his right foot and carried her inside.

"I would never force myself on you," he whispered, "because I respect you, Julie, as well as love you. If you want me to leave, say so."

She started kissing his face with the hungry kisses of a child that was rapidly transforming into a woman.

"Don't leave," she whispered. "Never leave. I want you, my darling. I'm mad for you."

He laid her gently on the bed, kissing her.

"Get undressed," he whispered.

He watched her as she wriggled out of her dress. When she was in her pantalettes, she said, "Look the other way."

"Don't you think it's a bit late for that?" he asked, suppressing a laugh.

"I've never undressed in front of a man before."

"I'm delighted to hear it. All right, I'll turn my back."

When they were both naked, he climbed in the bed next to her and took her in his arms.

"Julie," he whispered, beginning to make love to her, "my God, you drive me insane!"

"Lance, . . . I . . . don't know what's going to happen . . ."

"You'll soon find out."

"Will it hurt?"

"Perhaps at first. But you're going to love it."

"I shouldn't be doing this."

"It's too late now."

"I feel sure I'm going to regret this!"

"Julie, darling, my beloved, beautiful Julie: shut up."

8. "SHE'S MOVED IN WITH A PROFESSIONAL GAMBLER with a prison record!" Justin said, holding the telegram his butler had just brought into the drawing room of the Fifth Avenue house.

"Moved *in* with him?" Johnny said, thinking of his half sister's lack of sexual knowledge. "Julie? Do you think she's become his mistress?"

"Of course not," snapped his father, although Justin wasn't really so sure.

"What sort of prison record does this Lance Morrow have?" Fiammetta asked as she did her petit point. She was privately rather amused, though she didn't want to show it for fear of hurting Justin. Fiammetta's view of life and love was much more easygoing than her husband's.

"He served a year in a Missouri jail for cheating at roulette on a Mississippi gambling boat. He was the croupier."

"He's colorful," Fiammetta said.

"Colorful?" Justin snorted. "My daughter has moved in with an ex-convict."

"Now darling, don't be so stuffy. After all, you were a pirate once, which is certainly as colorful, if not more so. Maybe he's reformed, as you did. And maybe Julie doesn't know what he is."

"She'll soon find out," Justin said, crumpling the telegram in his fist. "Pinkerton's man was held up by more snow, but he'll be in San Francisco in a few days, and he's going to pay a 'call' on Mr. Morrow."

"Where does this Morrow fellow live?" Johnny asked.

"In a big mansion on Nob Hill."

"He sounds rich," Fiammetta observed.

"Rich? He's made a fortune from his gambling joints. And the Pinkerton man says he owns a chain of brothels as well. The man's a vice lord, and my daughter's living with him!"

Johnny's adrenaline was pumping at the thought of the brothels.

"Say, Father," he said, "maybe I should go out to San Francisco and talk to Julie . . ."

"You'll do no such thing!" his father roared. "That would be like sending the fox to the chicken coop!"

"Well at least," Fiammetta said, "it seems she's not going to China—for the time being."

Justin sank into a sofa.

"China's beginning to look better," he said, sourly.

On the morning of the last day of 1882, Pinkerton agent Leroy Seymour stood in front of Lance Morrow's fake–French Renaissance château at the very top of Nob Hill and marveled at the luxuries successful crime could buy. A philosopher might have pondered on the fact that Lance's more respectable neighbors—Mark Hopkins, Charles Crocker, and Leland Stanford—were, according to their many enemies in California, as crooked as Lance in the sense that their railroad monopoly was enriching them at the expense of poorer Californians. But Seymour, a balding, trim man in his forties, wasn't paid to marvel or philosophize. He climbed the stone stoop of the enormous house and rang the bell. After a moment, the heavy front door was opened by Hop Sing in a white jacket.

"Yes?"

"My name is Leroy Seymour. I'd like to see Mr. Morrow."

"He still in bed. Big party last night."

Seymour pulled his wallet from his jacket and extracted a card.

"Give this to Mr. Morrow. I think he'll see me."

Hop Sing glanced at the card, then stood aside.

"Come in, please."

Seymour came into the big stone entrance hall, which boasted a life-size marble statue of a nude woman.

"You wait, please," Hop Sing said, hurrying up the curved staircase. Seymour waited, peering curiously through two open doors into the drawing room of the house. Moments later, Hop Sing reappeared at the top of the stairs and called down: "Come up, please. Boss Man will see you."

Seymour climbed the stairs. Reaching the top, he followed Hop Sing down a hall lined with more paintings of voluptuous nudes to a tall wooden door. Hop Sing opened the door and led Seymour into a large bedroom overlooking the James Flood mansion. A big bed was unmade. Above it hung yet another nude painting, this one of a curvy Turkish *odalisque* reclining on a sofa, her *derrière* aimed at the viewer.

"Boss Man in bathtub," Hop Sing said, pointing to an open door. "Go on in."

Seymour went into a big tiled bathroom where, seated in a capacious, claw-foot tub smoking a cigar, Lance was reclining in suds. Lance took the cigar from his mouth and said, "Let me guess: Julie's father hired you to track her down."

"That's right. Is she here?"

"Absolutely. In fact, in her bathroom down the hall."

"Her father has authorized me to bring her back to New York."

Lance chuckled as he flicked his cigar ash into the soapsuds between his knees.

"That'll be a bit difficult unless I agree to it."

"Mr. Savage wants me to warn you that if you try to force her to remain against her will . . ."

"Let me tell you something, Seymour," Lance interrupted, "that may save a lot of jawing. Last night, Julie and I were married by the Mayor of this fair city, right downstairs in the drawing room. So Julie Savage is now Mrs. Lance Morrow, my bride. She's written her father a letter explaining all this, so it seems to me your job is over."

He smiled, showing his straight white teeth.

"I don't think," Seymour said, "that Mr. Savage is going to be very pleased with this news."

"I'm going to California to meet him," Justin said.

"I think that would be wise," his wife said. "When will you leave?"

"I'll have to talk to Ben, but it will be as soon as possible. I don't suppose you'll want to go with me?"

"Darling, you know I wouldn't go west of the Hudson, much less the Mississippi."

She stood up and crossed the room to him. "I had a long talk with Johnny," she said, "and we've made a compromise. He'll spend six weeks in the Badlands with Teddy Roosevelt this summer. Then he's coming to Rome to be with me."

"That keeps him away from the bank for a long time."

"Justin, you have to face the fact that the boy is restless and bored. He doesn't particularly like being at the bank, for which I can't say I blame him. What he needs is direction and a stable influence—in other words, he needs a wife."

"I agree with you about that. Johnny's gotten into some extremely bad habits."

"Everyone knows he drinks too much and plays around with loose women. I'll find him a suitable wife in Rome—that is, unless you're going to object to his marrying a foreign girl?"

Justin squeezed her hand and smiled.

"How could I object?" he said. "When I married the finest foreign girl in the world. But I'll miss you, darling. Will you miss me?"

Fiammetta hesitated.

."Of course."

She doesn't sound too convinced, he thought.

Julie stood before a full-length pier mirror in her and Lance's bedroom atop Nob Hill. She was examining her reflection, admiring the full-skirted blue silk ball gown he had bought her that morning.

I'm loved, she thought. Lance loves me, and I love him. Oh, God, how I love him, his touch, his smell, his body, his lovemaking! I never knew life could be so wonderful! Things have turned out so well, after all. . . . Lance is worth a dozen Norman Prescotts!

She saw in the mirror's reflection her husband coming into the bedroom. He was dressed in dinner clothes and carrying a black velvet box. She turned and smiled radiantly at him, holding out her arms.

"You've been gone two hours," she exclaimed, "and I've missed you like mad! Oh Lance, I'm so deliriously happy! Come here and smother me with kisses."

"With pleasure."

He came and took her in his arms, kissing her hungrily.

"I have a surprise for you," he said, after a moment.

"I adore surprises! What now?"

He handed her the black velvet box.

"This is your reward for being the perfect wife for two whole days."

"Lance, you wicked man, you're spoiling me dreadfully—and I love it!"

She opened the lid. Inside was a dazzling diamond-and-ruby necklace, the cabochon rubies surrounded by tiny pearls.

"Oh!" she gasped. "It's beautiful! But it must have cost a fortune . . . I know, you're rich, but still . . . Let me try it on! Here, hold the box . . . it's so beautiful . . ."

He took the box as she placed the necklace around her throat. The jewels felt cold against the skin of her breasts. She turned to look in the mirror again.

"I feel like an empress!" she said. He put his arms around her waist and kissed her bare shoulders. Suddenly, the jewels felt hot. "Fiammetta would be so jealous!" she said. "She's passionate about jewelry and has a magnificent diamond-and-ruby necklace, but it's not as nice as this."

"By the way, I received a telegram from your father. He's on the way to San Francisco. I think he wants to check me out."

"Father!" she said, excitement in her eyes. "When will he get here?"

"In four days. Will he like me?"

"Oh, I'm sure he will. That is, if you don't lie to him, as you did to me. 'Bible salesman' indeed! Really, darling, that was a bit thick."

He grinned as he exhaled.

"Well, I thought telling you the truth right off might have given you a bad impression."

She came and sat next to him, giving him a hug.

"I adore you."

He kissed her forehead.

"Will I like him?"

"No one could help but like Father. He's the most interesting person!" She thought a moment, frowning. "Well, he *used* to be. I suppose there are some people who could say he's gotten a bit stuffy now that he's older. But if you could have known him when he was young, in China . . ." She sighed. "He was so thrilling! But I suppose no one can stay thrilling forever."

"I can," Lance whispered, squeezing her left breast. "And I will."

He kissed her again. She loved his tawny smell of cigar smoke and cologne.

"Yes," she whispered, "I think you will."

"Shall we have a quick one before we go to the Maison Dorée?"

She shoved him away.

"Of course not! I'm all dressed. Besides, I'm hungry."

"I've got something that's not on the restaurant menu."

She giggled.

"You really *are* wicked," she said. "Maybe it's why I love you so much."

She stood up and started slipping off her shoes.

"By the way," she added, "I think it might help with my father if you took down some of your nude paintings. He might get the feeling he was coming into a bawdy house."

Lance laughed.

"You have a point. I'll have them all taken down tomorrow. I'll replace them with bucolic landscapes filled with nude . . ." he paused, mischievously. She looked at him. Then he added: "animals."

What will Father think of Lance? Julie thought nervously as she and Lance waited for the Silver Palace cars of the

Pacific Express to pull into the Oakland station. If only he'd sent a letter, so I'd have an inkling about how he's thinking . . .

"Nervous?" Lance asked.

"Yes, terribly. Are you?"

"No. Why should I be? We're all going to get along fine."

"I hope so."

A few minutes later, the engine came into the station, its bell clanging, smoke and steam issuing forth. After it squeaked to a stop, Julie looked down the platform as the passengers started disembarking.

"There he is!" she exclaimed, starting to wave at the tall man in the top hat and fur-collared black coat.

"Julie!" her father exclaimed, hurrying to her with open arms. "Thank God. My darling Julie."

As he hugged and kissed her, she was ashamed to see that there were tears in his eyes.

"Papa, can you forgive me?" she asked. "I mean, for running away?"

"Of course, darling. I wish you hadn't done it, but it doesn't matter now. As long as you're happy."

"I'm desperately happy!" she said, smiling. Then she turned to Lance. "And this is Lance. I know you two are going to get along so well."

Justin turned to the young man. Though he retained a smile on his lips, his blue eyes became a bit guarded.

"Ah, yes," he said, extending his hand. "The groom. How do you do?"

"Glad to meet you, Mr. Savage," Lance said, pumping his hand enthusiastically. "Or should I call you 'Father'?"

"You may call me whatever you like," Justin said. But his tone was a bit cool. He's pushy, he was thinking. Wonderful-looking, but definitely pushy.

As they drove to the house on Nob Hill, Justin told them about his train trip, which, unlike theirs, had been uneventful, the Horton Gang having been captured and summarily hanged. "Johnny's going out West, and Fiammetta is preparing to go to Rome, so I'm going to be all by myself," he went on. Julie squeezed his hand.

"Stay here with us," she said. "You'll love San Francisco."

"No, I can't stay more than a few days. Business. But I do want to see the city. And I'd like to see some of your establishments, Lance."

He leaned forward in the carriage looking at his new son-in-law, who was sitting on the other side of Julie.

"Be glad to give you a complete tour, Father," Lance said with a smile, thinking, I wonder if the old boy would like one of the girls? That should soften him up.

"I've been told the Palace Hotel is one of the biggest in the world," Justin went on, referring to the two-year-old seven-story hotel that covered an entire city block. It had been built by William Chapman Ralston, who founded the Bank of California and was found floating in the Bay weeks before the hotel opened after learning that his bank had failed.

"It's quite beautiful," Julie said. "Lance took me there for tea yesterday. But of course you're staying with us."

"You're sure I won't be in the way? After all, you're newlyweds. You could hardly want the old folks hanging around."

She hugged his arm.

"You're not 'old folks,'" she said. "You're my wonderful, wonderful father, and we're back together again. Oh, I do so love you!"

"And I love you. By the way, I have a wedding present for you." He pulled his wallet from his jacket. "I didn't have time to buy you anything, and I have no idea what you want or need. If you want a silver service, or anything, pick out your pattern, and I'll order it for you. But since you didn't let me plan a wedding for you, here's a check that I figure a wedding would have cost me."

He gave her the check. Julie looked at it and gasped.

"Look, Lance," she exclaimed. "It's for fifty thousand dollars!"

"Is everything all right?" Julie asked twenty minutes later as her father started to unpack his luggage in the big guest bedroom on the second floor. "Will you be comfortable?"

"Oh yes," Justin said, removing clean shirts. "The house is very grand."

"Lance doesn't have the best taste in the world, but I'm working on him. Do you like him, Father?"

"It's a little early to tell, but he seems nice enough. The important thing is, are you happy?"

"I've never dreamed of such happiness. For all one hears of love and romance, when you actually have it, it's like a miracle."

"You might have waited a little."

"But why? We were in love! And if it hadn't been for Lance, I'd have been shot by those bandits. I know we rushed into marriage, but you see, Lance doesn't think anything about the fact that I'm half-Chinese. He loves me for myself. That's another nice thing about San Francisco: even though there's a certain amount of anti-Chinese prejudice, the fact remains there are thousands of Chinese here, so I don't feel out of place, as I did in New York. I told you in my letter I was going to China, but this is much better, and I'm nearer to you. You'll come visit us often?"

"Yes."

"Lance is going to so much trouble to impress you. He's very proud of his chef at the Golden Nugget—that's his biggest casino on Portsmouth Square. The chef's a Chilean who trained in Paris, and he's coming here tonight to cook us dinner. We'll have a wonderful time!"

He smiled at her.

"I'm already having a wonderful time, just being with you again."

Julie ran into his arms and kissed him.

After he had washed off the grime of the train in his bathtub and changed into clean clothes, Justin felt improved physically. But as he walked down the wide staircase to the ground floor, his mood was positively foul. It didn't take a genius to see what he already knew from the background reports on Lance sent to him by Allan Pinkerton: the man was, at the very best, an extremely shady character. But Justin told himself to remain cool; after all, Lance held the trump, Julie, who was totally infatuated with him. Justin knew instinctively that if there were a showdown between him and Lance, Julie, no matter how much she might love her father, would probably side with her husband. So a showdown must be avoided at all costs.

Marveling at the vulgarity of the decor—the gilt furniture and the red-flocked wallpaper—Justin went into the big drawing room where his son-in-law was pouring himself a drink.

"Ah, Father!" he exclaimed. "Everything all right upstairs?"

"Yes, thank you."

"Care for a whiskey? I have Kentucky bourbon, Maryland rye, Russian vodka, English gin, and a very fine single malt Scottish whiskey. I also have beers, wines, and chilled champagne."

"You must either entertain a lot, or drink a lot."

"Both. Julie hasn't gotten in stride yet, but when we return from our honeymoon, she's going to be a very busy hostess. San Francisco's a party town. Yes, sir, life is one big party. But you didn't tell me what you want?"

"A glass of champagne, if it's handy."

Lance tugged on a fringed bell cord.

"Hop Sing will bring it."

"Where are you and Julie going on your honeymoon?"

"Well, of course, we got hitched so quick, we haven't had much time to plan anything. But I'm thinking of driving her down the coast to Santa Barbara. Beautiful place, Santa Barbara. I'm considering buying some real estate there. In my opinion, California real estate can go nowhere but up, in the long run. Ah, here's Hop Sing. Bring some champagne for Mr. Savage."

"Yes, Boss Man."

He nodded and returned to the central hall.

"Hop Sing's from Canton, like most of the Chinese here," Lance said, lighting a cigar. "He's a good man. Smart as a whip, and honest. Can't say that for a lot of the Celestials."

Justin gave him a cool look.

"Do you consider your wife smart and honest?" he said. "After all, she's half-Celestial."

Lance had the grace to turn slightly red.

"Hell, Julie's all American and the most beautiful girl in the world. I'm a mighty lucky man to have won your daughter, Father. But I'll admit at one time I had a sort of prejudice against Chinese. I'm anything but a saint. But the problem is, people say it's human nature to dislike people who're different. They don't understand human nature's got to be worked on, improved, because human nature's not very good. In fact, it can be downright nasty. Falling in love with Julie's taught me that love can do wonders for human nature. It sure as hell has improved mine."

He's really rather impressive, Justin thought. The man seems to have heart as well as brains.

"Here's Julie now," Lance said, smiling as Julie came into the room. Even Justin's heart skipped a beat as he looked at the loveliness of his daughter. She had pulled her hair back into a chignon and had slightly rouged her lips—something that shocked Justin, though he had to admit the effect was breathtaking. She was wearing a low-cut silver dress with a bustle in the back, and around her neck she had on the diamond-and-ruby necklace Lance had given her.

"My God," Lance muttered, staring at this vision. "What a pretty piece you are!"

He came to his wife and kissed her.

He looks like he's really in love with her, Justin thought. Maybe I'm being too harsh on him.

✦

Justin had to admit the dinner was first-rate, although the
dining room was, like the rest of the house, in bizarre taste—
bright yellow walls stenciled with a strange red design, thick
gold curtains over the windows, and on the big dining table
a pair of the strangest candlesticks he had ever seen, looking
like something out of a Greek or possibly Russian Orthodox
church. (True to his word, Lance had had all the nude paintings in the house taken down and replaced by a jumble of
third-rate farm scenes). But the food—from the Russian
caviar and sorrel soup through the fish course, meat course,
salads, and dessert—was topflight, and the wines superb.

And Lance proved to be an excellent host, able to talk in-
terestingly and amusingly, funded with an apparently endless number of jokes, most of which trembled like a
butterfly wing on the edge of bad taste, but which were genuinely funny, reducing both Julie and her father to howls of
laughter on several occasions.

He's got charm, Justin conceded, and he's smart.

"Isn't Lance wonderful?" Julie exclaimed as she hugged her
father an hour later in his bedroom upstairs. "Wasn't dinner
delightful? Didn't you have a wonderful time?"

It made Justin come close to tears as he saw how desperately his daughter wanted him to approve of her husband.
He took her in his arms and hugged her tightly.

"Yes, I had a very good time," he said. "And he's got
some funny jokes."

"He hears every joke in California at the Golden Nugget.
Of course, most of them are pretty bawdy. Anyway . . ." She
smiled at her father. "I'm so happy you're here and that you
like Lance. Everything's turning out so well! Did you see
my engagement ring? Isn't it beautiful? A sapphire and two
diamonds." She held out her hand, and Justin inspected the
ring, which was indeed beautiful. And expensive.

"Yes, it's lovely. Lance likes to spend, doesn't he?"

She shrugged.

"He makes a lot of money, and he spends a lot."

"I'll be most interested to see tomorrow how he makes it."
She frowned and held his hands.

"He's being very honest with you," she said. "He'll show you everything. You'll have to forget for a while that you're a very respectable banker. You have to give him the benefit of the doubt."

He smiled and kissed her forehead.

"You forget," he said, "that I'm a former pirate."

9. "YOUR FATHER DOESN'T LIKE ME," LANCE SAID at midnight. He was sitting up in bed next to Julie, smoking a cigar. As was his custom, which had shocked Julie at first, he was naked; he had just made love to her, but he always slept in the nude whether making love or not and would casually walk around the bedroom without a stitch. The Turkish *odalisque* whose *derrière* had been so daringly displayed above the bed had been replaced by a risible painting of four cute puppies in a wicker basket.

"That's not true!" Julie exclaimed. "He told me he's very fond of you."

"Then he lied." He exhaled cigar smoke as his left hand lazily scratched his smooth chest.

"Darling, how can you say that?"

"I feel it. I'm very good at sensing what people are thinking. He's being polite, but I can sniff that he hates my guts. Of course, I suppose I can't blame him: I'm hardly the ideal son-in-law. I'm sure what he wanted for you was some extremely proper banker or stockbroker."

Julie sat up, covering her breasts with the sheet—she, too, was naked.

"*He* may have wanted that, but *I* didn't!" she said. "More to the point, they didn't want *me*." She reached over and put her hand on his forearm. "*You're* what I want. Forever and ever."

He looked at her through the cigar smoke. Then he smiled slightly.

"Yes," he said, "I know that. We're a team your father can never break up."

"Well, I think you're imagining things. Where are you going to take him first in the morning?"

"The Golden Nugget."

"Portsmouth Square's where all the gambling action is in town," Lance said the next morning as he and Justin drove downtown to Portsmouth Square, which was situated between Chinatown and Telegraph Hill. "I bought the Golden Nugget five years ago—or, rather, I bought what was left of it, because most of the old saloon had burned down. I'm pretty proud of it. Without sounding like a braggart, I think it's the best damned casino in San Francisco."

Hop Sing pulled the carriage up in front of a large, three-story building, the facade of which had columns and pilasters, rather like a Greek temple. A big glass-and-steel marquee jutted out over the entrance, and an elaborately painted sign, illuminated at night by gas jets, read "GOLDEN NUGGET CASINO—SHOWS NIGHTLY!"

A tall, red-bearded doorman in a shiny top hat, green-and-beige knee-length coat, and leather boots opened the door to the carriage and tipped his hat as Lance climbed out.

"Good morning, John," he said. "This is my father-in-law, Mr. Savage."

As Justin got out, John tipped his hat again, and said, "Welcome to San Francisco, sir."

"Thank you."

"Follow me, Father," Lance said, taking Justin's arm. "I want you to meet my assistant, Jade Moon."

The two men went through two swinging wood-and-etched-glass doors into an enormous room which, to Justin's surprise since it was only ten-thirty in the morning, was packed with gamblers.

"When do you open?" he asked his son-in-law.

"We never close."

"But who are all these people? I mean, don't they work?"

"Some of them have jobs. Most of them just gamble."

"Do they win?"

"Some do in the short run. But in the long run, they all lose. The house always wins. Ah, here's Jade Moon."

Justin saw a beautiful Chinese woman, perhaps in her early thirties, making her way around the gaming tables toward them. For a moment, he thought he was back in the China of his youth, for the woman, whose face was heavily made-up, was wearing a traditional Chinese floor-length robe, and her black hair was coiffed in the elaborate Manchu fashion, with a wide black headpiece, from each end of which dangled colorful fringe. However, since the woman did not wobble in the infamous "lily walk," he knew that her feet had not been bound when she was young so that she walked normally. She nodded to Lance, and said, "Good morning, Mr. Morrow." Then she looked curiously at Justin.

"This is my father-in-law, Mr. Savage," Lance said. "This is Jade Moon. She'll give you a tour of the place while I go to my office and check the mail . . ."

He was interrupted by a yell from the rear of the gambling hall.

"You! Lance Morrow, you cheating bastard . . ."

Justin saw a young man, very drunk, leave one of the craps tables and stumble toward them. His red hair was a mess, and he wore a wrinkled tweed suit.

"Get that drunk out of here," Lance snapped to Jade Moon.

"Yes, Mr. Morrow."

Jade Moon signaled to a burly man smoking a cigar near the bar. The man, a former boxer Lance employed as one of his bouncers, dropped the cigar in a spittoon and started toward the young man, who was shouting at Lance, "The dice in this joint are loaded! I've been cleaned out by your goddamn thieves . . ."

The bouncer slugged him in the jaw so hard that the young man literally flew backward in the air, then crashed to the floor next to a roulette table. The other gamblers, the vast majority of whom were men, guffawed and applauded. The bouncer picked the young man up, threw him over his left shoulder, and carried him to a door in the rear, where they disappeared.

Lance turned to Jade Moon, and said, "Don't let him in the place again."

"Yes, Mr. Morrow."

Lance smiled at Justin.

"Sorry about the interruption, but there's only one way to deal with drunks."

"Is it true?" Justin asked.

"What?"

"What he said. Are your dice loaded?"

"Of course not. But every loser thinks they are. I'll see you later in my office."

Smiling, he patted Justin's upper arm, then started across the room toward a curtained doorway.

"What would you like to see first, Mr. Savage?" Jade Moon said, smiling.

Justin turned to her and spoke in Cantonese, which he had been fluent in since his childhood, having been taught by his Cantonese nanny, Ah Pin.

"I'd like to see what really goes on here."

Jade Moon looked surprised, whether by his fluent Cantonese, his question—or both. But her answer surprised him even more.

"Mr. Morrow has told me to show you everything—even the third floor. This way, please."

A half hour later, Justin came into Lance's large paneled office overlooking Portsmouth Square. Lance was sitting at his walnut desk reading some papers. When he saw Justin, he smiled and stood up.

"Well: Jade Moon gave you the tour. I hope you were favorably impressed."

Justin closed the door.

"What do you think?" he said. "I was impressed, but hardly favorably. Running a casino is one thing. But up on the third floor, you're running a damned whorehouse!"

"That's right. By the way, if you'd like one of the girls, it would be on me." He smiled and pointed to a cut-glass crystal decanter on a silver tray on top of a sideboard beneath a large oil painting of a nude. "Care for a drink?"

Justin had come across the room to the desk.

"Damn you," he said, softly. "I can't believe how any one man could be so totally corrupt. But worse than that, I can't believe you wouldn't try to hide your corruption. Instead, you actually flaunt it to me!"

Lance went to the sideboard and removed the crystal top from the decanter.

"I have nothing I'm ashamed of," he said, pouring whiskey into a glass. "My parents were dirt-poor farmers in Missouri who came out here in the Gold Rush and lost everything. My father committed suicide when I was five and my mother became a prostitute, so what I'm offering my customers upstairs is a big step up for me, socially. I've had to claw my way to the top, and I offer no apology for anything I've ever done." He took a sip of the drink. "You hate my guts, don't you? For marrying Julie? For being what I am?"

"I'm in no position to moralize to anyone. But I know Julie loves you."

Lance went back to his desk chair and sat down.

"And I love her. So, let's think about it now. Julie and I love each other, and we want to have a family. While I'm not ashamed of what I do, I'm no fool: I realize my business isn't 'respectable.' It might embarrass our children—and your grandchildren. I'll sell out all my businesses. It shouldn't be hard to find a buyer: the Golden Nugget is a gold mine, no pun intended."

Justin stared at him.

"And one day, I'm going to be governor of this state," Lance went on. "And you could hardly object to your daughter being married to the governor of California. Or, perhaps, a senator. Or . . ." he stuck the cigar in his mouth, sucked on it and exhaled a cloud of smoke as he smiled again, ". . . maybe even President."

Justin started to laugh.

"Did I say something funny?" Lance asked in a surprised tone. "I mean, you may think it's funny I might be President one day, but I sure as hell don't."

"I'm not laughing at that," Justin said. "I'm laughing that my daughter has married an absolute rascal whom I'm actually starting to like! So, damn you, yes: I *will* have a drink!"

He's honest, damn him, Justin thought. He's pulled no punches with me, he's shown me everything. He's even admitted he used to be prejudiced. Maybe he's not the ideal husband, but they're truly in love with each other. And Julie's happier than I've ever seen her, and I have to face the fact she was miserable in New York.

I hope San Francisco proves less prejudiced than New York . . .

PART TWO

THE HARVARD COWBOYS

10. "HEY, FOUR-EYES!" YELLED THE DRUNKEN COW-
boy, aiming his pistol at Teddy Roosevelt's face. "You prissy
dude from the East—you gonna buy us the next round of
drinks?"

The cowboy was standing next to the table in the Min-
gusville, Montana, saloon where Teddy Roosevelt and
Johnny Savage were drinking beer. Teddy, whose eyesight
was poor, was as usual wearing his pince-nez. Now he
looked at the cowboy and stood up.

"The name," he said in his squeaky voice, "is Mr. Roosevelt."

Then he slugged the cowboy on the jaw, knocking him
out on the floor and causing his gun to fire into the ceiling.
The other dozen or so cowboys in the smoky saloon stared at
him in awe for a moment. Then Johnny jumped to his feet
and pounded Teddy on the back.

"Bravo, Teddy!" he yelled. "Well done!"

The other cowboys burst into cheers and applause as
Teddy yelled: "Drinks on the house, that is, on me!"

It was the summer of 1884. Johnny's hunting trip West the
previous summer with Teddy had given him as deep a love
for the strange Bad Lands of North Dakota as Teddy, and,
like Teddy, he had invested money borrowed from his father's bank to buy a hundred head of beef cattle, an investment he was convinced was going to earn huge profits.
Many of their Harvard classmates were also investing in the
West, as well as rich dudes from all over the East and Europe. Cattle mania had swept the world with the opening of
the West by the railroads, and ranching had become the fashionable thing to do for young men with the means to afford
it. These Harvard cowboys, as they were laughingly labeled,
didn't consider themselves cowboys at all. They called
themselves ranchmen, and though they dressed somewhat
the same way as cowboys, their clothes were made of much

finer material, their saddles and guns were expensive, and, in the case of Johnny and Teddy, their hunting knives came from Tiffany's. Spurred by books like *The Beef Bonanza: or How To Get Rich on the Plains*, hundreds of young men went West, traveling in comfort by railroad. But it wasn't just money that attracted them. It was adventure. It was romance. It was getting away from cities and testing yourself in the wilderness. It was shaking off the elaborate rituals and rules of Victorian society and riding free on your horse over the limitless plains. Life became as heady as wine—with the proviso that you had enough money to take the train back East when the weather grew cold.

Also, the land was public domain, so your cattle could roam for free, feeding off the rich grass that grew everywhere: little bluestem grass, excellent for fattening the cattle, and curly buffalo grass, which was unexcelled for winter feeding. Teddy never bought any land, but he had built a log ranch house on some land on the Little Missouri River near the Montana border (the Little Missouri flowed north, and in summer was little more than a stream). He named the ranch the Elkhorn, and the ranch house was big by Badlands standards, sixty feet long and thirty feet wide, with eight rooms, a small cellar Teddy used as a darkroom for his photographs, a stone fireplace, and a porch where Teddy sat in the evenings reading poetry.

They might call themselves ranchmen, but they worked with the cowboys, and the work was strenuous, entailing long hours in the saddle. Johnny, who was a great horseman, found the work exhilarating as did Teddy, who was not such a good horseman and admitted that his roping was mediocre at best. But he threw himself into the work with his customary zeal. Only when they returned to the ranch house did he often sink into bouts of depression, for a double tragedy had altered his life the previous February.

On the same day, in the same house—the Roosevelt house on West Fifty-seventh Street in Manhattan—Teddy's beloved mother had died unexpectedly of typhoid fever. Eleven hours later, Teddy's beloved wife, Alice, had died a few days after giving birth to their daughter, Alice Roosevelt, of Bright's disease, a malady she hadn't even suspected she had. Teddy's mother had been only forty-eight; his wife had been twenty-two. This double tragedy in one day led Teddy to wonder if he were cursed. Though he never talked about it even to close friends like Johnny, the horror had brought home dramatically how short life could be. Remembering his asthmatic childhood—and he still suffered from the disease, though the attacks were much less frequent in North Dakota—Teddy worked with grim determination to build his frail physique. He was still a "light little fella," as one of his cowboys described him, whose waist you could surround with "two thumbs and your fingers." Particularly when compared to Johnny, a young giant, Teddy looked—and sounded—like a mouse. But as he had demonstrated in the Montana saloon when he knocked out the cowboy, Teddy was a mouse with guts and strength, and the "rough riding" on his horse was building himself into a much more rugged man.

But Teddy was depressed by politics, too. Earlier that summer he had attended the Republican Convention in Chicago and had worked against the presidential nomination of James G. Blaine, a former senator from Maine whom he—and many other Republicans—considered hopelessly corrupt. But when Blaine won the nomination, Teddy decided to back him in the fall election. Though being loyal to his party, Teddy thought he was betraying his principles. He retired to the ranch he really didn't own to devote himself to raising cattle and fighting the black moods of despair that assailed him by vigorous exercise and work.

In this, Johnny was the perfect companion. Johnny was not the intellectual that Teddy was, nor was his mind as brilliant. But when it came to action, to riding endless hours, roping cattle and all the many other activities of ranch life, Johnny was superb. The two young men, still in their mid-twenties, formed a bond that was deep and lasting. Johnny had incurred the wrath of his father, Justin, by quitting his bank job and going west to raise cattle. He had incurred the wrath of his mother, Fiammetta, by not proposing to any of the Roman beauties she forced on him the previous summer. Justin had called him "irresponsible" and "immature," and Fiammetta had called him "ungrateful" and "disloyal," but Johnny didn't care.

On his horse, Tumbleweed, in his chaps and sombrero, riding the rough landscape of the Badlands, he was his own man and having the time of his life.

Forty miles to the south of the Elkhorn Ranch lay the town of Medora, North Dakota, which was owned in its entirety by one of the most bizarre and flamboyant men ever to grace the Old West. His name was almost impossible to make up, much less pronounce: Antoine-Amédée-Marie-Vincent Manca de Vallombrosa, the Marquis de Morès (pronounced MorESS) whom his plain-speaking cowboy employees boiled down to the simpler Marquis (pronounced MarKEE). The most prominent figure in the territory, he had been dubbed by the local press "The Emperor of the Badlands," and not without reason. The Marquis, who was exactly Johnny and Teddy's age, was tall, sinewy, extremely fit, and dashingly good-looking, with black hair and a huge black mustache he waxed to a point on each end and which gave him the look of a stage villain evicting orphans in a storm. He was a Frenchman, although his title, awarded his ancestors in the fourteenth century, was Spanish. A graduate of St. Cyr, the French West Point, and Saumur, regarded as the finest cavalry school in the world, he was an excellent horseman and crack shot, as well as a superb fencer—he carried around a silver-headed bamboo walking stick filled with ten pounds of lead to exercise his dueling arm. He had killed two men in France in duels before coming to New York and marrying Medora von Hoffman, the beautiful daughter of a Wall Street multimillionaire. Fluent in English, French, and Spanish, the Marquis was brilliant, imaginative, and supremely egotistical, prone to bouts of fierce anger.

He was also a rabid Catholic, a rabid anti-Semite, and told people quite without embarrassment that he intended one day to mount the vacant throne of France. There were those who thought he was more than a little bit crazy.

"Guess what," Teddy said to Johnny one night as they sat before the fire in the ranch house eating supper. "We've been invited to dinner at the Château."

"What's the Château?"

"That's the house the Marquis de Morès built for himself and his wife down in Medora."

"Oh yes, my father knows the Marquis's father-in-law, Baron von Hoffman. I even think my father met the Marquis once, in New York. They live in the Brunswick Hotel on Fifth Avenue. I assume he named the town of Medora for his wife?"

"Absolutely, because her father is putting up all the money for the Marquis's meatpacking plants. I've run into the Marquis a couple of times—he's like a walking arsenal, by the way, carries two huge Colt revolvers on him with two cartridge belts across his chest, a heavy-caliber Henry rifle cradled in one arm and a bowie knife strapped to one of his legs. I personally don't like the man much—he's arrogant and difficult—but I'll admit that if he can pull off his idea, he'll make a killing out here."

"What's the idea?"

"Well, since they've invented refrigerator cars for the railroads, the Marquis decided to build a meat-processing plant out here where the cattle are and ship the meat already dressed to Chicago. It would make a considerable saving—no expensive cattle drives to Chicago—and presumably he could undersell the Chicago beef trust—the Armours and the Swifts and that bunch. As I say, if the Marquis can pull it off, he'll make a fortune. I think you'll like his wife, though. She's quite lovely—and a better shot than the Marquis. So, shall we accept the invitation?"

"I wouldn't miss it for the world."

"Just watch out for the Marquis," Teddy added. "He shot to death a young man last year he caught trying to pull down

one of his fences—the locals hate like the very dickens the
fact that the Marquis is fencing in his land. The Marquis was
tried for murder, but he claimed he acted in self-defense and
got off. There's some talk that he bribed either the judge or
the jury—or both."

"The Marquis sounds like a real charmer."

"Oh, he is. But the charm can kill."

11.   THE NEXT DAY AFTER LUNCH, JOHNNY AND TEDDY
set out on horseback to journey the forty miles south to the
new town of Medora. It was a broiling hot day, but the
young men's sombreros protected them from the merciless
sun. They brought along blanket rolls; although the Marquis
had invited them to spend the night at the Château, Teddy
had said the "crazy Frenchman," as the locals called him behind his back, could be capricious, and they should be prepared to camp out in case he changed his mind.

Many considered the Bad Lands of North Dakota a sort of
hell without brimstone—even though, in some places, un-
derground fires did burn naturally. But others, like Johnny
and Teddy, thought of it as a place of strange and haunting
beauty, with its cottonwood trees along the banks of the
Little Missouri rustling in the breeze. It was a sort of minia-
ture Grand Canyon, extending some two hundred miles
along the river. There were buttes and ravines, crisscrossed
by little streams, and strange, castlelike rock formations that
loomed before one suddenly, all caused by millions of years
of glaciers and erosion. Teddy, in one of his letters home,
had described it as country "that looks like Poe sounds"—a
peculiar, but apt, description. The artist Frederic Remington
described it as "a place for stratagem and murder, with nothing to witness its mysteries but the cold, blue winter sky."

The two men made good time, galloping for a while, then
slowing the pace to relieve the horses, and they reached the
Château at Medora at seven that evening. Johnny's first im-

pression of the place was that it looked like a big, frame farmhouse, rather than a château. Situated on top of a promontory overlooking the river below and, across the river, the town of Medora, it did have a rather baronial location. It was painted light gray, and had red shutters and a red roof, which Johnny thought was a rather odd color combination. A lawn had been planted, and a few scraggly trees and bushes put in around the house, but the place had a barren, almost forlorn, look about it, as if it were trying to be something better than it was. As Johnny dismounted, he heard from inside the building, which was girdled on two sides by a covered porch, a piano playing Verdi's "La Donna è Mobile" from *Rigoletto*—and played well.

"That's the Marquise," Teddy said as he tied his horse to the hitching stand next to Johnny's. "She plays very well. Had her piano shipped out from New York a few months ago. She also speaks seven languages and is a terrific horsewoman."

"And a good shot, you told me."

"That's right. She's killed a grizzly bear, which isn't for the faint of heart. The Marquis had a special hunting coach built for her, with folding bunks, a kitchen, and silver and china. Whatever you think of the man, he does things in style. And here he is."

A tall man in a black shirt, a sombrero, with a cartridge belt around his waist had come out of the house onto the porch. He had on leather riding trousers and shiny boots. He wore two revolvers in holsters at his sides and he carried a long-barreled rifle. Johnny thought he was one of the most striking-looking men he had ever seen, though there was something vaguely menacing about him.

"Ah, you're here," the Marquis said in his excellent English. "Welcome to the Château. How was your ride?"

"Uneventful, but hot," Teddy said, climbing the steps to the porch.

"Then we'll cool you with some champagne," the Marquis said, shaking his hand. "And this is young Savage? I've met your father in New York, Johnny. A superb man. And what a life he's led! On several occasions, I've thought of chucking it all and going to China to be a pirate, like your father. Delighted to meet you, sir."

Johnny shook his hand, noting that the man had a grip like a vise.

"Delighted to meet you, sir. And thanks for including me in the invitation."

"Nonsense, the pleasure is mine!" the Marquis said, putting his free arm around Johnny's shoulder. "It's a relief to entertain cultivated, civilized young men like you two. One gets so bored with these riffraff cowboys, who are the scum of the earth—half of them have criminal personalities."

"I happen to admire cowboys," Johnny said.

"Ah, but you're new out here. Once you get to know them, you realize that they're nothing but trash. Although if I'd had any idea what a fine-looking young man you are, Johnny, I might have hesitated inviting you here tonight. My wife has a liking for fine-looking young men. I'll have to watch you two!" He laughed heartily as he opened the screen door, but Johnny thought the "joke," if that's what it was, was maladroit at best, and at worst . . . some sort of clumsy threat? He exchanged looks with Teddy, who rolled his myopic eyes as if to say "What an arrogant boor!" Then they went inside the house.

The piano music had stopped. The Marquis put his rifle in a gun rack in the short hall, then led his guests into the parlor, which was large and refreshingly cool after the heat outdoors. Standing by a handsome spinet was a rather delicate young woman in a pink blouse and gray skirt. She was attractive without being a great beauty. She had a rather long nose and her dark red hair was set in curls. She smiled as the men came in the room, which was furnished with the usual clutter of the day.

"Darling, here are our guests," the Marquis said, leading them across the room. "Teddy you've met. And this is Johnny Savage, from New York. My wife, Medora."

Medora smiled prettily as her guests shook her hand.

"Welcome to our house, gentlemen," she said.

The Marquis yanked a bell cord.

"I've put champagne on ice," he said. "Veuve Clicquot, a favorite of mine. Of course, one has to bring the wines out from New York. In this godforsaken hole, all they have is cheap whiskey and beer."

Teddy looked rather stormy, Johnny thought.

"I say, de Morès," he said, "if you dislike it so much out here and think the cowboys are all trash, why did you come?"

The Marquis smiled and spread his hands.

"The same reason you've come: to make money! Greed! Nothing like plain, old-fashioned greed, which makes the world go round. We'll all enrich ourselves out here, then return to civilization. I guarantee you, my friend: within ten years, I'll be the king of France! And then, I'll start my real task in life: to cleanse France of the vermin who have infiltrated our ancient society. That's why God put me on this earth."

"What 'vermin'?" Johnny asked, beginning to think he really was a crazy Frenchman.

"What else?" the Marquis said with a shrug. "The Jews. Ah: and here's our champagne." A young man in a white jacket came into the room carrying a silver tray with four silver goblets on it. He was followed by another young man carrying a silver wine bucket with a bottle of champagne. "We have a staff of twenty here," the Marquis went on, "but they're ignorant brutes. My wife has had to teach them how to serve."

Johnny had known the Marquis less than five minutes. Already, he hated his guts.

He had to admit that the dinner, which was served on blue Minton china, was the best food he'd had since coming West, and the wines were excellent.

"It's my own lamb," the Marquis said, carving into his chop. "I've brought in five hundred head of sheep. Of course, as Teddy knows, the locals are all howling at me for fencing in my land, but I've got a huge investment out here. I can't afford to let every fool rancher graze his cattle on my land; there won't be enough grass to go around. It's my land, bought and paid for, and I have the right to fence it in. Except I don't believe you agree with me, do you, Teddy?"

"You have a right to protect your investment," Teddy said. "But you know as well as I do that you've made yourself unpopular out here. Ever since the ranchers came out here, the land has been open."

"Hah! As if I care about popularity! And the ranchers—and I include you, sir—have no right to moralize. You stole the land from the Indians."

Which shut Teddy up, not an easy thing to do.

As the meal progressed, Johnny noticed that both the Marquis and his wife were drinking heavily of the wine. He also noticed that Medora was shooting him occasional rather bleary-eyed glances. She didn't say much during the meal, but then, neither did anyone else, since the Marquis was something of a monologuist. At first, he went on at length on the arts and literature, about which he was knowledgeable. Then he switched to the subject of opera. He turned out to be a passionate Wagnerian. He rattled on about the brilliance of Wagner's music—and then also about the brilliance of his political and racial views. Since Johnny knew little about either opera or Wagner, he didn't pay much attention to his host, but rather sneaked looks at his hostess. The wine and the monologue were making him feel drowsy, when something the Marquis said snapped him to attention.

"The worst idea that's come out of France is that ridiculous Statue of Liberty they're talking about putting up in New York harbor," the Marquis growled, signaling for one of the servants to refill his wine glass from the crystal decanter. "I can't believe the stupidity of the whole project."

"What's stupid about it?" Teddy said, sounding rather ominous.

"The whole idea. What a twisted, degenerate scheme! Why would America want to invite the riffraff of the world to come here? All it will do is ruin the country."

"The country," Teddy said in even tones, "was founded by the riffraff of the world."

"Yes, of course, religious fanatics and criminals, but that can't be helped now. Why in the world continue the same stupid practice? At least, the riffraff that founded the country have now become respectable, industrious people. Why pollute the water by throwing open the floodgates to a bunch of scum from east Europe and Italy? That's what you'll get: Jews and wops, Czechs, Serbs, and God knows what else. The scum. I don't understand you people."

"My father's partner is a Jew," Johnny said, "who saved my father's life in China. His daughter, Rachel, I've known all my life and is very dear to me. I happen to think, Monsieur de Morès, that your views on Jews—and just about everything else I've heard tonight—are distinctly repulsive." He put down his napkin. "If you'll excuse me, I'm going to head back to the ranch." He bowed to Medora, at the other end of the table. "Thank you for dinner, madame. It was excellent. Teddy, are you staying?"

Teddy also put down his napkin.

"No, I'll come with you." He stood up, turning to the Marquis, who was watching his guests with a stormy look on his face. "Monsieur, you are a man of many qualities. But when it comes to this country, you are totally misinformed and quite wrong. Good evening, madame."

He bowed to the Marquise, then followed Johnny out of the dining room.

"It's a relief to get out of there," Johnny said as they left the house, emerging onto the porch. "The man makes me want to vomit."

"Yes, he's some sort of dinosaur, politically. But don't fool yourself, Johnny. There are a lot of people in this country who agree with him."

They walked to their horses. The night air had turned refreshingly cool, and a clear sky revealed a dazzling panoply of stars.

"You may be right, Teddy. But I'd rather camp out with the rattlesnakes than spend a night in the house of the Marquis."

The two men mounted and started north, back toward the ranch.

12. ON THE SAME NIGHT JOHNNY AND TEDDY HAD
their unpleasant dinner with the Marquis de Morès, Lance
Morrow came out of his private office to survey the action at
the Golden Nugget in San Francisco. The place was packed,
as usual, with drinkers, gamblers, whores of a variety of
races—including Chinese, known as "singsong girls"—
tourists, and young men looking for a little action of any sort
they could find. The saloon, which was almost two hundred
feet long, was filled with gambling tables—poker, black-
jack, craps, and roulette—and Lance's croupiers were con-
ducting business briskly as, at the far end of the room,
Mabel Chisholm, Lance's star "songbird," stood on the
small stage and sang a bawdy tune to the accompaniment of
the five-piece band. She could hardly be heard over the hub-
bub. Smoke from a hundred cigars curled up to the tinplate
ceiling and coiled around the five big glass-bowl chande-
liers with their dripping crystal pendants which Lance had
imported at great expense from Germany.

When Julie had forced him to take down from the walls of
their Nob Hill mansion Lance's collection of nude paintings,
Lance hadn't objected. Actually he had fallen in love with
her because she was one of the most beautiful women he had
ever seen, as well as cultivated. She had class. All his colorful life, Lance Morrow had hungered for a little class, and he
had finally gotten some by marrying Julie.

But this was the bar, after all, and he hadn't taken down
the eight-foot-long nude painting over it. Lance's customers
liked nudes.

Lance was smoking a Havana cigar. He was wearing a
well-cut serge suit with a doeskin vest under the jacket. He
was on top of the world. And though he had told Julie re-
peatedly that he would sell off his "enterprises," the truth
was that he wasn't constitutionally able to sell anything. The
Golden Nugget made a fortune. Besides, he enjoyed the
place.

Jade Moon, in a red silk robe, came up to him.

"Business is very good tonight, Lance," she said. "I've got a long waiting list."

"Good," Lance said, puffing his cigar.

"The man in Number Four is drunk, but he's buying our best champagne."

"Is Number Four Lily?"

"Lily has a cold tonight. He's with Flora."

"How long has he been with her?"

"An hour."

"Tell him he has to pay overtime if he stays any longer."

"I'll go up and knock on the door."

She left Lance and started through the crowd toward the rear stairs.

Upstairs, in Room Number Four, a naked Flora, a voluptuous blonde, was struggling to ward off the drunken advances of her client, a prospector named George McNamara.

"George, honey," she was saying as he tried to pin her to the bed, "you've got to pay extra for another time."

"Then I'll pay it!" he roared. "Goddammit, Flora, you drive me crazy!"

George was a heavyset man with a dark beard who had panned five hundred dollars in gold the past week and was blowing it all on a night on the town.

"Let's see your money first," Flora said, giving him such a shove that he fell off the bed, knocking over the bed table and the oil lamp. The lamp smashed on the floor, spilling its oil on the carpet. The oil burst into flame.

"Now look what you've done!" Flora cried, as the flames started licking the lace curtains.

"I'll put it out . . ." he muttered, getting to his feet and taking his pants off a chair. He started hitting the fire with his trousers, but he was so drunk he only whipped up the flames with the breeze his pants created. By now, Flora was off the bed and throwing a robe over her nudity.

"I'll get help," she said, opening the door and running into the hall. She almost bumped into Jade Moon, who had just come upstairs.

"There's a fire!" she cried.

"Oh my God . . ."

Jade Moon hurried to the door and looked in to see that George's underwear had been ignited by the sparks. He was drunkenly trying to beat out the fire, but he was becoming a human torch. The room was now filled with smoke, becoming an inferno. Jade Moon yelled to Flora, "Run downstairs and tell Mr. Morrow! Hurry!"

Flora ran down the hallway to the stairs. Despite the fact that San Francisco had been subjected to a number of devastating fires since its founding, the vast majority of the buildings were made of wood, as was the Golden Nugget, and the Fire Department was still rudimentary even by the primitive standards of the day. The plain fact was that wood was cheap, and people were used to fires: fires, like earthquakes, were a way of life in California. By the time Flora had made her way through the crowd of gamblers to Lance, the smell of smoke was beginning to permeate the heavy fog of cigar fumes.

"Mr. Morrow, there's a fire upstairs," she said, in a low voice. "Room Number Four."

"Damn," he muttered. "How bad is it?"

"Pretty bad."

"Go get the fire brigade. I'll clear the place. Where's Jade Moon?"

"Upstairs."

Flora headed for the front door as Lance stood on a chair, signaling to the band to strike a chord, which it did.

"Ladies and gentlemen," Lance exclaimed as the crowd became silent, "I don't want anyone to panic, but we have a small fire upstairs in the entertaining rooms. . . ."

"You mean the whorehouse!" one old geezer yelled, drunkenly, and the crowd whooped with laughter. Lance grinned, signaling for silence.

"All right, the whorehouse," he yelled. "Anyway, for everyone's safety, please go out on the street until we can bring it under control.

"What about our chips?" a young man yelled.

"Take your chips with you. I guarantee you'll be able to cash them in, even if the joint burns down. Charlie," he yelled to the chief bartender, "take the booze outside. Drinks on the house!"

The crowd cheered as the customers started surging toward the front entrance. By now, smoke was curling down the staircase, becoming thick enough to cause eyes to sting. Lance jostled his way against the current of the crowd toward the stairs. "Jamie," he called to one of the croupiers, "go outside and hook up a hose. Get the other boys to help you."

"Right, Mr. Morrow."

Some of the "entertaining rooms" customers were hurrying down the stairs in varying states of undress, followed by the girls, most in their underclothes.

"Where's Jade Moon?" Lance yelled to one of them.

"Upstairs, throwing water on the fire!" she yelled back. "Don't go up there, the whole place is on fire!"

"I've got to get Jade Moon out!"

He pushed his way through to the stairs and started up.

"Goddamn place is a tinderbox!" one of the customers yelled.

When Lance made it to the top of the stairs, there was so much smoke he couldn't see anything.

"Jade Moon!" he yelled. "Get the hell out!"

He heard a scream from down the hall, and Jade Moon staggered out of the smoke. Her robe was on fire, and she was trying to tear it off. Lance ran to her to help. He had torn off most of the burning silk when the horsehair plaster ceiling, weakened by the flames, collapsed on both of them, burying them in a pile of rubble.

"We were very much in love and very happy," Julie said a week later as she stood at one of the tall windows in the drawing room of her Nob Hill house. Raindrops trickled down the glass like tears. "I know you never particularly liked him . . ."

"That's not true," her father said. Justin had come West to be with his daughter when she wired him the news in New York. "I thought Lance was all right in many ways. He was a self-made man, sharp, charming, charming being perhaps a euphemism for stretching the truth . . ."

"Oh yes, he was 'charming,' all right," Julie interrupted with a sad smile. "He said he was going to sell off his saloons, and of course he never could. He enjoyed them, he loved the life. And it finally killed him."

"It didn't bother you that he couldn't give up the life?"

She turned to look at her father, who was sitting in one of the overstuffed chairs. Julie was wearing a plain black dress.

"I loved him," she said, simply. "And he loved me. He saved my life, he was funny and warm and tender, and . . ." She shrugged. "What more is there to say? It never bothered him at all that my eyes were different from his. I don't have a single regret, except that he's dead."

"What are you going to do now, Julie?"

"First, I'm going to have the baby."

Her father looked surprised.

"You mean, you're in the family way?"

"Yes. I just found out two weeks ago. We'd tried so hard for two years, and then when it happens, my poor Lance dies. God can be terribly cruel at times."

"Then you'll stay here in San Francisco? Do you need money or anything . . ."

"I'll stay here for the foreseeable future. No, I don't need money. Lance has left me extremely well-off."

"What will you do with his . . . businesses?"

"I'm going to do what Lance could never do. I'm going to sell them."

"And then what?"

She came over and sat next to her father, smiling at him. "I don't know yet."

"Won't you come home with me?"

"Papa, when I left New York it was forever. It doesn't mean that I don't love you . . ."

"But, Julie, we all love you and miss you."

Julie's jaw set. "I'll never go back."

"Won't you reconsider?" Justin was pleading.

Julie got up and crossed the room.

"And how's Johnny? Is he having fun on the ranch with Teddy?"

"Too much fun. He's behaving irresponsibly."

"Well, I ran away, and so has he. Maybe you'll have to resign yourself to the fact that you have irresponsible children. And how's Fiammetta?"

A sad look came over Justin's face.

"She's spending a great deal of time in Rome," he said. "I suppose I can't blame her. She loves it. Rome is so much a part of her life . . . and I hear she has a friend over there."

"Do you mean a lover?"

Justin smiled sadly. "I'm afraid so." He shrugged.

"Do you still love her?"

Her father looked at her, and there was such sadness in his eyes.

"Very much," he said, softly. "And I will till the day I die."

"Then you'll have to fight for her," Julie said. "Love's the most important thing there is."

"Johnny, I know you love it out here as much as I do," Teddy said as he and Johnny sat around a campfire one night, a week after the dinner with the Marquis de Morès. They had left the ranch for a three-week hunting trip to Wyoming in the hope of finding a grizzly bear. "But I don't think you intend to stay out here forever. Will you eventually go back to your father's bank?"

Johnny was slowly turning a handmade wooden barbecue over the fire on which he had impaled two plump grouse he had shot that afternoon with his No. 16 hammerless shotgun built for him by Kennedy of St. Paul, one of the finest gunmakers in the West.

"I wish you hadn't asked me that, Teddy," he said, "because that's the same question I keep asking myself over and over. My father wants me back, he expects it of me, but I don't know: so far, it's been pretty boring. For some reason, I can't burn with excitement over spending my life involved with money. I know it's important, but still."

"I know what you mean. Did you ever consider going into politics?"

Johnny, who was squatting by the fire, chuckled.

"Politics? Me? Who'd vote for me?"

"You might be surprised. You're an attractive fellow, you speak well, you've got money behind you—which, believe me, is a big asset in politics. People are cynical about machine politicians, and let's face it, most of them are corrupt. But someone from your background . . . well, people would assume you had no reason to steal. They'd assume you'd be honest because you don't need money. We've been lucky, Johnny, but there's a lot of misery in this world. And politicians could alleviate some of that misery if they . . . Oh my God . . ."

He started gasping and wheezing. Johnny, alarmed, stood up.

"What's wrong?"

"An asthma attack . . ."

He was trying to stand up. Johnny hurried to him and grabbed him under the arms.

"What can I do?" he cried, terrified. Teddy was turning red in the face. His pince-nez had dropped off his nose onto the blanket.

"Help me to the . . . top of the hill . . ." He was wheezing. "A change of air . . ."

Johnny picked him up with both arms and carried him up the steep stone path to the top of the hill they had camped under. When he reached the top, he gently set him on his feet. Teddy leaned on him with both hands, gasping to get air into his lungs. There were tears in his eyes.

After about fifteen minutes, he started breathing more easily. He straightened, gulping the cool night air into his lungs.

"Are you better?" Johnny asked, truly concerned for his friend.

Teddy nodded.

"It wasn't so bad," he said, his chest moving in and out. "Or at least, I've had a lot worse. The damnable thing is, one never knows when it's going to happen. Asthma's a curse, Johnny. You should thank your lucky stars you're healthy and fit." Taking another deep breath, he squeezed Johnny's arm. "Thanks, my friend. I appreciate your help. Now, shall we have supper? Unless my wretched health caused the grouse to burn."

He started down the steep path. Johnny followed him, feeling guilty for never having to think even once about breathing.

"Look!" Teddy whispered, pointing to the huge pawprints of a grizzly bear. It was a week later. They were near Ten Sleep Creek at an altitude of nine thousand feet near the Wyoming border. They were in a part of the forest that had been burned by a lightning fire a month before. The faint stench of burnt wood still lingered in the afternoon air.

"A grizzly," Johnny said. "And by the looks of it, a big one."

"This may be our lucky break. Let's follow the pawprints. Get your gun at the ready. I'm told they can charge quickly, and they're the most dangerous animal on the North American continent. My brother shot tigers in India, but I'd bet on a bear over a tiger any day."

"Shall we mount?"

"No. Let's go over yonder where the fire didn't burn. We'll tie the horses to a tree and go in on foot. We'll have more maneuverability."

Johnny followed Teddy perhaps two hundred feet, to where the dense pine forest began. They tied their horses, then started into the forest, walking over soft pine needles. They both carried Winchester rifles, loaded. Johnny had never felt such a thrill. But he was also tense and, despite the cool air, sweating with nerves. He had heard stories of grizzlies tearing off arms, legs, and even heads. The fact was, he had never seen a grizzly. But, despite all his extensive knowledge of birds and wildlife, neither had Teddy.

The bear's trail was easy to follow: besides its prints in the needles on the forest floor, there were bent twigs and branches that pointed the way like a road sign. They came to a small clearing.

"Look!" Teddy whispered. In the clearing was the half-eaten carcass of a deer. Standing over it, its snout buried in the deer's ripped belly, was a monstrous brown bear.

Johnny, his heart pounding, raised and cocked his rifle. The bear heard the noise. It turned and reared up on its haunches, the deer's blood dripping from its mouth like a vampire. The beast was a monster, almost nine feet tall, weighing at least twelve hundred pounds. It was a magnificent animal, but a terrifying one.

As the two young hunters tensed, the bear dropped back on all fours and started charging them.

"Wait till he's close," Teddy whispered. "I'll fire first."

Johnny, who was trembling from nerves and fear, watched as the huge animal charged them, its beady, sinister eyes almost burning with bloodlust. When it was perhaps eight feet in front of them, Teddy fired.

"My God, I missed!" he gasped, starting to reload. "Johnny, he's yours!"

Johnny aimed his trembling rifle at the monster, cursing himself for not having steadier hands. The beast was almost on him when he fired.

The huge grizzly dropped to the forest floor. It shook for a few seconds, then lay still.

Gulping, Johnny went over to it, staring down. Blood was pouring from a hole directly between the beast's dead eyes. Teddy came up behind him and clapped him on the back.

"Good show, Johnny!" he said. "My God, that was a close one! What a fine fellow you are! What cool nerves!"

"Cool?" Johnny gulped. "I about shat in my pants!"

Teddy, who never used foul language, burst into his ungreased squeak of a laugh.

13. THE SAME DAY JOHNNY AND TEDDY WERE HUNT-
ing their grizzly, a half world away Rachel Lieberman got
out of the carriage behind her mother, Hildegarde, and
stared at the huge stone building in front of them, Blenheim
Palace. Lady Randolph Churchill, née Jennie Jerome of
New York City, hurried down the steps of the Great Court of
the palace.

"Welcome to Blenheim," she said, kissing Hildegarde's
cheeks as several servants started unloading the Liebermans'
luggage from the carriage. "Was your crossing pleasant?"

"Quite pleasant," Hildegarde said. "Unfortunately, the
weather in London has been bad."

"Yes, it's been a terrible June. But it looks as if it's going
to be a lovely weekend." She turned and kissed Rachel's
cheeks. "Darling, you look glorious," she said. "It's so wonderful to see you again! And this summer, we have for the
weekend an extremely handsome French count and a Rothschild, both single. You couldn't ask for better hunting."

Rachel blushed, but couldn't help but laugh.

"Jennie, you're outrageous. You know neither Momma
nor I has any interest in husband-hunting."

"Of course, dear. Nor does any other unmarried girl in
England or America. Come: we'll put you in the same room
as last year. I'm terribly sorry there's no adjoining bathroom, but you know how Blenheim is: three hundred and
twenty rooms in the place, and not one of them really liv-
able. This weekend, we figure the waiting time for a proper
bath will be forty minutes, so you'd best get your name on
the list."

Jennie led the Americans up the stone stairs to the imposing
main entrance of the house, which looked like a Roman
temple with its triangular stone pediment supported by two
Corinthian columns and four Corinthian pilasters. Blenheim's
architect had been the brilliant Sir John Vanbrugh, and the
palace, a gift from Queen Anne to the first Duke of Marlborough as a reward for his brilliant victories against the French

on the Continent at the beginning of the eighteenth century, was meant to inspire awe. This it did extremely well. But Vanbrugh had little interest in comfort or bathrooms.

They entered the huge Great Hall of the palace, which was made of stone and soared sixty-seven feet to a series of windows below the ceiling. Rachel craned her neck to grasp the enormity of the place which, with its double tier of arches, reminded her somewhat of a Roman aqueduct.

"Impressive, isn't it?" Jennie said. "But it's ghastly to live in. It's cold, damp, and has mice. The servants will take you to your room. We'll meet in the Long Library at eight, and I'll introduce you to Felix and Maurice. Good hunting!"

She winked.

"Lady Randolph's so beautiful," Rachel said that evening as she put on a lovely champagne silk evening gown in the room she was sharing with her mother. Unlike the magnificent state rooms in the palace, the guest rooms were fairly ordinary. Hildegarde and her daughter had brought two steamer trunks and six valises from New York. They knew that the rule in the great country houses of England was to change clothes as often as four or five times a day.

"Yes, she's very beautiful," her mother said, fastening on two diamond-and-pearl earrings. "But her sense of humor is rather coarse. It's embarrassing how blunt she is about why we're here."

"Oh Momma, everyone knows. That's what country houses and weekends are for: to find husbands for the unmarried girls, and lovers for the married ones."

"Rachel, you shock me!"

"Well, it's true."

"Nevertheless, one doesn't *say* these things. Now, my dear, I want you to wear your pearls and the diamond star I bought you at Asprey in London."

"Don't you think the diamonds are a bit showy for someone my age?" Rachel said, loving, as always, to tease her stuffy mother.

"Not at all. I wouldn't have bought it if I thought it were showy. You know I have perfect taste in jewels and clothes."

"Yes, Momma."

Actually, Rachel loved jewels as much as her mother. She pinned the two-strand necklace of pearls her father had given her for her eighteenth birthday around her long, swan-like neck. Then she attached the diamond star into her raven hair, where it glittered in the gaslight.

She's ravishing, her mother thought. And with a Rothschild downstairs . . . I mustn't get my hopes up, but a Rothschild!

Lord Randolph Churchill, Jennie's husband and Winston's father, looked at the rash on his wrist and shuddered.

"It's back," he told himself. "Oh my God, it's back!"

He remembered that horrible moment years before when, as an undergraduate at Oxford, he had awakened after a drinking party to find himself in bed with a grinning, tooth-less hag of a whore. He didn't remember how he had gotten there—his classmates had spiked his champagne—but he knew what might happen. As soon as he could he went to a doctor, but it was too late: the spirochetes of syphilis were in his blood. At the time, the only cure for the disease was the so-called Greek water, an arsenic treatment that had been patented in the eighteenth century and which killed many people by arsenic poisoning. Lord Randolph had been given the slightly more modern mercury treatment when a syphilitic sore appeared on his penis; but even though the doctor declared him cured, the disease was to reappear.

The doctor in New York had told him what the rash on his wrist confirmed: the disease was still in his blood. He knew what would happen: in time, the disease would rot his brilliant brain and he would die, hopelessly insane.

Which is exactly what did happen, years later. But tonight, he told himself to keep the proverbial stiff upper lip.

He was a slender young man with bulging eyes and a thick mustache, and was smoking a cigar in the Long Library when Rachel and Hildegarde came downstairs at eight. The Long Library was a magnificent white room some 40 feet high and 180 feet long, with a pipe organ at one end and a life-size marble statue of the first duke's benefactress, Queen Anne. Standing with Randolph were two young men, one rather short and pudgy, the other quite tall. There were over two dozen other houseguests seated and standing around the room chatting while footmen passed trays holding champagne glasses.

"Ah, here are our Americans," Randolph said as Rachel and Hildegarde started toward them. "The mother's a bit of a dragon, but the daughter is a beauty, don't you think?"

"Extraordinary," said the shorter man who, like all the men in the room, was wearing white tie and tails. "You tell me the mother is the niece of August Belmont, our man in New York?" The speaker was Felix Rothschild.

"That's right."

Randolph kissed Hildegarde's hand, then introduced her and Rachel to Felix. Then he introduced the women to the tall, thin man who had curly blond hair and blue eyes.

"May I introduce Comte Maurice de Belleville?" Randolph said. The Count kissed hands.

Rachel thought, I certainly hope I sit next to him at dinner.

She did.

Twenty minutes later, the party, led by the gray-bearded seventh Duke of Marlborough, Randolph's father, entered the dining room, which was called the Saloon, and which, again, was a cavernous room, its soaring walls painted with frescoes by the eighteenth-century artist Laguerre. Behind each red velvet, stiff-backed chair stood a bewigged footman, who pulled the chair back as the guests arrived at the tables to seat themselves.

"I'd love to see America," Maurice said to Rachel after they unfolded their napkins. "Especially the West. I have a cousin who's bought a cattle ranch out there."

"Really? Where?"

"It's in what's called the Dakota Territory. A little town named Medora. He has the rather interesting idea of butchering the beef *in situ*, then sending the dressed meat on to Chicago."

"Yes, that is interesting. What's his name?"

"The Marquis de Morès. He's rather crazy. Loves to fight duels, but he's bright."

"He sounds fascinating. Did you ever fight a duel?"

"Oh no." Maurice chuckled.

"Would you if you had to?"

"Well, I suppose I would if I had to, but duels are to be avoided, in my opinion. However, my cousin lives mentally somewhere in the fourteenth century. How long are you staying in England?"

"Another week, then we're going to the Continent."

"Paris?"

"Yes."

"Is it your first visit?"

"Oh no, we were there last year, and Mother's been there often. She adores Paris."

"Then you must come to my place outside Paris for dinner."

"I'd love to."

"Excellent. I'll talk to your mother and arrange it."

The footmen served the first course.

"Your English is so fluent," Rachel said. "How did you learn it so well?"

"I had an English nanny and spent two years at Oxford. Do you speak French?"

"Not as well as you speak English."

"Perhaps we could ride together in the morning? That is, if you ride?"

"I'd love to."

Is he interested in me, she thought, or is all this merely French gallantry?

"That Felix Rothschild is such a sweet young man," Hildegarde said later in the evening as she and Rachel prepared for bed. "It's a pity you were seated next to that dreadful Frenchman, because you didn't get much of a chance to talk to Felix."

"Why in the world would you call him 'dreadful'?" Rachel said, getting into her bed. "Maurice couldn't be nicer."

"Oh, so it's 'Maurice' already?"

"Yes. He told me to call him that."

"That's rather presumptuous of him, but I suppose that's all one could expect from a person of that sort."

"What are you talking about?"

"He had the unmitigated gall to ask me if we would like to stay at his place in Versailles while we're in Paris."

"And you said no?"

"Of course. Such an arrangement would be totally out of the question."

Rachel stared at her mother, who was sitting in front of a dresser brushing her long black hair.

"Why?"

"Rachel, dear, you're quite sophisticated for a girl your age, but when it comes to men you're very naive. This Count de Belleville obviously has designs on you. Oh, he was very suave about the whole thing. He asked us to dinner first, and then casually suggested we could stay with him if we wished. Once he got you under his roof, heaven knows what he'd do next."

"But you'd be with me!"

"That wouldn't matter. Men like him know how to get around even the most careful parent. We will stay at our hotel, as your father planned. Besides, we won't be going to Paris just yet."

"Why?"

"Felix Rothschild asked us to stay at his place in Sussex, Blackthorn Manor. Jennie told me it's one of the most beautiful homes in England, and . . ."

"Mother!" Rachel interrupted angrily. "If we can't stay with Maurice, how can we possibly stay at Felix Rothschild's place?"

"It's a completely different situation. Felix is an Englishman and a gentleman. You'll be perfectly safe with him."

"I've never heard of anything so ridiculous! I won't go to Felix's place unless we go to Maurice's too!"

"Rachel, I refuse to bargain with you. And your behavior is unladylike and distasteful." She put down her brush and stood up. "It's all been settled. Monday we go to Blackthorn Manor with Felix. He's a perfectly charming young man, and he's a Rothschild. I need hardly say more."

She went to her bed.

"You're planning to marry me off to him!" Rachel exclaimed.

"I'm planning no such thing. However, if such a marriage did come about, it would be a brilliant turn of events. Your father would be absolutely thrilled, as would Uncle August. Turn out the light, dear. I'm very tired."

"If you don't let us stay with Maurice, I'll run away, like Julie Savage did!"

"You'll do no such thing. Now, I don't want to discuss it further. Turn out the light."

"I won't go!"

"You'll do what you're told. Turn out the light."

Her dark eyes blazing with anger, Rachel obeyed.

I'll make her take me to Maurice's! she thought as she turned on her side, her back to her mother's bed. I can be just as stubborn as she!

14. JOHNNY AND FOUR OF TEDDY'S COWBOYS WERE roping heifers for branding on a grassy plain not far from the ranch house. Teddy had had to go back to New York for a week on family business and to see his baby daughter Alice, who was being raised by Teddy's older sister, Bamie. It was a broiling hot afternoon, and the men were shirtless. Johnny, who had mastered the art of roping, was chasing a terrified young cow on his horse, Tumbleweed. Johnny twirled his lasso, then threw it, bringing the heifer down, its hooves neatly caught by the rope. Johnny jumped off Tumbleweed and ran to the cow, yelling at the cowboys to bring the brand as he held the frightened animal. The men hurried over and one of them, Joe, put the searing iron brand on the heifer's side. As the animal squealed in pain and terror, Joe removed the brand.

"Well, that's the last of 'em," he said. "Good ropin', Johnny. I'm sweatin' like a pig. Think we could have a beer?"

"Good idea," Johnny said. "Let's go back to the ranch house. It's hot as hell."

"Hotter."

"You been there?" Johnny asked with a grin as he re-mounted Tumbleweed.

"Oh sure. Went there for a family reunion."

The men guffawed as they remounted and headed toward the river and the ranch house. The deathlike stillness of the great, green undulating plains that stretched like an endless ocean was broken only by the song of an occasional mead-owlark and the squawking of the gaudy black-and-white magpies that were so common to the Badlands. Far above their heads, a magnificent golden eagle soared, searching for prey.

It may be hot as hell, Johnny thought. But this surely is heaven.

"Looks like you got a visitor," Joe said twenty minutes later, as they rode up to the log ranch house. In fact, a hand-some white horse was standing by the river, drinking, while a woman in a leather skirt with a white blouse, her face pro-tected from the fierce Dakota sun by a huge black sugar loaf sombrero, held its reins.

"Go on in and help yourself to beer, boys," Johnny said. "I'll see who it is."

He spurred Tumbleweed, and the bay horse started down the gently sloping hill to the cottonwood-lined river. When he was near enough to make out the woman's face, Johnny saw that it was Medora, the Marquise de Morès.

"Hello!" he called, dismounting and letting Tumbleweed also go to the river for a drink. He walked over to Medora. "What brings you to these parts?"

Medora smiled prettily.

"I wanted to see Mr. Roosevelt's ranch," she said. "It's quite lovely here."

"Yes, isn't it?"

"Is Mr. Roosevelt home?"

"No, he had to go back to New York for business and to see his daughter. You'll pardon my appearance, but we were branding some heifers."

Medora looked at his smooth, bare chest.

"Oh, but I like your appearance very much," she said as a horsefly buzzed around Johnny's blond head. There was an awkward silence. "Are you going to invite me in?" she went on. "I'd love to see the inside of the house. It's so charmingly rustic."

"Um . . . yes. Of course. Would you like some tea?"

"I loathe tea. But I'd love a beer. Or even something stronger, if you have it."

Johnny looked at her, wondering what game she was playing. There were so few women in the Dakota Territory, and the cowboys were in such a state of permanent ruttiness, that only a very foolish, or determined, woman rode alone. But he saw that she carried a shotgun in her saddle, and he remembered that she had a reputation as an excellent shot.

"We have some fine bourbon whiskey," he said.

She smiled at him.

"I love fine bourbon whiskey."

"Well then, let's go."

They took their horses' reins and started walking to the farm house.

"How's the Marquis?" Johnny asked.

"As unpopular as ever. My husband has a real talent for making himself disliked, as you undoubtedly noticed that night at our house. I admired the way you stood up to him, although he was furious at both of you for leaving the way you did. He cursed and swore and vowed he'd get even with both of you for being so 'Goddamned morally superior,' as he put it in his elegant way."

"I'm sorry if I offended him, but I disliked his opinions."

"Oh, his opinions are despicable. My husband's more than a little mad, you know."

"Doesn't it bother you that he's more than a little mad?"

She smiled at him.

"Of course. Why do you think I'm here?"

He looked at her as he tied Tumbleweed's tether to the hitching bar.

"I thought you wanted to see the ranch?" he said.

"I do. But I want to see other things too."

Her eyes traveled down his chest to his navel, then to his chaps, then back up his chest again to his eyes.

"It's very lonely for a woman out here," she said. "There are so very few diversions. It's not like New York, where a woman can shop, or go to parties or . . . other things."

A bumblebee attacked some flowers by the porch steps.

"Yes, you're right," Johnny said, sweat trickling down his ribs. "It's not like New York. Shall we go inside?"

He watched Medora as she tethered her horse. He told himself to be careful. The Marquis was a time bomb. But that old primal urge, dormant for so long in the womanless West, was stirring.

"Where is your husband?" he asked as they climbed onto the porch.

"Oh, Antoine's in jail," she said, casually.

"In jail? What for?"

He held the screen door for her, and she went inside. He followed her. From the kitchen came the sound of the cowboys talking.

"Is someone here?" Medora asked, rather nervously.

"Just some of the hands having a beer."

"Then perhaps I should stay on the porch. We wouldn't want people to gossip."

"There's nothing for anyone to gossip about—so far. But I'll tell them to leave. Take a seat. I'll put on a shirt and get us some whiskey."

"Oh, leave your shirt off. I like looking at handsome young men, and you're certainly that, Mr. Savage."

Again, he eyed her.

"The name's Johnny," he said.

"And I'm Medora."

"Be back in a moment."

He went into the kitchen.

"Do you boys mind leaving?" he said. "There's a lady here on private business."

The cowboys grinned lecherously.

"Got yourself a gal, Johnny?" Joe said.

"Oh sure. We're having a hot love affair. Now, scram."

"Who is she? Ain't many wimmen round these parts, and she's a looker."

"She's an old friend from New York. Actually, she's a cousin."

"A kissin' cousin?" Joe snickered.

"Go on, the lot of you. Take some more beer if you want. See you all in the morning."

Chuckling, the cowboys took more beer from the icebox Teddy had imported from Chicago and left by the back door. Alone, Johnny took a dish towel and wiped the sweat off his face and torso, wondering how to handle the situation. While a romp with Medora held its obvious attractions, it was fraught with dangerous possibilities. He was somewhat amazed by how brazen Medora was—she was, after all, a lady of "refinement," or at least he assumed she was. But she was practically throwing herself at him. Deciding caution was the better part of valor, he took his shirt off a peg and put it on. Then he filled two shot glasses with bourbon and went back into the living room. Medora was examining some of Teddy's family photographs on a table.

"Who's the baby?" she asked.

"That's Teddy's daughter, Alice. Isn't she cute?"

"She certainly is." She set the photo back on the table and took the drink from Johnny. "You put your shirt back on," she said.

"It's chilly."

She smiled.

"Positively icy. Cheers."

They clicked glasses and took a drink.

"Now, tell me about your husband. Why is he in jail?"

"Well, there was a certain unpleasantness last year. Antoine found some men taking down one of his fences, and he fired at them. Antoine has a fierce temper—he can go into absolute rages. Anyway, he killed one of them, a nineteen-year-old named Riley Luffsey . . . shot him through the neck. Of course, it was an accident, but he was charged with murder." She sat in one of the two large wicker sofas Teddy had bought in St. Paul. "There were several hearings and the charges were ultimately dropped. But there are those— Antoine has his enemies, as you know—who say my husband bribed the judge. That's a terrible calumny, but there's a new judge now, and he wants to bring Antoine to trial. So he's in jail, without bail. I take him cigarettes every day, and our chef prepares his food, so it's really not so bad for Antoine. I'm sure it will all work out well in time. Meanwhile"—she smiled at Johnny—"I'm free. Or, let's say, on vacation from marriage."

"That's an interesting concept. I thought the idea about marriage was, you know, fidelity . . . through good times and bad . . . that sort of thing."

"Yes, they say that, don't they." She took another sip of the whiskey. "Well, Johnny, are you going to make love to me, or are you just going to stand there, looking gorgeously indecisive?"

Johnny stared at her. Don't be a fool, he thought. Get her out of here. She's nothing but trouble.

He set his glass on a table.

"I think, madame," he said, "you'd better go home. I wouldn't want to take advantage of your husband's incarceration or your . . . shall we say . . . momentarily being overcome by the heat?"

Her smile vanished.

"You don't find me attractive?" she said.

"I do. That's the problem."

She stood up.

"You disappoint me, Johnny. Your reputation as a ladies' man led me to hope for a somewhat more exciting afternoon. Obviously, you're all talk and little action. Don't bother to see me out."

She went to the screen door and left.

Alone, Johnny finished his whiskey, then went to the door to watch her gallop away.

Maybe, he thought, I'm finally growing up.

Felix Rothschild lifted the cover of the silver chafing dish and stared at the rasher of crisp bacon inside. Felix loved to eat, as his portly body testified. Now he put five pieces of bacon on his plate and moved to the next chafing dish, which was full of creamy scrambled eggs. His plate already held two sausages, a grilled tomato, and a spoonful of fritata, the dish the Duke of Marlborough had grown fond of on a visit to Spain. Except for two footmen, Felix was alone in the breakfast room of Blenheim Palace, and he was having a wonderful time. The chafing dishes of the hunt-style breakfast on the sideboard held treasures of food, and Felix loved treasure hunts. Aside from lunch and dinner, breakfast was his favorite meal.

He took his plate to the long, Jacobean-style table and seated himself as one of the footmen poured him hot coffee and the other placed a rack of toast by his plate along with a selection of marmalades, jellies, and jams. Unfolding his damask napkin, Felix dived in. At twenty-four, he had auburn hair, beautiful skin, and delicate features except for his lower lip, which protruded somewhat, a gene inheritance from his great-grandfather, Nathan Rothschild, who had founded the English branch of the Rothschild Bank during the Napoleonic wars. The Rothschild lip was as well-known in Europe as the Hapsburg jaw. It was also well-known in Europe that the Hapsburg emperors frequently came to the Rothschilds hat in hand to borrow money. This one family completely dominated the finances of Europe in a way that no other family had done before or since.

Felix was buttering his third slice of toast when Rachel came in the room. He looked at the beautiful American and desire surged through him. He had been captivated by her at first sight.

"Good morning, Miss Lieberman," he said, standing up. "Lovely day, isn't it?"

"Yes, isn't it, Mr. Rothschild. Did you sleep well?"

"Very well, thank you. I can highly recommend the bacon. It's excellent."

"You don't observe the dietary laws?"

"Oh no. I'm quite liberal about that. I'm so looking forward to having your mother and you to Blackthorn Manor. She told you?"

Rachel was at the sideboard, piling her plate with everything in sight.

"Oh yes, she told me."

"It was built in the seventeenth century," Felix said, going back to his food. "I'm told it's one of the finest examples of Jacobean architecture in England. And the gardens are just coming into full bloom. I have some absolutely first-rate rhododendrons."

"How nice. Momma tells me that you're a brilliant botanist."

"Your mother is too kind, but I am proud of my greenhouses. At risk of boring you, I'd love to show you around."

Coming up to take the seat beside him as a footman pulled out her chair, she "accidentally" tipped her plate to the side, spilling her breakfast into Felix's lap.

"Oh, how terribly clumsy of me!" she exclaimed. "I'm dreadfully sorry! Momma is always telling me I'm so clumsy, like an absolute clod. Can you ever forgive me?"

Then, as a shocked Felix tried to wipe the mess off his lap, she hurried out of the room, not waiting for an answer.

Twenty minutes later, she was walking past the magnificent Column of Victory in the park outside the palace when she saw a man come out of the building and start toward her.

Her heart jolted a bit when she recognized Maurice, who was in a riding outfit. It was a warm June morning with hardly a cloud in the sky.

"Well, you caused a bit of a stir," he said as he joined her. "Did you really spill your breakfast on Felix's lap?"

"Yes. It was very clumsy of me."

Maurice grinned.

"You don't look very clumsy to me. Why is it I think it wasn't an accident?"

"Well, perhaps it wasn't a *total* accident."

"I believe you're a devil. Why did you do it?"

"Because I want him to take back his invitation to his country house. Oh Maurice, I do apologize for my mother! She told me she declined your kind invitation to stay with you at Versailles. Momma's so stubborn about some things, she drives me to distraction! But I want you to know that I would love nothing better than to stay with you."

"Does your mother have something against me?"

"No, it's just that she's out to catch Felix Rothschild as a son-in-law, and it's so embarrassing to me."

"Ah, so she's *that* kind of mother!"

"Is there any other kind?"

"I can understand why you poured your breakfast on Felix's lap. But you have miscalculated."

"Why?"

"He just told me he's fascinated by you. He loves women with spirit."

Rachel groaned.

"Have you forgotten about our ride?"

"Not at all."

"Then you'd better change. I'll arrange for the horses. Shall we walk back to the house together?"

"Mother's going to kill me."

"I'll face the firing squad with you."

When they returned to the palace, they met Hildegarde, Felix, and Jennie, the latter looking somewhat amused, in the Great Hall.

"Rachel, you will apologize to Felix for your manners," her mother said.

"I'm terribly sorry, Felix. I'll try to be more careful in the future. Momma, I'm going riding with Maurice."

"Please come to our room."

"Yes, I have to change anyway. Maurice, when shall I meet you?"

"In a half hour?"

"Lovely."

As Rachel started across the hall, Felix hurried up to her and put his hand on her arm.

"I say, did I do anything to offend you? Because if I did, I'm frightfully sorry."

She sighed.

"No, you did nothing, Felix. I suppose I have to explain. You see, I'm subject to certain fits. There's a streak of insanity in my family, and . . ."

"Rachel, that's not true!" her mother exclaimed.

"Oh Momma, why try and hide it? You see, Felix, my poor mother despairs of ever finding me a husband, because who in the world would want to marry a lunatic? Unhappily for you, you were the victim of my mental disorder. I'm so sorry."

Smiling at Maurice, who was snickering, she continued on her way.

"Felix, dear, this is some foolish game she's playing," Hildegarde said, almost desperately. "There's no madness in our family! I can't believe this is happening!"

She hurried after her daughter. Felix turned to Jennie, and said, "Rachel may be mad, but by God, she's gorgeous."

Upstairs in her room, Rachel began to change into her riding clothes when her mother bustled into the room. After closing the door, she said, in a low voice, "Are you trying to ruin us all? This monstrous lie . . . that there's insanity in the family . . . oh dear, I think I may be ill . . . Of course, you're behaving like a maniac! Why did you spill your breakfast in his lap?"

"I think that must be obvious. And I'll throw my lunch on him if you don't give in. And if that doesn't work, I'll throw up at dinner, right in the middle of the table."

"Rachel, if your father were here . . ."

"He'd tell you that you're behaving like an ogre! You're being completely unreasonable about Maurice. Now, if you want me to be nice to Felix and go to Blackthorn Manor and behave like a lady, fine, I'll do it. As long as you agree that we can go to Maurice's afterward. Does that seem unreasonable?"

Her mother fumed a moment.

"You're not falling in love with him?" she finally said.

"Mother, I love you dearly. But that's my business."

What damnable luck, to have a daughter with a will of her own! Hildegarde thought.

"Very well, I agree. We'll stay at Maurice's château."

Rachel smiled prettily and kissed her cheek.

"A château's not exactly a hardship," she said. "See you at lunch."

Blowing her mother another kiss, she left the room. Hildegarde thought a moment. Then she, too, left the room.

"Tell me about Maurice," she said to Lady Randolph ten minutes later in the Long Library.

"Oh, he's almost ostentatiously eligible," Jennie said. "He's enormously rich and absolutely gorgeous, don't you think?"

"Yes, he's good-looking," Hildegarde admitted. "Are his parents alive?"

"No, they were both killed in a train accident several years ago. He inherited everything."

"What is 'everything'?"

"One of his ancestors owned what is now the east part of

Paris. Of course, it's mostly slums, but Maurice still owns a lot of it."

"Then he's a slum landlord?"

Jennie laughed.

"Well, yes, I suppose you could say that. So are the Astors, for that matter. But he has more than that. His grandfather bought textile mills in Lyons and founded a bank. As we Americans say, he's stinking rich. He also owns one of the best vineyards in Bordeaux. I believe it's directly next door to Felix's cousin, Château Lafite-Rothschild. Felix and Maurice have known each other since childhood. Believe me, Hildegarde, you could do much, much worse if you're thinking a romance may be blooming between Maurice and Rachel."

"I suppose he's Catholic?"

"Of course."

Hildegarde's face became stony.

"I thought as much. Thank you, Jennie."

They galloped across the rolling green fields, Rachel riding sidesaddle with a top hat, green jacket, and long black skirt. When they reached a small pond, they both stopped and Maurice got off his horse to help Rachel off hers.

"Beautiful, isn't it?" he said, as they stood beside the pond, on which a white swan was gliding.

"Yes. The swan's beautiful too, but I'm told they have mean tempers. A friend of mine's brother almost had a finger bitten off by a swan."

"Are you a swan?"

"What do you mean?"

"You're beautiful, and I imagine you have a temper."

She laughed.

"It's true I have a temper. But what I did to Felix was calculated—and it worked. Mother's agreed to let us stay with you at Versailles—that is, if the invitation still holds."

"Of course it still holds. And I'm delighted you're coming. Are you still going to Blackthorn Manor?"

She sighed.

"Yes, that's part of the bargain, though I'm not looking forward to it."

"You're much too hard on Felix. He's really a decent chap. And he has the most extraordinary greenhouses. He's quite a botanist."

"I know nothing about botany, and I think it would probably bore me to death."

"Plus, he has a first-rate kitchen and wine cellar."

"You've been there?"

"Oh yes. And I'll be there next week."

Her face lit up.

"You will?"

"Absolutely. Now that I know you're going to be there, I'll invite myself. Felix is always after me to stay with him. He's a wonderful host. Don't move: there's a bee on your hat."

"I'm not afraid of bees."

"I imagine you're not afraid of anything. Ah, the bee's gone."

She reached down and picked a wildflower, which she sniffed as they strolled along the pond's edge.

"Surely a man as attractive as you must have many lady friends?" she said, trying to sound cool.

"Actually, I'm engaged."

Oh my God, no! she thought.

"Oh?" she said. "Might I ask to whom?"

"She's a second cousin. We've known each other since childhood. It's always been more or less understood that we'd marry someday. She's very nice."

Rachel threw the wildflower on the ground and started back to her horse.

"I'm sure she is. Congratulations. We'd better get back. Lady Randolph said lunch is at noon, and I have to change . . ."

He took her hand and pulled her into his arms, kissing her so hungrily that her top hat fell off, landing in the grass.

"You little vixen," he whispered, "you wanted that, didn't you?"

She pushed him away and slapped his face.

"Yes, I wanted it," she said, hotly, "but don't think I'm easy, and I certainly have no interest in a man who's engaged to his third cousin."

"Second."

"Don't be petty." She picked up her hat and put it on her head. "Now please help me up."

"You're enchanting."

"You're too kind. Come to think of it, maybe I should give Felix another look. After all, being a Rothschild might be fun."

"Are you trying to make me jealous?"

She smiled slightly.

"Perhaps."

He laughed as he helped her on her horse.

"I find myself hopelessly . . . liking you," he said.

"Don't get carried away with emotion. Race you back."

She smacked her horse with her crop and started galloping back to Blenheim Palace. He jumped on his horse and started after her, thinking, My God, am I crazy? She's Jewish! But she's irresistible!

15. **"YOU WERE SMART NOT TO GET INVOLVED WITH** Medora de Morès," Teddy Roosevelt said as he cut into his buffalo steak. He had returned from New York that morning, and he and Johnny were eating supper in front of the fire in the ranch house. Outside, a storm was pouring fierce rain, and occasional flashes of lightning were followed by claps of thunder that actually shook the house.

"I figured that if her husband killed a man for taking down his fence," Johnny said, "God knows what he'd do to a man who made love to his wife."

"Good thinking."

At which point, Teddy sneezed.

"*Gesundheit,*" Johnny said. "Do you have a cold?"

"I picked up a sniffle on the train."

"Anyway, the Marquis was let out of jail two days ago," Johnny went on. "They're saying that he bribed the new judge, but I don't know if that's true. It wouldn't surprise me, though. What did surprise me was how unsubtle Medora was."

"Remember what her husband said about keeping his eye on you. And I've heard stories about Medora in New York. She's no nun."

"Yes, obviously. By the way, did you see my father in New York?"

"Yes, I went to the bank as you asked. I told him you're fine. He wanted to know when you plan to come home."

"What did you tell him?"

"I said I didn't know when."

"Good."

"Your father misses you."

"I miss him."

"I got the impression he's quite lonely. This may not be any of my business, but are he and your mother permanently separated?"

"I don't know if it's permanent, but for the time being they're pretty much going their separate ways."

"Does that bother you?"

"Very much. I'd give anything to get them back together again, but . . ." He put down his knife and fork. "This is very confidential, Teddy, but I know I can trust you to keep a secret."

"Of course, old man."

"My mother has a lover in Rome. A certain Count Fosco. He's from quite an old family, but he has no money. I met him last summer in Italy. He's quite charming. I, uh . . . well, this is rather embarrassing to admit, but I think she sort of keeps him. I mean, financially, if you know what I mean."

"I do."

"You must realize, in Rome they look upon these things differently than we do."

"No, I understand. And I hate to tell you this, Johnny, but

it's not exactly a secret. You know what a tight little world New York society is. Everybody seems to know about it."

Johnny winced.

"I'm not happy to hear that," he said.

There was a loud banging from outside. Johnny looked at the window.

"That wasn't any thunder," he said.

"It sounds like the barn door came loose."

Johnny got up.

"I'll go take a look."

"I'll go with you."

"No, stay here, Teddy. It's miserable out, and you've got a cold and with that asthma . . ."

Johnny went to the door and put on a slicker and hat. Then, buckling on a holster and putting his Colt into it, he lit a bull's-eye lantern, opened the door and went out into the storm.

A fierce wind was blowing the rain in sheets. Closing the door with some difficulty, Johnny leaned into the wind as he shone the lantern around. When the beam hit the barn door, he saw that it had come loose and was banging against the side of the building. Sloshing through the mud, he went to the barn. Hanging the lantern on a hook, he started to push the door shut when he smelled cigar smoke coming from inside the barn.

He had just started to turn around to look inside the barn when something banged down on his head.

He fell into the mud, unconscious.

When he regained consciousness, his first sensation was pain. His head was pounding.

His second sensation was cold. Though he was in total darkness, so he couldn't see anything, the temperature was below freezing. Someone had taken off his rain slicker and hat and tied him to a chair, his wrists behind the chair and his ankles to the legs. He had absolutely no idea where he was. A sense of panic gripped him.

"Hello?" he said, softly. "Is anybody here?"

His words echoed slightly. He wondered if he were in a cave or—even more terrifying—in some sort of tomb. Had he been buried alive?

Now his panic turned to terror.

"Help!" he yelled with all his strength. "Somebody help me!"

He tried to break the ropes binding his wrists, but it was no use. Whoever had tied him had done a good job.

"Help!" he yelled again.

It was then he heard a noise. A door started to open, and a beam of light pierced the gloom.

"You're awake," said a familiar voice. A tall figure had appeared in the door. Whoever it was held a lantern. Its beam blinded Johnny for a moment. The man came into the room and closed the door behind him. As Johnny's vision unblurred, he saw that it was the Marquis de Morès. He also saw that he was in the middle of a cold storage room. Beef carcasses hung from hooks on a ceiling rack. Large tubs, hoses, and butchering equipment were around the sides of the room or hanging from walls.

The Marquis walked over to Johnny. He was wearing black trousers and a hand-embroidered leather vest over a white shirt.

"What the hell is this?" Johnny said, angrily. "Let me out of here!"

"I intend to, Johnny. But only after I've given you a little present. My beloved wife has told me what you did to her. How you raped her . . ."

"Raped her? Are you mad? She almost raped me!"

The Marquis slapped him twice in the face.

"You'll watch what you say, you bastard, or you may be hanging up there with the rest of the carcasses!"

"I didn't touch your wife! She came to the ranch last week and asked me to make love to her! I told her to go home . . ."

The Marquis slapped him again, even harder.

"Don't tempt me, Johnny," he said, softly. "You have no idea how much I want to kill you. I even considered challenging you to a duel, but I would have an unfair advantage. But you have to be punished for what you did to my wife."

"I'm telling you, I didn't touch her!"

"Who do you think I believe, you or Medora?"

"Believe *me*! I swear to you, nothing happened!"

"Whatever you think of me, I'm no fool. A friend of mine in New York was in your class at Harvard. He told me all about your schoolboy antics, how you love to whore around. Well, my wife is no whore!" He shouted this with sudden manic rage, and Johnny realized the man was indeed mad.

The Marquis walked over to a wall and took a large butcher knife off a hook. He returned to Johnny, and a look of sadistic glee came over his face.

"I hear they called you Goldenballs in college. Well, Goldenballs, you're about to lose them."

He touched the point of the knife to Johnny's crotch. Johnny burst into a cold sweat.

"You can't do this," he said, his voice quavering.

"You forget I've already gotten away with murder, Johnny. This town is owned by me. The Judge is owned by me. Nothing will happen to me, and you'll never molest a woman again. I'm a very good butcher. I took a course in Chicago before I built this plant. I'll do a very neat job, and it shouldn't hurt too much." He placed the knife on the cement floor and started to unbuckle Johnny's belt. "I'll have to pull your pants down . . ."

"Don't touch him!"

The voice. Johnny sighed with relief when he saw Teddy Roosevelt in the doorway. He was holding a Colt pistol. The Marquis straightened, a look of surprise on his face.

"Untie him!" Teddy ordered. "You crazy fiend! By God, sir, if you had gone through with this foul act, I would have shot you in cold blood!"

"He raped my wife!" the Marquis yelled.

"He did no such thing, and there are witnesses to prove it."

"Who?"

"Four cowboys," Johnny said. "They were in the ranch

house when Medora came to me. They can testify that nothing happened."

"Your wife, sir, is a Jezebel," Teddy said. "If you punish anyone, punish her. Now, untie Johnny. We'll keep this madness of yours a secret, for everybody's sake. But by God, sir, never try to harm us again or you'll pay for it. I'm a damned good lawyer, and I can sue you for every penny you're worth."

The Marquis looked nervous.

"Of course I wasn't really going to harm Johnny. I was just trying to scare him . . ."

"Untie him."

"Yes, of course. Then we'll all go to my house and have some champagne . . ."

"I don't like your champagne," Johnny said, "I don't like your wife, and I hate your damned guts! Now untie me before Teddy shoots. He loves to kill things. He's a great hunter, and . . ."

The Marquis picked up the knife and cut the ropes on Johnny's wrists.

"I get the point," the Marquis said.

"Jesus, was I glad to see you!" Johnny said fifteen minutes later as he mounted Tumbleweed, whom Teddy had brought with him. "That guy's a maniac!"

"He is indeed," Teddy said, mounting his own horse, Manitou. The rain had slowed to a drizzle.

"How did you know where to find me?"

"When you didn't come back to the house, I went out to look for you. I found a cigar wrapper just inside the barn door. The Marquis's name was on it—he has his own brand made for him in New York. I immediately rode to his house. The servants told me he'd gone to the packing plant, and so there I went."

"In the nick of time. Teddy, you'd make a first-rate detective."

"The Marquis is a third-rate criminal."

"I'll pay him back for this one day. I'm going to take fencing lessons. The next time, by God, he won't have the advantage over me."

The two men started riding back to the ranch house just as first light began to appear in the east.

"I have to go to Rome," Johnny said the next week. "I got a letter from my father. My mother's very sick."

"I'm sorry to hear that," Teddy said.

"I'll be leaving for New York in the morning. What are your plans?"

"I'll stay here until the first frost. Then I'll be going back to New York too. The winters out here are punishing. I'll miss you, old man. You saved my life with that bear."

"And you saved the family jewels. You know, Teddy, this summer has taught me what fear is. I've never really been afraid in my life before—I guess both of us have had a pretty privileged childhood—but when that grizzly was coming at me like a locomotive, and when the Marquis put that knife to my crotch . . ." He took a deep breath. "You know, he really would have maimed me if you hadn't been there."

"Oh yes, definitely. I have no doubt he would have, and probably gotten away with it too."

"At any rate, it's caused me to do a lot of thinking about myself. My father's called me irresponsible, and I guess in a way I have been. I have an obligation to him, and to my mother too. So, as much as I've loved it out here, I think I'll be going back to the bank soon. As dreary as that sounds, I guess it's my duty."

"You'll think about what I said about politics?"

"That's nice of you, Teddy, but I don't think politics is for me. They're for you, though. You're good at it, and it's in your blood. You mustn't let a few setbacks keep you out of the game. You can excite people, Teddy, and you've got all the right instincts."

"You're kind, Johnny. I don't know . . . sometimes I have the old itch to get back in the fray."

"I hope you do. And the other thing I've decided . . . well, when the Marquis stuck that knife at me, I thought, 'Johnny, you'd better start looking for a wife and having some kids. Life's awfully short, and God knows what can happen.' "

"Yes, life is short," Teddy said, softly, thinking of that horrible day when his young wife died. "And God knows what can happen." Feeling another bout of black despair coming on him, he forced a smile and squeezed Johnny's arm. "Well, old man, it's been a summer to remember, hasn't it? And we've had some splendid times."

16. HAVING CHECKED—IF NOT CHECKMATED—HER mother, Rachel began to feel rather self-confident. The news that Maurice was engaged was a setback. But she sensed—or perhaps hoped—that the engagement to his second cousin was not a passionate affair, but rather a family arrangement. The memory of his kiss by the swan pond not only made her burn with hunger for him, it also confirmed her conviction that he was as attracted to her as she was to him. And the fact that he was going to Blackthorn Manor to be with her buoyed her hopes.

Meanwhile, the weekend at Blenheim Palace dragged on. The Duke and Duchess were amiable enough, less condescending to Americans than most English of their class, perhaps because the son, Randolph, had married one. To please her mother, Rachel paid more attention to Felix Rothschild. Felix seemed to have completely forgotten the ignominious affair of the dumped breakfast and followed her around like a lovesick puppy. This pleased Hildegarde, who whispered to Jennie that she thought "something was happening" between her daughter and the Rothschild heir. Worldly-wise Jennie made no comment. But she could see that the beauti-

ful young New York girl had fallen head over heels in love
with the dashing Frenchman. And from the looks of things,
Maurice was falling just as head over heels with Rachel.

The two young people lost no opportunity to walk or ride
together, and the magnificent two-thousand-acre property
surrounding Blenheim Palace was a sumptuous setting for
their perambulations. Rachel's favorite spot was the lake,
with its glorious beech trees and the avenue of huge elms,
planted in triplicate on both sides of the Grand Avenue that
stretched from the Ditchley Gate to the Column of Victory.
There were nearly two miles of the elms, supposed to repre-
sent the embattled armies as they faced each other in the
Battle of Blenheim. Rachel and Maurice walked down this
elm-shaded avenue talking about life, gossiping about the
other houseguests, enjoying the glorious summer weather. It
was under one of the elms that Maurice took her in his arms
again and kissed her. This time, Rachel put up no resistance.

However, the words she was longing to hear from him—a
commitment of love—he failed to utter. She couldn't resist
quizzing him about his fiancée. But he was maddeningly
vague about that topic, saying only that her name was Adele,
she was attractive, and came from an old and respected family. Rachel was typically American in that she liked things to
move quickly. Maurice was typically French in that he liked
things to take their time. Over and over again she asked herself if he were merely toying with her.

However, she was by nature an optimist. She began considering what it would be like married to a European. And
since she had grown fond of beautiful Jennie, one afternoon
she approached her on one of the terraces of the palace and
asked her about her experiences being married to Lord
Randolph.

"Well," Jennie said, "of course his parents would have
preferred it if he'd married an English girl, but they've accepted me now. The English will never think me quite as
good as they—they're terribly smug, but they own so much
of the world I suppose that's natural. But they can't very

well snub the daughter-in-law of one of their dukes, so I get along quite nicely. Why do you ask?"

"I was just curious."

"Thinking about Maurice?" she asked with a sly smile.

"Well, perhaps."

Jennie laughed.

"You're not very good at hiding your thoughts, my dear. You'd make a terrible poker player. Every time you look at him, it's as if you're about to swoon with desire. It's rather sweet and terribly romantic—like when Randolph and I first met."

"Was it love at first sight with you two?"

"Oh yes. It happened so quickly. He told me the second day he knew me he wanted me to be his wife."

Rachel sighed.

"That hasn't happened to me—at least not yet. Oh Jennie, I'm mad for Maurice, I won't try to hide it from you. But so far he's said nothing."

"But surely you know why?"

"No, I don't."

"Maurice's family is very Catholic. His uncle is the Bishop of Lyons! If he marries you, it could make him an outcast with all his relatives and many of his friends. It's all about religion."

Rachel stared at her. She had forced herself not to think about religion. But she knew, with a sinking heart, that Jennie was probably right.

The following Monday, Rachel, her mother, and Felix were driven from Blenheim Palace to the nearby Woodstock railway station, where they entrained for London, thence to Brighton on the English Channel. There they were met by one of Felix's carriages, and the party was driven to the village of Blackthorn where, a few miles outside, they entered through an imposing wrought iron gate the park of Blackthorn Manor, proceeding on a winding drive through what seemed to Rachel to be miles of luxuriantly planted gardens and groves, including an alley of sixty-foot-high rhododendron bushes which were ablaze with huge blossoms in what seemed to be every color of the palette.

"They're absolutely beautiful," Rachel said to Felix as she stared out the carriage windows.

Felix, sitting opposite her, smiled with delight.

"Rhododendrons are a special hobby of mine, although these were planted in the last century. I've won several medals in international competitions. I breed azaleas as well. We've produced some beautiful hybrids in my greenhouses."

Finally, the carriage rounded a turn in the drive and entered a great lawn of lush green. In the distance rose, behind a large fountain, an extremely beautiful manor house made of mellow brick. Unlike Blenheim Palace, it did not impress by its massiveness, but rather by the soft blending of its architectural elements. The main section of the house, in front of which the carriage stopped, rose three stories and was highlighted by an impressive oriel window that went to the second floor. On either side, the house stretched in wings of varying shapes, the brick softened by ivy. As Rachel got out of the carriage, she turned to Felix and said, "Oh Felix, it's breathtaking. I love it!"

Felix purred.

Unlike the Churchills, whose family fortune had over the years been depleted by spendthrift dukes, forcing Lord Randolph's father to sell off many treasures to keep the family afloat financially, Felix had at his disposal almost unlimited funds. Consequently, Blackthorn Manor was sybaritically luxurious. Rachel was assigned a large, airy room on the second floor with sweeping views of the sea, for the house was on a cliff overlooking the Channel. She was also given a personal maid, who unpacked for her as Rachel inspected the bathroom, which was made of seafoam green marble and included a capacious, claw-foot tub. She lost no time in filling the tub, undressing, and climbing in, where she luxuriated in the sweet-smelling bath foam that her host had provided—along with the finest soaps and scents from London and Paris. As she washed her arms with an oversize sponge, she thought that being mistress of all this beauty had its temptations.

After putting on a peppermint silk dress, she went downstairs, where she found Felix in the paneled library. He looked at her with wide, hungry eyes.

"You look so very beautiful," he said. "Is your room comfortable?"

"Oh yes, thank you. And I love the bathroom! It was such a luxury not to have to wait in line to take a bath."

"Maurice will be here in a few days, I'm not sure exactly when . . . he can be rather vague about dates, but he does have a lot of business interests to tend to. I hope you won't be too bored until he gets here?"

"Oh no," she said, thinking, I wish he were here now! "What's this?"

She pointed to a large, leather-bound book resting on a wooden stand.

"A history of my family."

"Tell me about it."

"My family? Are you really interested?"

"Of course."

"Well, it's a bit complicated. Things got started in the last century. My great-grandfather, Mayer Amschel Rothschild, was a merchant in the Frankfurt ghetto, which was a dreadful place called the Judengasse, or 'Jews' Alley.' It was very bad for Jews then. My great-grandfather had to wear a yellow patch on his coat, and when he crossed the bridge over the River Main he had to pay what was called a 'Jew tax.' And when he walked the streets, to anyone who yelled, 'Hey, Jew, do your duty!' he was forced to take off his hat and bow."

"How horrible," Rachel said, sitting in a chair.

"The idea of the ghetto was to protect Jews from pogroms, but the reality was that it was a sort of prison. Anyway, Mayer finally made enough money to buy a house for his family, which was big. The family, I mean."

"How many children?"

"Ten in all. They all slept in one bedroom. Mayer and his wife slept in the other bedroom. And the one other room was used as a money exchange room. The building was called the House of the Green Shield, and the Rothschilds shared it with the Schiff family, who are bankers in New York today. One advantage was that the new house had a pump."

"I can see why Rothschilds like big houses today."

Felix chuckled as he sat in a chair near hers.

"Yes, I suppose so. At any rate, my great-grandfather was doing quite well exchanging money. And one day, he rode north to a small town called Cassel, where a very rich prince, William of Hesse, whose family made a fortune selling soldiers to foreign armies, lived in a fancy palace. The Hessians that fought in your revolution came from him."

"You mean the Prince could force his people to be soldiers?"

"Yes. It was a form of slavery, I suppose. And the Prince got all the money. At any rate, my great-grandfather did some business for the Prince. And over the years, his business grew. And then along came Napoleon. The Prince kept all his treasure in chests in the basement of his castle, and when Napoleon's army came near, he panicked and fled to Prague. But he couldn't take all his money with him, so what he couldn't take he entrusted to my great-grandfather, who put it in the basement of his house in the ghetto. He then sent his middle son, Nathan, my grandfather, to London. Nathan used the Prince's money to build his own fortune. And he was so clever, he ended up more or less financing the Napoleonic wars for England. He had a system of carrier pigeons that kept him informed of what was going on in the Continent—he knew more than even the army or the government. In fact, he knew that Napoleon was defeated at Waterloo even before the English Foreign Secretary, who was literally taking a nap when my grandfather came to tell him the news. So my grandfather bought all the government bonds he could get his hands on. When the news broke the next day, the bonds skyrocketed."

"Your grandfather must have been a very clever man."

"Oh, he was. After Napoleon was defeated, all of the Prince's money was returned to him with interest. My grandfather not only saved the Prince's fortune, he made him even richer. And he made himself rich to boot. I could never be what my grandfather was."

Rachel's heart felt a pang of sympathy for him.

"I don't know you very well, Felix," she said, "but I know one thing about you. You have a good heart."

He looked at her almost worshipfully.

"That's the nicest thing you could say to me."

"I say it with all sincerity."

He was staring at her with that puppy-dog look.

"After dinner," he finally said, "I'd like very much to show you my greenhouses."

The second generation of Rothschilds, perhaps remembering that overcrowded bedroom back on the Judengasse, began a palatial building spree that dazzled Europe. The Paris Rothschild, Baron James, built an enormous château in nineteen thousand acres of farmland at Ferrières, nineteen miles east of Paris; he also bought the great house off the Place de la Concorde that once belonged to Prince Talleyrand. The Vienna Rothschild, Baron Ferdinand, not only owned several castles in Austria, but at the time was building a gigantic French château-style mansion near Aylesbury, in Buckinghamshire, called Waddesdon Manor, made of Bath stone, which was transported up the hill by a specially constructed steam tramway. Mayer, one of Nathan's sons, had built twenty years before a fantastic house in Buckinghamshire called Mentmore Towers. All of these dream palaces were filled with treasures, and Blackthorn Manor was no exception. However, Felix did not go in for showy eighteenth-century French furniture, as his cousins did, but rather the much more subdued Jacobean furniture that agreed with the architecture of the manor. He also had fine collections of contemporary paintings and medieval armor, as well as an extensive collection of butterflies—all of which he showed Rachel after dinner that night. But his true passion was his greenhouses, through which he toured Rachel. Almost a half acre of glass housed hundreds of shrubs and flowers, enabling him to have fresh flowers all through the year.

"I have a young assistant who works with me," he told Rachel later that evening as he led her through one of his greenhouses. The enormous place was filled with a bewildering assortment of flowers and shrubs. "He's something of a genius at botany. We crossbreed azaleas and come up with some startling new colors. It's most fascinating, at least to me. I studied botany at Oxford: it's always interested me more than banking."

"Really?" Rachel said.

"I worked at the family bank for a few years, but was so bored the rest of the family politely suggested I devote my time to my passion. So I do. Of course, all this botany probably bores you."

"Not at all."

"Are you in love with Maurice?"

She was surprised at his bluntness.

"Felix, I'm not sure that's any of your business."

Felix looked uncomfortable.

"Uh . . . yes. I mean, Maurice is so very dashing, I suppose all women find him very attractive, unlike me."

"You shouldn't say that, Felix."

"Why? I have mirrors, I know what I look like. I have the Rothschild lip. You see, my great-grandfather, Mayer Amschel, wrote in his will that only sons with the Rothschild name could be associated with the family business, so Rothschilds tend to marry Rothschilds. I mean, I look too much like my grandfather. Consequently, I want very much to marry someone who isn't a Rothschild. On the other hand, I don't think it would be a good idea for me to try and marry a total stranger."

"But one never knows who one will fall in love with."

"That's true. But you see, you're not a total stranger, since you're related to August Belmont. And of course, you're not a Rothschild. And, you see . . . what I'm trying to say is, I've fallen desperately in love with you. Would you be my wife?"

. She almost gaped at him.

"I'm terribly honored, Felix . . ."

"I know I'm not handsome, like Maurice . . . but please don't say 'no' yet. Think it over, I beg of you!"

He looked so anguished, her heart went out to him.

"Yes, I will think it over. But perhaps we should go back to the house."

"If . . . if you'd let me kiss you just once, it would make me the happiest of men."

She stared at him.

"I suppose one kiss couldn't hurt anything. But we mustn't give people anything to talk about."

"No, of course. I would never want to sully your reputation. I . . . I honor you . . ."

He took her in his arms and gave her a hungry kiss on her lips. When he finally released her, he stepped back, looking at her nervously.

"I . . ." he swallowed, ". . . adore you."

She thought, That wasn't bad at all. Of course, Maurice's are better, but still . . .

When she came downstairs the next morning, she found her mother and Felix eating breakfast in the Jacobean-style dining room.

"Good morning, dear," her mother said, sipping her coffee.

Felix stood up and kissed her hand.

"Did you sleep well?" he asked.

"Oh, yes. The bed's wonderfully soft, and the sea air makes one sleep like a log."

As at Blenheim Palace, here the English country-style breakfast was observed, with an elaborate buffet on the sideboard. After Rachel had served herself and sat down, she asked, "Has Maurice arrived yet?"

"He's not coming," Felix said.

"Not coming? But why?"

"He sent this note for you."

He pulled an envelope from his jacket and handed it to Rachel. A sense of panic growing in her, she tore it open and pulled out the card. It read:

> "*Dear Rachel:*
>
> *I have been called away on urgent business. Since I have no way of knowing when I can return to Paris, I may not be able to meet you in Versailles. My invitation for you to stay at my place is, of course, still open. I have instructed my servants to expect you and your mother.*
>
> *Rachel, perhaps things are working out for the best. I have never met anyone more beautiful or adorable than you. But because of my engagement, there could be no real, honorable future for us, and I care for you far too much to tempt you into a dishonorable one. Forget me, my angel. You will find happiness with another—of this I am sure.*
>
> *Believe me, I am, etc. etc.*
>
> *Maurice.*

She put down her napkin and stood up, barely choking back her tears.

"Excuse me," she said, and hurried out of the room.

Felix and Hildegarde exchanged looks.

"I'd better talk to her," Hildegarde said, standing up.

When she entered her daughter's bedroom a few minutes later, Rachel was lying facedown on the bed sobbing her heart out. Hildegarde quietly closed the door and came over to the bed.

"My dear, what did he say in the note?" she asked, gently.

"Here . . . read it." Rachel shoved the note across the counterpane. Her mother picked it up and read it quickly. Then she looked at her daughter.

"At least he's being honest with you," she said. "There never was any future for the two of you."

"I love him!" she sobbed. "He's the only man I've ever loved!"

"Well, you're a bit young. Besides, what do you know about love?"

"I *know*! I want him!"

"My dear, what you're talking about is desire, not love, and believe me, desire passes soon enough. Love is mutual respect, it's companionship, it's friendship."

"Don't you desire Papa anymore?"

"Your father has had a series of mistresses. I accept that he has other women, but I'm his *wife*. *That* he'll never take away from me."

"But don't you believe in romance? Don't you believe in love? They're the most important things in the world!"

"My dear, you're sounding like the heroine of a dime novel. Felix has told me he has proposed to you—news that has thrilled me. What are you going to tell him?"

She sat up and wiped her eyes.

"I can't marry Felix. I don't love him."

"That word again! You could never find a better husband. And Felix is one of *us*, unlike Maurice. You know I would never have spoken to you again if you'd been so foolish as to marry outside of our faith. But Felix? With his magnificent heritage? You will bring honor to your father and me. And Felix will bring you the world on a platter. Think about it, my dear. Opportunities like this don't happen often."

She went to the door and opened it, looking back at her daughter.

"I know," she said, "that you'll make the right decision for all of us."

17.   WHEN JOHNNY GOT BACK TO NEW YORK, HIS father explained to him that his mother had had a bad bout with typhoid.

"Your mother's very depressed," Justin said. "She writes that she wants to see both of us. She's convalescing out of the hospital now."

"I want to see her, too. I've missed her—and you."

"Do you think you've got the Wild West out of your system yet?"

"I don't think it will ever be completely out of my system. I love it out there. But I'm ready for a change."

"Good. While you were out there, did you ever encounter a man named the Marquis de Morès?"

"I certainly did. He's insane. Why do you ask?"

"His father-in-law, Baron von Hoffman, is very powerful on Wall Street. As you know, several years ago, Ben and I made a public offering of the bank stock. Recently, von Hoffman put together a syndicate which has been buying up as much of the stock as they can get their hands on. It's gotten to the point that they are demanding seats on the Board. Ben and I are worried about it. Ben thinks there may be something personal behind this."

"It's the Marquis. He hates me. He accused me of seducing his wife, which was total nonsense, but as I told you, he's mad."

"Then Ben's instincts were right."

They were in the library of the Fifth Avenue house. Now Justin stood up and went to a window, looking out at the street a moment. Then he turned to his son.

"Johnny, what are your feelings toward Rachel Lieberman?"

"I think she's a very beautiful girl. I think she's fabulous. I always have, ever since we were kids."

"Do you have any romantic feelings toward her?"

Johnny looked thoughtful.

"Well, I . . . Yes. But I would never do anything about it. I was afraid I might offend you in some way, or hurt your relationship with Uncle Ben."

"Then Ben was right again. He tells me you two have always been attracted to each other. Would you consider marrying her?"

"I don't think her mother would allow her to marry a gentile, would she?"

"Ben thinks in your case, she might be persuaded to go

along with it. He's not happy that Hildegarde is going around Europe practically offering Rachel on a platter. At any rate, we'll be spending a few days in London before we go to Rome. Rachel and her mother are at Claridge's. In my opinion, you couldn't hope for a better wife than Rachel."

Johnny was speechless. Rachel! Beautiful Rachel . . . Is it possible . . .

Yes, by God, he thought. I've been in love with her all these years!

"Now, you'd better get packed," his father went on. "We'll leave for the dock at nine in the morning. By the way, Julie sends her love."

"How is she?"

"She's fine. She's leaving her baby, Edgar, with his nurse while she takes a trip to China."

"Why China?"

"She writes that she wants to see it again, not to run away this time. I suppose she'll be safe enough, though I'd prefer it if she didn't go. But she's as stubborn as her mother. She considers it her homeland, even after all these years. By the way, she sold off all of her husband's somewhat shady businesses. She's quite wealthy now."

"Is she seeing anyone?"

"Not that I know of."

When they got to London the next week, they learned that Rachel had already announced her engagement to Felix Rothschild. Johnny was bitterly disappointed. But now he knew that he was in fact in love with Rachel.

How could I have been so stupid? He asked himself over and over again. How could I have been so blind? The most beautiful girl in the world sitting right there. And we had such good times together. There I was running to whore-houses! Am I a total ass?

He went into a bleak depression . . . but it was difficult to be depressed in Rome. And his mother had a surprise in store for him.

PART THREE

ON A SLOW BOAT
TO CHINA

18. ON THE SECOND NIGHT OUT FROM SAN FRANcisco, Julie stood at the starboard rail of the freighter *Polar Star* and gazed at the full moon. The Pacific Ocean was as calm as its name, and the moon's reflection shimmered on the surface of the black water like a million diamonds.

"Beautiful, isn't it?" said a voice behind her.

Startled, she turned to see a young man in a black suit standing behind her. He was over six feet tall and quite lean. He wore a neat shirt and tie and a black bowler hat, which he now removed as he bowed slightly to her. In the moonlight, she saw that he had thick black hair and a strong, handsome face with smooth skin and eyes even more slanted than her own.

"The moon," he said. "And the sea. They're so beautiful."

"Oh . . . yes. Are you one of the passengers?"

"Yes. My name is Tim Chin from San Francisco, bound for Shanghai. Since I am told there are only a few of us passengers aboard, and it is a long voyage, I hope I would not be presumptuous in getting to know you?"

He spoke perfect English, though she sensed it was not his native tongue. There was a slight formality to it, and she thought he probably spoke Cantonese, as did the vast majority of Chinese in San Francisco. She smiled and extended her hand.

"I think that's a very good idea. My name is Julie Morrow."

"I know, Mrs. Morrow." He shook her hand, again rather formally.

"You do? How so?"

"Everyone in Chinatown knows the beautiful Widow Morrow who lives on top of Nob Hill and never comes to Chinatown."

"Since my husband's death, I don't go out very much. Do I sense an implied criticism in that I never go to Chinatown?"

Tim hesitated. Then he smiled.

"Perhaps a slight criticism," he said. "But very slight. May I inquire why you are going to China?"

"To see it again. I was raised there."

"Yes, I know the story of your childhood. Most interesting."

"And why are you going to China?"

"I have formed a group of businessmen who see great profit to be made in China. I have been delegated to travel to Shanghai and explore the possibility of opening a department store there, to give competition to such great stores as H. Fogg and Company and Jardine-Matheson."

"Well, Mr. Chin, you certainly don't lack ambition. Those stores are huge, as I understand it, and extremely well financed."

"I suppose you could say we are somewhat like David taking on Goliath. But our financing, while not comparable to theirs, is not without a certain strength."

"I'm glad to hear it, and I wish you luck."

"Of course, there are many difficulties. The corruption of the government officials—the 'squeeze' one must pay everywhere and everyone to get the proper permits from the authorities."

The ship's bell rang eight times.

"That's dinner, the double hour of the dog," Julie said.

"I'm impressed you remember our ancient way of time telling. Is there a formal seating arrangement?"

"No. There being only eight passengers, the Captain said, 'Sit where you like.' "

"Then might I be so bold as to ask if I might sit next to you?"

"I'd be delighted."

He offered her his arm. She studied his face a moment in the moonlight and thought that it was as intelligent as it was handsome. Then she took his arm, and they headed up the deck toward the saloon.

The *Polar Star* was anything but luxurious. The dozen cabins aboard reserved for passengers were small and cramped, and there were only two heads available for the passengers. The so-called saloon, a combination dining room and living room, was airless and unattractive. The ship carried manufactured goods shipped to San Francisco by rail from Chicago, Boston, and New York, thence taken by sea to Shanghai with stops at Hawaii and the Philippines. Since not many passengers went to China, the *Polar Star* was one of the few ships available to Julie.

The eight passengers, the Captain, and three officers squeezed themselves at one table in the saloon, Tim Chin managing to find a seat next to Julie. Among the other passengers was a missionary couple from Montgomery, Alabama, the Reverend and Mrs. Palmer, who looked uncomfortable eating with a "Celestial" like Tim even though his soul, and the souls of his fellow Chinese, were ostensibly the goal of the Reverend Palmer's converting zeal. As Billie, the Chinese steward, served the first soup course, Mrs. Palmer, a rather bucktoothed lady with salt-and-pepper hair who was wearing a prim gingham dress, said to Tim in a deep-fried Southern accent, "I didn't realize we had a Chinaman aboard, sir. Do you speak English?"

"Yes I do," Tim said. "And if I may be so bold as to correct you, ma'am, 'Chinaman' is not a proper word. I am a Chinese."

"Indeed. I stand corrected."

She whispered something in her husband's ear, and he nodded affirmatively.

"Something tells me," Tim whispered to Julie, "this voyage is going to be torture."

Julie suppressed a giggle.

"It's odd," she said a half hour later as she and Tim once again stood by the rail on the main deck watching the moon. "For the first time that I can remember, I didn't take offense at that foolish woman's remark. All I thought was how remarkably provincial she is. And to think they're going to China to 'convert the heathens,' as I'm sure they think of it."

"If I may suggest without seeming to aggrandize myself, perhaps you did not take offense because you were with me, a full-blooded Chinese. Perhaps I gave you a feeling of solidarity."

She turned to him and smiled.

"Yes, perhaps you're right, come to think of it. I've always been alone before in a sea of roundeyes. But having you next to me took the sting out of the bite."

"I believe you have a son?"

"Yes, Edgar. I've left him home with his nurse."

"Does he look Asian?"

"Only very slightly. He's a beautiful boy, and very sweet. My poor husband wanted a son so very much."

"Look!" Tim exclaimed, pointing to the sky. "A shooting star!"

An arc of white light fell out of the heavens.

"It's beautiful," Julie said. "I wonder if it's an omen?"

"I'm sure it's a good omen. It means you will soon find great happiness."

She looked at him. In the moonlight, with the soft hissing of the ship's wake below them, he seemed like a tower of strength. She reached out and squeezed his hand a moment.

"I hope you're right, Mr. Chin," she said, releasing his hand.

"Please: Tim."

"All right, Tim. Now I must go to bed. Good night."

He watched her as she walked down the deck in the moonlight, the veil of her straw hat fluttering lazily behind her.

During the next week, they became friends, then close friends. Julie found Tim possessed a steely strength of character mingled with a gentleness that she found immensely appealing. But Tim also had a pride in being Chinese that she had never felt and which excited her. For the first time, she began to feel that she was part of an ancient and wonderful culture far superior in many ways to the American culture she had spent most of her life in, a culture that worshiped material success over almost any other factor, especially in New York.

But Tim was ready to take the best of all cultures to help modern China, about which he had extensive knowledge.

However, when it came to Julie's old nemesis-guardian, the Dowager Empress, the young Chinese-American had nothing but scorn and anger. "She's an old whore and a thief," he said one night after dinner. "She steals all the money from the Naval appropriations to put in her own pocket, so China is militarily weak. She's letting the European powers descend like vultures and pick China to pieces. It's a crime."

"Perhaps she has no choice?" Julie said rather timidly, feeling a need to defend somewhat the woman she remembered so vividly from her childhood.

"She has choices, but she doesn't want to give up any power. She's ruling China as if it were the twelfth century instead of the nineteenth. She could introduce some democratic reforms, she could throw out the old system of Imperial Examinations which is totally outdated, she could encourage education—but what does she do? Plays with her silly eunuchs in the Forbidden City. It's disgusting. But someday . . ." A look of angry excitement came into his eyes. "China is a sleeping giant, but someday it will wake up and shake the world!"

The muted fire in his voice excited her.

There was nothing faintly resembling organized entertainment on the ship. There were playing cards, a chess set, parcheesi, and a few dozen outdated novels and travel books; but otherwise, nothing. Aside from the Alabama missionary couple, there were a brewer from Milwaukee, who was hoping to buy a brewery in Shanghai, and his wife, and a pair of antique dealers from San Francisco, who were hoping to buy jade and other antiquities from China. Hardly stimulating company, so Julie and Tim spent hours together. He was so gentle and polite, he never pressured her in the aggressive fashion Lance had on the train years before. But their intimacy was growing each day. And on the evening of the eighth day, as they took a turn on the deck after dinner as had become their custom, he stopped beside one of the ship's stacks, took her in his arms, and kissed her.

She had been longing for him to do it. All of the hunger in

her for love had been fired by her proximity to him day after day. She didn't even make a pretense at resisting him. She took his hand, and whispered: "Come."

She led him to her cabin door. They went inside. She closed and locked the door, but lit no light. They stood in the middle of the tiny cabin, embracing in the dark. Then he started unbuttoning her blouse.

"You've never told me," she whispered. "Are there others?"

"There have been," he whispered back. "But not now. Now there's only you."

She didn't care whether it was the truth or not. Now all she wanted was him.

When they were both naked, they still stood in the middle of the dark room exploring each other's bodies with their hands. His hands squeezed her full breasts, then ran up and down her back, gently massaging her buttocks as he rubbed his stiff penis up and down against her belly. She loved his smooth, sinewy body. She loved his smell. She loved his lips with their fiery kisses. When he picked her up in his arms to carry her to her bunk, she thought: The shooting star was an omen after all! I've never been so happy!

Of course, on such a small ship as the *Polar Star*, it was impossible to keep the romance a secret. Within a few days, the Palmers from Alabama were cutting off both Julie and Tim, which couldn't have pleased either of them more. The brewer from Milwaukee seemed mildly shocked, but also a bit intrigued, while the antique dealers kept to themselves.

But the ship's captain, a beefy Dane named Lund who drank gin neat, seemed delighted.

He whispered to Tim one night before dinner, "You've given us something to talk about. It's usually so damned boring out here." Then he added, thoughtfully, "If you and Mrs. Morrow would like to have a ceremony at sea, I'm empowered to marry you."

"I haven't proposed to Mrs. Morrow," Tim replied.

"Ah, I see. Bit clumsy of me. Sorry. But it's nice having

you two young lovebirds on board. And don't pay no attention to the Palmers. Those damned missionaries give me a pain in the behind."

That night, Tim didn't come to her cabin. Nor had he been to dinner. At eight o'clock, a worried Julie let herself out of her cabin and hurried down the passageway to Tim's, knocking quietly on the door. After a moment, he opened it.

"Darling," she whispered, "are you sick? You weren't at dinner . . ."

"Come in," he whispered.

Glancing down the passageway and seeing no one, she obeyed. He closed the door.

"I've made a terrible mistake," he said. "Except I was so in love with you, I suppose I didn't think about anything else, about the future . . ."

"Who cares about the future? We've made no mistake. I've never been so happy."

She put her arms around him and kissed him; he hugged her to him, tightly.

"No, it's all wrong," he said.

"What's wrong?"

"I only realized it this afternoon when Captain Lund said he could marry us."

"I'm not thinking about marriage . . ."

"But I am. I adore you, Julie, but you don't know anything about me . . ."

"I know you want to start a department store in Shanghai."

"That's not true. I mean, it is to a certain extent, but I lied."

She looked at the face she had come to adore, unable to believe what she was hearing.

"Lied? How? What are you talking about?"

"Julie, I'm a dangerous person for you to know."

"Are you a criminal?" she asked, fearfully.

"Yes, that's it. I murdered someone in San Francisco. It's a long story, a stupid one . . . you don't want to hear it . . ."

"But I do! Tim, I love you! I want to help you if I can . . ."

"You want to stay away from me! Believe me, stay away! If I didn't love you, I wouldn't be saying this. You must forget me."

She sank onto his bunk, starting to sob.

"Oh my God, just when I was so happy. . . ."

He looked at her with pity. He pulled a handkerchief from his pocket and knelt beside her, gently drying her eyes.

"I was selfish not to have told you before," he said. "But I didn't want to get you involved with my problems."

"Whom did you murder?" she asked.

"A man. It was a fight over some money. The point is, I was wrong. Please forgive me, Julie. You're the most wonderful woman I've ever met. Under different circumstances, I would have been honored to be your husband if you'd have me. But as it is . . ."

"As it is, what?" she interrupted, angrily. "I won't let you go! Whatever it is you've done, I won't let you go. I have plenty of money, I'll hire lawyers in San Francisco. Anything can be fixed with enough money. When we get to Shanghai, we'll take the first boat back and we'll clear your name. Then we can talk about marriage."

"All right," he said. "If that's what you want, we'll go back to San Francisco."

And he started making love to her.

The next two weeks were the happiest time she had had since Lance's death. By day, Julie and Tim were inseparable, by night they made love. From her childhood in the Forbidden City, Julie remembered hearing the concubines talking about the classic erotic manuals. One day in a San Francisco bookstore she had come upon a copy of *The Secret Codes of the Jade Room*, and read with fascination the classic Chinese variations of physical lovemaking: "The Dragon Turns," "The White Tiger Leaps," "The Fish Interlock Their Scales," "The Butterflies Somersault," "Approaching the Fragrant Bamboo," and more. Now she and Tim tried them all.

By now, even the Palmers had accepted the situation to a certain degree, since the boredom on the steamer was palpable. When the Milwaukee brewer organized a bridge tournament, Mrs. Palmer even agreed to play against Tim and Julie, achieving a level of broad-mindedness that stunned her missionary husband.

The weather continued calm, with only a few minor squalls to impede the progress of the ship as it plowed across the Pacific toward Asia, stopping to refuel and revictual at Manila, which was witheringly hot even in January.

But as the ship neared China, Tim became increasingly tense. When Julie asked him what was the matter, he shrugged it off as nerves. But she sensed something was bothering him.

But his "nerves," if that was what was the matter, were the only thing that marred her happiness. Otherwise, she was blissful.

The *Polar Star* arrived in the Yangtze Delta late on a February night, and Captain Lund dropped anchor off Paoshan at the mouth of the Huangpu River, eight miles downstream from Shanghai. He explained to his passengers that the ship would sail up the Huangpu in the morning and anchor off the Bund, the Shanghai waterfront, to be boarded by the Imperial Customs Officers before they would be allowed ashore. "Be prepared for a certain amount of unpleasantness from the officers," he advised. "If you want things to go smoothly, I would suggest you all contribute to a general pool of 'squeeze' money that I can slip to the Customs men. It will make things move much more quickly. The Manchus love American dollars."

There was a certain amount of grumbling in the saloon as fifty dollars was collected. Then the passengers went off to bed, glad that the long voyage was almost at an end. Julie was about to go into her cabin when Tim came up to her.

"I have to pack," he told her, "so I won't be with you tonight. Where are you staying in Shanghai?"

"I was told in San Francisco that the best hotel is the Imperial on the Bund."

"I've made other arrangements, staying with family friends, but I'll look you up at the Imperial tomorrow. Do you know that you really are the most beautiful, wonderful, lovable woman I've ever met in my life?"

At which point, he took her in his arms and kissed her. It was a long kiss, long enough for Mrs. Palmer, returning to her cabin from the head in her bathrobe, to give them a shocked glance. Then Tim released Julie.

"I love you with all my heart," he whispered. Then he hurried down the passageway to his room and disappeared inside.

Julie went into her own cabin and closed the door, her heart still pounding from his kiss. She leaned her back against the door a moment, her eyes closed, a smile on her lips.

Then she started to pack.

That night, she dreamed she was back in the Forbidden City as a little girl. She was being led across one of the five marble bridges that spanned the Golden Water River by An Te-hai, the Dowager Empress's Chief Eunuch, then across broad terraces through the Gate of Correct Conduct to the west of the T'ai Ho Men, or Gate of Supreme Harmony, then across the largest terrace in the Forbidden City to the Throne Hall of Supreme Harmony, standing on the Dragon Pavement Terrace. The great hall with its gabled roof of golden tiles was the very heart of the Celestial Kingdom, the seat of the Dragon Throne.

An Te-hai was about to lead her up the steps of the hall when she heard a noise behind her. She stopped to look back. She heard the sound of waves lapping against the side of a boat in the distance. She started running back across the courtyard in the slow motion of dreams, as if weights were tied to her ankles and feet.

When she returned to the great Golden River, she saw Tim standing in a small boat. He was waving at her.

Then he disappeared, and she woke up.

She sat up in her bunk, listening. First light was creeping through the port. All was silent except for the soft creaking of the ship as it rolled slightly at anchor in the Yangtze. She got out of her bunk and went to the port to look out. A few fishing boats were going out to sea on the muddy water of the river. A few seemingly deserted small islands were to the port side of the ship and, beyond them, the very big Ch'ung-Ming Island, on which she could discern a few shacks. Otherwise, everything seemed peaceful and calm.

Still, she couldn't shake the feeling that something was wrong.

Two hours later, she was wakened from a fitful sleep by a knock on her door.

"Yes, who is it?" she called.

"Captain Lund. We're almost at Shanghai. The Customs men will be coming aboard in a half hour."

"Yes, I'm up. Thanks."

She got out of the bunk when she heard the Captain add: "May I speak to you for a moment, Mrs. Morrow?"

She put on a negligée over her nightgown and opened the door. The Captain came in, closing the door behind him.

"I thought you should know," he said, "your friend, Mr. Chin, left the ship about two o'clock this morning."

"Left it? How?"

"It was all arranged by friends of his. A small boat came out from the shore rowed by several men. He climbed down a rope from the side of the ship, got in the boat, and they rowed away in the darkness. I happened to have come up on the bridge for a smoke and heard them. I didn't try to stop them because . . ." he shrugged ". . . well, it was none of my business, and I like that young fellow, Chin."

"But I don't understand! Why would he do it?"

"As to that, one can only speculate. I've thought all along there was something not quite right about him. He may be in some sort of trouble with the Manchus. If so, I can understand why he sneaked out. They're a rough bunch."

"The murder," she whispered.

"What murder?"

"He told me he had killed a man in San Francisco, but maybe the truth is he killed someone here, in China. But then, why would he come back? It makes no sense . . ."

"I have no idea, but I thought you should know."

He opened the door.

"Yes, thank you . . ."

"Be topside with your bags in a half hour. I'll send Billy to help you."

He touched his cap and left the cabin, closing the door.

"What has he done?" Julie whispered to herself, despair all over her face. "Oh Tim, will I ever see you again?"

Not for the first time, her heart started to crack a little. But she realized, rather angrily, that the reason he had agreed so quickly to returning to San Francisco with her was that he never intended to do it.

"Was the whole damned thing a lie?" she muttered to herself. She remembered Lance on the transcontinental train back in America. His lying to her, telling her he was a Bible salesman. Of course, that had turned out wonderfully, but . . .

Have I fallen for more lies again? she thought, furious at her gullibility.

19.   WHEN JOHNNY AND HIS FATHER ARRIVED IN Rome, they found that Fiammetta was already up and about from her convalesence, proceeding with her life with her usual gusto and vitality—so much so, that Johnny privately wondered if she hadn't exaggerated her depression just to get them all over to Italy. Whether true or not, he was glad to see his mother again, and she greeted Justin with such warmth that Johnny began to wonder if there might not be some *rapprochement* possible between his parents, something he longed to see happen. However, Justin was given his own bedroom in Fiammetta's palazzo on the Via del Corso. Whatever Fiammetta's feelings toward her husband at this point, she was obviously keeping separate bedrooms. Still, there was no mention of Count Fosco. Johnny had no idea whether the man was still her lover, or had fallen from favor. Whatever game she was playing, Fiammetta obviously was holding her cards close to her voluptuous chest.

She was less mysterious with her son. "So you were thinking of proposing to Rachel Lieberman?" she said at lunch the day Justin and Johnny arrived in Rome. "But Hildegarde already landed her a Rothschild?"

"Yes. We met him in London," Justin said. "He seems quite nice and very much in love with Rachel. I'm not so sure Rachel's that much in love with him, but . . ." He shrugged.

"Mother," Johnny said, forking his delicious penne with clam sauce, "it's very possible Rachel wouldn't want me. Who knows?" As he struggled out of his depression over having missed the boat with Rachel, Johnny had started rationalizing his own mistake.

"Why wouldn't she want you?" his mother said, rather grandly. "You're a very desirable catch. But never mind, things may have worked out for the better. I'm not at all sure Hildegarde Lieberman would let her daughter marry a gentile anyway. By the way, I've invited a very lovely girl to dinner tonight. She's from Florence, and her name is Clarissa Chalfont-Volpe. Her father was an Englishman—he died two years ago, poor man. He had a bad heart—and her mother's the sister of one of my dearest friends, Princess Serafina Volpe. Clarissa is totally charming and very sweet."

"Mother," Johnny said, "are you matchmaking, like Hildegarde Lieberman?"

His mother smiled at him.

"And what if I am? It's time you got a proper wife, and

the Volpes are one of the finest families in Italy. I think there were two Popes in the family—maybe three—and who knows how many Cardinals? The Cardinals did quite nicely, thank you, so there's plenty of money too."

Justin looked amused.

"I thought Cardinals were supposed to worry about the soul?" he said.

"Of course, darling, but Italian Cardinals think about other things, too, thank heavens. How long can you stay?"

"Well, I have to get back to the bank."

"Ah, the dreary bank. Oh well." She reached over and took Johnny's right hand, squeezing it. "But you'll stay, won't you? You owe it to your poor mother, whom you've neglected shamefully."

Johnny glanced uncertainly at his father across the table from him. On the way over from New York, Johnny had told him he was ready to return to work at the bank. But his memory of the Marquis's attempt to castrate him, as well as his dejection over losing Rachel to Felix, made him more than open to his mother's matchmaking.

"Well," he said, tactfully, "we'll see."

"My mother tells me your father was a painter?" Johnny said that evening, sitting next to Clarissa in the dining room. Her aunt, Princess Volpe, was seated opposite them next to Justin, while Fiammetta sat as usual at the head of the table.

"Yes, Father was quite a wonderful painter in my opinion," Clarissa said. "Unfortunately, the critics didn't seem to agree, but critics are so often wrong, aren't they? I mean, they never seem to recognize a genius until he's dead. Now that Father has died, unhappily, I'm sure his reputation will start to climb."

"I'm sure it will. I'd love to see some of his paintings," Johnny said, looking at the stunning blond girl in the iridescent bronze gown. "I know so little about art, but I must say, Clarissa, you remind me of a Botticelli."

She turned her gorgeous blue-green eyes on him and

smiled. "Dear me, Mr. Savage, you do have a way with words." She spoke with an English accent. Her voice was most pleasant, almost musical.

"Please, call me Johnny."

"All right, Johnny. Is New York as exciting a city as I read?"

"Yes, I think so."

"I'd love to see it some day."

"Perhaps you can visit us. I'd show you around."

"Perhaps I will."

One of the white-gloved footmen removed the chilled seafood salad and placed in front of him a delicious-smelling cod, potato, and fennel cannelloni. Johnny sipped the heady Mastrobernadino Greco di Tufo wine, thinking that Clarissa had so far lived up to his mother's advance billing. She was as charming as she was beautiful. Thirty feet above the diners, a cloud of angels and putti painted by Tiepolo in the eighteenth century stared down at the sumptuous setting, the huge baroque silver candelabra and tureens, and the women in their beautiful gowns. The pale pink marble pilasters of the walls were separated by elaborate gold console tables, piled with even more silver.

Fiammetta was very much of her time, but she loved the eighteenth century setting she lived in.

Johnny was about to climb into his bed three hours later when there was a knock on his door.

"Yes?"

His mother opened it and came in. She still had on the aquamarine gown she had worn at dinner. It displayed a good deal of her bosom, which still looked amazingly youthful.

"So, what did you think of Clarissa?" she asked, closing the door.

"I liked her a lot," Johnny said, pulling the blankets over his nightshirt.

"I thought you would. I'll admit I've been looking the field over for some time now before you fell for some overfed New York girl with bad skin. . ."

"Mother, there are a lot of beautiful girls in New York."

"But you know I want you to have an Italian wife. It's certainly no secret. Don't worry: I'd never force anyone on you. But I know you better than anyone else in the world, because you're my son, my flesh. And I felt sure you'd like Clarissa. Now we must plan the next step."

"Shouldn't that be my business?"

"It's much too important to be left to you, my darling. I'll talk to Serafina. I think she might give a ball next week in honor of Clarissa, and you could be her escort. Yes, that seems a good idea. Of course, you'll have to stay. You can't run off to New York with your father."

"I'll stay a while longer. But he wants me back at the bank. He's terribly lonesome, you know. With Julie in China and you here . . . I mean, that big house in New York is practically empty. And you never come home anymore."

She came over to the bed and kissed his forehead.

"Rome is my home now," she said.

"Are you in love with Count Fosco?"

"I'm not sure that's any of your business."

"But it is! You're my mother. I'd give anything in the world if you and Father would get together again and we were a family once more."

She straightened, eyeing him rather guardedly.

"Well," she said, "things may work out. Who knows? Good night, darling."

She blew him a kiss and left the room.

The next morning, Johnny awoke early, shaved and dressed, then hurried out of his third-floor bedroom down the upstairs hall to the arched grand staircase of the palazzo with its mural of yet more gods and putti (Johnny was amused by his ancestors' passion for fat-bottomed cupids). He hurried downstairs to the *piano nobile*, then down yet another flight to the kitchen, where Carla, his mother's two-hundred-pound chef, who adored Johnny, gave him a big bowl of her fabulous coffee and a slice of the blood orange *crostata* left over from the dinner the previous night. As Johnny seated himself at the wooden kitchen table and began wolfing down the sweet cake, Carla said, "So, you young rascal, what are you up to today?"

"I'm going to St. Peter's to be blessed by the Pope."

"Ah, you youngsters have no respect," she said, standing at the black coal stove and stirring a pot of soup. "I know you haven't been in a proper church for years. When you get to be my age and can feel the heat of Hell breathing down your neck, that's when you'll start getting religious."

"Carla, you'll never go to Hell. You're going to Heaven and cook for Saint Peter."

The old woman chuckled.

"Carla," he went on, "if you were my age, do you think you could fall in love with me?"

"You're fishing for compliments. I'm half in love with you at *my* age. Why do you ask? You got a girlfriend?"

"Maybe."

He saw a tall young man pass by a window. Then the back door opened, and the man came in. He was young—Johnny judged him to be his age—with thick black hair and very white skin. He was wearing a rather dusty black overcoat and a black cap, which he now removed.

"Ah," Carla said, "there you are. Want some coffee?"

The young man closed the door and looked at Johnny curiously. He crossed the room, extending his hand.

"You must be Johnny," he said in Italian. "I'm Count Fosco."

Johnny stood up, looking rather confused.

"My mother's friend . . . ?"

The young man smiled.

"His son. My father's gone to the country for several weeks. So you're Johnny. I've heard a lot about you from my father. I'm glad to meet you."

Johnny shook his hand.

"So am I. Your name is . . . ?"

"Franco," said Carla, carrying him a bowl of coffee. "Do you want some of the cake? It's from last night."

"Yes, thanks, Carla," Franco said, taking the bowl and sitting down opposite Johnny. "How was the dinner last night?"

Johnny was surprised at how at home Franco seemed.

"It was very nice," he said.

"And Clarissa Volpe? Is she as beautiful as they say?"

"Yes . . . You knew she was coming?"

"Oh yes. I don't mean to brag, but I know everything that goes on around Rome. What your mother forgets to tell me, Carla does."

He smiled at the cook, who had returned to the stove.

"He's a sly one, this Franco," Carla said. "And a heart-breaker. Can twist women around his little finger, but they'd be fools to trust him."

Franco smiled as he sipped his coffee.

"Carla knows me pretty well," he said. "So, Johnny, my new friend: How is your mother getting along with your father? Are they falling in love all over again?"

"They seem to be getting along quite well," Johnny said, coolly. "Why are you interested?"

"That's simple. If my father loses favor with your mother, he and I are in rather serious trouble. I suppose that's hard for you to understand, having all the money in the world. But the Foscos are . . ."—he spread his hands and smiled slightly, as if to say, "that's life"— ". . . poor as church mice. By the way, if you'd like to take me to lunch, I know the best new restaurant in town. I think we should get to know each other better, don't you?"

Johnny stared at him, flabbergasted by Franco's casual self-invitation. Then he laughed.

"What's so funny?" Franco asked.

"You! You're outrageous!"

"I have to live by the few wits I have, my friend. Haven't got much else."

"Don't let him fool you," Carla said from the stove. "He's got the face of a saint, but he's headed for Hell."

Franco smiled.

At the same time upstairs, in her big white-and-gold bed-room, Fiammetta had just awakened when her bedroom door opened and Justin came in, dressed in a business suit.

"At least," he said, "you don't lock your husband out—yet. Where's your lover?"

"I sent him away to a villa I own in the country. I thought it would be awkward if you both were in town at the same time."

He closed the door and came across the room to the bed.

"That was diplomatic of you." He stood by the bed, his hands in his pockets, looking at her. "You know, you're still so beautiful."

"Thank you, darling, you're very sweet. But if you're thinking about trying to make love to me, forget it. The doctor tells me I shouldn't do that for at least several more weeks."

"A convenient excuse."

"It's not an excuse. It's a fact."

"Is it all over between us?"

She looked at him.

"I don't know," she finally said. "I still love you . . . in a way. But as one goes through life, relationships change. And I certainly don't want to go back to New York. I'm Italian. This is my home."

"Is this Count Fosco that exciting to you?"

"He's charming. He's sweet." She shrugged. "We're *simpatico*. Perhaps you should take a mistress. I won't be jealous. Well, maybe a little." She looked at him and smiled slyly.

"Do you want a divorce?"

"You know that's out of the question. The Pope hates me because I was so close to Garibaldi. When this Pope dies, perhaps something can be worked out. It will take money. Lots of money."

"I'm taking the train this afternoon back to Calais, then on to Southampton to catch a boat home."

"But you've only just gotten here!"

"I can see you're fine, and I'm not wanted."

"That's not true! You're always welcome here, anytime. This is your home."

"New York is my home. It used to be yours." He went back to the door, looking at her again. "Good-bye, Fiammetta. And maybe I'll take your advice . . . about a mistress."

He walked out and closed the door. She glared at the door for a moment.

Then she sank down her pillows and sulked.

"Damn him," she muttered to herself. "I'm going to lose him to some pretty young face."

She bit her lip. She was amazed at how upset she felt. She twirled one of her dyed-blond curls as she remembered her first meeting Justin so many years before, when Garibaldi had brought Justin to her castle on her private island off the coast of Sardinia. The young American was then a penniless fugitive from justice, wanting to learn the art of war from Garibaldi, the famous Italian general and revolutionary who had been Fiammetta's lover. She remembered the intensity of the passion she felt when she first saw Justin in the ragged suit Garibaldi had bought him. She had wanted to devour the young American, and she had begun her pursuit of him that led, shortly afterward, to one of the most intensely passionate nights of love she could remember.

And now . . . so many years had passed, so much had happened . . . now they were almost like strangers. Was it her fault that their marriage seemed to be falling apart?

She snuggled farther under her duvet, feeling a strange cocktail of emotions: remorse, guilt, longing . . . and nostalgia for a past that could never be recaptured.

Or could it?

20.   THE IMPERIAL HOTEL ON THE SHANGHAI BUND was not as grandiose as its name implied, but it was the best in town. Julie checked in, taking a room on the second floor overlooking the ship-clogged harbor. After the porter had put her luggage in the closet and left the room, she took off her hat and raised the mosquito netting on her four-poster bed to lie down, staring at the small green lizard on the ceiling that the porter had told her was a local variety known as *tjik-tjak*. She felt miserably alone and she ached for Tim, as at the same time she kept wondering if everything that had gone on between them on the ship had been a lie.

She cursed herself for falling in love with a man she knew so little about. But she couldn't deny that she was in love.

"Oh God," she mumbled to herself as the *tjik-tjak* darted across the ceiling and out the window, "I wish there was no such thing as men."

But it was a lie.

She fell asleep. When she was awakened by a knock on the door, it was already dark . . . the hour of the rooster. Surprised by how long she had slept, she sat up, raised the mosquito netting, and lighted the bedlamp. Then she went to the door and unlocked it. When she opened it, Tim hurried in. She was surprised to see that he was dressed in Chinese clothes and was wearing a pigtail beneath his black hat.

"Close the door," he whispered. "Hurry!"

She obeyed.

"Where have you been?" she asked as he took her in his arms and kissed her. "And why are you dressed that way?"

"So I won't be obvious in the streets. Do you like my pigtail? It's fake."

"Tim, what's going on? Why did you leave the ship that way, sneaking out in the dark?"

He took her hand and led her to the bed, raising the netting so they could sit by each other.

"Do you know what Triads are?" he asked.

"No."

"They're clubs, rather like the tongs back in San Francisco. Like the tongs, some of them are criminal. But there are also political Triads, and I belong to one of them. It's only partially true that I came to China to start a department store—I fully intend to do that one day. But I'm also helping organize a revolution to overthrow the throne and set up a democracy. That's why I had to sneak off the ship—and by the way, it's a good thing I did. Someone in the Triad is a traitor and tipped off the Manchus that I was coming to China."

"You're a revolutionary?" Julie said in a stunned tone.

"That's right. There are many of us in America who want to bring democracy to this country, and it's not only altruistic motives about democracy. We think that if China can be made to work properly, there's enormous potential profit to be made, and who's in a better position than us Chinese-Americans? If we can get rid of that old whore, Tz'u-hsi, we can run this country, which is the biggest on earth and with the greatest potential."

"It's a wonderful idea, but where does that leave us?"

He took her in his arms and hugged her.

"In love," he said, kissing her. "Now that I've delivered the money . . ."

"What money?"

"I brought a bank draft for a hundred thousand dollars to finance the Triad—we raised the money in Chinatown back home. Now that I've delivered that, I'm going back home to raise more. We'll go back together and get married—that is, if you'll accept my proposal. I didn't feel that I could propose to you on the ship, because I wasn't sure I might not be killed by the Manchus."

"Is this a serious proposal? You're not fooling me?"

"It's extremely serious, a bona fide, honest proposal. My darling Julie, I'm asking you to be my wife because I love you with all my heart."

"You know, you're completely mad. A revolutionary?"

"Do you have anything against revolutionaries?"

"Of course not. And before you withdraw your proposal, I accept."

He kissed her again, slowly lowering her to the bed.

"You're bad for the revolution," he whispered. "I've thought about nothing all day except you, when I should be plotting to overthrow the Empress."

"You won't kill her?" Julie said, anxiously. "I know she's corrupt and bad, but she was nice to me . . ."

"We won't hurt her. She's got millions stashed away in a London bank. We'll retire her to someplace in Europe. She'll love spending all that money."

She giggled as she ran her hands through his thick hair.

"I sort of like your pigtail," she said. "And I'm wild about you."

Then he tore her clothes off, literally.

"Tim," she gasped. "Oh, Tim . . ."

They were in the middle of "The Butterflies Somersault" when the door to the hotel room burst open and four Imperial Guards, called Bannermen, charged into the room. As Julie screamed, one of the soldiers tore the mosquito netting off the bed and grabbed Tim's left arm.

"What are you doing?" Julie screamed.

"Go to the American Consul!" Tim yelled as the soldiers tugged him off the bed. "I've been betrayed!"

"Tim, Tim . . . oh my God . . ."

As she covered her nudity with a sheet, the soldiers dragged Tim out of the room into the corridor.

The Forbidden City in the heart of Peking, the capital of the vast Celestial Kingdom, as China was known, was a box within a larger box called the Imperial City, which was within an even larger box called the Tartar City which was bordered on the south by the rectangular Chinese City. Each of these cities was surrounded by high walls pierced by a number of gates that were closed at night for protection; the Forbidden City was also surrounded by a moat.

All this Julie knew when, two months after Tim's abduction by the Bannermen in her Shanghai hotel room, she finally was given permission to address the Dragon Throne in the Hall of Supreme Harmony in the heart of the Forbidden City. She had spent fruitless hours arguing with, first, the American Consul in Shanghai and, later, with the American Minister, or Ambassador, in the Foreign Legation in Peking. They both told her they knew nothing of the fate of her lover. When she angrily proclaimed that Tim was an American citizen and therefore not subject to Chinese laws, they threw up their hands and agreed. "We know that," the American Minister said, "but what can we do? We have no idea where he is, the government refuses to discuss the matter with us, and he's a revolutionary. It's very difficult for us to deal with the official Chinese government about an American citizen who's trying to overthrow it."

"What you're really saying," she exclaimed, sharply, "is that Tim is a Chink from Chinatown, and why would Washington want to get involved with trying to save him?"

At which point, the Minister got red in the face.

Julie knew that if she were to save Tim, she'd have to do it on her own. But she had one invaluable advantage: she knew the supreme ruler of China, the Dowager Empress.

After having traveled from Shanghai to Tientsin and then taken the newly built train to Peking, she had sent a message, including a promise of one thousand dollars cash, to the man who was, in effect, the Prime Minister of China, Prince Ch'un. He was the Dowager Empress's brother-in-law and father of the present Emperor, the teenage Kuang-hsu Emperor who was terrified of the Dowager Empress. Weeks passed before she received an answer. She knew that Tz'u-hsi was toying with her. But finally, the answer arrived at Julie's boardinghouse: she was to present herself at the Ch'ien Men, the central gate of Peking's Tartar City, the next day at noon, where she would be led to the Hall of Supreme Harmony and granted an interview with the Dowager Empress of China.

Julie had been staying at a small boardinghouse in the Legation Quarter of Peking, which was where the principal embassies of the foreign powers were located in the southeastern section of the Tartar City. At eleven-thirty, she set out on foot from the boardinghouse to walk to the nearby Ch'ien Men. She was understandably nervous. She had no idea whether the Dowager Empress would be hostile or not. If Tim were alive, which was problematical, he could be anywhere in the enormous Celestial Kingdom, and only the Dowager Empress had the power to free him. There were a dozen reasons why she wouldn't. But what kept hope alive in Julie's mind was the thought that there was one reason she *might* free him: Money.

It was a clear spring day with a warm breeze blowing in from the Gobi Desert. All around her, the sights and sounds and smells of Peking assaulted her in a slapdash jumble of humanity and animals that she remembered from her childhood. Especially the smells: of roasting meat and game, of ginseng and soy, of garlic and tobacco, and of human and animal night soil which the thrifty Pekingese collected in jars to use as fertilizer and, dried, as heating fuel.

When she reached the main gate of the Tartar City, she looked north along the sixty-foot-wide main street of the city, which was lined on both sides with mat-shed booths and shops three rows deep, flags fluttering in the breeze announcing their wares. Peddlers carrying baskets of everything from sewing needles to candy jostled with Peking carts—wheelbarrows pulled by one or two men—heaped with all sorts of goods for sale. Horses, dogs, cats, and camels from Mongolia created a never-ending stream of traffic, while mandarins in sedan chairs were protected from the dirty throng by attendants who whacked the traffic with bamboo rods to clear their master's way. Whatever the political and economic ills plaguing the Celestial Kingdom, the teeming humanity of its capital city seemed oblivious to them. Life might have been dirty and hard for the vast majority of the Dowager Empress's subjects—and the severed heads of criminals hanging in wire baskets from poles along the street reminded the Pekingese just how hard life could be—nevertheless, life went on.

Julie waited a half hour, being constantly besieged by peddlers and beggars. She was beginning to wonder if her interview had been called off when she saw approaching her a sedan chair with a dozen bamboo rod–wielding attendants before and behind it. The number of attendants indicated that this sedan chair belonged to a mandarin of high rank. The chair's green color indicated a mandarin of the first or second rank. One of the attendants bowed to her and said:

"You are the American lady?" Julie was wearing a western suit of white linen, as well as a white hat with an ostrich plume in it and was the only westerner in sight.

"Yes," she answered in Mandarin, her native tongue.

"Please get in the sedan chair. We will take you to the Forbidden City."

As the passersby gawked, the attendants set the chair on the street and held the curtain as Julie climbed in. Then the retinue reversed its direction and started north toward the Tien An Men, the Gate of Heavenly Peace, which was the main entrance to the Forbidden City.

With the curtains drawn, Julie saw nothing more until a half hour later, when she felt the sedan chair being set down with a gentle thump. Then the curtains were drawn open by the lead attendant, and she saw that she was outside the Hall of Supreme Harmony. She was flooded with memories as she got out, memories of that cold morning years before when she had been summoned to the Dragon Throne by the Dowager Empress. Then it had been to tell her that her father, Justin, was taking her to America. Now she was the supplicant, praying for the life of the man she loved, in a poker game where her opponent held all the aces. She knew the Dowager Empress loved to frighten people, and the more frightened they looked, the happier the old woman was, so Julie told herself to remain calm. She certainly didn't underestimate Tz'ŭ-hsi: the woman had played the game of court intrigue brilliantly and had climbed from the lowest ranks of the Emperor's many concubines to the position of supreme power. Admire her or hate her, there was no doubt that she was the most powerful woman in the world.

Julie saw one of the palace eunuchs standing on the bottom step of the great hall with its many-tiered roof of golden tiles; she remembered that all palace eunuchs wore green coats embroidered with dragons. Now the eunuch bowed to her and said, "Follow me, please. The Empress awaits."

Julie followed him up the steps into the great throne hall, which was 200 feet long and 110 feet wide, its roof soaring 100 feet. Then she walked behind him toward the Dragon

Throne. Everywhere stood carved five-claw cloisonné drag-ons, the imperial symbol, holding the Flaming Pearl of knowledge and power. Finally reaching the throne, the eu-nuch whispered "Kowtow." Julie obeyed, getting on her knees, removing her hat, and touching her forehead to the floor three times. Then she stood up again, put her hat back on, and looked up at the elaborately carved dais where, on a gilt throne flanked by life-size statues of pale blue cranes, symbols of longevity, sat the Dowager Empress of China. She was wearing one of her many Dragon robes, this one yellow. With her tasseled Manchu headdress, her long fili-greed gold nail guards, her raised pearl-encrusted slippers, and the cherry dewdrop painted on her lower lip, as was the Manchu custom of cosmetics, she looked as lurid and vaguely sinister as Julie remembered her. She also looked much older.

"So," she said, "you have returned to China. We have thought of you from time to time. Do you like America?"

"It's all right, Your Majesty. But most Americans don't much like me."

"Because you are a mongrel. We told you this would happen."

"I know, Your Majesty. I was foolish not to appreciate your infinite wisdom."

"Mmm." She paused. "Why do you plead for this miser-able dog who dares to attack me and my government?"

"Because I love him, Your Majesty."

"Then you're a bigger fool than I thought."

"Is he . . ." Her heart was pounding. "Is he alive, Your Majesty?"

"The dog lives, though he pleads for the mercy of death. We have not made life pleasant for him."

"Your Majesty, I will remind you that he is an American citizen."

"Do you threaten us?"

"No, Your Majesty."

She was so nervous, she thought she might faint.

"We have made inquiries about you," the Dowager Empress continued. "We know you are rich. How much do you love this cur? Can you put a price on him?"

Money! Julie thought. I knew it would come to this! Just as Father bought me away from her!

"How can anyone put a price on love?" she said, aloud.

The Dowager Empress's eyes narrowed.

"You dare to haggle with me?" she shouted. "As if I were a common merchant in a shop?"

"No, Your Majesty."

The old woman clapped her hands. Julie saw four eunuchs come out from behind a screen. Two of them carried wicker baskets, while the other two dragged a thin young man dressed in filthy rags. Julie cried:

"Tim!"

She started to run toward him, but the Dowager Empress roared: "You have not been dismissed!"

She froze. Tim, whose hands were tied behind his back, looked haggard and pale. He said to her, "Julie, I love you."

"Silence!" howled the Dowager Empress. "You dog, who dares to undermine my throne! Show the woman the scars on his back," she commanded the eunuchs, who turned Tim around and tore open his ragged shirt. Julie gasped as she saw the scars crisscrossing his back. "We had him whipped," the Dowager Empress said, smiling cruelly. "And it gave us pleasure to watch him in agony. Even though he is an American, he cannot escape our power! Nor can his friends. Open the baskets: show what's inside."

The eunuchs set the baskets on the floor, opened them, reached in, and pulled out two human heads by their pigtails.

"Butcher!" Tim yelled as Julie cried out in horror. The heads were of two young men.

"Your so-called Peony Triad no longer exists!" the Dowager Empress exclaimed, with a gloating smile. "All the conspirators have been executed after suitable torture. The money you brought them from San Francisco has been expropriated by the Imperial Treasury." She stood up from the Dragon Throne and pointed her long nail guard at Julie.

"You: American woman. When you pay us one million American dollars, this mongrel will be freed and allowed to leave our kingdom. Until then, he will remain in the windowless cell we have consigned him to. This audience is at an end. Take him away."

As she started down the steps of the throne, the eunuchs dragged Tim back toward the screen. He yelled, "Julie, don't do it! Go to the American Minister! Don't let her blackmail you!"

She didn't have the heart to tell him she had already gone to the American Minister.

"Don't worry, darling," she cried. "You'll be free soon!"

And then, Tim and the eunuchs vanished behind the screen as the other eunuchs casually put the heads back in the baskets and carried them away. The Dowager Empress came up to Julie and smiled.

"We like your dress," she said. "Is it fashionable?"

"Yes, Your Majesty," Julie sniffed.

"You will make the arrangements to pay us the million dollars?"

"Yes, Your Majesty. It will take some time."

The Dowager Empress's smile faded.

"Every day he will not see the sun until we are paid. Every day he will eat wormy gruel until we are paid. However," she put her hand on Julie's arm, "since we are such old friends, we will not have him whipped again. Good-bye, American girl. Tell your father hello." She chuckled. "We remember with pleasure making him crawl to us without any clothes on. It was very amusing. The eunuchs still talk about it."

Chuckling to herself, she walked away and vanished behind a black-and-silver screen.

21. *"EN GARDE!"* FRANCO FOSCO ANNOUNCED AS HE adjusted his fencing mask over his face. He and Johnny saluted each other with their foils, and then began a half hour practice session in a fencing club off the Piazza del

Popolo in Rome. When Johnny told Franco he wanted to take up fencing in order to avenge himself against a "certain crazy Frenchman," as he referred to the Marquis de Morès, Franco volunteered to give him lessons "for lunches," as he said with a smile. After a few days, Johnny had come to like the impoverished but shrewd Franco. He might be a first-class freeloader, but he was an excellent fencer, and he taught Johnny much. Being a natural athlete, Johnny picked up the sport quickly.

After showering and getting dressed, they went to the Via Condotti near the Spanish Steps for lunch at the Caffè Greco, one of the oldest restaurants in Rome.

After Franco chose the wine (he might be poor, but his tastes were expensive), Johnny said, "Some friends of mine are coming to Rome today. Since you know Rome so well, do you think you could give them a tour? They're here on their honeymoon. They've chartered a yacht for a Mediterranean cruise . . ."

"A yacht?" Franco interrupted.

"Yes, at Ostia."

"Who are they?"

"The wife is an old friend of mine from New York. She just married a Rothschild. Her name is Rachel. I . . ." He paused, thinking again of his frustration at having lost Rachel, of his stupidity at not realizing how strongly he felt about her. Franco watched him with interest.

"I have an idea you were in love with this 'old friend' of yours," Franco said.

"Yes, I was. And too dumb to know it."

"You grew up with her?"

"Yes. Her father is a business partner of my father's."

"When you grow up with someone, very often you don't see the jewel because of its setting."

"If you mean by that what I think, then you're right. I didn't realize what I really felt about her, and when I finally did, it was too late. Felix Rothschild beat me to the punch."

"Is she beautiful?"

"Very. I think you'll like her. Will you do it?"

"With pleasure. I've never met a Rothschild."

"I'm sure they'll buy you a nice lunch."

Franco laughed as the waiter poured the wine.

"I can practice my terrible English," Franco said as he tasted the wine. "Yes, that's fine," he told the waiter. Then he asked Johnny, "How's your romance progressing with Clarissa?"

"Franco, I'm crazy about her. In fact . . ." He pulled a small black velvet box from his pocket. "Look what I bought this morning."

He opened the lid to reveal a diamond ring. Franco looked at the stone, impressed by its beauty.

"So you're going to propose to her?" he said.

"Tonight's the big night."

"Congratulations. Are you nervous?"

"I'm scared to death."

"She'll say yes. Better put that ring away. Rome is full of thieves."

Letter from Johnny Savage to his father, Justin, dated December 24, 1885.

> *Dear Father:*
>
> *I bring you news that I hope will please you as much as it excites me. I am engaged to be married! Clarissa, whom you met in Rome, accepted my proposal last night. Her aunt gave a ball in her honor at the Palazzo Volpe, which is not far from Mother's on the Corso. Mother and I arrived a bit early and we went up to the piano nobile, where Princess Volpe was standing with Clarissa and her mother to greet us.*
>
> *Dear Father, I wish I were a poet so as to properly describe how beautiful Clarissa looked last night. She had piled her exquisite hair into a mass of curls on top of her head and put three small carnations in them. She was wearing a peach-colored dress and carried a plumed fan. I*

whispered to her, with what I suppose is a profound lack of originality, "You look beautiful." She smiled at me and my heart pounded till I thought it was going to pop out of my chest.

There were about sixty people at the ball, and promptly at nine the majordomo banged a staff three times on the floor, which was a signal for everyone to go to the big dining room for dinner. After dinner, everyone went to the Galleria, which is one of the major sights of Rome, Mother tells me. It's something like 150 feet long and maybe 60 feet high, and it was built in the seventeenth century by one of the Princess's ancestors who had defeated the Turks in a great sea battle somewhere—there's an allegorical painting on the ceiling showing the Admiral being carried to Heaven by a bunch of angels. An orchestra was seated at one end of the hall, and at a signal from the Princess, the Maestro started playing a waltz. I led Clarissa out on the dance floor. She waltzes like a dream. She told me how her parents used to hold tableaux vivants in the room and how she enjoyed appearing in them. An hour later, I led her out onto a balcony overlooking the city and proposed to her. To my euphoric delight, she accepted! We plan to be married in Florence next April.

I start back to New York in three days. Mother is thrilled with the news about Clarissa and has promised to buy us a house in New York as a wedding present. I'd appreciate any ideas you might have on the subject of where would be a good neighborhood for us to live. I'm looking forward to seeing you. By the way, Felix and Rachel Rothschild are in town. Franco is taking her sight-seeing tomorrow; poor Felix has a cold and is staying in his hotel.

Your loving son,
Johnny

Justin handed the letter to his Aunt Adelaide Savage, who was dining with him in the Fifth Avenue house. "He's finally done it," he said. "Read this."

Adelaide, who was now in her sixties and had worn nothing but black since the death of her husband, Sylvaner, quickly read the letter. "This Clarissa sounds delightful!" she said. "You must be pleased."

"Yes, I am. I'd always wanted him to marry an American, but as long as he's in love, it doesn't matter." He checked his gold watch. "We'd better get to the theater. The curtain goes up in a half hour, and I know Robbie Phillips is your favorite actor. I hope the play's a hit. I've put some money in it."

Fifteen minutes into the first act, a most extraordinarily beautiful brunette came on stage. She was playing a soubrette named the Countess of New Orleans—the play was a wickedly "racy" comedy—and she wore an extremely tight-fitting satin dress with a long train that showed off her ex-tremely sexy figure to full advantage. On her head was a huge hat piled with ostrich plumes, and she carried a gold-headed walking stick. As Justin sat up, he borrowed his aunt's opera glasses and took a close-up look at the girl, whose voice was rather breathy and seductive. Her eyes, he saw, were big and a curious hazel-green color. Though she wore heavy makeup, which was still frowned upon by "Society," he could tell that her skin was flawless except for a small mole to the right side of her chin, which might, he realized, be a beauty mark. He lowered the opera glasses a bit and stared at her bosom, which was lushly full and displayed to the full extent of the law. He felt his heart pumping with desire.

I'm going to meet that one, he thought as he gave the opera glasses back to Adelaide and fumbled for the playbill. He opened it to read:

"Countess of New Orleans. . . . . Miss Kitty Kincaid."

"I suppose one might call the Via del Corso the Fifth Avenue of Rome," Franco said as he and Rachel Rothschild sat in the backseat of the open carriage driving down the arrow-straight, very narrow street lined with elegant buildings and cafés. It was a sparkling Christmas Day, with a cloudless blue sky. Rachel looked beautiful in a celadon Empress Eu-génie–style hat with an ostrich plume and a rich sable coat, her gloved hands in a sable muff. The carriage was pulled by two magnificent matched horses. The Via del Corso was crowded with carriages and pedestrians as all Rome turned out to celebrate this champagnelike Christmas. "They call it the Corso because during Carnival there are many races held on the street," Franco went on, adjusting the mink lap robe over Rachel's knees. "Are you comfortable?"

"Yes, thank you."

"There are many important palazzi on the Corso," he went on. "Besides Johnny's mother's, there's the Palazzo Rondinini, the Palazzo Fiano, which has a small puppet theater, and the Palazzo Bonaparte, which was the home of Napoleon's mother. Those are all open to the public. Then there are several magnificent private palazzi, again like Johnny's mother's: the Palazzo Ruspoli, the Chigi— Agostino Chigi was the rich banker who helped Pope Julius II finance the building of St. Peter's—the Palazzo Doria Pamphili and the Palazzo Odescalchi. We'll drive by what used to be the Imperial Forum during the Empire. They've started excavating it, but there's still not much to see except the tops of arches. Still it's interesting—at least to me. I hope I'm not boring you?"

"On the contrary, it's all fascinating. To imagine how old everything is here! To be in the city of Caesar and Nero and the Popes—it's thrilling!"

He smiled at her.

"Thank you, signora, for enjoying my city. I am very proud of it. Of course, we Romans take so much for granted. Someone said that Rome is like a man who makes a living by putting his grandmother's corpse on display, which is true. But what a corpse!"

Rachel laughed. She was having a great time with this fascinating young man on this beautiful day in the Eternal City. She was also amused to see that the city was filled with goats, pigs, sheep, and horses, many of the animals squatting placidly in the piazzas, oblivious to the traffic swirling around them. Franco explained that farmers still brought their animals into the city to sell on the hoof.

During the next several hours, Franco showed her many of the most obvious tourist attractions—the Piazza Navona, the Trevi Fountain, the Colosseum, the Quirinale Palace, home of the royal family—while he sketched in with light strokes the highlights of the city's recent history. "After King Victor Emmanuel and Garibaldi united Italy thirteen years ago," he said, "Rome became the capital of Italy again after centuries of being only the capital of the Papal States. The Vatican didn't like being shoved aside to second place, so to speak, so the Pope and his Cardinals have been sulking ever since. The Cardinals used to travel around the city in gaudy coaches draped with red, but now they're draped in black—it's all a bit silly. Still, a lot of people take it very seriously. The so-called black nobility—most of whom made their fortunes by being related to various Popes—snub the Royal Family. These include the Barberini and Chigi, the Borghese and Aldobrandini, and my family. Of course, we're so poor, we hardly count anymore."

Rachel felt a twinge of pity for him.

"Where do you live, Franco?" she asked.

"I would take you to St. Peter's, but today the Pope makes his appearance on his balcony to bless what they call *urbi et orbi*, to the city and the world, and there will be so many people there you won't be able to see anything."

"You didn't answer my question."

He looked at her with his big, dark eyes, and she thought she saw sorrow in them.

"Please don't ask me that, signora," he said.

"You must call me Rachel. We are friends."

"Yes, Rachel."

"But I don't understand. Why can't I ask you that?"

"Because you are a very rich lady. I would be ashamed to show you my home, and if I tell you where I live, you will want to see it."

"Franco, my father's father was a poor Jewish peddler in Alabama. My husband's great-great-grandfather was a poor Jewish peddler in the Frankfurt ghetto. You surely have nothing to be ashamed of!"

He stared at her with a frown, as if trying to see into her soul. Then he turned to the driver and said something in staccato Italian.

"Very well, Rachel," he said, settling back in his seat. "I'll show you my home."

The carriage rattled across the Tiber River.

"We are now in Trastevere," Franco said, "which means 'across the Tiber.' In the sixteenth century, the Popes created the first Jewish ghetto here. It is also the home of writers and artists—all poor."

Rachel said nothing, but she was feeling uncomfortable. She was truly curious about Franco, but she knew she had made a blunder asking where he lived. As the carriage drove into ever poorer neighborhoods, she became even more uncomfortable. Finally, she turned to him, and said, "Franco, if you don't want to show me your house, I'll understand. Perhaps it's better if we go back. I'm sorry I insisted."

"We're almost there now," he said. "So, you will see."

After a few moments, the carriage stopped in front of a three-story house that looked fairly much like the other houses on the winding street, except that it had a new coat of ocher paint and there were flowerpots in the windows. As a crowd of street urchins gathered, the kids ogling the splendid carriage, Franco got out and held the door for Rachel, who stepped down, feeling conspicuous in her sables. She smiled at the children as Franco unlocked the front door. Then she followed him inside. The house was neat and comfortably furnished, the ground floor consisting of a large parlor and, behind, a kitchen that opened out into a small garden.

"Why, it's charming," she said, looking around. "Perfectly charming. And I love the garden."

"You're very kind. Yes, it's not a bad place, and it has indoor plumbing, which is unusual in Trastevere. She insisted on that."

"Who's 'she'?"

Franco indicated a wooden chair by the fireplace.

"Please," he said. "Would you like a glass of wine?"

"No thanks." She took the seat. Franco stood in front of the empty fireplace.

"Let me tell you about my father," he said. "He's very charming and well-read—he's really quite erudite in many subjects. He's extremely handsome and has the most beautiful manners of any man I've ever known. I don't think he would ever knowingly hurt any person. He is also extremely lazy, totally uninterested in making money, and a compulsive gambler. In short, he is perfectly suited for one profession: to be the lover of a very rich and indulgent lady. And that is what he is."

Rachel squirmed slightly with discomfort.

"You mean, he is a kept man?"

"Exactly. The lady in question is very generous, and we live as well as we do because she insists on it. She also paid to send me through the university and pays our clothing and food bills. So what little I have, I owe to her. And I am grateful to her. But what a degrading life this is. If only my father had a little pride! But he doesn't. He's happy just as things are."

"Well, yes . . . But why can't your father marry the lady in question?"

"She already has a husband, and the Church has so far refused to give her an annulment. She has many enemies in the Vatican, because over the years she has helped the Church's enemies—in particular, Garibaldi. Now she's trying to ingratiate herself with certain influential Cardinals, and perhaps she'll be able to succeed. But for the moment, my father is nothing but her lover. In some ways, it's a very Roman situation. But I'm considered something of a joke in this city."

"Does this woman love your father?"

"Yes, I think she does. Very much, in fact. She is a very strong-willed woman, so my father's many weaknesses don't bother her. In fact, I think it's one reason she loves him: he's so easygoing, so pliant."

"Is the woman in question by any chance Mrs. Savage?"

Franco diplomatically pulled out his gold watch and checked it. He had no intention of answering her question, but he knew she knew.

"It's getting late," he said. "Your lunch is at two o'clock. We should get back to the palazzo."

Rachel stood up and put her hand on his arm.

"I'm glad you've told me all this, Franco," she said, softly. "I will tell no one. But you must always consider me your friend, and anytime you need help, come to me."

"You are very kind."

He led her out of the house back to the carriage.

As they drove back, Rachel said, "Johnny told me you want to be a doctor."

"I've changed my mind about that," Franco said. "I find I have no calling for it after all."

"Then what is your calling?"

"Money, if you can say there's such a thing as a calling for money. I want to work with money somehow or other. In a bank, perhaps. Johnny works for his father's bank and tells me he's beginning to like it. I wish I were he. I think I'd be completely happy surrounded by money."

"Then perhaps my husband can help you," Rachel said. "I mean, if there's any family that knows money, it's the Rothschilds. Would you be interested in working with them?"

Franco stared at her.

"Signora, that would be the best thing in the world for me!"

"Remember: Rachel. Then I'll talk to my husband. I'm sure he can be helpful."

"Rachel, I will be forever in your debt!"

She smiled at him. "We won't talk about debts," she said. "If I can help you, it will give me great pleasure. You will owe me nothing—but success! You must work hard!"

"I am not afraid of work—unlike my father."

It took Julie two agonizing months to arrange for the transfer of one million dollars from her San Francisco bank to the Imperial Treasury. During that time, she stayed at her boardinghouse in the Legation Quarter, terrified that some harm would befall Tim in the Dowager Empress's prison, haunted by the thought that each day that he spent in his cell prolonged his agony. But finally, word arrived that he would be released the next day at noon. Though doubts gnawed at her that the Dowager Empress might pull some last-minute treachery (she even fantasized that now that she had the money, she might, out of sheer perversity, have Tim killed), in fact the next day at noon a sedan chair arrived in front of her boardinghouse and a haggard Tim stepped out.

Julie ran into his arms, sobbing, "Thank God you're free!"

He kissed her, then hugged her.

"They treated me better after you saw the Old Buddha," he said, using the Dowager Empress's nickname. "But I'll tell you one thing: I'm through with politics."

Julie was laughing and crying, almost drunk with excitement at having recovered her lover.

"We're leaving China," she said, "and never coming back. We're going to get married and be blissfully happy!"

"I know exactly where we're going. I figured it all out in that damned prison."

"Where are we going?"

"We're going to Hong Kong, where that old bitch, the Dowager Empress, can't touch me. And we're going to start that department store there."

PART FOUR

MURDER

22. "JUSTIN, MY DEAR MAECENAS, GENEROUS PATRON of the arts, welcome to my humble abode!" exclaimed Robbie Phillips, Broadway's leading actor as he embraced Justin in the drawing room of his house on East Thirtieth Street, not far from the Rialto, the theater district. Robbie, who was somewhere in his forties, was a handsome man whose looks were being slowly ravaged by his nonstop consumption of alcohol. Already, an hour after the final curtain of his opening night, Robbie was well on his way to oblivion. "Tell me," he said, in a private tone, "did you enjoy the play?"

"Very much. And you were terrific."

"Ah, you are a man of infinite taste, but alas, I fear doom! The laughs weren't there, the audience was stony. Can you ever forgive me for inveigling you into investing in my disaster?"

"Robbie," Justin said with a smile, "it's a positive pleasure to lose money with you. But I think you're being pessimistic. I had the feeling the audience was having a good time. And that brunette, Kitty Kincaid . . ."

"A find, a true gem! I predict a dazzling future for her! She's over there, by the piano. Would you like to meet her?"

"Very much," Justin said, peering through the smoke-filled room that was packed with actors, actresses, theater-goers, and theatrical hangers-on.

"Come, sir. First, a libation . . ." He took two glasses of champagne from a passing waiter and gave one to Justin, taking a generous sip from the other for himself. "I must warn you, dear Justin," he continued in a guarded tone, " 'tis said she has a rich boyfriend who keeps her in a certain style. Whether that's true is another question. In the words of the Immortal Bard, 'We in the world's wide mouth live scandalized and foully spoken of.' *Henry IV*, Act One, scene three. Mayhap you saw my production of the play a few seasons back? The critics were savage, but what do critics know? A pox on them all! Kitty, my dear, I have brought you a fan. This estimable gentleman, a titan of finance, has rhapsodized about your performance tonight. Justin Savage, Miss Kitty Kincaid, the belle of Hartford, Connecticut."

Kitty, who was almost as tall as Justin, turned and smiled at him, extending a hand.

"Not the famous Justin Savage?" she said. "The man who was a pirate?"

Justin smiled, staring at her perhaps a bit too obviously.

"These days I restrict my pirating to Wall Street," he said, kissing her hand.

"All Wall Streeters are pirates, aren't they?" she said, as the man at the piano segued into the hit tune from *H.M.S. Pinafore*, "Poor Little Buttercup." A number of people around the piano, mostly young and drunk, started bellowing out the song. Kitty, who was wearing a low-cut red dress that displayed to advantage her magnificent bosom, made a face. "It's so noisy here, Mr. Savage. Let's go in the next room where we can talk, and you can tell me how you liked the play. Or, more to the point—" and she flashed him another dazzling smile, "—how you liked *me*."

"Isn't she a beauty?" Robbie warbled as he took another glass of champagne. Then he declaimed in his rich, hammy baritone, " 'Oh, she doth teach the torches to burn bright! It seems she hangs upon the cheek of night like a rich jewel in an Ethiop's ear!' *Romeo and Juliet*, Act One, scene five."

Several hours later, Kitty sat up in bed and yawned.

"I'll have to ask you to leave soon," she said to the man next to her, who had just made love to her. "I'm worn out, what with first night and Robbie's party. Oh, by the way, guess who I met at Robbie's?"

"Who?"

"Justin Savage."

Her lover sat up and looked at her.

"Really? How extremely interesting."

"Don't you know him?"

"I've never met him, though I know his son well enough. Tell me: was he interested in you?"

"Oh, I think so. He asked me to dinner tomorrow night after the show. I think he has certain ideas, if you know what I mean. Of course, darling, I'd never, never cheat on you." She leaned over and kissed his nose.

"No, go to dinner with him. Better yet, ask him here to your suite. Have Véronique cook him something, one of her West Indian specialties."

"But why?"

"I'll tell you what I want you to do."

Kitty's lover was Antoine-Amédée-Marie-Vincent Manca de Vallombrosa, the Marquis de Morès. Kitty had become his mistress several months before, after the Marquis's wife, the same Medora who had thrown herself so brazenly at Johnny back in the Dakota Bad Lands, had run off with a cotton planter from Mississippi. The Marquis had threatened to kill both his wife and her lover—murderous threats were part of his *modus operandi*—as he set Kitty up in a suite in the Brunswick Hotel, a convenient two floors below his own digs.

The next evening, as per Kitty's instructions, Justin arrived at the Brunswick Hotel on Fifth Avenue and went to her third-floor suite. The door was opened by a handsome woman in a pale blue turban who wore an apron over her blue dress. *"Bon soir, monsieur,"* she said. "I am Véronique. Miss Kitty just got back from the theater and she's changing."

"Did the flowers come?" Justin asked as he went into the nicely furnished living room of the suite.

"Yes, and they're beautiful," said the maid, who was from Martinique, indicating a large vase filled with lilies on a table. "May I get you a drink, Mr. Savage?"

"No thanks. I'll wait."

"Then I'll go back to the kitchen. I'm making a special chicken and fish gumbo, the recipe from Martinique."

"Sounds wonderful," Justin said, with a smile.

"And we start with oysters—food for lovers!" she said, winking at him as she left the room. Alone, Justin inspected the many framed photographs of Kitty that were everywhere. Shortly, the actress came into the room from her bedroom, putting an earring in her right ear. She was wearing a green dress that showed off her spectacular figure to advantage. Justin was dazzled by her beauty.

"Good evening," she said. "Did Véronique get you some champagne?"

"I didn't want any till I saw you."

She smiled. "That's sweet. Well, I'm dying for a drink. Tonight was terrible news. The play got dreadful notices, and Robbie told us he's closing it, so I'm out of work. I hope you didn't lose too much money?"

She went to a sideboard on which was a silver bucket holding a bottle of champagne in ice.

"I'll survive. And it was worth every penny because I met you."

She smiled as she carried two glasses of champagne across the room.

"You're a very romantic man, Mr. Savage."

"Please: Justin."

"And a very handsome man, too, Justin. So: here's to us."

She gave him a glass, and they clicked before sipping. Kitty sat in a sofa, arranging her skirts to show her small feet, on which were a pair of expensive black shoes.

"You have a nice place here," Justin said, taking a seat opposite her. "The Brunswick's one of the best hotels in town."

"By which you're saying, how do I afford it? My father's a doctor in Hartford. He sends me the money. He disapproves of my being an actress—you know how people are about the 'wicked' stage—but I have him wrapped around my finger. Oh, by the way, thanks for the lovely flowers."

"I have something else for you," Justin said, pulling a black velvet box from his jacket pocket. He handed it to her. Kitty set down her glass and opened the box. Inside was a diamond flower pin with an emerald in the center.

"You play very fast, Justin," she said, holding the pin up

to the light, which flashed off the diamonds. "No lady could possibly accept such an expensive present."

"I hope you're not a lady."

She laughed. "I am—up to a point. It's lovely, Justin. I'll keep it, even though it's very naughty of you to tempt me into wicked ways. I hope you're not going to be too wicked too soon. I don't like to be rushed."

"I'm a patient man—up to a point."

Véronique rolled into the room a small round table.

"Dinner's served."

"Most women are bored by business," Kitty said twenty minutes later as they finished the delicious oysters. "But business fascinates me. I hope, if our relationship . . ." she smiled coyly at him, ". . . matures, you'll tell me about your business. Do you play the stock market?"

"Not personally, but my partner and I have a number of stock portfolios that we manage."

"How fascinating. I hope you can give me some stock tips now and then. I have a little money my grandmother left me, and I love to play the market."

"I'd rather not, Kitty. If I gave you a bad tip, you'd resent it, and I wouldn't want anything to come between us."

"That's sweet of you, Justin, but I wouldn't hold anything against you and I'm not a sore loser. And I certainly could use a little extra money."

Véronique came in to clear the oyster plates as Kitty refilled their champagne glasses.

"Well," Justin said, "if you put some money in Union Pacific stock, I think you'd be quite happily surprised in a few days. But please, Kitty, don't tell anyone else. It's really very confidential information."

She smiled as she reached over and squeezed his hand.

"You can trust me, you darling man," she said.

"Buy Union Pacific," she told the Marquis de Morès ten minutes after Justin had left the hotel.

"You may be amused to know," Justin said to his son the next morning at breakfast, "that your old friend, the Marquis de Morès, is back in town."

"Hardly any friend of mine," Johnny said, drinking his grapefruit juice.

"I realize that. I found out, by slipping some money to a certain hotel clerk, that the Marquis is paying a certain lady's hotel bills."

"You mean, he has a girlfriend?"

"Exactly. The lady in question has been asking me for some investment counseling, which I'm convinced she's passing on to the Marquis. So I'm giving her phony stock tips."

Johnny looked at his father with admiration.

"Father," he said, "you're a sly one. And who's this lady?"

"That's none of your business, young man. But she's very beautiful." He sighed. "It's too bad she can't be trusted. Anyway, the Marquis's father-in-law has had some financial reverses lately. And if I cause the Marquis to lose a bundle in the market, they may be forced to sell their stock in the bank, and I can get the rascals out of my hair. They've been demanding a seat on the Board, as I told you. So things may be working out very nicely."

23.   ON A SPRING DAY IN 1886, FRANCO FOSCO FIN- ished filling in his entry in his ledger in a tiny office in the back of an unprepossessing, three-story brick building on St. Swithin's Lane in the City of London. Then he put the ledger away, said "Good day" to his coworkers, put on his coat and hat and went to the front door of the building, where a porter let him out. Beside the door, on the exterior, was a shiny brass plaque that read "N. M. Rothschild & Sons." The building was known as New Court, which was the name of the Rothschild bank in London. In its holy of holies, the Partners' Room, the destinies of nations were directed by the three Rothschild brothers, Nathaniel, Alfred, and Leo. A "yes" or "no" response to a request for loans from a foreign government could mean life or death to the economies of the countries in question. The Rothschilds had arranged the financing for the English government to buy control of the Suez Canal, merely the most well-known of their many dealings.

Franco had never been in the Partners' Room, but in his dreams he thought some day he might.

Shortly before eight that evening, as a heavy fog swirled around the great mansions of Piccadilly, reducing the gas streetlights to blurry blobs of yellow, a cab pulled up in front of Number 109 Piccadilly, and Franco got out. After paying the cabbie, he looked up at the four-story stone mansion that belonged to Felix and Rachel Rothschild. Franco knew they weren't the only Rothschilds in the neighborhood. Nathaniel, soon to be Lord Rothschild, lived at 148 Piccadilly, his cousin Hannah, Lady Rosebery, was at 107, Ferdinand at 143, his sister Alice at 142. Around the corner, Leo Rothschild lived at 5 Hamilton Place and Alfred at 1 Seamore Place.

Going to the front door, Franco rang. The door was opened by a balding butler.

"I am Count Fosco," Franco said.

"Please come in."

After taking Franco's hat and coat, the butler led him into an enormous room cluttered with fine furniture and palms in huge Chinese vases. The walls were red damask with matching curtains that had been pulled over the windows. Standing in front of the marble mantel was Rachel, looking beautiful in a rather severe black dress. Next to her stood Felix, who smiled when he saw Franco and advanced to him, extending his hand.

"Well, it's our young friend from Rome," he said. "Welcome, Felix. How are you enjoying life in London?"

"Aside from the weather, sir, I'm enjoying it a lot."

"Ah, the weather: it's been a bad winter, it's true. But my cousins tell me you're doing quite nicely at the bank."

"For your help, sir, I will be eternally grateful."

"Please, none of this 'sir' business. You make me feel ancient. I'm Felix. And you remember my wife?"

"Who could ever forget such a beautiful lady?" Franco said, kissing Rachel's hand. "It's a true pleasure to see you again, signora. I mean, Rachel."

"And it's delightful to see you, Franco. We've been meaning to have you to dinner since you arrived in London, which was . . . when?"

"Five weeks ago. I'm finally beginning to understand how to get around this great city. London is so alive! It makes me realize how . . . what is the word? Unimportant Rome is."

"Rome will always be important, but in terms of business I suppose London is more vital than Rome," Felix said. "Have you found a place to live?"

"Yes. I rent a room in a boardinghouse in Earl's Court."

"Excellent. Shall we go in to dinner? And you can tell us all about yourself. When the weather gets better, you'll have to spend a weekend with us in the country."

"You're very kind, Felix," Franco said, looking at his wife. "Very kind."

Tim and Julie Chin stood on one side of Queen's Road in Hong Kong and watched as the workman raised the sign on the three-story brick building. The sign read "T. Chin & Co. Department Store."

"It's happened," Tim said, squeezing his new wife's hand. "It's finally happened."

"We're in business," Julie replied. "And darling, it's going to be the best department story in Hong Kong."

"Why not Asia?" he retorted, and she laughed.

Queen's Road was the main street of the flourishing colony, thirty square miles of mountainous stone on the north lip of the huge Pearl River in South China. Forty years before, Hong Kong had been uninhabited except for a tiny fishing village on the south side of the island. The local mandarin had considered the island almost useless, if not even a place of bad *joss*, or luck, because it lay directly in the path of the monstrous storms that plagued the Pacific.

But the British, always with an eye to trade, particularly the immensely profitable opium trade, saw that Hong Kong also had one of the most magnificent natural harbors on earth. The British forced the Emperor to lease them the island, and soon English ships were filling the harbor, English sailors were getting drunk in English gin shops on Queen's Road, English businesses were beginning to thrive, and English fortunes were beginning to build.

It was Tim and Julie's dream, now that she had paid off the Dowager Empress to obtain her husband's freedom, to build their own empire of business in Hong Kong. And if further financing were needed, Julie knew she could always call on her beloved father, Justin.

The Marquis de Morès slapped Kitty Kincaid's cheek, hard.

"You bitch!" he roared. "I bought ten thousand shares of Union Pacific stock on your tip, and it's gone down six points!"

Kitty put her hand to her cheek. The slap had hurt.

"I only told you what Justin told me!" she yelled back. "And I sure as hell don't like being slapped!"

The Marquis grabbed her shoulders with both hands and shook her, angrily.

"You must have gotten it wrong! And I've lost sixty thousand dollars! Now listen: if you want to stay in this suite, you'd better start getting me correct information, or I sure as hell will have you thrown out of here!"

She pushed him away.

"Let go of me," she snapped. "He's taking me to Robbie

Phillips's house tonight for dinner. I'll ask him what went wrong."

The Marquis, his waxed black mustache trembling, shook his finger at her.

"You get it right this time—understand?"

He put on his coat, took his gold-headed walking stick, and slammed out of the room.

"I'm rather put out with you," Kitty told Justin an hour later as they drove to Robbie Phillips's house. "I bought Union Pacific, as you told me, and it's gone down six points. I've lost a good deal of money."

Justin took her gloved hand.

"I told you not to ask for stock tips," he said. "I could be wrong, and then you'd be mad at me, and that's exactly what's happened. I won't do it again."

"Oh no, darling . . . I mean, I said I wasn't a sore loser, and now that's exactly what I'm being. I take it all back."

"How much did you lose?"

"Oh, it was only a few hundred dollars."

"Then I'll pay you back."

"No, really, I couldn't accept it. Just . . . give me a better tip."

"No. Listen, Kitty, I'll not lie to you. I'm a lonely man, and I've fallen for you, hard. So I'm not going to do anything more that would chance aggravating you. I hope, sometime very soon, that we can become more intimate."

"As to that, Justin, I don't want to rush things, as I told you. I wouldn't want you to think of me as cheap or easy. Actresses get enough of that as it is. On the other hand, I'm becoming so very fond of you."

He put his arm around her, pulled her to him and kissed her. It was a long, passionate kiss. When he released her, he said, "Buy Central Pacific stock. And here we are, at Robbie's house. I hope he can stay sober tonight."

Justin got out of the cab and helped Kitty out after him. It was a cool night, and she wore a silver cloak. They went to the door of the house and rang the bell. The door was opened by an aging actor who had bushy white Dundreary whiskers, the fashion of a generation before. His face lit up when he saw Kitty.

"Miss Kincaid!" he warbled. "Come in, you lovely creature."

"Good evening, Sylvester." She turned to Justin. "Sylvester was in the cast of *Our American Cousin* the night Lincoln was shot." She went in the house.

"That I was," said the old actor, closing the door. "I knew John Wilkes Booth. The crazy man thought life was a play, he was Brutus and Lincoln was Caesar. What a pity. Here: Give me your wraps."

After doing so, Justin and Kitty went into the parlor, which was hung with oil paintings of Robbie Phillips in many of his various stage roles, including a large painting of him as Hamlet holding Yorick's skull. Robbie, holding a wineglass instead of a skull, was embracing a pretty young girl on a sofa. When he saw Justin and Kitty, he released her and stood up.

"Kitty! Justin! Welcome, dear friends! I was just getting acquainted with this lovely young wench who aspires to a career on the stage. Justin, I've had a brilliant idea! I'm thinking of mounting a revival of *The School for Scandal*. Would you perchance be interested in a small investment in the production? It's so difficult to finance a classic. All New Yorkers want is drawing room comedies and vaudeville. Culture, alas, is caviar to the general on these barbaric shores."

"Robbie," Kitty said, "you might offer Justin a drink before hitting him up."

"A libation! Indeed! Come, sir, to the bar. 'We'll teach you to drink deep ere you depart.' *Hamlet*, Act One, scene two."

24. AS THE WINTER WEATHER BEGAN TO WARM INTO spring, Felix and Rachel Rothschild invited Franco Fosco to several weekends at their country home, Blackthorn Manor, the handsome Jacobean manor house perched on a cliff overlooking the English Channel. Franco was the ideal houseguest. Young, ingratiating, charming, and funny, he displayed intense interest in Felix's greenhouses, he took daily morning walks with Felix, regaling him with his stories of life in London and the business activities of the Rothschild bank that he worked for. More importantly, Felix could see that the handsome young Italian made Rachel happy. Franco was always perfectly correct with his hostess, who came to treat him almost as a member of the family.

But by the fourth weekend, the bloom for Felix began to fade from the rose. He was no fool. As much as he adored Rachel, he knew that his wife loved him but did not reciprocate his passion. Rachel continued to be childless—through whose fault, no one knew—and she was often restless and bored, except when around Franco. Slowly at first, and then not so slowly, the suspicion began to grow in Felix's mind that his wife was forming an attachment to Franco that could only spell trouble. And even though he was certain nothing physical had occurred between the two, he began to think of how to ease Franco out of his life in as diplomatic a way as possible.

It was at this point that something extremely unusual happened.

"Felix has received a death threat," Rachel said to Franco as she welcomed him to Blackthorn Manor.

"A death threat? Surely you're joking."

"I'm afraid not."

"From whom?"

"Something called 'the Committee of Six.' Felix has hired a private detective in London to find out something about them. Apparently, it's one of the radical Socialist movements that seem to be springing up all over Europe these days. The note said that the Rothschilds were the leading capitalists of the world, that they exploit the masses, and one of them must pay with his life. Of course, it could all be some stupid prank, or some demented person acting out his fantasies. But on the other hand, it might be the real thing."

"Is Felix worried?"

"A little. But I think he tends to write the whole thing off as some sort of . . ." she shrugged, ". . . joke. I've tried to get him to hire some private guards, but he says that would just make us all prisoners."

"But he's wrong!" Franco exclaimed. "He absolutely should hire private guards!"

She looked at him.

"Oh Franco, would you say that to him?" she asked. "I'd feel so much more at ease if we had some sort of protection. I think he'd listen to you."

"Of course I will. I'll talk to him tonight. I'm Italian. In Italy, we take assassination threats seriously."

Since it was an unusually warm day for late March, tea that afternoon was served on the terrace outside the library of Blackthorn Manor.

"I think," Felix said, accepting a cup of tea from his footman, "that we may have an early spring this year, which would be nice. That is, if this day is any indication of what's to come."

Rachel, who was looking lovely in a gray-and-white-striped dress, the big skirt of which billowed over the wrought-iron bench she was seated on, poured Franco's tea.

"You still prefer milk, Franco?" she said.

"Yes, please."

"Jersey, Hereford, or Shorthorn?"

"I think I'll try Jersey this time."

Rachel poured from the magnificent silver service and handed the cup to the footman, who brought it to Franco. Franco was wearing a casual country suit and a wide-brimmed brown hat. He stirred his tea, waiting for the footman to go back inside the house. The setting sun gave the wide lawns, just beginning to wake up, a lush look. The tall trees were showing the first stirrings of budding, and the leaves of the rhododendron bushes had de-drooped, their big buds starting to expand.

"Rachel tells me you've received a death threat," Franco said.

Felix waved his hand in a dismissive manner.

"Yes, but it's probably some crank."

"What makes you so sure?"

"My dear Franco, if someone wanted to kill a Rothschild to make some sort of political statement about the evils of capitalism, the last Rothschild they would pick would be me. Very few of the general public know I even exist. No, surely they would go after my cousin Natty, or one of his two brothers. They are the celebrated Rothschilds. It would be a waste of a bullet to shoot me."

"Nevertheless, if I may be so intrusive into your private business, don't you think it would be wise to hire some bodyguards?"

"A total waste of time and money. No bodyguards can protect you if someone truly wants to murder you. Look at the late Tsar of Russia! Surely no one has better protection than the Tsars, but, as you know, several years ago Alexander II was blown up in the middle of St. Petersburg by a bunch of Nihilist students. The bomb went off right between his legs! Absolutely horrible—and the poor man lived on for several hours in utter agony. No, there's no way to protect against assassins. I could surround myself with bodyguards and be shot strolling down Piccadilly. I refuse to live that way. Besides, as I said, it's the work of a crank."

"But surely you could have some guards here, where it's so easy to get access to the grounds."

"I have the night watchman. He's good enough."

"Darling, he's almost stone deaf and well over seventy years old!" Rachel said. "I do wish you'd listen to Franco."

"I appreciate your concern—both of you—but I choose to leave my protection in the hands of God, who is a far better bodyguard than anything one can hire. Besides, I'm told that many so-called bodyguards turn out to rob the houses they're hired to protect."

"Then," Franco said, "may I suggest you carry a gun—just in case?"

"No. I don't like guns. They cause accidents to happen. Who knows how many people get hurt—or killed—in shooting parties? One reads about it all the time in the newspapers. Some poor fool houseguest up in Scotland last summer had his eye shot out by one of the other guests, who was probably tipsy."

Rachel looked at Franco and shrugged slightly, as if to say, "What's the use?"

Dinner was held, as usual, at eight that evening in the big dining room with its elaborate plaster ceiling—one of the finest Jacobean ceilings in England, Felix had boasted. The linenfold paneling on the walls was dark with the patina of time, but beautifully carved, and the Jacobean furniture, so very masculine with its intricate carving, gave the room a solid air. The dark red velvet curtains hung on either side of the mullioned windows, the largest of which overlooked the Channel. In fact, in the distance could be heard the muted roar of the surf as it beat against the stone cliffs in front of the house and some sixty feet below it.

As the three sat down to the table, Franco had the definite feeling that Rachel looked strained. She seemed more pale than usual and rather tense. However, in the soft candleglow she looked even more beautiful in her Prussian blue velvet gown. And the smell of the hothouse flowers that were everywhere in great profusion lent an orchidaceous hint of decadent luxury to the scene that Franco rather liked. There was something almost oriental in Felix's love of the sensual. Franco had read that many of the numerous Rothschilds shared this trait, and of course their fabulous wealth enabled them to indulge it in a way the world had not seen since before the French Revolution.

The dinner was magnificent, as always. Afterwards, Felix mumbled something to Rachel, then excused himself, telling Franco that he had a slight headache and was going to bed. "I'll be taking my usual walk in the morning," he added as he started out of the room. "Will you be joining me?"

"I'm looking forward to it," Franco said, standing up from the table and wiping his mouth with his napkin.

"Excellent. See you at nine. Good night."

After Felix had gone and the footmen had served coffee in the library, Franco said, "Is something the matter? You look rather strained . . ."

Rachel put down her demitasse cup. Her hands were trembling so much, the cup clattered against the saucer.

"It's Felix," she said, softly. "He told me before dinner tonight he's going to talk to you in the morning."

"About what?"

"He . . ." She wrung her hands, her face a study in despair. "Oh Franco, you know how close we've become . . . and even though Felix knows full well that our friendship is platonic, I believe he's become jealous of you."

"He has no reason to!"

"I know, but . . . Felix was bound to want to be the only man in my life, which I suppose is his privilege, but . . ."

As tears formed, Franco, who was seated next to her, stared at her.

"What does he intend to do?" he asked.

She wiped her eyes.

"He's going to ask you to limit yourself to one weekend a month here."

"But of course. I do not wish to take advantage of his hospitality . . ."

"It's *my* hospitality, too!" she blurted out, angrily. "I want you here! And I've done nothing to be ashamed of!"

"You are so kind," Franco said, softly, setting down his cup. "So good, so noble. It breaks my heart to see you unhappy."

He took her hand and raised it to his mouth. She looked at him with tear-filled eyes.

"I threatened to stay in London, to see you there," she said. "But he said he can undo what he did . . ."

"What does he mean?"

"I think he means that he got you your job with his cousins, and he can get them to fire you! I don't know what to do . . . I don't want to lose you . . ."

"Rachel, we'll always be friends. Don't worry."

"Yes, I suppose you're right . . ."

She turned and left the room.

Franco moved to the fire and stared into the burning logs.

"Do you have any lady friends in London?" Felix asked Franco the next morning as they walked from the Jacobean manor house toward the Ledge, Felix's favorite spot to view the English Channel. It was another beautiful early-spring day, and the sky was cloudless.

"I'm afraid I have neither the time nor the money to be much of a man-about-town," Franco said. "But I do see a young lady now and again. Her name is Sybil, and she works in a draper's shop. She's quite nice, but I don't think one could call it much of a romance. Why do you ask?"

Felix walked in silence for a while. The two men were now out of sight from the house, walking through a wood that bordered the sea for a short period. Then he said, "I find myself in a rather delicate position, Franco. I'm quite fond of you, actually. And my wife, as we both know, is devoted to you. While I don't believe there have been any improprieties—and I say that with total sincerity—still we have become what many people must view as a *ménage à trois*. Given the fact that people in general have suspicious minds and love to gossip, I think we must assume your continued presence here must generate much malicious comment. If you were not quite so young and attractive, it might be another matter. But as it is . . ."

"Please," Franco interrupted, "Rachel already mentioned this to me last night. The last thing I would want is to repay your kindness and hospitality with any cause for gossip. I of course will limit my visits here to once a month—or never, if you would prefer."

The two men emerged from the wood and started toward the rocky precipice that was known locally as the Ledge.

"How very delicate of you, Franco," Felix said. "Of course, I have known all along that you are a gentleman. No, I would not want to banish you from Rachel's company—or mine, for that matter. We both enjoy having you here. But now that you understand my worries, I will appreciate it if you limit your visits here to once a month."

"It is done, Felix. And please: if ever I cause you any more consternation, please speak to me frankly. I value both your and Rachel's friendship much too highly to wish to damage it."

"Well said, Franco. And we won't speak any more about it. By Jove, what a splendid day! And look at the Channel! It positively sparkles in the sun." They had stopped on the rocky ledge, a few feet from the cliff. Some sixty feet below them, the sea swirled in white foam around the jagged rocks at the bottom of the precipice. In fact, it was a breathtaking view of the Channel. Beyond Felix, a rocky path led down the side of the cliff to the stony beach. "Most of my family prefers Buckinghamshire," Felix was saying. "But I fell in love with this place when I first saw this view. You know, I actually believe we can see France today."

Franco, standing slightly behind him, watched Felix intently as the breeze blew his thick hair.

Then Felix turned and smiled at him.

"Well," he said, "shall we go back to the house for breakfast? I'm absolutely famished."

"Felix has received another death threat," Rachel said a month later as Franco came for the weekend. "I don't know what to make of it, but Felix continues to shrug the whole thing off."

"You know my feelings about that," Franco said. "I think you should take it seriously."

"Yes, I know." She sighed. "Dear Franco, I'm so glad to see you again. I missed you. Felix has spoken so highly of you. He says over and over again what a gentleman you are, and how well you reacted to his fears. He actually likes you, you know."

"And I'm so very fond of him."

That evening passed pleasantly enough, with Felix and Franco discussing the events of the day. But at the end of the dinner, Franco declined coffee and brandy and, saying he had a headache, excused himself and went upstairs to bed. Before he left, Felix asked him if he would be walking with him in the morning as usual, and Franco said he hoped he would be better and be able to accompany him.

The next morning, though it was drizzling slightly, Franco and Felix started out for their walk, heading for the woods and the Ledge. "Your headache is better?" Felix asked as they tramped across the wet lawn in their Wellies.

"Yes, thanks, it's gone. They've been working me fairly hard at the bank."

"You'll be glad to know that I was speaking to my cousin last week, and he spoke very highly of you. They're quite pleased with you."

"I'm delighted to hear that, Felix. It means that your faith in me has, so far, been justified."

"I feel exactly the same. Blasted weather, isn't it? But they say the rain is good for the lungs."

They squished through the woods until they arrived at the Ledge. Felix walked up to the edge of the cliff and stared out to the Channel, which was foamy with whitecaps.

"Ah, the English Channel," he exclaimed, "never so beautiful as when it's in an angry mood! Do you agree with that, Franco—what in God's name?"

Franco had stepped up behind him and given him a

mighty shove. Felix fell over the side of the cliff. He screamed a moment as he plummeted to the rocks below. Then all was silent as his broken body was washed into the sea by a wave.

Franco stood at the edge of the cliff a moment, looking down. Then he pulled a carving knife he had stolen from the kitchen from his jacket pocket. He started yelling "Help! Help!" as he tore his jacket and shirt open in front. Then he plunged the knife into his right shoulder, his knowledge of fencing being sufficient for him purposely to miss any major muscle that could cripple him permanently. As blood gushed from the wound, he threw the knife over the cliff.

On top of the cliff, Franco started running back toward the wood. He was still yelling as he began slapping his face with his left hand. By now, his torn clothes were drenched with blood from the shoulder wound. Feeling slightly dizzy from the loss of blood, he stopped long enough to catch his breath and lean down to grab some mud, which he smeared on his face. Then he punched his right eye with his left fist hard enough to cause it to start turning black-and-blue.

He started yelling again, running through the wood toward the house. As he emerged from the wood onto the broad front lawn of Blackthorn Manor, he saw several of the servants coming out of the house, hurrying toward him.

"What is it?" one of the footmen yelled, as Franco fell face forward onto the grass. He and the other footmen ran down the lawn. "It's Count Fosco!" the first footman cried out, kneeling beside him. "He's wounded! Go for Dr. Metcalfe!"

Gently, the first footman turned Franco over on his back. The blood was still surging from his shoulder wound, although more slowly now as it began to clot. But with his torn clothes and bruised and muddy face, he looked as if he had been in a terrific fight.

"Mr. Rothschild," he gasped. "A man appeared at the Ledge and pushed him over . . . I tried to stop him, but he . . . stabbed me. . . ."

"Who was it, sir?" the footman asked.

"I don't know . . . Some foreigner with a black beard . . . he said 'Death to all capitalists' as he pushed Mr. Rothschild over the cliff . . . Then he ran down the path to the beach . . . I . . . I'm so dizzy . . ."

He passed out from loss of blood. His fainting was the only thing that was not an act.

"Dearest Franco," Rachel said. There were tears in her eyes. She was sitting next to the bed in Franco's room on the second floor of Blackthorn Manor. Franco, his right shoulder bandaged, was just regaining consciousness.

"Where am I?" he whispered weakly.

"Dr. Metcalfe was here," Rachel said, taking his hand. "He dressed your wound. You're going to be all right, but you must rest, you've lost a lot of blood."

"Felix!" he said, his eyes widening. "Did they tell you?"

"Yes, I know everything. Oh Franco, I can only thank God that this villain—whoever he is—didn't kill you too! To lose Felix is bad enough, but if I had lost both of you . . ."

Franco was trying to sit up, but he was too weak. He fell back into his pillows.

"Did you tell the police?"

"Yes. Everything. The detectives want to ask you some questions when you're strong enough, but there's no hurry. You must gain your strength first."

"The man must have been waiting for us . . . he ran out of the woods before I even saw him and pushed Felix over the cliff. Then he attacked me with a knife . . . We struggled for a few minutes, then he ran away . . . if only Felix had listened to us!"

"I know, I know. We both urged him to hire bodyguards. I've told the police everything. I fear that Felix's stubbornness has cost him his life. But I have you. Thank God, I have you."

She leaned down and kissed his hand. Franco, watching her through half-closed eyes, suppressed a smile.

25.   KITTY WALKED INTO THE LOBBY OF HER FIFTH AV-
enue hotel, having been out shopping, when one of the assistant managers hurried up to her.

"Miss Kincaid," he said, "might I have a word with you?"

"Yes, of course."

"Will you be staying at your suite after the end of next
week?"

"Why wouldn't I be?"

"Well, you see, the Marquis has told the Management that
he won't be paying . . . ah . . . for the suite after the end of
this month, if you see what I mean."

"This is news to me!"

"Naturally, we have to make arrangements to rerent the
suite, unless you wish to remain."

Kitty, who was wearing a smart wool suit and a feathered
hat, pulled off her leather gloves and put them in her purse.

"I'll let you know," she said, "in the morning."

"Thank you, Miss Kincaid. You are, of course, one of our
most valued clients . . ."

"As long as someone pays the rent. Don't give me any of
your applesauce, Mr. Drew. I'm no babe in the woods."

She crossed the gaudy marble lobby to the wrought-iron
grilled elevator cage and took the lift to the third floor.
Walking down the hall to the door of her suite, she pulled
out the key and unlocked it, going inside. It was a rather
chilly afternoon, but a clear one, and sun poured through
the windows overlooking Fifth Avenue. She had just
locked the door from the inside when someone grabbed her
from behind and she felt cold steel at her throat. It was a
knife.

"You two-timing bitch," she heard a familiar voice behind
her, and she smelled a familiar smell: whiskey. " 'Buy Central Pacific.' You're in league with Savage, aren't you?
You're both playing me for a fool, feeding me phony stock
tips. Is he making love to you?"

"Antoine, let me go . . ."

It was the Marquis de Morès, and he was drunk. He pressed the knife blade harder against the skin of her throat.

"I have half a mind to slit your pretty neck," he whispered. "You've cost me another twenty thousand, you bitch. Did they tell you downstairs you're out of here after next week?"

"Yes . . ."

"It's the end of the free lunch, sweetheart. You'll be out on the street, where you can earn your keep the old-fashioned way: the oldest profession, for which you're extremely well suited."

He pressed the knife even harder against her throat. She was panicking. She told herself to bluff him, not show her fear.

"Antoine, stop it," she whispered. "You're not scaring me, and you're not going to risk hanging. You're just drunk."

He removed the knife and pushed her away from him. She fell onto a sofa. She picked herself up and looked at him. His white shirt was open, revealing his hairy chest, and he was weaving. He threw the knife on the floor and poured himself another shot of whiskey.

"You didn't answer me," he said, taking a drink. "Have you gone to bed with Justin Savage yet?"

"It's none of your business," she said, taking off her hat and hanging on to the hatpin in case he got frisky again. "Now get out of here. I want to clean up."

He started toward her, finishing the whiskey.

"You've cost me a lot of money," he said, slurring his words. "Sixty thousand here, twenty thousand there, it starts to add up. But I've figured out your game."

"I don't have any 'game.' I did exactly what you told me. I passed on his tips. I don't know anything about the damned stock market, I wish to God I did!"

"All right, I figured out *his* game. He's played me for a sucker twice. But the next time, he's going to give you a straight tip, figuring that by now I'll have caught on and that the third time, I'll bet against him. But the third time, I'll bet *with* him, and recoup all this money I've lost. So you've got one more chance, sweetheart. You can make this all up to me, and I'll keep on paying the rent. All right?" He leaned over her, supporting himself with his left hand on the back of the sofa while his right hand finished the drink. "You know, I still think you're special, Kitty. You still excite me." He set down the glass and put his right arm around her, pulling him up against her, pressing his lips against her.

She jammed the hatpin into the crotch of his pants. He yelped and released her, jumping back.

"Your breath stinks," she said, getting up. "Now, get out of here and sober up."

He was holding both hands over his crotch.

"You could have hurt me!" he exclaimed.

"But I didn't. And yes, I'll give Justin one more try. And no, I haven't slept with him yet." She gave him a cool look. "But I'm considering it."

"I've lied to you," Kitty said to Justin that night as they returned from dinner at Delmonico's to the Brunswick Hotel.

"Oh?" Justin said, beside her. "In what way?"

"I'm a kept woman. My father doesn't pay my hotel bills. He doesn't make enough money delivering babies to pay his own mortgage in Hartford, much less an expensive hotel suite in New York."

"I see. And who's keeping you?"

"A crazy Frenchman named the Marquis de Morès. I think your son knows him."

"Oh yes. He met him out West. They had a bit of a problem. The Marquis tried to castrate my son."

"My God! Well, it doesn't surprise me. He's a violent man with a terrible temper, and when he gets drunk he can be abusive. He tried to slit my throat this afternoon."

"You're not serious?"

"Oh, I'm very serious. I don't think he would have done it, but then, you never know. At any rate, those stock tips I've been prying out of you, I've been passing on to him."

"I'm aware of that, Kitty. I've known all along."

"You did? Why didn't you tell me?"

"I have my reasons. But I appreciate your telling me the truth now, at last. I hate being lied to, Kitty."

"Well, you may not believe this, but I feel ashamed about what I've done. I'm not the world's most moral woman by a long shot, but I'm not as bad as you must think I am."

"You're looking better." He took her hand and kissed it.

"At any rate, Antoine told me he thinks he's outwitted you. He thinks he can recoup all he's lost by betting with you the next time, instead of against you. I'm so damned mad at him for the way he's treated me that I decided to come clean with you and tell you. If you give him a third phony tip, he's going to go with it."

"Unless he's told you this to get me to go the other way, which is certainly a possibility. The Marquis's no fool."

"He's not *that* smart."

"You may be right. At any rate, I appreciate your honesty, Kitty. I hope that maybe we can start our relationship on a new footing."

"I have champagne in the kitchen."

"I don't want champagne. I want you."

Twenty minutes later, she came out of her bedroom wearing a filmy negligée and nothing else. He looked at the contours of her body, so tantalizingly veiled by the material, showing just enough to make him want to rip it off to see the rest. She smiled as she came to him and put her arms around him. She smelled of a subtle perfume.

"You know something?" she said. "I think you're quite wonderful, Justin Savage. In fact, I think I'm falling in love with you."

She slipped the negligée off her shoulders and it slid down her body, landing in folds at her bare feet. He gazed at the milky splendor of her flesh and felt as rutty as a teenager. He picked her up in his arms and kissed her mouth. Then he carried her into the bedroom, kicking the door shut behind him with his shoe.

✦

Two nights later, a smiling Justin fixed himself a whiskey and soda in the library of his Fifth Avenue house and said to his son, "Well, Johnny, I think we've gotten rid of the crazy Frenchman for good. He and his father-in-law sold all their bank stock today, so they're out of our hair. I hear the Marquis is moving back to France."

"That certainly is good news," Johnny said. "I take it your phony stock tips had something to do with this?"

"That, and a very charming young lady. I didn't want to tell you this before, Johnny, but I've fallen in love. I know you'll probably think it strange that a man as old as I am could fall in love with someone, but it's happened."

He sat next to his son.

"Who's the lady?" Johnny asked, quietly.

"A very beautiful young actress named Kitty Kincaid."

"An actress?"

"Is there something wrong with that?"

Johnny shrugged. "And what about my mother?" he asked.

"Your mother chooses to live in Rome. She told me to get a mistress, and that's what I've done. She's charming, Johnny. I want you to meet her. I know you'll like her."

"I don't think I want to meet her, Father."

"Why? Do you disapprove of my having a mistress?"

"It's just that . . . well, I was hoping someday you and Mother could get together again, and we'd all be family once more. But I guess that's not going to happen, so . . . I don't know. Maybe someday I can meet her, if you want me to. But let me get used to the idea first."

"Fine. Now, let's talk about you. You asked me in your letter from Rome to think about where you and Clarissa could live here in New York. I've discussed this with Ben, who knows New York real estate better than I, and he said there's a house on Gramercy Park that's on the market and is a good buy. I thought this Saturday you and I could go down and take a look at it, if that would suit you."

"Sure. That sounds like a good idea."

"There's something else. I take it that you and Teddy

Roosevelt have pretty much given up your Wild West adventures, since Teddy's back in New York politics and you're working at the bank?"

"Yes. The cattle business hasn't worked out as well as we'd hoped."

"In that case, I want you to start studying French. Being fluent in Italian, it shouldn't be hard for you to pick up."

"Why French?"

"Ben and I are thinking of opening an office in Paris. We both agree that you'd be a perfect choice for running it. I'm not talking right away, but perhaps in a few years. Would you like living in Paris?"

Johnny, who had been looking rather glum, brightened up.

"Oh, yes, Father! I'd like that a lot! But what about the house on Gramercy Park?"

"Real estate's always a good investment. If you and Clarissa go to Paris, you can rent it out, and it would always be waiting for you when you come back to New York. . .Yes, Oswald?"

The butler had appeared in the doorway.

"Excuse me, sir, there's a gentleman here to see you. A Detective Walter O'Malley of the Metropolitan Police. He's with a police officer."

Justin stood up.

"Show them in."

Oswald left as Justin looked at his son.

"I wonder what this is all about," he said. "At any rate, I'll set up an appointment to look at the house Saturday morning, and I've asked a friend of mine who teaches at Columbia University to recommend a French tutor for you."

A balding man in a brown suit appeared in the doorway, followed by a policeman with a thick mustache.

"Mr. Savage, I'm Detective O'Malley, and this is Sergeant Pierce."

"How do you do, gentlemen?" Justin said, shaking their hands. "This is my son, Johnny. What can I do for you?"

"Do you know a Miss Kitty Kincaid, resident in the Brunswick Hotel?"

"Yes, I know her. Is something the matter?"

"When was the last time you saw her, sir?"

"As a matter of fact, I saw her this afternoon. I had a drink with her in her hotel suite."

"At what time?"

"It was about . . . let's see . . . I'd say five-thirty."

"And how long were you with her?"

"About an hour." Justin noticed that the policeman had taken out a black notepad and was writing in it. "Excuse me, but what's this all about?"

"I'm getting to that, sir. But there's one more question. Did you and Miss Kincaid have a personal relationship?"

Johnny was watching his father. He saw him get red in the face.

"I don't think that's any of your damned business!" Justin said, stiffly. "Now I'd like to know what this is all about!"

"Miss Kincaid was found by her maid, Véronique Dubois, at eight this evening. She had been raped and stabbed four times and left on the floor of her bedroom. Before she died, she managed to write a word with her own blood on the wall. The word was 'Justin.' "

Johnny rose to his feet. His father's face had turned from red to ashen.

"Kitty . . . murdered?" Justin whispered.

"Yes, sir. I have here a warrant for your arrest."

PART FIVE

DETECTION

26. THE MOMENT FRANCO FOSCO PUSHED FELIX Rothschild over the cliff, sending him plunging sixty feet to his death on the rocks of the English Channel, he made Rachel Rothschild the second-richest woman in England after the Queen herself—a fact Franco was well aware of. He had worked at New Court, the Rothschild bank, long enough to grasp the enormity of the Rothschilds' collective fortune, and he had a fairly shrewd estimate of what Rachel would inherit. In fact, her inheritance amounted to £2,000,000 at a time when one English pound was worth five American dollars, and there were no death duties or income tax.

The rich were celebrated in the popular press, and the mystery surrounding Felix's murder was like catnip to the Fleet Street reporters. And when Rachel began to be seen in public with Franco, the penniless young Italian employee of the Rothschild Bank, the press exploded in a frenzy of speculation—a fact that Rachel's mother was only too well aware of as she climbed the steps of Number 109 Piccadilly and rang her daughter's doorbell. It was a drizzly day. Hildegarde and Ben had just arrived in London on the boat train from Southampton and checked into Claridge's. Hildegarde told her husband she wanted to speak with Rachel alone first. Hildegarde knew Ben was nowhere as religious as she and felt much less strongly on the matter of Rachel's being involved with a gentile than his strong-willed wife. Hildegarde was ready for war.

One of the fifteen footmen employed by Rachel opened the front door of the mansion. One of Felix's odder requirements for employment had been that his footmen all had to be at least six feet tall. This gentleman was a strapping six-foot-two, looking imposing in his black silk breeches, white silk stockings, and crimson-and-gold swallowtail coat with white tie.

Hildegarde was admitted into the immense entrance hall, which featured busts of the twelve Caesars standing on marble columns, Felix having bought the busts from a dealer who had dated them to the first century A.D. She was then led to the red drawing room, where Rachel ran into her arms.

"Momma!" she cried. "I'm so glad to see you! You're looking wonderful. Was your crossing successful?"

"I wouldn't be here if it weren't," Hildegarde said, stiffly.

Rachel was no fool. She knew there were stormy seas ahead.

"You informed your father and me in your last letter that you actually intend to marry this Franco person," Hildegarde said twenty minutes later, after she and Rachel had been seated in the dining room for lunch.

"Yes, and I'm so eager for you to meet Franco!" Rachel exclaimed.

"I have no intention of meeting him."

"Momma, you can't be so horrid! I know you'll come to love him in time."

"Among other things, he's not Jewish."

"I've discussed that with him. He's willing to convert to Judaism . . ."

"Who wouldn't for two million pounds sterling?"

"Oh Mother, what an awful thing to say. Besides, other Rothschilds have married gentiles who converted . . . and look at Uncle August! He married Caroline Perry!"

"We've been over that. The marriage is not a success."

"I can't believe you could be so totally narrow-minded!"

"My dear child, when it comes to religion, one *has* to be narrow-minded. How can it be otherwise? People speak of tolerance to other religions. If you truly believe, how can you be tolerant? Do you think Catholics are tolerant of Protestants, or vice versa?"

"Franco is a Catholic and couldn't care less."

"Then he obviously is a man of no character or conviction. But setting religion aside, darling Rachel, surely you must see that he's after your money? You're enormously rich—he doesn't have a penny!"

The footmen brought in the soup course. Rachel kept silent until they had left.

"Listen, Momma," she said in a soft voice. "I married Felix

to keep you happy, and I didn't love him, though I did care for him a great deal. This time I'm marrying for love, and I don't care whether he's a Catholic or a Buddhist or even if he's after my money. Yes, you're right: I'm enormously rich. But this is going to be a consideration with any man I marry, so why should I be concerned with it about the man I truly want?"

"You truly want this Franco creature?"

"Oh, stop talking about him as if he were a toad! He's beautiful, he's warm, he's gallant . . ." She shrugged. "I adore him. And I'm going to have him!"

Hildegarde eyed her coldly, then took a sip of soup.

"You have told me in your letters," she went on, "that Scotland Yard has given up on trying to find Felix's murderer."

"I didn't say they've given up. They simply have no leads or clues."

"As you know, I read a fair amount of detective fiction. The foremost rule of detection is to look for the motive. Who stood to gain the most by killing Felix?"

"Momma, it was a terrorist—a Socialist fanatic."

"Whom nobody has seen, and who has not been heard of since. Socialism hasn't gained by Felix's murder, nor have the Rothschilds been attacked by the press. In fact, from what I have read of the case in New York, the public's sympathy has gone out to the entire family. No, I don't believe the terrorist theory, and I've given the matter a great deal of thought, believe me. The terrorist theory is poppycock. There were only two people on earth who stood to gain from Felix's murder: you and Franco Fosco. And I assume *you* didn't push Felix over the cliff."

Rachel laughed as she wiped her mouth with her napkin that was embroidered with the Rothschild coat of arms.

"Momma, are you saying that Franco pushed him?"

"Exactly. He murdered your husband, knowing you were in love with him and would marry him."

"Oh Momma, this really is too absurd! The man stabbed Franco! He could have been killed himself!"

"Oh yes, that was the cleverest part of the scheme. Everyone assumed that because he was wounded, he was innocent. The man is clever, I'll give him that. Did it ever occur to you that he stabbed himself?"

"Momma, that's so absurd I refuse to discuss it any further. Franco, a murderer? Ridiculous. He wouldn't harm a flea, and I strongly resent your saying these things to me!"

"My dear, I am only trying to save you from making a tragic error! If he killed Felix to get you, mightn't he kill you someday to get the money? One has to think of these things! He's Italian! Their history is filled with assassinations."

"Yes, he said the same thing when we tried to get Felix to hire bodyguards, and Felix pooh-poohed the whole idea. Actually, if anyone is at fault in this whole miserable affair, it's Felix, who brought about his own death by refusing to be careful, and he almost caused Franco's death, to boot. He was warned! And I find it extremely distasteful that you try to accuse Franco of some heinous plot against Felix, when it was *he* who did everything in his power to prevent what happened—and what almost cost him his life!"

"Oh, my dearest daughter, it breaks my heart that you've so completely fallen under the spell of this young Italian enchanter!"

"I don't want to speak about it anymore. How's Papa?"

"He has a bad cough—I can't get him to stop smoking those foul cigars!—and don't change the subject. I'm warning you, Rachel, that unless you call off this unholy alliance with Franco, I'm going to hire a detective agency to investigate Felix's murder. I'll bring this Franco creature to justice and see him hanged!"

Rachel's eyes filled with rage.

"You do," she said, "and I'll never talk to you again!"

"You marry this miserable Italian schemer," her mother retorted, hotly, "and I'll never talk to *you* again!" She threw down her napkin and stood up. "Think about it, my dear. When you've come to your senses, you may call on your father and me at our hotel. I have nothing further to say on the subject."

She stalked out of the dining room as Rachel burst into tears.

That night, in Rachel's enormous bedroom in the Piccadilly mansion, Franco ran his hands over her naked thighs as he kissed her full, luscious breasts.

"How did it go with your momma?" he asked between kisses.

"I don't want to talk about it."

"You keep saying that, but I want to know!"

Rachel was not only trying to push the unpleasant lunch out of her thoughts, her body was responding passionately to Franco's lovemaking. His smooth, sinewy body drove her crazy with desire. When he made love to her for the first time a month after Felix's funeral, it had been the first time she had ever enjoyed sex. Now her passion for the young Italian was unquenchable—she couldn't get enough of him. She dug her fingers into his firm buttocks and moaned with pleasure. "Do it, darling," she whispered. "Make me happy again. I love you so much, Franco—so much. You're everything to me, and I don't give a damn what Momma says."

He sat up next to her in bed. The frilled and bowed pink silk shade of the bedlamp filled the room with a soft light.

"I don't feel like it," he said, standing up to cross the room to his pants. Rachel sat up, a look of alarm on her face.

"What's wrong?" she said. "What are you doing?"

"Getting dressed. Going home."

"Darling, what's the matter? Don't leave me! I'm in a wretched state of nerves . . ."

Franco pulled on his underdrawers.

"Rachel, all night you've been dodging my questions about your mother. Obviously, she's making trouble—we knew she would. But until I know exactly what kind of trouble she's making, I'm in no mood for love. Just because I'm Italian doesn't mean I can perform on demand, like Casanova."

She sighed.

"You're right. I'm sorry. Please stay: I want you to be near me tonight. I want . . . I *need* you . . ."

He looked at her a moment. Then, smiling slightly, he dropped his drawers and stepped out of them, naked again. He came back to the bed and crawled in beside her.

"She's against me because I'm not Jewish," he said. "Am I right?"

"Yes, that's part of it."

"Did you tell her I'd convert?"

"Yes, but . . ." She shrugged.

"Well, damn her, what does she want?"

Rachel burst into tears and buried her face in his chest.

"It's so crazy," she sobbed. "I can't believe it . . ."

"What's so crazy?"

She looked up at him, tears streaming down her beautiful face.

"She thinks . . ." she sniffed, ". . . that you murdered Felix."

His eyes widened.

"*I* murdered Felix?" he repeated, softly. "Didn't you tell her that I was almost killed too?"

"Yes." And she continued to sob.

"Did you tell her I urged him to hire bodyguards?"

"Yes . . . oh, it's so terrible . . . she's convinced you murdered Felix . . ."

"But why?" he almost shouted.

"So I'd marry you and . . . and . . . oh, and Franco, I know she's wrong about this, I don't believe a word of what she said . . ."

"She thinks I'm after your money?"

"Yes."

"I suppose that's understandable. She doesn't believe I love you?"

"No. And the worst part is . . . oh God, I can't even bring myself to tell you . . ."

"What?" He grabbed her arms and shook her. "Tell me! What?"

"She's going to hire a detective agency to prove you murdered Felix."

Yet again, she burst into sobs. Franco, a look of concern on his face, released her.

"This is more serious than I thought," he said. "She must be mad."

"Yes, she is . . . I know it! She's gone crazy! Oh, hold me, my darling—love me! I'm so miserable!"

He took her in his arms and kissed her, smoothing her hair with his right hand.

"We must talk to your father," he said. "You tell me he's a sensible man. Invite him to lunch tomorrow. Tell him you want him to meet me. But don't invite your mother!"

"She refuses to meet you anyway," she sniffed.

"This will all work out," he said, soothingly. "You'll see." He kissed her tenderly.

"Oh God, I love you so!" she cried as he began making love to her again.

At noon the next day, Ben Lieberman got out of a cab and walked into the Café Royale, one of the favorite haunts of Oscar Wilde, who had recently returned from his triumphant lecture tour of the United States and was about to marry the lovely Constance Lloyd. Ben was still youthful-looking, and he was known for his great style in clothes. He was dressed in a well-cut greatcoat, a silk hat, and he was carrying a gold-topped walking stick. The maître d' led him through the packed restaurant to a corner table, where Rachel stood up to hug him.

"Papa," she said as she kissed his cheek, "thanks for coming."

"Of course I came," her father said. "I want to see for myself this paragon of virtue you tell me you've lost your heart to. You must be Franco?"

Franco, who was wearing a well-cut bespoke suit Rachel had bought for him, stood up and shook Ben's hand.

"Yes, sir," he said. "I'm delighted to meet you."

After Ben had sat down and ordered an aperitif, he said, "Hildegarde has told me what she's doing. I want you both to know I think she's wrong, but I can't stop her. My wife has a mind of her own." He went into a short coughing fit, covering his mouth with his napkin. "Excuse me," he said. "My wife's trying to force me to give up cigars. I suppose I should, but . . ." He shrugged. "I'm weak, I guess."

"But Papa, it's so unfair!" Rachel said. "She thinks Franco . . ." she looked around the restaurant and lowered her voice, ". . . murdered Felix. It's crazy!"

"I know," her father said. "She's seeing a detective at this very moment."

"Sir, if I can make a suggestion," Franco said. "If you could prevail on her to at least meet me . . . I mean, this is terribly unfair to me."

"Oh Papa," Rachel added. "Can't you please do something?"

Ben sighed.

"I'll talk to her again."

And he started coughing again. Rachel looked concerned.

"Father, shouldn't you see a doctor about this cough?"

"It'll go away," he said, shaking his head. "And you know I'm scared to death of doctors."

"I spent two days at Brighton," detective Sam Cooper said to Hildegarde the following Monday. Cooper was in his forties, with sandy hair and a thick mustache. He was seated at his desk in his office on the ground floor of a private house on the Fulham Road. "As you know, Blackthorn Manor is only a few miles outside Brighton, on the sea. I made inquiries at the little village of Blackthorn. The only thing of any interest I found was that the six-year-old son of one of the cooks at Blackthorn Manor found a knife on the beach below the cliff where your son-in-law fell to his death. The boy recognized the knife as coming from the kitchen of the manor house—he spends a good deal of time there with his mother, and the knife is of French manufacture with a steel blade, very different from any English knives. He brought the knife to his mother, who recognized it. It had been missing from the kitchen since the night before Mr. Rothschild was killed."

"It must be the knife he used to stab himself!" Hildegarde exclaimed.

"Yes, that occurred to me. The blade was stained, but unfortunately the boy's mother cleaned it. I have the knife here."

He opened the desk drawer and pulled out something wrapped in a cotton cloth. He placed the cloth on the desk in front of Hildegarde and unfolded it. Inside was a carving knife with a carbon steel blade approximately six inches long. Hildegarde, who was looking formidable in a black dress with a huge black hat, reached out her right hand to pick it up. "No, don't touch it!" Cooper exclaimed.

"Why not, pray?"

"Let me explain. Some quite extraordinary developments are occurring in crime detection, developments which the general public is as yet unaware of. Have you ever heard of a Frenchman named Alphonse Bertillon?"

"No."

"He is a clerk working for the French police who several years ago developed a system of identifying criminals by anthropometric measurements."

"My dear Mr. Cooper, I have no idea what you're talking about."

"Monsieur Bertillon discovered that if you took fourteen measurements of the human body—the height, the size of the nose, the size of the foot and so forth—the odds were over 286 million to 1 that any two humans would share the same measurements. So far, the French police have not endorsed his findings."

"I fail to see how that helps us?"

"It doesn't. But what I'm getting at is that there is another theory called dactyloscopy that may help us. This theory, which has been around for some time, is that human fingerprints are totally individual, in other words, no one on earth has the same fingerprints as anyone else. Scotland Yard has not accepted this theory yet, but I do. If Fosco stole this knife to stab himself, then his fingerprints may be on the handle. I've dusted the handle with aluminum powder and ground carbon, and there are a number of smudged prints on it. I took the boy's fingerprints, as well as his mother's, and matched them with prints on the handle. But there is another set of prints. If those prints were Fosco's, we'd be a good deal closer to pinning the murder on him."

"But you say this dactylo . . . whatever, fingerprinting is not accepted by the police? Would it be accepted in a court of law?"

"Let me say this: Scotland Yard has the death threat that was sent to Mr. Rothschild. If Fosco's fingerprints were also found on it, then I think that would certainly be enough to make Scotland Yard take notice."

"You told me Scotland Yard still believes in the terrorist theory?"

"Yes, they don't suspect Fosco at all. This certainly would make him a suspect, in my opinion. There are some people at the Yard who believe in the fingerprint theory. But I need Fosco's fingerprints. Would you be able to obtain a set of them? You'd need something he has touched—a glass, a plate, almost anything, though something with a hard surface would be best."

Hildegarde thought a moment.

"That would be difficult for me," she finally said, "since I've refused to meet the creature. And I don't trust my husband, who's taken a fancy to him."

"Then perhaps you should change your attitude. Meet him, pretend you've changed your mind about him so that he drops his guard, and then get something that he's handled. It could be extremely useful to us."

Hildegarde frowned, and Sam Cooper reflected that she would be a terrifying mother-in-law.

"Perhaps you're right," she said. "I'll pretend to change my mind. I'll do anything to catch the villain and see him hang."

She stood up.

"Excellent," Cooper said, also standing.

"You've done very good work, Mr. Cooper. I'm impressed. Do I owe you any more money?"

"Just the expenses for the trip to Brighton, which I'll put

on my next bill. By the way, Mrs. Lieberman, are you or your daughter aware that Fosco has a girlfriend on the side?"

She looked startled.

"No!" she exclaimed. "The scoundrel! Who is it?"

"A young woman named Sybil Cranford. She works at a draper's shop on Bond Street. She's quite attractive. I've tailed Fosco for several days. As you know, he's moved into a flat at Queen Anne's Gate . . ."

"Paid for by my daughter," Hildegarde sniffed. "She's such a fool!"

"On two occasions, Sybil has come to his flat for several hours during the evening. I assume they're not playing chess."

"He is a man of no moral character at all," Hildegarde said. "I'm ashamed that my daughter has been so blind as to be taken in by this blackguard, but apparently he is a person of considerable charm. How sad that my daughter, who was raised in the most correct of homes, should be so taken in by these superficialities."

"By the way, I wouldn't say anything about the Cranford woman for the time being, at least until we can get his fingerprints."

"You are very wise, Mr. Cooper. I appreciate your advice. It is very difficult for me, as a mother, to have to deal with this situation, but your help is invaluable. Good day, sir. I can let myself out."

27. "THIS IS CRAZY!" JOHNNY EXCLAIMED TO DETECtive O'Malley. "My father's been here with me since six-thirty. When was the last time Miss Kincaid was seen alive?"

"A waiter brought her a small supper at seven," the detective said.

"So my father couldn't possibly have killed her! And the servants here will back me up. So you can put away that arrest warrant."

The detective looked confused.

"But why would she have written your name on the wall?"

"As to that," Justin said, "whoever murdered her might have been trying to put the blame on me."

"By the way, sir, how do you spell your name? Is it with an 'e'?"

"No, an 'i.' J-U-S-T-I-N."

The detective and the police sergeant exchanged looks.

"It was spelled with an 'e' on the wall," O'Malley said. "Miss Kincaid knew how to spell your name?"

"Of course. Gentlemen, this news has come as a terrible shock to me. Kitty was . . . a very dear friend. I take it I'm no longer a suspect?"

The detective folded the warrant and put it back in his pocket.

"No, sir," he said. "And I'm sorry we jumped to conclusions about you. It was just, with your name on the wall . . . Well, we'll have to rethink this case. Do you have any idea who might have done it?"

"Yes. The man who was paying Kitty's hotel bills was also her lover. He's a Frenchman who happens to live in the Brunswick. His name is the Marquis de Morès. Kitty told me that he attacked her on several occasions, and that he's a very violent man. He attacked my son a few years ago out West. I definitely think you should question him."

"How do you spell that?" asked the policeman, who was writing this in his pad.

Justin spelled it for him. Then, after again apologizing, the detective and the policeman left the house, Johnny showing them out.

When he returned to the library, he found his father slumped in a chair, tears in his eyes.

"It's my fault," Justin said. "If the Marquis killed her, it was to get back at me for losing all that money on the market."

"You really cared for Kitty, didn't you?" Johnny said, feeling awkward because of his father's grief.

"She made me feel young again." He dried his eyes with a

handkerchief, and a cold look came into them. "But if the Marquis did it, by God, I'll pay him back for this one day. I don't know how I'll get him, but I'll do it, one way or the other. I'll make him pay."

Johnny had no doubt that his father meant every word.

"Darling!" Rachel exclaimed as Franco came into the drawing room of her Piccadilly mansion. "Did you get my note?"

"Yes. It's wonderful news."

A smiling Franco came across the room and took her in his arms, giving her a kiss.

"I could have cried for joy when the note came from the hotel," Rachel went on. "They're both coming to dinner tonight, and Momma wants to meet you. Papa must have finally beaten her into submission."

"I told you everything would work out, though I must say I'm a little nervous about meeting the old dragon."

"She'll fall madly in love with you! Who couldn't? Oh, and I have something for you. I was so thrilled at the news, I went out and bought you a present. Here."

She took a beautifully wrapped gift off the mantel and handed it to him."

"*Cara,* you shouldn't have," Franco said. "You're much too good to me."

"I want to spoil you! I want to give you everything in the world, because I love you absolutely madly, you beautiful, beautiful man. Go on: open it."

He took off the wrapping, revealing a leather box marked "Asprey." He opened the lid. Inside was a set of shirt studs and cuff links, each holding a diamond surrounded by sapphires. Franco's eyes widened.

"They're beautiful!" he exclaimed. "Gorgeous!"

"You must wear them tonight. Here: let me put them in your shirt for you."

"When are your parents arriving?"

"Eight."

"Then we have time for me to thank you properly." He took her hand and started leading her to the entrance hall.

"Where are you taking me?" she asked.

"Upstairs to bed, of course."

"But I have to bathe!"

He grinned at her.

"Then we'll bathe together."

She laughed.

"Franco, you're an absolute pagan!"

"I come from Rome—remember?"

That evening, when Ben and his wife arrived at Number 109 Piccadilly, the New York banker thought he had never seen his daughter look more beautiful. At the same time, he was somewhat shocked by her dress, which was certainly daring. It had been designed by Redfern, the up-and-coming young tailor with shops in London and Paris who outfitted the *"dolce vita"* world of the time, competing with Charles Frederick Worth, an Englishman whose shop was in the rue de la Paix in Paris. Rachel's dress was violet silk that matched her extraordinary eyes. Its top was held by two slender silver chains, exposing entirely her arms, shoulders, and bosom. With her black hair pinned up by the diamond star her mother had bought her on their trip which seemed so long ago, and a rope of pearls around her slender neck, she was, Ben thought rather nervously, almost voluptuously indecent. Or perhaps, he corrected himself, "sensual," which sounded a bit nicer. Whatever the word, she was a stunner.

After kissing her parents, Rachel took her mother's hand. "And now," she said with a smile, "it's time for you to meet Franco."

"I'm looking forward to it," Hildegarde said, trying to sound infinitely more congenial than she felt. "I must say, my dear, that dress of yours displays a bit too much flesh. Is it quite proper, especially for a widow? Shouldn't you still be in mourning?"

"Momma, I shocked enough people by seeing Franco in

public so soon after Felix's death—especially his Rothschild cousins. It would be ridiculous for me to be in mourning now, under these circumstances. Come: Franco is eager to meet you. And be sweet to him, he's terribly nervous. I know you'll learn to love him, in time."

"I'm sure."

Hildegarde, who was wearing a dark blue dress that showed as little of her aging flesh as possible, crossed the hall with her daughter, her imposing diamond necklace and tiara twinkling in the gaslight. Rachel led them into the drawing room, where Franco was standing before the fire, his back to them. When he turned around, Hildegarde took a long look at her nemesis.

"Isn't he handsome? Rachel whispered.

"In a rather obvious way," her mother commented, determined not to give too much ground.

"Oh Momma, he's a god, and you know it. Darling," she said to Franco, raising her voice, "here she is: my mother."

"Signora," Franco said, raising Hildegarde's hand to his mouth to kiss. "I am honored."

"I will not try to disguise the fact that I have been against you, young man," Hildegarde said. "We must keep hypocrisy to a minimum. But my husband's glowing report of you has led me to reconsider my first decision to refuse to meet you. Perhaps I have been wrong about you. I certainly will try to keep an open mind on the matter. My daughter's happiness and well-being are foremost in my priorities. If, in fact, I conclude that you will make her happy, I will withdraw my objections to this marriage. Provided, of course, that you convert to Judaism."

"Signora, I am already taking instruction from a rabbi."

"Indeed. I assume it is one of those 'Reform' rabbis. I don't particularly approve of the Reform movement and conversion, but I suppose it will have to do."

"Franco," Rachel said, "pay no attention to Momma when it comes to religion. She's as intolerant as the Pope."

"As to the rest, signora," Franco continued, "I can only be myself. You must judge me as I am. I only know—" he smiled as he took Rachel's hand, "—that I love your daughter with all my heart and will pledge the rest of my life to making her happy."

"Indeed. Those are beautiful shirt studs, young man. And quite expensive, by the look of them. In fact, I paid a visit to Asprey the other day and could swear they were on display there. Is it your custom, on a clerk's salary, to frequent such expensive establishments as Asprey?"

"They were a gift from me, Momma," Rachel said, rather defiantly. "Franco has never asked for a thing from me."

"The fact that I am poor, signora," Franco said, "is as undeniable as the fact that Rachel is rich. I suppose anyone would say I love her for her money—that's only human nature. You must judge for yourself the truth, which is that I love her for herself."

"You must be an extraordinary young man not to have some slight interest in two million pounds."

"Momma," Rachel snapped, "I will remind you that you are my guest this evening. I don't want to get into a quarrel about money."

"Quite right, my dear. To discuss money is, of course, always vulgar."

He's exactly what I knew he'd be, she thought. Out after her fortune.

Is he also a murderer?

The dining room of Number 109 Piccadilly was perhaps the apotheosis of what had come to be known as *"le style Rothschild,"* opulence mixed with discrimination. It was a reproduction of an eighteenth-century French interior, gilt pilasters against a white background with a ceiling that was elaborately carved, a mass of swirling gold in a classic setting. The table was set with Felix's collection of vermeil candlesticks and épergnes, the latter heaped with fresh fruit from Felix's greenhouses, and the dinner, the main course of which was *gigot Rothschild*, lamb cooked for twelve hours until it was so tender it melted in the mouth, was served on a white-and-gold dinner service that had been made for Catherine the Great.

Rachel, who was seated at the head of the table flanked by her father and Franco, was tensely nervous at first. But as the meal progressed, she relaxed as it seemed that things were going smoothly. And as the Lafite-Rothschild flowed, Franco reduced Ben to tears of laughter by his demonstration of the hand and face gestures that were such an important part of Italian communication. Hildegarde, who was seated next to Franco, didn't say much during the meal. But she didn't seem hostile to Franco, and on several occasions when he addressed her, she replied civilly. Rachel was beginning to think that her troubles might soon be over, when a curious incident happened.

Her mother had carried a small silver handbag which, rather to Rachel's surprise, she insisted on bringing with her into the dining room, placing it on her lap after sitting down. Now, as the dessert was being served, the purse fell out of her lap onto the floor between her and Franco, spilling its contents. Franco immediately leaned down to pick it up, returning several small pillboxes and a comb back in the purse then handing it to Hildegarde.

"Thank you, Franco," she said with a smile.

Now I have your fingerprints!

28.   THREE EVENINGS LATER, WHEN FRANCO CAME TO Number 109 Piccadilly to have dinner with his fiancée, he was met in the entrance hall by an excited Rachel, who threw her arms around him and kissed him.

"Darling," she whispered, excitement making her violet eyes flash, "you're going to be a father!"

A look of joy came over him.

"Is this true?"

"Yes. I was at the doctor this afternoon. I'm pregnant! Isn't it wonderful? Are you as thrilled as I am?"

He kissed her.

"Absolutely! This is very exciting. But now it's more important than ever that we marry. I want no scandal when the child is born."

"I'm thinking the same thing. And since Momma seems to have quieted down, I think we should go ahead and do it as quickly as possible."

He took her hands and smiled.

"I agree. Let's go inside and make our plans."

The next evening, a hansom cab pulled up in front of a row of affluent private houses at Queen Anne's Gate, near the new Albert Memorial. Hildegarde looked out the window at a four-story red brick house trimmed with white stone. The ground-floor windows were lit, although lace curtains had been closed over them.

Telling the cabbie to wait for her, Hildegarde got out and crossed the street, climbing the stairs to the front door, where she rang the bell. A few moments later, the door was opened by Franco, who was wearing a sweater. On his feet were a pair of slippers.

"Signora," he said, "to what do I owe this honor?"

"May I come in?"

"Of course."

He stood aside as Hildegarde came into a narrow entrance hall with a stair.

"This way, please," Franco said, closing the door. "I must apologize for my appearance. I've been studying my Hebrew."

Hildegarde said nothing as he led her into a tall-ceilinged room that was casually furnished. In front of a fire was an overstuffed chair with an ottoman on which was a Hebrew grammar book.

"May I offer you something?" Franco asked. "A glass of wine? Some tea?"

"No thank you. This is not a social call." Hildegarde spoke in icy tones. "My daughter tells me you have put her in the family way and that you both intend to marry next Tuesday."

"That is true, signora. I hope this pleases you?"

"You know it does not, you scoundrel." She sat in a chair and glared at him. "You have not asked Rachel's father or me for permission to go through with this shocking marriage, and you know full well you would not receive mine."

Franco put the grammar book on a table and sat on the ottoman, folding his hands as he leaned forward, his elbows on his knees.

"It would be more shocking, signora, if we did not marry quickly, considering that Rachel is, as you say, in the family way."

"As I believe you know, I have hired a private detective by the name of Mr. Cooper, a man highly regarded in his profession. He has come up with evidence that links you without question to the murder of Felix Rothschild."

"Ah, we are back to that interesting fable. And what is the evidence?"

"Fingerprints."

"Fingerprints? What are you talking about?"

"If you had any knowledge of modern criminology—a subject you might explore with profit—you'd know that there is growing acceptance of the theory that no two sets of fingerprints are alike. Mr. Cooper has obtained a kitchen knife that was found on the rocks below the cliff where you pushed my poor son-in-law to his death. Your fingerprints are on the handle of that knife. Mr. Cooper has also examined the death threat Felix received, supposedly from a fanatic Socialist. There are clear sets of fingerprints on that document that reveal the author was a fanatic capitalist— namely you, sir, an adventurer twisted by greed for my daughter's millions. I warn you: if you do not back out of this marriage by tomorrow and promise never to bother my daughter again, I will turn the evidence over to Scotland Yard and you will be brought to justice and hanged for murder."

Franco tapped his fingers thoughtfully.

"I think, signora, you may be a bit optimistic about a jury

convicting me on the basis of some fingerprints. But even if
you are right, let us think this through. If Scotland Yard
thought I had murdered Felix, surely they would start to
wonder if Rachel had not been my accomplice."

"Rachel? Preposterous."

"Perhaps not. If one considers the unseemly speed with
which Rachel began to be seen in public with me after
Felix's death, and the fact that she is now carrying my child
and will soon be my wife . . . well, this surely would lead
people to wonder if she had not been involved with the
murder to get rid of an unwanted husband so she could
marry a wanted one: me. Given the press's fascination with
the Rothschilds, this would be trumpeted all over the newspapers. Rachel at the very least would be ruined for the rest
of her life. And, though I don't know the English policy on
hanging females, she might very well end up on the gallows
next to me. I don't think you would want that, would you?"

Hildegarde looked pained and frightened.

"How cold your heart is," she said, softly. "To make such
a cruel accusation! Have you no gallantry at all?"

"When a man is accused of murder, he becomes somewhat less gallant than usual. Let me add that if you go to
Scotland Yard with this flimsy evidence, I might be forced
to suggest to the authorities that Rachel was my accomplice.
It could get very ugly."

She stared at him. Finally, she said, "How can Rachel be
so blind to what you really are?"

Franco stood up.

"I'm getting a bit tired of your name-calling, signora. I
have never lifted my hand against you. I have tried my best
to behave as a gentleman. But if you persist in these manic
accusations, it will be you who leads us all to ruin and woe.
Now, I'll ask you to leave. Even the intricacies of Hebrew
are less tiresome than you."

Hildegarde stood up.

"I would try to buy you off," she said, "but I know it
would be useless. Rachel is far richer than I. But I will write
her a note telling her all I know, and the threats you have

made against me. If this is not enough to deter her from marrying you, then so be it. I will never speak to her again. And may you rot in Hell."

She left the room. When Franco heard the front door slam, he ran back to his bedroom to change into street clothes.

A half hour later, he let himself into Number 109 Piccadilly with the house key Rachel had given him and ran up the huge staircase to the second floor. When he burst into Rachel's room, she was sitting up in bed reading a novel.

"Darling, what's wrong?" she exclaimed, putting down the book.

"Your mother's gone completely mad." He hurried across the room to the bed, where he sat beside her and embraced her. "Darling, we have to be strong or she will ruin us!"

"What are you talking about?"

"She came to my flat an hour ago. She claims she has some strange evidence that proves I murdered Felix . . ."

"What kind of evidence?"

"Fingerprints."

"Fingerprints? What do fingerprints have to do with anything?"

"Apparently, there's a theory that claims that no two sets of fingerprints are alike. The detective she hired says my fingerprints are on the death threat Felix received and also on the handle of a knife they found at the bottom of the cliff. Your mother and the detective think this could prove that I killed Felix, and she threatened to go to Scotland Yard with it. I tried to make her see how ugly this could get for all of us—how Scotland Yard might begin to suspect that you and I were involved in a murder plot together . . ."

"Me?"

"Yes, you. She's going to write you a letter . . . She'll do everything in her power to turn you against me . . ."

"That she could never do!"

"She'll even say I threatened to tell the police you were my accomplice, which is a lie. I'd never do that because it isn't true. None of it's true! But you must be resolute against her, for she can destroy us all! The only thing that can save us against her is our love for each other."

And he kissed her, hungrily, passionately. She responded in kind. Then she threw her arms around him, digging her fingers into his back.

"Oh my darling," she said, tears in her eyes, "I'll never forgive her for saying these horrid lies! I love you with all my heart."

"The last thing she said before she left was that you were dead to her if you married me."

"Then my mother is dead to me. And I won't even read her letter."

Franco smiled.

"I adore you," he whispered, kissing her again as he unbuttoned her nightgown.

Rachel and Franco had decided to be married in Paris to avoid the complications of inviting all Felix's Rothschild relatives to the ceremony, many of whose noses were well out of joint because of his widow's precipitous remarriage. Two mornings later, Rachel was standing in her bedroom trying on one of the new dresses Mr. Redfern had designed for her trousseau when her butler knocked on the door.

"There is a young lady to see you, madame," he said. "She claims to be a friend of Count Fosco."

Rachel turned from the mirror.

"Oh? Who's that?"

"Her name is Sybil Cranford."

Rachel looked a bit perplexed.

"Show her into the drawing room: I'll be right down as soon as I change."

Ten minutes later, Rachel came into the drawing room of the Piccadilly mansion. An attractive young blonde in a stylish tweed suit was leafing through a magazine on one of the tables. She had on a small black hat with a half veil. She put the magazine down as she looked at Rachel.

"Miss Cranford?" Rachel said, coming into the room.

"That's right. Are you Mrs. Rothschild?"

She spoke with a rather overrefined accent, as someone whose native English might not be as tony as required in expensive shops.

"Yes. You wanted to see me?"

"That's right. Your mother came to see me yesterday afternoon."

"My mother? Whatever for?"

"She wanted me to talk to you about Franco. She offered me five hundred pounds to tell you the truth about Franco and me, and I took it. I mean, why not? It's a lot of money, and Franco couldn't care tuppence about what happens to me once he marries you. I have no illusions about that."

Rachel turned pale.

"Pray enlighten me as to what this is all about," she said. "You have the advantage over me."

Sybil smiled.

"Well, can't you guess? Franco and I have known each other ever since he came here from Rome. Those Italians . . . well, I hardly have to tell you how romantic they are, do I? And Franco certainly has a way with the women, as you well know. He can wrap a girl around his little finger, that rascal. By the way, would you be interested in buying these back? Franco told me they could fetch another five hundred pounds from a jeweler, but I thought you might want to keep them in the family, so to speak?"

She pulled a small box from her purse and extended it to Rachel, who came over and took it in her hand. The box was marked "Asprey." She opened the lid. Inside were the diamond-and-sapphire studs and cuff links she had given Franco. She gasped softly.

"Where did you get these?" she asked.

"I won't try to pretend I'm a saint in all this," Sybil said. "After your mother paid me to tell all, I thought, 'Well now,

maybe Franco would cough up something to shut me up.'
He's hardly been generous with me in the past—I've paid all
the restaurant bills. He's a tight one with money, that Franco
is. So I paid him a little visit last night, and told him what I
was up to. Well, he went into a real panic. Said I mustn't
come to you—even threatened to hit me, he did. You know
he's got a real mean streak."

"No, I didn't know."

Sybil smiled.

"You'd better open your eyes a bit wider, if I do say so. At
any rate, he gave me these pretty little baubles to shut me up.
Asprey—that's a very nice store, but I hardly have to tell
you that, do I? Being a Rothschild, I'm sure you know the
best. At any rate, if you want them, the price is five hundred
pounds."

Rachel slowly shut the box as she closed her eyes a moment. She was fighting back the tears. Then she opened her
eyes.

"Yes, I'll give you the money," she said in a hoarse voice.
"But if you ever try to blackmail me again, I'll report you to
Scotland Yard."

"Oh dear, 'blackmail' is such an ugly word. Your mother
led me to believe I would be doing you a great service
telling you the truth. I think you could be a bit more genteel
the way you treat me." She lowered her voice, smiled and
winked at Rachel. "He's good in bed, isn't he, that Franco?
Eh? He really knows how to make a girl happy. Ah, those
Romans! It must be in their blood."

Franco was sitting in his bathtub shaving his face with a
shiny straight razor when the door to his bathroom opened
and Rachel came in.

"*Cara!*" he exclaimed, putting the razor on the enamel
tray of the elaborate steel shaving rack attached to both sides
of the tub. The rack, which featured a round shaving mirror
on a double post, had been a present from his fiancée. "What
has happened?"

She pulled the Asprey box from her purse and tossed it to him. Surprised, he caught it with both hands, barely saving it from falling into the foamy bathwater.

"This," she said in tones so icy they reminded him of her mother, "is the first time in my life I've had to pay for a gift twice. I hope you enjoy those cuff links. They're the last things you'll ever get out of me, you despicable cheat."

"Rachel, what is this? How did you get these . . . ?"

"Can't you guess? Your mistress, that Sybil what's-her-name, came to me and sold them back after cheating my mother out of five hundred pounds and trying to blackmail you. Oh Franco, it speaks volumes about your character that you could fall in love with a woman as common as Sybil."

Franco calmly put the Asprey box on the shaving tray next to his razor.

"In the first place," he said, "I'm not in love with Sybil. She was merely my mistress."

"How odd that you never mentioned her to me. And what else did you fail to mention? Is my mother right about you? Did you murder Felix?"

"Of course not. And I find it insulting that you should say such a thing."

" 'Insulting'? You have a marvelous sense of proportion! After humiliating and insulting me by bedding this woman behind my back, you're insulted that I suggest you might have murdered Felix—a charge that apparently has a good deal of evidence to support it?"

"So you believe this fingerprint nonsense? Very well." He shrugged. "Go back to your mother. You've always had the advantage over me, Rachel, with your millions. I suppose you always will. I'll always be suspect in your eyes because I'm poor . . ."

"That's not true!" she cried out.

"Isn't it? You've always had money—obscene amounts of it. You have no idea what being poor is like, the awful, igno-minious inability to do what you really want because you can't snap your fingers and write a check . . ."

"Stop it!" she shouted. "Stop trying to play on my guilt!

This has nothing to do with money! It has everything to do with character—a quality you apparently are sadly lacking!"

"*Cara,*" he said, picking up the razor from the shaving tray, "I have made one great mistake in my life. I fell in love with you, and I was romantic enough to think you loved me also. Now I see the truth. Now I see what you really think of me. I'm just a poor beggar who can keep you happy in bed. Well, that's not enough for me."

He placed the razor against his left wrist and cut a gash in it. Blood squirted out in a gusher, spraying onto his soapy chest.

"Franco!" she screamed. "What are you doing?"

He lowered the bleeding wrist into the water.

"I have lived like a Roman," he said, "and I'll die like one."

"Oh my God, stop it! Oh—!" .

She grabbed a bath towel off a rack and ran to the tub. He pushed her away as she tried to take his left arm out of the water.

"Let me alone!" he shouted. "Get out of here! I want to die with dignity."

She was sobbing hysterically.

"You can't do this . . . oh please, I'm sorry, Franco . . . oh God, I love you . . . let me wrap your wrist . . . please . . . don't do this!"

Again, she grabbed his arm and tried to pull it out of the reddening water. Again, he shoved her away.

"I'm sick of you!" he shouted. "Sick of your mother, sick of these cheap accusations! I'm no murderer! My only mistake was to fall in love with you! Yes, I was sleeping with Sybil, so what? I even told Felix about it. Is a man not supposed to be able to satisfy his natural desires?"

"I don't care about Sybil!" she cried. "I only care about you! Franco, if you die, I'll kill myself too! I'll kill our baby! Oh please, my darling love, please let me stop the bleeding—for our baby's sake, if nothing else! Please don't do this! I forgive you for everything! I don't care! You're everything to me—everything! Oh please . . ."

She sank to her knees beside the tub, sobbing uncontrollably. Franco, who was beginning to feel weak as his lifeblood continued to pour into the bathwater, lifted his left wrist out of the water.

"Bind it," he whispered, closing his eyes as he leaned back against the tub. "I love you, my darling. Stop the blood and let's start over."

Tears streaming down her face, Rachel took his arm and started tying the towel around the razor wound.

Five nights later, in a suite in the Intercontinental Hotel in Paris overlooking the Tuileries Gardens, Franco finished making love to Rachel, then got out of bed and put on his new red silk bathrobe, part of over five thousand dollars' worth of wedding presents his wife had bought for him on a two-day shopping binge. Then he filled two flute glasses with champagne and brought them back to the big, ornate gilt bed where Rachel lay back against the pillows, a smile on her face.

"So, bride," Franco said, handing her a glass, "are you happy?"

"Very much so, groom," she said, almost purring. "Although it would have been nice if someone had been at our wedding besides the Judge."

"You wish your parents had come," he said, sitting beside her on the bed.

"Of course. But Momma . . ." She sighed.

"Give her time. When we start having children—and we're going to have many beautiful children—she'll come around. But I've been thinking about the future."

"Why, when the present is so wonderful?" She ran her hand through his thick hair.

"Yes, but I have responsibilities now. I must plan for our family. I don't think we should stay in England."

"Why?"

"The Rothschilds have turned against us, and there will always be a cloud over us."

"You mean, Felix's death?"

"Yes. As long as his murder is unsolved, people will talk.

People love to be cruel. It would be very difficult for our children."

"Then, where do you think we should go?"

"To New York. The New World. I've always wanted to see America, and New York is your home. We'd be close to your parents there, and I could start a business."

"What sort of business?"

"I don't know yet. But I'm a good businessman, *cara*. I could make a lot of money."

"We already have a lot of money."

"Yes, but it's yours. I want to make my own money. What would you think of going back to New York?"

"Oh, I'd be delighted to go home. And you're right about my parents: once we start a family, they'll give in. Yes, Franco, that's a good idea. We'll go home! And everyone in New York will adore my handsome, wonderful husband!"

He smiled and kissed her cheek.

"No regrets?" he said, softly.

"None in the world. I'm floating on a cloud."

In contrast to Rachel and Franco's wedding, which had taken place in a suburban town hall, Johnny and Clarissa's wedding the next month was a joyous, splendid affair in the private chapel of Clarissa's mother's villa in the hills above Florence. A fair sampling of Italian nobility was present in their finest plumage. But what delighted Johnny was the fact that it was a Savage family reunion. Not only were his father and mother brought together again under happy circumstances, but Julie and her husband, Tim Chin, attended; they had arranged their European buying trip for their successful department store in Hong Kong around his wedding. Johnny hadn't seen Julie for so long, he had almost forgotten how beautiful she was. But this new Julie was a happy woman, unlike the tortured girl he remembered in New York.

When Julie had a moment to be with her father alone, she said, "The store is doing tremendous business. I think we'll be able to pay you back the money you loaned us with interest in a year."

To get the store started, Julie had borrowed a million dollars from her father's bank.

"There's no hurry, believe me," Justin said. "I have the utmost confidence in you and Tim and feel the money is safe in your hands. The important thing to me, Julie, is that you're happy, and I can tell from looking at you that you are."

"Oh, Papa, everything has turned out so well for me. Yes, I am happy. Tim's a wonderful husband and a wonderful father to Edgar. As soon as we finish building our house, we're going to enlarge our family."

"That's the best news, Julie."

Everyone agreed that Clarissa with her Botticellian blond beauty was as beautiful a bride as had been seen for some time in the ancient city on the Po River.

"Aren't they a handsome young couple?" Fiammetta said to Justin at the reception as Johnny led his bride onto the dance floor. "This is the fulfillment of a dream for me: that my darling son marries an Italian. Now I can die happy."

"You're not about to die," Justin said, with a grin. "And how about a waltz?"

"I'd love to."

He led her onto the dance floor, which was filling up.

"And how's Count Fosco?" Justin asked as he twirled her around.

"I retired him," Fiammetta said.

"You retired your lover? What in the world do you mean?"

"I got tired of him. Besides, after his son married Rachel, I thought it was better if I got rid of him. I bought him a nice villa outside Rome, and he's very happy. He tells me he's fallen in love with a girl young enough to be his daughter. What fools men are."

"They are if they deal with you. So now what happens? Will you find another lover?"

"Who knows? At my age, I'm living one day at a time. Johnny told me you found a mistress, but that she was murdered."

"That's true."

"Do they know who killed her?"

"The police don't, but I do."

"Were you in love with her? Johnny said she was an actress."

"She made me feel young again."

"Ah, if I could only find someone who could make me feel young again! Not that I'm old, mind you."

"You look as young as the spring, Fiammetta."

She chuckled.

"Well, let's say summer," she remarked. "You know, I'd forgotten what a good dancer you are, darling."

He put his cheek against hers and whispered, "Have you forgotten what a good lover I am? You used to love 'Approaching the Fragrant Bamboo.' "

"Is that an indecent proposal?"

"Extremely indecent."

"I haven't had an indecent proposal for a shocking long time. I may have to think this over."

And they continued their waltz.

"Have I told you recently that I love you?" Tim Chin said to Julie as they whirled around the same dance floor.

"Not for at least ten minutes," Julie replied with a smile.

"Well, I do. Madly, passionately, insanely."

"Darling, the feeling is reciprocated one thousand percent."

"By the way, I got a cable this afternoon from the office. We've been invited to Government House again, and I wonder if this time we shouldn't accept."

"Absolutely not. I won't toady to the Governor until they let us into the public library, take away the curfew papers, and invite us into their damned racetrack and clubs. The English are worse than the New Yorkers, but they're going to find that I am the most stubborn woman in Hong Kong.

It's total surrender or nothing. Besides, the food at Government House is terrible."

The British in Hong Kong had a terrible prejudice against the Chinese. Though very slowly, and with the insistence of liberal-minded English governors like Sir John Pope-Hennessy, some of the most odious anti-Chinese restrictions had been lifted—most importantly, allowing Chinese to buy property on the island—there were still enough restrictions remaining to remind the Chinese, even rich American-born Chinese like Tim and Julie, that they were second-class citizens.

"I ran away from prejudice in New York," Julie went on, "but this time I'm not running. I'm staying put. And I'll fight them until I win."

"Good for you," Tim said, admiringly. "No one could ever say you haven't got guts."

That night, in the hotel suite Johnny had rented, he began making love to his bride, kissing her passionately in the big double bed. But as he started to insert himself into her, she gently pushed him away.

"Wait a minute, darling," she said. "We haven't talked about this yet, but now is the time. I want you to use a *préservatif.*"

"A what?" Johnny, who was in the heat of passion, almost groaned with frustration.

"You know."

"Oh *no*!" Now he actually did groan. "Why?"

"I don't want children yet," she said, firmly.

"Clarissa, this is a helluva time to mention it!"

"Perhaps, but we have to get this straight before an accident happens."

"Don't you want a family?"

"Not yet. I'm not going to ruin my figure."

"But darling, a lot of women have children and keep their figure—or get it back!"

"Not in my family. You've seen my mother. She's fat as

an old woman, and I'm not going to let that happen to me—
at least not yet. Later on, we can have children."

"But darling, I don't have any!"

"Call down to the concierge. He can get you some."

Covering his annoyance with masterful control, Johnny
sat up in bed and pressed the newly installed electric button
to summon a bellboy.

"I'll do it," he grumbled, "but this is a damned bad way to
start a marriage!"

"Johnny, darling, it's not as if I'm denying either of us
pleasure! You know I love you with all my heart. It's just
that I refuse to get fat." ·

After a two-month honeymoon on the Continent and in England, Johnny brought his new wife home to New York, a
city that delighted Clarissa almost from the moment she
stepped ashore. They were met by Justin, who drove them
uptown to Gramercy Park, where the house Fiammetta had
bought for them along the west side of the handsome park
that had been developed in 1845 had been restored at
Justin's expense (he had wired the handsome four-story
house for electricity, a new development that was transforming life in the city). When Johnny carried Clarissa over the
threshold and into the front hall, they saw a crowd of people
on the stairs, who burst into cheers and applause. It was a
surprise reception arranged by Johnny's father, and included
Teddy Roosevelt and Robbie Phillips.

While Clarissa was caught up in the gaiety of the moment, there was one person, she later told Johnny, who really impressed her.

"You must mean Teddy Roosevelt," Johnny said. "He's
one of the most extraordinary men in New York."

"Oh no," Clarissa said. "I mean, he's interesting, but not
fascinating."

"Then who do you mean?"

"Robbie Phillips. I adore actors! That's been my dream all
my life, to go on the stage. Of course, I never will. But I

loved talking to him. We must have him over to dinner, soon."

Johnny looked at his lovely bride.

"You're serious?" he said. "You want to go on the stage?"

"It's been my dream, but as I said, I'll never do it. At least, I don't think I will."

"What's that mean?"

She smiled and kissed him.

"One never knows what will happen."

PART SIX

A STAR IS BORN

29. ON A COOL APRIL EVENING IN 1890, FRANCO
Fosco was walking his pet cocker spaniel in Central Park in
front of the Dakota apartment building when a man stepped
out from behind a bush. He held a gun, which he pointed at
Franco.

"Vampiro!"' the man yelled. *"Sanguisuga!"*

He fired the gun, hitting Franco in the stomach. Franco
fell forward, facedown on the grass. The man fired at him
again, hitting him in the back. Then, as a policeman started
toward him, blowing a whistle, the attacker ran north, out of
sight.

"Your husband's in critical condition," Dr. Goodwin told
Rachel several hours later in a waiting room in Bellevue
Hospital.

Rachel, who was pale, asked, "Is he . . . going to live?"

"It's too early to tell, but if he does live, he probably will
be paralyzed from the waist down. The second bullet hit his
spine . . ."

"Dear God!" She sat down on a bench and pulled a
handkerchief from her purse to wipe her eyes. "My darling,
paralyzed!"

"The first bullet went into his stomach. He's lost a great
deal of blood. I wish I could give you some good news, but
there isn't any."

"No, I understand. Will I be able to see him?"

"Not yet. He's still unconscious."

Johnny was informed of the shooting by a phone call from
his father. Johnny and Clarissa had just gone to bed when
the call came through.

"Franco's been shot," Johnny said as he started to put his
clothes on.

"Shot? By whom?" Clarissa said.

"I don't know, but Father wants me to go to Bellevue and be with Rachel. I don't know when I'll be back."

After he was dressed, he left his Gramercy Park house and hailed a cab, which took him to the hospital. He found Rachel in the waiting room. She looked exhausted. Johnny gave her a hug.

"How is he?" he asked.

She shook her head.

"It doesn't look good," she said. "And the doctor told me he'll be paralyzed . . . that is, if he survives. One of the policemen on the case was here a while ago. They've caught the man who shot him, but he doesn't speak any English, so they haven't been able to question him yet."

"What is he?"

"An Italian immigrant named Sandro Benedetti. They've got him down at police headquarters on Mulberry Street."

"My Italian's pretty good. Maybe I should go talk to him."

"Oh Johnny, that's a wonderful idea. That would be a big help."

"Do your kids know?"

"No, I haven't told them yet."

"I'm terribly sorry, Rachel. The moment I learn anything, I'll tell you."

She smiled sadly.

"You're very sweet, Johnny. And thanks for coming. I appreciate it."

Sandro Benedetti was around thirty years old, a rather small man with a big mustache and ragged clothes. He was being held in a detention cell at police headquarters. When Johnny was led to the cell, he spoke to him through the bars.

"My name is Johnny Savage, I know the man you shot. Why did you do it?"

Benedetti got off his bunk and came to the bars, grabbing them with both hands.

"He was a bloodsucking vampire," the man said, almost

spitting the words. "I'm a poor man who don't speak English. I've only been in this country three months, but this Fosco, he suck me dry with his interest payments. My wife, my two kids—we live in filth, we got hardly no food at all, but each week I gotta pay the interest. So I kill the bastard! And if they hang me, at least Fosco won't ever hurt no one else again."

"What are you talking about? What interest payments? Did Fosco make you a loan at the bank?"

"What bank? I never go to no bank. No bank would even let me through the door. I go to his loan company down in Little Italy. . ."

"What loan company?"

"The Vesuvius Loan Company, not far from here. Fosco owns it. They give loans to poor immigrants like me, then they kill you with the interest—fifty percent! I had no money when I got here, so I borrowed five hundred dollars from Vesuvius, and now they suck me dry!"

"Wait a minute: did Fosco himself give you the loan?"

"Course not. The guy who runs the company is named Marco Passante. But Fosco owns the business, I found that out. Passante told me that if I didn't make my payments, something would happen to my children. So I shoot Fosco, and I'm glad. Let the bastard die."

And he spat on the cell floor.

Like the Rothschild Bank in London, the Savage Bank on Wall Street had a Partners' Room which Justin and Ben Lieberman shared. The next morning, Johnny went to the Partners' Room to confer with his father and Ben.

"Did you know," Johnny began, "that Franco has a loan company on the side down in Little Italy? And he makes loans to immigrants and charges them fifty percent interest?"

His father and Ben exchanged startled looks.

"I had no idea," Ben said, speaking in a hoarse whisper. The cough that had plagued him for years had developed into something much worse. "What's it called?"

"The Vesuvius Loan Company. And Vesuvius just

erupted, because that's why Benedetti shot your son-in-law last night. Franco's interest payments drove him crazy."

"I wonder if Rachel knows about this," Ben said.

"I'll bet she doesn't. Franco would be smart enough to keep that from her. But he must be making a tidy little fortune with this outrageous interest."

"Franco's not the only person making money off the immigrants, but that's no excuse," Ben said. "Franco must have gotten the idea from running the Loan Department here. By the way, Johnny, can you take over his job? Your father and I were discussing this before you got here. I know it puts a lot on your plate, but you're the best qualified man for the job. And we'll raise your salary."

"I like the sound of a raise. Clarissa has little respect for a budget," Johnny said. "By the way, Rachel wants to know why Benedetti shot Franco. Should I tell her the truth?"

Ben considered this a moment.

"Yes," he finally said. "She should know."

In 1880, a real estate speculator named Edward Clark, who owned half of the Singer Sewing Machine Company and could well afford to speculate, decided to build the biggest and most luxurious apartment building in New York. Having bought two acres of land from Hildegarde's uncle, August Belmont, for $200,000, with two hundred feet of frontage on Central Park West between Seventy-second and Seventy-third Streets, Clark began construction of the massive brick building. When it was finished, the building was so far uptown and out of the way that some wag told Clark it was as far from civilization as the Dakota Territory. Clark liked the idea so much, he named the building the Dakota.

When Johnny entered the courtyard later that morning, he was thinking of his own failed investment in the Dakota Territory. The cattle he and Teddy Roosevelt had bought had been wiped out in the extremely severe winter of 1886–87, a winter so cold that freezing cattle broke into farmhouses desperately seeking escape from the howling winds. The financial loss had been particularly heavy for Teddy, who had remarried and was starting a new family. But Johnny had taken a hard hit too.

When Rachel and Franco had come to New York four years before, they bought one of the biggest apartments in the Dakota, on the second floor overlooking Central Park. Johnny was admitted to the apartment by Rachel herself, who looked exhausted.

"How is Franco?" Johnny asked, coming into the entrance hall.

"I just came from the hospital," Rachel said, closing the door. "He's still unconscious. It doesn't look good."

"Have you told the children?"

"Not yet."

She led Johnny into the parlor, which was twenty-five by forty feet, with a high ceiling. Sunlight poured in through the windows. Rachel had furnished the place with many of her treasures.

"Did you talk to Benedetti?" she asked, sitting down in a window seat, motioning to Johnny to sit next to her.

"Yes. What I found out came as a surprise. Did you know that Franco owns a loan company in Little Italy?"

"Vesuvius. Yes, he told me about it a year ago. Apparently, he was making a great deal of money from it. You know that Franco wants desperately to have his own money."

"Did you help him get it started?"

"Yes. I put up the working capital. But what does that have to do with Benedetti?"

Johnny told her. She looked amazed.

"He was charging fifty percent interest?" she exclaimed.

"Yes. You didn't know?"

"I had no idea. He told me he wanted to help immigrants who couldn't get loans at regular banks, but fifty percent? That's outrageous! And this man, Benedetti—that's why he shot Franco?"

"Yes. He couldn't make the payments. And Vesuvius threatened to harm his children."

"But that's criminal!"

"Yes, I'm afraid it is."

"Franco was using my money to make these outrageous loans to poor people, and threatening their children . . . ? Oh Johnny, I wish you hadn't told me this. Oh my God, how could Franco have done it?"

"I'm sorry, but your father felt you should know."

She stood up, looking out the window at the park. Then she looked at Johnny.

"I'm lying," she said. "I've lied to myself all these years, and now I'm lying to you, my oldest, dearest friend. I've suspected all along that Franco was up to something . . . But I didn't want to ask any questions because I was afraid he'd lie to me—and even more afraid that he might tell me the truth. Oh Johnny, I fell so madly in love with a man who's . . . I even think . . ."

She hesitated.

"What?"

"I even think my mother might be right about him. I think Franco may have pushed Felix Rothschild off that cliff. Is that a horrible thing to say about one's husband? About the father of one's children? But if it is true, Franco's finally paying for what he did. And the price is high, very high. Dr. Goodwin doesn't think he'll live through the day."

"It's that bad?"

She nodded.

"I came home just to check on the children. I'm going back to the hospital soon. I only hope that he regains consciousness before he goes, but perhaps it would be better if he doesn't. And I'm so afraid to tell the children! They adore him, you know. For all his faults, Franco is a wonderful father. How can I ever tell them that their father is really a crook and possibly a murderer?"

"Don't tell them. Why should they know?"

She reached out and put her hand on his shoulder.

"Thank heaven for you," she said. "Yes, you're right. Why should they know?"

30. CLARISSA SAVAGE HAD INHERITED FROM HER ARTIST father a love of color and beauty that had turned her into a passionate redecorator, which meant, much to Johnny's financial woe, that she never stopped decorating the house on Gramercy Park. Once she had finished doing a room, she would go on to the next and start all over. The result was constant upheaval, not to mention expense, which irritated her husband. But since this was the only flaw he could find in his lovely Italian wife, aside from her continued putting him off about starting a family, he let her go her merry way because he loved her deeply. She was also a charming and popular hostess, and she set one of the best tables in New York, although her love of pasta kept Johnny in a nonstop war with his bathroom scales. Everyone in New York envied their marriage; and Johnny's Harvard classmates joked, in private, that "Goldenballs" had hit a home run.

When Johnny got home that evening, he put on a clean shirt and went downstairs to the parlor that overlooked Gramercy Park to join Clarissa for what had become a popular New York institution, the cocktail hour.

"How's Franco?" Clarissa asked, as Johnny handed her a glass of Orvieto, one of her favorite wines.

"He's hanging on, but it will take a miracle to save him, and no one's expecting the miracle to happen. Father and Uncle Ben have given me his old job, running the Loan Department. I was looking through some of his loans this afternoon, and there are a couple that stink to high heaven."

"What do you mean?"

"I mean, I think Franco was taking bribes under the table to approve loans."

"Not really? You mean, he's a crook?"

Johnny sat next to her in the sofa she had just had reupholstered in a bright chintz.

"Well, we've already found out he was running an illegal loan operation in Little Italy, so yes, he is a crook. The question now is, how big a crook? For instance, he approved a

loan of a hundred thousand dollars two years ago to a
Malatesta Cement Company in Secaucus . . ."

"Where's that?"

"Across the Hudson, in New Jersey. None of the principal
of the loan has been paid off, although the interest has been
paid. But every time the loan comes up for renewal, Franco
has approved it."

"Is there something wrong with that?"

"It's not very sound banking, although it's done. I think if
Uncle Ben and Father had been paying closer attention, they
would have asked some questions at the very least. At any
rate, I'm going over to Secaucus in the next few days and
take a look around. I don't know what I'll find, but I'm
smelling the proverbial rat."

"Then you'll be careful?"

"Don't worry, I'll be careful." He paused a moment, sipping his drink. "In fact, I'll take my gun."

"That's a good idea. May I have another glass of wine?"

"Oh . . . of course."

Johnny got up and refilled her glass from the decanter.

"Robbie Phillips has come up with the most interesting
idea," Clarissa went on as Johnny sat back down. "You
know he's putting on a production of *Hedda Gabler*, the
Ibsen play that's caused such a stir in Europe."

"Yes, I read about it in the paper."

"Now, I want you to promise not to laugh, but he's offered
me a tiny part in it. It's the maid . . . there are hardly any lines at
all, but it would be such fun! Say you wouldn't mind, darling."

"But you told me you'd never go on the stage . . . Won't
you have stage fright?"

"Robbie's going to coach me. You know how mad I am
about the theater: it would be such a thrill for me."

"Well . . ." He squeezed her hand. "If you want so much
to do it, I guess you should try."

"Franco has regained consciousness," Dr. Goodwin told
Rachel in the Bellevue waiting room. "You may see him

now for a few moments. But he's very weak. It's really . . ." He shrugged.

"Does he have a chance?"

"Well, there's always a chance. I don't know how religious you are, but a prayer certainly couldn't hurt. Follow me, please."

He led her down a corridor to a door, which he opened. Rachel, who was wearing a plain brown suit with a matching hat and fur piece, entered a private room. Franco, in a white hospital smock, was lying in a bed. She was shocked by how pale and gaunt his once beautiful face was.

She came to the bed, took his hand, and leaned down to kiss his forehead.

"How," he whispered, "are the children?"

"They miss their father," she said, sitting in a wooden chair Dr. Goodwin had pulled up for her.

"I miss them . . . Did you tell them what happened?"

"I told them a bad man had shot you in the park."

"I want to see them . . ."

Rachel looked at the doctor, who shook his head "no."

"Later, darling, when you're stronger."

He had closed his eyes. Now he opened them and looked at her.

"You've never really understood me," he whispered. "I'm a realist, always have been. There isn't going to be any 'later.' It's all right. I've had a good life. And we had a good marriage, didn't we? Despite your mother."

Franco started to gurgle slightly. Rachel, alarmed, looked at the doctor, who said, "Perhaps you'd better go now. He needs to sleep."

She stood up. Franco opened his eyes again.

"Does your mother," he whispered, "still think I pushed Felix off the cliff?"

"I suppose." She hesitated, then added, "Did you?"

He smiled slightly.

"What do you think?" he said.

The doctor led her out of the room.

The Malatesta Cement Company was in an ugly factory building on the outskirts of Secaucus, next door to a trash-littered
field. Three days later, Johnny got out of a cab in front of the
factory and went into the reception room, which reeked of
cigar smoke. A big calendar advertising root beer hung on one
wall. A young man in a pin-striped suit was seated at a desk
reading a copy of *The Police Gazette.* He looked at Johnny.

"Yeah?" he said. "Whaddya want?"

"I'm Mr. Savage from New York. I phoned yesterday. I
have an appointment with Mr. Malatesta."

The young man stood up.

"Oh yeah, you're the guy from the bank. Wait a minute."

He went to a door with a frosted glass panel on which
was painted "President." He knocked, then opened the door.

"The guy from the bank's here," he called in. Then he
turned to Johnny. "Go on in."

Johnny went into a medium-sized office that also reeked
of cigar smoke. Seated at a rolltop desk was a man in a black
suit who must have weighed three hundred pounds. He had
thinning black hair and a thick black beard. He was smoking
a cigar. He looked at Johnny.

"You're Johnny Savage," he said. "Franco's mentioned
you. Take a seat. Pardon me for not getting up, but with my
weight, getting up and down takes more effort than it's
worth. How's Franco?"

Johnny sat in a chair next to the desk.

"He died last night."

"Huh. Well, that's a shame. Imagine, a young fellow like
him getting shot in the park by some crazy immigrant. Well,
New York's a strange city where strange things happen.
What can I do for you, Johnny?"

"I've taken over Franco's responsibilities in the Loan Department. I've gone through your portfolio. The Malatesta
Cement Company has an outstanding loan of one hundred
thousand dollars that's up for renewal this week."

"That's right. Is there any problem? I've made the interest payments on time."

"The problem is, I hired a private detective to investigate your relationship with Franco. Franco was funneling bank funds through you into the Vesuvius Loan Company, charging five times the interest he was paying the bank. You got your cut of the action, and you and Marco Passante handled the rough stuff, shaking down the poor suckers who couldn't come up with the interest payments. Well, that little game is over. I'm not going to renew the loan." He stood up. "I'll expect you at the bank on Friday with a cashier's check for payment in full."

He gave Malatesta a searching look. The fat man returned the look as he sucked on his cigar.

Then he removed the cigar and said, softly, "You're making a big mistake, my friend."

"That's your opinion."

He turned and walked out of the room.

31. AFTER CLARISSA HAD READ SEVERAL LINES FROM *Hedda Gabler*, Robbie Phillips remained thoughtfully silent for a few moments. He was standing in front of the fireplace beneath his Hamlet portrait in the parlor of his town house. Clarissa, her heart pounding, watched him anxiously. Finally, she said, "Was I *that* terrible, Robbie?"

"Hmm? Oh no, my dear," said the tall matinée idol, whose shoulder-length hair was turning silver—which on him looked good. "Of course, the part is inconsequential, but you brought something to it . . . And of course, you're such a radiant creature, your beauty may steal the show from the star, which could cause grave consequences for me, as you may well guess. That's what I was considering. One must tread delicately when one deals with stars! They're temperamental, the shrews. I need a drink. Willst join me for a libation?"

"Yes, thank you, Robbie. So you really liked me?"

"My sweet angel, you were incandescent," he said, going to the sideboard to fill two glasses with champagne.

"Robbie, I know it's a small part, but don't toy with me! Do I have it?"

"Ah, the part," said the actor, carrying her glass to her. "The theater, as we all know, is not pure art, alas. We humble players who follow in the footsteps of Thespis must come to grips with harsh commercialism from time to time—'tis the reality of the stage. You are not a well-known name, Clarissa—a draw, in the parlance of the box office. This is a fact which I, as the play's producer, must bear in mind."

"Then I don't have the part?" she said, bitterly.

"You rush to judgment, my sweet. On the other hand, you are married into a well-known family, which should create some fodder for the harlots of the popular press to scribble their drivel about. So I would say the part is yours to illuminate the Rialto's firmament—on one condition."

"Which is?" she asked, trying to hide her anxiety. She really did very much want to be in the play.

"Again, alas, I must stoop to the vulgarities of commerce. Your father-in-law, Justin, is not only a prince among men, he is also a Medici. If you could convince him to invest a pittance toward the production of this play, then almost certainly the part would be yours—though, unhappily, I could not pay you much; but of course, you are doing this for art."

"How much is the pittance?"

"A small sum, a mere trifle when compared to the estimable Mr. Savage's net worth. Let's say, ten thousand dollars."

"I'll talk to him. He's such a sweet man, and he loves the theater almost as much as I. I'm sure he can be persuaded."

"Alas, his lovely friend—a most talented actress, Kitty Kincaid—met such a horrible end!" Robbie refilled his glass, then carried the champagne bottle to Clarissa.

"He doesn't like to talk about it," she said, "but he says he knows who did it. Some Frenchman."

"Ah, the mad Marquis!" Robbie filled her glass. " 'Tis true the gendarmerie questioned him before he left for France, but he had an alibi—or so 'tis said. I suspect that he used influence to get off, but I could be wrong. She was an angel, that Kitty! An angel. Almost as lovely, my dear, as you."

He smiled as he touched the rim of his glass to hers.

"We must," he went on, "talk about my coaching you. It could be done here, in this house. There's so much I want to teach you about the theater. I feel in my very bones that you have a great talent, waiting to be warmed by the sun, as 'twere, into full bloom."

"Do you really think so, Robbie?"

"I would not say it, if it weren't so. So you are stagestruck, my sweet. There is no greater vice. 'The play's the thing wherein I'll catch the conscience of the king.' *Hamlet*, Act Two, scene two."

Dio, she thought, he is wonderfully attractive!

She left Robbie's house a half hour later, feeling more than a little giddy from the champagne. It was much later than she thought; the sun was already setting. She looked up and down the street for a cab when a black cab parked down the street started toward her, its driver flicking his whip on his horse's haunch. When the cab stopped in front of her, she said "Gramercy Park, please." She opened the door to get in, when both her arms were grabbed from the inside and she was tugged into the cab.

The cabbie whipped his horse again, and the cab roared off down the street as a hand reached outside to slam shut the door.

Athough Rachel was not particularly religious, and Franco had been anything but, in fact he never did convert—they both considered themselves members of two worlds—their children, three-year-old Cesare and two-year-old Beatrice— were Jewish because their mother was. But Rachel decided Franco should be buried in a Catholic cemetery, whatever his sins; and he was duly laid to rest in Calvary Cemetery.

It was a chilly, drizzly morning, and few people attended the service. Rachel's father was there, though her mother wasn't. And Justin was there, without Johnny. After the service, as they trudged through the mud to their carriages, Justin told Rachel, "Johnny's sorry he couldn't be here, but something terrible has happened. Clarissa has been kidnapped. We think Agostino Malatesta is behind it."

"Oh no!" Rachel exclaimed. "If that's true, this is Franco's fault."

"I didn't want to say that at his funeral . . ."

"No, it's too important—these things must be said! Have you contacted the police?"

"No. Johnny wanted to. He also wanted to contact his old friend, Teddy Roosevelt, but I told him not to. For everyone's sake, including the bank's reputation, I told Johnny we must forgive Malatesta'a loan and get him out of our lives. Needless to say, we want Clarissa home safe."

"Of course. But there's a better way."

"I'd be delighted to hear it."

Two hours later, after taking Cesare and Beatrice back to the Dakota, Rachel pulled up in front of Johnny's Gramercy Park house. She got out, still wearing her black widow's veil, and went to the front door to ring. The door was answered by Gibson, Johnny's balding, Cockney-accented Englishman who ran the house, cleaned it, did the shopping and the cooking, and was a general factotum.

"Is Mr. Savage home?" she asked.

"Yes, he's in the drawing room. He's very upset."

"I'm Countess Fosco. Might I see him?"

"Yes, of course. Come in."

After Rachel came into the entrance hall, Gibson closed the door and took her hat. Then Rachel went upstairs into the newly redecorated drawing room, which Clarissa had lined with pale yellow silk. Johnny was standing at the end of the room in front of one of the French windows that gave out onto the wrought-iron balcony overlooking the park. When

he turned to look at her, Rachel could see that he was upset.
His thick blond hair was tousled, and he looked awful.

"Did you get that rotten bastard of a husband of yours
buried?" he said as she crossed the room to him. "I know:
'Speak no evil of the dead.' But he's to blame for my wife's
kidnapping."

"Johnny, I don't blame you. Your father told me about
Clarissa."

"If I don't hear anything from Malatesta by three this afternoon, I'll call him and tell him I'll renew his damned loan."

"You'll do nothing of the sort. I went through Franco's
papers at the apartment and found his address book. I've already called Malatesta and told him Franco had willed him a
hundred thousand dollars, so he won't need the loan re-
newed. He's releasing Clarissa right away—she's all right,
by the way, though a bit upset."

Johnny stared at her.

"Is this true? Did Franco leave him money?"

"Of course not. I'll send him the money. It's the least I can
do to make up for some of the mess Franco created with his
shady dealings. I don't want the bank to be involved with
crooks any more than you do."

A look of joy came over Johnny's face.

"God bless you, Rachel! And Clarissa's all right?"

"Yes."

He put his arms around her, kissing her cheek as he
hugged her.

"God bless you," he repeated.

Promptly at five that afternoon, Clarissa got out of a cab in
front of the Gramercy Park house. She hurried to the front
door and started to let herself in with her key, when Gibson
opened the door. "Gibson, thank God!" she exclaimed, hurrying inside. "I've had the most ghastly experience!"

"But you're home safe now, mum," he said, taking her
coat and hat.

"Where's my husband?"

"Upstairs in the parlor, mum."

When Clarissa arrived in the parlor, Johnny was asleep in a chair. She hurried over to him and slapped his face. Johnny woke up, almost bolting out of the chair.

"Clarissa!"

"Why didn't you call the police?" she cried, bursting into tears. "I could have been killed by those awful people!"

Johnny stood up.

"Which is exactly why I didn't call the police! We were concerned for your safety."

He took her in his arms and hugged her as she wept uncontrollably.

"Who are they?" she sobbed. "What was it all about? I was terrified! They kept me locked in a dark room off the kitchen somewhere . . ."

"But they didn't hurt you, and you're home safe."

"No thanks to you!" she sniffed, pushing him away. "I've never gone through such an ordeal! You haven't answered me: who were they?"

"It's rather complicated, but it has to do with the bank, which is another reason we didn't want to involve the police."

"But surely *now* you'll involve them! They're criminals! They might have done God knows what to me!"

"There's no point now to bring in the police. Everything's been settled—it all had to do with Franco, but Rachel's fixed it all. She's been terrific . . ."

"You mean, these people are going to get away with kidnapping me? I can't believe it! They should all be sent to jail for twenty years!"

"Clarissa, you're upset, naturally. Why don't you go take a bath and calm down, then we'll have a drink and try to forget all this."

Clarissa stood up. "You don't care about me," she said, softly. "All you care about is that precious bank."

"That's not true! God, Clarissa, you're taking this all wrong . . ."

"I was in danger, and what do you do? Nothing! I won't forget this, Johnny. I have a very long memory!"

She started out of the room.

"Clarissa, you're hysterical! You've got this all wrong. . ."

But she was gone.

"Here's a check for ten thousand dollars," Clarissa said two mornings later, handing it to Robbie Phillips. The actor's eyes lit up as they scanned the zeros.

"Od's blood, Clarissa, you have toiled well in the vineyards. I will have my lawyer, that scoundrel, draw up papers of partnership in the production."

"Justin was very sweet about it," Clarissa said as she pulled off her kid gloves, "but then he should have been. I'm so furious at him and Johnny! Are you going to offer me a drink?"

"Yes, of course! I'm a clod, a veritable clod!" Putting the folded check in the pocket of his dark blue velvet smoking jacket, he hurried to the sideboard to pour drinks. "I heard about your adventure. You escaped the villain's clutches! Were you scared?"

"Terrified. And Johnny didn't lift a finger to save me."

"Ah, perhaps you're being unfair. The young man has the courage of the lion! Why, he told me himself how he shot a ferocious grizzly bear in the Dakota Territory."

"Hah. That's *his* story. He and Teddy Roosevelt probably made it all up. Thank you, darling. My nerves are a wreck."

She took the champagne glass and drank some.

"Well," she said, "I've delivered the money. Are you delivering the part?"

"It is yours, sweet angel!"

"I've been doing some thinking. For ten thousand dollars, it would seem I could get a better part than the maid. And Berta is supposed to be rather middle-aged—it's hardly a glamorous part."

Robbie clutched his heart with one hand.

"Experience, Clarissa! You must have some little experience! Even Sarah Siddons didn't start out in the starring role!" He leaned over her chair. "We'll get you on the boards first. And then, as I coach you, we'll graduate you to better parts. Why, within a year, you could be playing Hedda Gabler instead of the maid."

She smiled at him.

"Do you really think so, Robbie?"

"I know so. In the theater, connections mean everything. And, my angel, in me you have the finest connection in town."

"Oh Robbie, I adore you," she exclaimed. "I also adore your new cologne. It's so strong! What's it called?"

" 'Nuit d'Amour.' I bought it in London. Would I be over-stepping the bounds of friendship if I told you I thought you are particularly lovely today? That the excitement of your adventure has brought roses to your cheeks and fire to your eyes?"

She purred.

"Why Robbie, I do believe you're making advances."

He raised one of her hands to his lips and kissed it, watching her intently.

> " 'My bounty is as boundless as the sea,
>   My love as deep; the more I give to thee
>   The more I have, for both are infinite.'

Romeo and Juliet, Act Two, scene two. I am mad for you, Clarissa. Become my love and with my guidance, you will be a star."

He gently raised her to her feet and took her in his arms, planting his lips firmly on hers.

For a moment, she resisted him.

Then she didn't.

32. THE DAY AFTER FRANCO'S FUNERAL, RACHEL received a note from her mother—the first communication with Hildegarde in four years. The note read:

> *"My dearest Rachel:*
>   *Now that your husband is gone and an unfortunate*

chapter in your life closed, I am most anxious to meet with you and your children. As you know, my beloved husband, your father, is ill. I fear that his time is limited—the doctors give us little hope. Please bring the children to our house tomorrow for lunch at noon. I am looking forward to seeing you after these long years. I hope you are aware that my love for you has always been foremost in my thoughts, even though I couldn't accept your husband.

Your loving mother."

The next morning, she dressed Cesare and Beatrice in their best outfits and took them across Central Park to Fifth Avenue. Four years earlier, Ben and Hildegarde had decided they wanted to build a newer, grander house, particularly after they had been offered a handsome sum for their old house. They bought a hundred-foot-by-hundred-foot lot at Seventy-fifth Street and Fifth Avenue and hired the firm of McKim, Mead, and White to design them a classic limestone mansion five stories high surrounded by an elaborate wrought-iron fence. The house turned out to be one of the most beautiful dwellings in the city, with a balcony projecting from the second floor across the entire front, and beautiful pedimented windows. As Rachel's carriage stopped in front of the mansion, she had a strange sensation: to be entering her parents' home for the first time at her age.

She led her children to the front door and rang. When the door was opened by a properly stiff butler, they were admitted to a marble entrance hall. There stood her mother, looking rather forbidding, as usual, in a black dress. But when she saw her daughter, she smiled and opened her arms.

"My dearest Rachel," she said, "welcome home."

Rachel ran to her and they embraced.

"And now, Momma," she said, "here are your grandchildren."

Hildegarde looked at the two children, who were remarkably beautiful, with their father's patrician nose and their mother's violet eyes.

"Come meet your grandmomma," Rachel said.

Cesare came to her and bowed, stiffly, as his sister tried to curtsy, but succeeded in falling on the marble floor instead. Hildegarde picked her up in her arms and kissed her, then leaned down to hug Cesare.

"They're adorable," she said to Rachel. "Absolutely adorable. Come, my darlings. We'll take you upstairs to meet your grandfather. And you must understand that he has a very sore throat and has to speak in a whisper."

The sore throat was cancer, caused by Ben's lifelong addiction to cigars, and the disease killed him almost exactly one month later. As befitting a man who had become one of the pillars of the "Our Crowd" world of wealthy East Side Jews, his funeral at the Lexington Avenue Synagogue was heavily attended, and his obituary listed the many charities he had contributed to, including the Hebrew Orphan Asylum, the Montefiori Home, the Hebrew Charities, and the Metropolitan Museum of Art. Rachel sat with her mother and her children. She saw Johnny and his father in the congregation.

But she thought it rather odd that Johnny's wife was missing.

"Clarissa couldn't come because she's in rehearsal," Johnny explained to Rachel an hour later. Hildegarde was sitting *shiva* in her Fifth Avenue mansion, and cakes and sweets were being served to everyone who had gone to Ben's funeral. Hildegarde had not gone so far as to rend her clothes in grief for her dead husband. Rather, she had clipped a small piece of torn cloth to her dress.

"Clarissa's only playing Berta, the maid," Johnny went on, "but Robbie Phillips has made her the understudy for Hedda Gabler. Robbie tells me Clarissa has real star quality, much to my surprise. I mean, I knew that Clarissa had always been fascinated by the theater, but for her to be recognized like this by Robbie is quite extraordinary. At any rate, I hope you'll understand and forgive her for not being at the funeral."

"Oh, absolutely," Rachel said. "And I'm looking forward to the first night. When will it be?"

"A week from tonight. Clarissa's a bit frantic. And she tells me that Robbie and his star, Olga Inwood, are fighting like cats and dogs."

"Oh well, that's the theater."

"Robbie's fired Olga Inwood!" Clarissa told Johnny on the phone to his office. "I'm going on tonight as Hedda Gabler!"

"You're kidding! You have no experience!" Johnny said, sitting in his Wall Street office.

"Well, darling, I think it's rather unkind of my own husband to say Robbie's wrong. After all, he has total confidence in my acting talent."

"Yes, I know . . . And so do I . . . I mean, are you nervous?"

"Not a bit. I'm going to be great. And make a reservation at Delmonico's for an after-theater supper. We'll celebrate as we read the reviews."

"I already have. And Rachel's joining us."

"Fine by me. Wish me luck, darling."

"Yes, of course. All the luck in the world. And this is fantastic news!"

"In the theater, you say 'break a leg.' "

"All right, break a leg."

He hung up, thinking that an actor-manager as canny as Robbie Phillips would hardly fire an established star like Olga Inwood on opening night unless . . . unless there were some other reason he wasn't seeing.

He leaned back in his desk chair, staring at the ceiling.

Is it possible, he thought, my wife is having an affair with Robbie? No. She loves me. And yet . . .

" 'A hit! A very palpable hit!' *Hamlet*, Act Five, scene two. By Gad, sir, listen to this review in the *Herald*—a newspaper I heretofore deemed unfit for any but the Great Unwashed, but now, sir, a veritable competitor to the London *Times*!"

Robbie Phillips stood up at the table in Delmonico's and read to Johnny's guests. " 'Tonight at the Majestic Theater, a star was born! Hats are in the air, and cheers fill the Rialto! Actor-Manager Robertson Phillips, who has graced our stage for lo, these many years . . .' " Robbie cleared his throat, ". . . lo, these *few* years . . ." The table rocked with laughter. Clarissa, who was sitting between Robbie and Johnny, signaled to the waiter to refill her glass. " 'Robertson Phillips, the *distinguished* actor' . . . I can't refrain from editing this review a bit . . . 'has pulled off one of the coups of the theatrical season with his handsome production of the Norwegian playwright Ibsen's latest, and perhaps most profound, drama, *Hedda Gabler.* But not only is Gotham celebrating a distinguished new play, it has a new star to clasp to its collective bosom. Going on at the last minute to replace the star, Olga Inwood, her understudy, a hitherto unknown young actress named Clarissa Savage, wife of Wall Street banker Johnny Savage, turned in such a commanding performance as the vixenish Hedda Gabler as to leave this critic gasping with admiration. Not only is Clarissa a blond beauty, but she has the poise and confidence of a true star, as well as the magnetism that should ensure her a niche in the Theater's "Hall of Fame." ' I ask you, my friends," Robbie said, putting down the newspaper, "is this the stuff of dreams?"

The table, which seated fourteen, burst into applause and cheers as the actor leaned down to hug and kiss his new star, Clarissa.

Johnny watched this with cool detachment.

"Aren't you thrilled?" Rachel said to him. She was seated to his left.

"Yes, I guess I am," Johnny replied, with notable lack of enthusiasm. "I never realized when I married her this was what she really wanted. I always thought she wanted me."

A week later, on a warm early June evening, Rachel was sitting in her bed in her Dakota apartment reading the *Saturday Evening Post* when something hit one of the bedroom windows. Startled, she put the magazine down and got out of bed, hurrying across the room to the window, which was half-open. She looked out to see Johnny standing on the sidewalk of Seventy-third Street. He was in white tie, wearing a top hat tilted at a crazy angle, and was weaving. He had thrown some pebbles at the window, and was about to throw more. Rachel raised the window farther and leaned out.

"Johnny," she called down, "what are you doing?"

"I wanna talk to you, Rachel," he said. "Can I come up and talk to you?"

"Of course, but you look a bit looped."

"I'm drunk out of my mind. Can I come up and talk to you?"

"Yes. I'll put some coffee on."

Putting on a negligée, she hurried through the apartment to the kitchen and put on the kettle. Moments later, she heard her doorbell. She went back through the labyrinthine corridors of the apartment to the entrance hall and opened the door. Johnny stumbled in, almost falling into her arms.

"Whoops!" he giggled. "Didn't mean to fall on you."

"Johnny, what's the matter?"

"The matter? Oh, nothing much is the matter. It's just that my beautiful wife has left me for that damned actor, Robbie Phillips."

"No!" She closed the door.

"Oh, yes indeed. It doesn't seem possible, does it? Clarissa leaving me—me, Johnny Savage, the Golden Boy of Harvard—for that flea-bitten ham, Robbie Phillips? Oh Rachel."

He leaned against the wall, tears running down his cheeks. She took his hand.

"Come on, I'm going to give you some coffee."

"Don't want any coffee. I wanna forget. Forget everything! Rachel, I've been cuckolded—can you imagine . . . me?"

She was leading him to the kitchen.

"Did she tell you she wants a divorce?" she asked.

"Yes, or an annulment. We were married in the Catholic Church . . . I suppose I'll have to get my mother to help me, except she's going to be furious 'cause she set this whole thing up, I mean me and Clarissa . . . Oh boy, oh boy, do I look like a fool . . ."

She set him down at the kitchen table and started to make the coffee.

"You mustn't judge her too harshly . . ."

"Why not? She cheated on me!" He started laughing, drunkenly. "You and I, we make a great pair, don't we? You married a crook and maybe even a murderer, and I married a goddamn whore! Well, at least we've got one thing in common: a pretty rotten sense of judgment. What a joke. What a dirty, rotten joke."

He laid his head down on his arms and started sobbing. She looked at him with pity. After a moment, she came over and smoothed his hair.

"Poor Johnny," she said, softly. "I hate to see you hurting so."

He looked up at her with a tear-stained face. "What's it all mean, Rachel? Here are you and me, kids of two of the most successful people in the city, and we've messed up our lives. So, what's it all mean?"

She thought a moment, looking at him.

"Well," she said, "perhaps it means we should start all over again."

He stared at her, her face blurring in his drunken vision.

"You know, if I were sober, I wouldn't have the nerve to say this," he slurred. "But God knows, I'm not sober, so I'll say what I'm thinking. And what I'm thinking is that ever since I was a kid, I've always wanted to make love to you."

She stared back a moment. Then she laughed.

"Oh my God, Johnny," she said, "you really are drunk!"

"Drunk as a lord! But whaddya think about that?"

She thought a moment. Then she took the coffeepot off the stove and filled a cup, placing it beside him on the table.

"I'm thinking," she said, "that perhaps you should stay the night. I mean, to sober up." She smiled. "You can use Franco's pajamas."

"I wouldn't wear anything that bastard touched."

"Well, then—" she shrugged, "—wear nothing."

Four hours later, he woke up on a sofa in the drawing room. The sky over Central Park was just beginning to glow with early light. He sat up, shaking his head and trying to remember where he was. He was covered by a sheet, and he was naked. He saw his tail suit neatly folded over a chair, with his shoes, shirt, tie, and underwear piled on the seat. As he looked around the elegant, high-ceilinged room, his memory began to come back in bits and pieces. Rachel . . . he was in Rachel's apartment, he could remember coming there from the restaurant where he had drunk himself into near oblivion. Clarissa . . . Robbie Phillips . . .

Rachel. He got off the sofa and wrapped the sheet around his waist. Had he destroyed their relationship by coming to her drunk and propositioning her?

Rachel, beautiful Rachel.

He had been in the apartment several times before and had a vague memory of its layout. Now he started through the dark rooms toward her bedroom. Would she throw him out?

But then he thought of Rachel. Her dark hair, her pale skin, her violet eyes, her voluptuous body. Rachel, beautiful Rachel . . .

He started moving again, stubbing his toe on a table leg, gasping at the pain. A light went on at the end of the hall.

"Johnny?"

It was Rachel. He limped toward the light. When he reached her door, he leaned against it. She was sitting up in bed, her hair down over her shoulders.

"I stubbed my toe," he said.

"How romantic. Come in and close the door. I don't want to wake the children."

He closed the door quietly, then walked across the room to her bed.

"Have I made a fool of myself?" he whispered.

"Yes." She pulled back the covers and patted the mattress beside her. "Let's both make fools of ourselves."

He climbed in beside her and took her in his arms, kissing

her. She put her arms around his torso and hugged him to her, reveling in the warmth of his strong body.

Three months later, Rachel invited her mother to her apartment for lunch. Johnny was there also.

"Momma, guess what?" Rachel said as they sat down at the dining room table. She smiled and reached over to take Johnny's hand. "Johnny and I are going to be married! Now, before you start harping on the fact that he's not Jewish . . ."

"We're very much in love," Johnny interrupted. "I do hope you'll approve."

Hildegarde took a drink of ice water, then dabbed her lips with her napkin.

"My late husband often mentioned to me," she said, "that it was a pity you two hadn't married, as he believed you were very much in love—but just didn't know it . . . and it would be wonderful to unite our two families. Johnny is a fine young man. And after all we've been through . . . it's too bad he's not Jewish, but . . ." she sighed, ". . . nobody's perfect."

PART SEVEN

THE MAD MARQUIS

33. TWO YEARS AFTER JOHNNY AND RACHEL WERE married, Justin sent them to Paris to open the first European office of the Savage Bank. They took with them, along with five steamer trunks, twelve suitcases, and an English nanny, Cesare and Beatrice, whom Johnny had adopted, as well as their baby girl, Brook. The bank office was in the Place Vendôme, across the square from the newly opened Ritz Hotel. Johnny rented a handsome house in the suburb of Neuilly, which had a lovely garden, and he and his family moved in. Life in Paris started off pleasantly enough.

But several weeks after they had moved in, Rachel had a strange visitor. It was a sunny spring morning. Johnny had just left for the office when Claude, their French butler, came into the morning room where Rachel was drinking her coffee and said, "Madame, there is a Count Esterhazy who has just arrived. He is asking for a chance to talk to you. He says it's very important."

"Who is he?" Rachel asked.

"I have no idea. But he wears the red ribbon of the Legion of Honor in his lapel."

"How strange. Show him into the drawing room. I'll be right in."

A few minutes later, she went into the drawing room of the house to see a slightly built man in a well-cut suit standing by a window, looking out at the garden.

"You wanted to see me?" Rachel said.

The man turned and bowed rather stiffly. He had deep-set eyes and a large mustache over a drooping chin.

"Mrs. Savage, I am Major Count Esterhazy, an officer in the French Army."

"Are you related to the Hungarian Esterhazys?" Rachel asked, coming over to him and giving him her hand to kiss.

"I have that honor, madame. However, I am married to a Frenchwoman and am loyal to France."

"Yes, I'm sure you are. Please take a seat." After they had

seated themselves, Rachel said, "Now, what can I do for you?"

"Madame, you were married to a Rothschild."

"This is true."

"The Rothschild family is famous for its devotion to Jewish causes."

"This is also true. Members of my late husband's family are, among other things, investing large sums of money for Jewish settlement in Palestine."

"I must tell you, madame, that there is much sentiment against the Jews in France and that the anti-Semitism is growing every day."

"I am unhappily aware of that."

"I wish to work against this anti-Semitism, this boil on the soul of France. But this will take time, organization, and money. Your name was suggested to me as a possible contributor to this cause by the Marquis de Morès, who is acquainted with your husband."

"The Marquis is hardly a friend of my husband, since he tried to mutilate him in the Dakota Territory some years ago. However, what is it I'm supposed to be contributing to?"

"My organization does not yet have a name. First, I need money to get it started. Unfortunately, I have personal debts that must be satisfied before I can take up the glorious work of fighting French anti-Semitism. If you could see fit to donating twenty-five thousand francs, you would enable me to free myself of my personal obligations and begin the work that is so important to all Jews and to France."

This man is a common swindler! she thought.

"Count Esterhazy, while I sympathize with your efforts to combat anti-Semitism, I am an American, and I already donate considerable sums to Jewish causes at home. Knowing nothing about you or your work, I could not possibly give such a large sum of money. Now, if you'll excuse me . . ."

She stood up, as did the Count, whose face had frozen into a cold glare.

"I thank you for your time, madame," he said. "I have already approached other Rothschilds and have received the same hostile reception as yours."

"I am not hostile . . ."

"You Jews," he interrupted, "will one day wish you had helped your friends instead of refusing them. You, with your vast wealth, will someday pay for your greed."

"Count, I will ask you to leave."

"I will leave, madame. Gladly. And I will tell the Marquis de Morès, who is not without influence in this country, that you and your husband are as unfriendly to me as to him."

Bowing stiffly, he left the room.

That night at dinner, Rachel told Johnny about the strange Count Esterhazy.

"I've heard about him," Johnny said. "He gets around in certain circles—including the mad Marquis. Esterhazy speaks seven languages fluently, married a rich wife and went through her fortune. He's always trying to borrow money and is a rotten risk. But I find it strange that he told you he wants to fight anti-Semitism, because he and the Marquis are pals of Edouard Drumont, the editor of *La Libre Parole*."

"Isn't that the newspaper that's violently anti-Semitic?"

"Exactly."

"Then I don't understand . . ."

"Nor do I. But I'll tell you one thing: I don't like the idea of the Marquis de Morès being back in my life. The man's a lunatic, a dangerous lunatic. And if my father's right, the Marquis murdered Kitty Kincaid."

Rachel put down her fork, looking nervous.

"The children . . ."

"Exactly what I'm thinking."

"Should we send them back to Mother in New York?"

"No. I'll talk to a man I know in the Sûreté in the morning. He can tell me more about the Marquis and whether we should hire guards. I hate the idea of guards, but after what happened to Felix . . ."

"The Marquis fought a man in a duel just last week," Johnny reported to his wife the next night, "and he killed him. It was a Jewish officer named Captain Armand Mayer. Mayer had trouble with his right arm, but was too proud to admit it. He could hardly lift his sword. The Marquis stabbed him to death in three seconds."

"Good Lord! Isn't dueling illegal?"

"Everybody duels at the drop of an insult. Authors duel critics who give them bad reviews. It's like some *opéra bouffe* in Paris. But the point is, the Marquis is as crazy and violent as ever. My contact with the police says we definitely should hire guards for the children. It's expensive, but I feel we have to do it. I've made arrangements for the first guard to show up in the morning at eight."

Rachel sighed.

"What a terrible way to live in France," she said.

"We'll only be here for a few years," Johnny said. "Then we can go home and lead a halfway normal life. But I think to be on the safe side, I'm going to take up fencing again."

Two years later, on July 20, 1894, a visitor was announced to Colonel Max von Schwarzkoppen, the military attaché of the German Embassy in Paris. The colonel, a Prussian nobleman, watched as a slightly built man in civilian clothes wearing the red ribbon of the French Legion of Honor came into his office. The man introduced himself as Major Count Esterhazy. He told the German that he was an officer in the French Army, he had worked in Algiers and on the Italian front, that he had worked in the intelligence department of the Ministry of War, and that he wanted to sell valuable military secrets to the German government because he was desperately in need of money. Although the German Colonel at first refused to deal with Esterhazy, when he reported back to Berlin the German government jumped at the chance. The deal was made, and Esterhazy began turning over documents to the German Embassy in Paris—documents that proved to be authentic and as highly valuable as the spy had declared.

The following September, Esterhazy delivered even more documents to the Germans, but he included with them a handwritten *bordereau*, or itemized list of all the documents he had delivered so far—a sort of laundry list. The *bordereau* was put in a wastebasket in the Embassy. What the Germans didn't know was that one of their cleaning ladies was actually a French spy—the French being enormously paranoid about the Germans after the German victory in the Franco-Prussian War twenty-five years before. The cleaning lady brought the *bordereau* to the French Intelligence, who by now were aware that a spy high up in the French Army was selling secrets to the Germans. They also thought they knew from another source that the spy's name began with a D—a fact that was later proved to be untrue. Anxiously, the authorities poured over the names of officers high enough in the French Army to have access to the information sold to the Germans.

After several false starts, they found the name of an artillery officer who had just recently been appointed to the General Staff. To the immense relief of the investigating officers, almost all of whom were rabid anti-Semites as were almost all the top officers of the French Army, the man, whose name was Alfred Dreyfus, was a Jew. The investigating officers exclaimed: "It's the Jew!"

And thus began the Dreyfus Affair, which for ten years tore France into two factions, Dreyfusards, who believed Dreyfus was framed, and anti-Dreyfusards, who believed Dreyfus was a traitor who deserved death.

Dreyfus's first trial, held in a military court, convicted him on the flimsiest of evidence, and he was sentenced to life imprisonment on Devil's Island.

Of course, neither Rachel nor Johnny had any idea that the real spy for whom Dreyfus was taking the rap was the same

Count Esterhazy who had tried to swindle money from Rachel when they first moved to Paris. But though Johnny cautioned Rachel that, as Americans, they must remain neutral about the case for the sake of the bank, they both were convinced Dreyfusards. It was impossible to escape the case; the newspapers were full of it. Johnny usually ate lunch at the Ritz across the street from his office, and he often entertained clients there. But even at business lunches, the case was hashed over and over. Friends of his with "inside" information about the case told him that the Army's evidence was built solely on the now-infamous *bordereau*, or laundry list, found in the waste basket, and that the French Army was using Dreyfus as a scapegoat to deflect attention from their own miserable performance in the war.

But it was the mounting clamor of anti-Semitism that made the whole affair so increasingly ugly; it was as if the worst demons in the French soul had been let out of the bottle. And as a Jew, Rachel was horrified at what she read and heard.

The night before Dreyfus was to be publicly drummed out of the army, she told Johnny, "I've done my best to stay out of this, as you wanted. But I want to go see this tomorrow. Will you mind?"

"Of course not. We'll go together."

The next day, January 5, 1895, dawned cold and windy, with leaden skies threatening snow. Johnny and Rachel took a cab to the Champ de Mars, where the punishment was to be carried out on the parade grounds of the École Militaire.

But such a huge crowd had gathered, they had to get down from the cab. The mob was in a lynching mood. Cries of "Death to the Jew!" were heard on all sides. The Army had put a double line of guards around the outside of the iron railing which fenced in the quadrangle where the proceedings were to take place. Being pushed and jostled, Johnny and Rachel nevertheless managed to get close enough to the guards to be able to see what went on.

Finally, a trumpet sounded, commands were barked, and

a door was thrown open. A tall sergeant of the Republican Guard emerged from it, leading four soldiers with drawn swords, in whose midst walked Captain Dreyfus. The crowd became so silent, the heels of the soldiers could be heard as they marched up to General Darras, who was on horseback. The General drew his sword and called out, "Alfred Dreyfus, you are unworthy of carrying arms. We herewith degrade you in the name of the people of France."

Dreyfus was a thin-haired man who wore glasses and had a small mustache under his sharp nose. His face was understandably white. He shouted: "Soldiers! An innocent is dishonored! Long live France!"

This caused the crowd to roar, almost in one voice, "Death to the Jew!"

Rachel winced at the almost palpable hatred that filled the cold January air.

Then the sergeant rushed at Dreyfus and tore the epaulets from the Captain's shoulders and ripped off the red stripes on his trousers that denoted his position on the General Staff. Finally, the sergeant took Dreyfus's sword, broke it in two, and threw it on the ground.

Another person viewing the ceremony was a young journalist from Vienna, the Paris correspondent of Vienna's leading newspaper, a moderately successful playwright named Theodore Herzl. Herzl was so repulsed by what he saw that the next day he formulated the plan that was to become known as Zionism.

Still another man in the crowd was a tall, theatrically handsome man with a big, black-waxed mustache. But he wasn't only watching Dreyfus. He was also watching Johnny and Rachel.

The man was the Marquis de Morès.

"Now I know Dreyfus is innocent," Rachel said as she and Johnny returned to the Place Vendôme in their cab. "I know it in my heart! The look on his face as they tore off his epaulets and broke his sword . . . A terrible injustice has been done."

"I absolutely agree with you," Johnny said. The ceremony had shaken him as much as it had his wife. "I wish there was something we could do about it."

"Maybe there is. We have money, and money is power!"

"We don't have enough money to take on the French Army."

"I'm going to do something. I don't know what it is yet, but I'll do something. A person can't stand by and let horrible injustices be committed without doing *something*."

"Death to the Jew!" the Marquis de Morès said that night as he, Count Esterhazy, and Edouard Drumont celebrated Dreyfus's downfall with champagne toasts in the offices of Drumont's *La Libre Parole* (which had been partially financed by the Jesuits).

"Death to the Jew!" chorused Drumont and Esterhazy as the three men clicked glasses.

"I heard a good joke this afternoon at the club," the Marquis went on. "Someone said that Dreyfus must have been worrying about his tailor bill when they ruined his uniform."

"I'll put that in tomorrow's paper." Drumont chuckled.

"By the way, guess who was there, watching today?" the Marquis said. "The two Americans, Johnny and Rachel Savage."

"Her!" Esterhazy snorted. "The damned bitch threw me out of her house when I tried to get money from her."

"Well, we may be able to get some revenge for you," the Marquis said with a smile. "The Rothschilds are lying low about Dreyfus, but from the look on Mrs. Savage's face, she sympathizes with the traitor. She was married to a Rothschild once. I'll keep an eye on her. We may be able to get a lot of useful publicity from the Jewess from New York." He chuckled. "I almost cut off her husband's balls once. A pity I didn't do it. They have a pretty young daughter named Brook. Yes, it's a definite pity."

Such a dark look came over the Marquis's face that even Esterhazy and Drumont were a bit chilled.

34. IT WAS SEVERAL MONTHS BEFORE RACHEL FIGURED out how she might help the Dreyfuses. In the meantime, Johnny had gone to Rome to see his mother and set up the opening of a Rome branch of the bank, for the Paris branch had been a success, and Justin was talking about a London branch as well. When Johnny returned to Paris, Rachel told him she was going to pay a call on Mme. Dreyfus. She had read in the newspapers that she had been refused permission to go to Devil's Island at least to be near her suffering husband.

"Just try and be careful," Johnny said. "I've heard that she gets hecklers from time to time. If you were spotted going in to see her, it might be bad for you."

The next day, she took a cab from Neuilly into Paris to the rue du Trocadéro, where the unfortunate Captain Dreyfus had once lived happily with his family. Telling the cabbie to wait for her, she went to the front door and rang the bell. After a moment, Mme. Dreyfus answered the door. She was a small, birdlike woman who looked haggard.

"Yes?" she said.

"My name is Rachel Savage. I wondered if I could talk to you? I'm convinced of your husband's innocence."

Mme. Dreyfus looked nervously out at the street. A few pedestrians were strolling by.

"Come inside—quickly," she said. "There are usually reporters watching this house. You wouldn't want them to know you came to see me."

Rachel obeyed, hurrying into a small foyer as Lucie Dreyfus closed the door.

"You're the American?" she asked, leading her into the parlor. "The one who was married to a Rothschild?"

"Yes. How did you know?"

"I've read about you in the papers. Sometimes they write about something else beside my poor husband. May I get you some tea?"

"No, thank you."

After the two women had taken seats in the cluttered room, Rachel said, "I read that the War Department turned down your request to join your husband."

"Yes. I thought they would, but I felt I had to try. The poor man writes me that he is being held in the most terrible conditions. Of course, one could hardly expect Devil's Island to be pleasant, but they're being inhumanly cruel to him. It's almost as if they're afraid he'll escape, which is impossible. You know, the government had abandoned Devil's Island as a prison because the conditions are so unbearable. It was taken over as a leper colony, but even the lepers couldn't stand it and left. But there is my poor husband. He says the heat is ghastly. He's kept in a stone hut and watched day and night by two guards. He's never let out except for a daily walk, and then no one is allowed to talk to him." For a moment, Rachel thought the woman was going to burst into tears, but she brought herself under control. "It's inhuman," she said. "And he is, as you say, innocent. But you are kind to tell me you believe in him. There are not many people in France these days with the courage to come to this unfortunate house."

"I came because I wanted to help, if I can," Rachel said, opening her purse. She pulled out a check. "I have no idea what your finances are, or what the legal expenses of your husband's defense was. But I thought this surely would be of some help to you."

She handed the check to Lucie Dreyfus, who looked at it.

"Ten thousand francs!" she exclaimed. "You are most generous, madame, but I couldn't accept this money. My husband's attorney has been paid, and we are not lacking for funds. But I appreciate your gesture. Thank you."

She handed back the check.

"I hope I haven't offended you," Rachel said.

"Oh no, it was very kind of you. The one thing my husband doesn't need is money. What he needs is vindication!"

Rachel replaced the check in her purse and stood up.

"You have no idea who the real spy is?" she asked.

"None. But someday he'll be found. I know that in my heart. Someday, my husband will be free."

Outside the house, a young man came up to the cab.

"Who's visiting the traitor's wife?" he asked the cabbie, pointing to the house.

"I don't know. Some woman from Neuilly. She's an American. Her name's Sauvage, I think. Or Savage. That's it, Mrs. Savage. Why?"

"Just interested," the young man said, jotting something into a small notepad. When he saw Rachel appear in the doorway with Mme. Dreyfus, the man, who was a freelance reporter, put the notepad back in his pocket and continued down the street.

That evening at seven, Rachel finished dressing in the second-floor bedroom of her house and looked in a full-length mirror, inspecting the ravishing gunmetal gray silk gown with puffed sleeves that she had bought from Monsieur Worth on the rue de la Paix. Around her throat was the diamond-and-emerald necklace Johnny had given her as a wedding present, with matching diamond-and-emerald pendants on her ears. Her black hair was pinned up in the prevailing Gibson Girl fashion, held in place by her diamond star. Satisfied that she looked her best, she put a pale pink chiffon scarf around her shoulders and went downstairs, where her carriage was waiting to take her into Paris.

A half hour later, the carriage stopped in front of the Ritz Hotel. She got out and went inside to the main restaurant, where she met Johnny, who had reserved a table for the evening: it was their custom to dine one night a week at the renowned hotel, whose food and wine, under the management of César Ritz, were the finest in the world. The dining room was filled with the rich and glamorous, but even the most jaded Parisian eyed Rachel with admiration as she was led to her table by the maître d': she was breathtaking. As she sat next to Johnny, the young American couple were without a doubt the best-looking people in the room, despite the fact that several of Paris's most notorious *grandes horizontales*, as the most beautiful and successful professional courtesans of the day were known, were also in the magnificent dining room.

Johnny's years in Paris had made him a passionate gourmet and a devotee of French cuisine, which, in that Escoffier era, was at its peak of richness, sauces seduced with cream and butter. After studying the enormous menu, he ordered as a first course a *Jambon Persillé relevé de bonne Moutarde forte de Dijon* with a Bourgogne Aligoté. As a second course, he ordered a *Loup Farci en Croûte Brillat-Savarin* with a *Pouilly-Fuissé*.

"No more," Rachel groaned, thinking of her waistline.

"Well, we'll look at the desserts later, after the cheese tray," Johnny said, handing back the menu to the maître d'.

They were halfway through the first course when a tall, distinguished-looking man in impeccable tails entered the dining room. He muttered something to the maître d', then came into the room, navigating the tables until he was standing in front of Johnny and Rachel. Then, the Marquis de Morès removed one of his white gloves and slapped it across Johnny's astonished face.

"I challenge you, sir, to a duel," the Marquis proclaimed in a loud voice that silenced the room.

Johnny jumped to his feet and slugged the Marquis on the jaw, sending him reeling backward onto the neighboring table.

"What the hell do you mean, you lunatic?" he yelled, his face red with rage.

The Marquis, holding his jaw, got back on his feet, the rear of his tailcoat smeared with the omelet he had landed in.

"Do you deny," he roared, "that your wife—that Jewess—visited the wife of the traitor Dreyfus today? You and she are collaborating with the man who has betrayed France to Germany, and you will answer for this infamy to me, sir! My seconds will call on you in the morning."

Then, as the stunned diners watched, he started out of the room, yelling: "I say to all true Frenchmen: do not do business with the Savage Bank across the Place Vendôme! Boycott the bank, for it is run by traitors to France!"

As a pride of waiters scrambled to clean up the mess at the next table, Rachel said, "Johnny, let's go!"

"No," Johnny said, sitting down again. "I won't give that maniac the satisfaction of ruining my dinner."

"But I'm a wreck!"

"Don't show it," Johnny said through clenched teeth. "Act as if nothing happened."

He smiled at the maître d', who hurried up to the table, looking shocked. "I am so sorry, monsieur," he gushed. "I had no idea . . ."

"It's perfectly all right," Johnny said in a voice loud enough for the whole room to hear. "Everyone knows he's crazy. The *jambon* was excellent, though perhaps a trifle too salty."

The other diners, many of whom were anti-Dreyfusards, burst into applause at this wonderful display of Yankee coolness.

"Darling, you were magnificent," Rachel said an hour and a half later as they returned to Neuilly in their carriage, "and I'm terribly proud of you. But the Charge of the Light Brigade was magnificent too, and most of them ended up dead. I hope you're not thinking of accepting his challenge?"

"Absolutely I'm going to accept it."

"Johnny, the Marquis is the best duelist in France!"

"I'm pretty good, myself."

"Oh please, be serious! I know you're courageous, and I love you for that, but this is senseless! If you won't think of yourself, think of me and the children. He's a killer!"

"Rachel, I have to fight the man. It's not only to defend your honor, though that certainly is the main thing . . ."

"I don't care for my honor!" she exclaimed.

"Well, I do. And I care for my reputation, as well as the

bank's—I mean, if I refuse him, every anti-Dreyfusard in France will call me a coward, and God knows what it will do to the bank's business. I'm worried enough about his calling a boycott of the bank, but we'll see in the morning if that has any effect. But it's more than that. You yourself said someone has to do something. You tried by offering help to Madame Dreyfus. Well, if I take on this anti-Semitic bully, maybe that will help the Dreyfuses too. Besides, I owe him for what the bastard tried to do to me in Dakota—not to mention what he did to poor Kitty Kincaid. I owe him one for my father too."

Tears were streaming down Rachel's face as she clutched his arm.

"Oh darling," she whispered, "I love you so! And everything you say is right. But please don't do it! Please! You said we should stay out of this whole mess . . ."

"Well, we can't. We're in it now, for better or worse."

"But I'm afraid!"

He kissed her.

"You know something?" he whispered. "So am I."

It was late in the afternoon New York time when Justin's carriage pulled up in front of Hildegarde's Fifth Avenue mansion. Justin got out and hurried to the door. After a moment, the butler let him in, telling him that Hildegarde was in the drawing room. Justin went directly to the room overlooking the Avenue and Central Park, where Hildegarde was reading a book.

"Dear Justin," she said, smiling as she put the book down. "How nice to see you. How are you?"

"I'm extremely upset," he said, coming over to give her a kiss on the forehead. "I just received a cable from Johnny. He tells me the Marquis de Morès challenged him to a duel in the dining room of the Ritz—of all places!—and the young fool is going to fight him! I can't believe how idiotic this is! Here we are, almost in the twentieth century with telephones and electricity—and my son is fighting a duel like something out of the *Three Musketeers*!"

"Why did this Marquis challenge him?"

"Apparently, Rachel tried to help Madame Dreyfus."

"Ah, that deplorable situation in France. Well, then, I can understand why Johnny was challenged. And I must say I admire him for fighting this despicable Marquis."

"But he'll probably be killed! The Marquis is the best swordsman in France! He's killed lots of people! I can't believe this is happening. I'm sailing to Paris tomorrow. I'll be too late to stop him, but at least I can be with Rachel and the children if . . ." He stopped a moment, trying to control his emotions. "Oh my God, if he's killed—!"

Hildegarde reached out and took his hand.

"Justin, I've known Johnny all his life," she said. "All his life he's been trying to fill your shoes. They're very big shoes to fill, you know. You're a quite formidable father to have—I never have envied Johnny. He went out West to try and duplicate the adventures you had when you were a young man in China, and that didn't work out. He's had to be in your shadow and dear Ben's at the bank. His first marriage didn't succeed. But now, he's fighting for something important. I think it's quite wonderful. If he fails at this, well, he will die a man. But I'm not so sure he'll fail. Rachel has written me how hard he's been training over the years. She says he's stronger than he's ever been, so this odious Marquis may well have met his match."

Justin was staring at her.

"I never thought of it that way," he said, quietly. "How wise you are, Hildegarde. And I hope you're right. But I'm still going to Paris in the morning."

The Paris papers carried the story of Rachel's visit to Lucie Dreyfus the next morning, the anti-Dreyfusard papers playing up the story more than the Dreyfusard papers. But, predictably, the anti-Semitic *La Libre Parole* blew the story out of all proportion by screaming this headline: "American Rothschild Visits Mme. Dreyfus: Do Jews Plot World Domination?" The Marquis de Morès's fight with Johnny in the

Ritz Hotel was also duly reported, once again the anti-Dreyfusard papers making the Marquis out as the hero and Johnny the villain. When Johnny got to the bank that morning, a crowd had already gathered in the Place Vendôme. Policemen forced an opening through the crowd for Johnny to get to the bank doors. But while there were shouted threats and many clenched fists raised, by noon only three depositors had removed their funds, and it was becoming evident that the Marquis's proposed boycott of the bank was going to be a fizzle.

Johnny spent every spare hour training with his fencing coach, a Roman named Dino Moretti, who had watched a number of the Marquis's fencing matches and even refereed one. "The Marquis has extremely good footwork," Dino said, "and is very strong, physically. He's a very aggressive fencer, good on the attack. Are you using saber or épée?"

"I'm choosing the épée because the Marquis is taller than I, by about an inch."

"Yes, I think that's wise. Now, you're right-handed, but the Marquis is left-handed, which gives him a certain advantage because you, like most fencers, are used to right-handed opponents. First rule: don't turn sideways!"

"Good. I'll remember that."

"Don't attack deep to his right side. His quarte-parry will open you up to ripostes to neck, back, and flank. When you guard/invite sixte, keep your hand fairly high and forward. Avoid pulling your arm back. And keep your distance!"

They were on the second floor of the fencing school. Now Johnny and Dino put down their face masks, saluted each other, and Dino said, *"En garde!"* He attacked Johnny with his foil in his left hand. Johnny took his advice and parried sixte.

The two men fenced for an hour, after which Johnny removed his mask and wiped the sweat off his face.

"Have you chosen your seconds yet?" Dino asked.

"I'd like you to be one, if you would."

"I'd be honored."

"And my Cashier, Edmond la Motte, will be the other. I

expect the Marquis's seconds will show up at the bank this afternoon. So what do you think, Dino? Do I have a chance?"

"Yes."

"Would you bet good money on me?"

"Well . . ."

Johnny laughed, rather nervously.

"I take that back," he said. "You don't have to answer."

Johnny was honest enough with himself to admit he was nervous about the duel, which the seconds of the two parties agreed would take place the next morning in the Bois de Boulogne at eight o'clock, the Bois being the favored locale for duels. Johnny was a good fencer, but he had always fenced with face masks, proper protection over his body, and buttoned tips. The impending fight with the Marquis was without any protection at all and was a duel to the death, something the Marquis had experienced numerous times. To face the best swordsman in France with one's life on the line was a daunting experience: just the previous month, a champion German fencer had been killed when an épée pierced his face mask and went directly through his right eye, coming out the back of his skull. Johnny ate dinner that night knowing the probability was that within a few hours, he might be dead. Rachel knew it too. She tried to make small talk, but her heart wasn't in it. Halfway through the meal, she started sobbing. Johnny got up and came around the table, hugging her.

"It's going to be all right," he said, soothingly.

"I can't help it . . . all this is my fault! This wouldn't be happening if I hadn't gone to Mme. Dreyfus! I should have stayed out of it. And now I may lose you!"

He hugged her tightly as she put her face on his arm and cried her heart out.

"It's not too late, darling," she sobbed. "You can back out. Let the Marquis say what he likes! Please . . . it's not too late."

Johnny kissed her, smoothing her hair.

"I'm afraid," he whispered, "it is too late."

"Oh God, I can't go . . . I can't watch . . . I'll stay here with the children."

"I may be the underdog, but you never know: underdogs can win."

"If you do . . . win, will you kill him?"

Johnny, who had been stooping beside her, now stood up.

"As to that," he said, "I don't know. But right now, it's the least of my worries."

35.   At seven-thirty the next morning, Johnny, dressed in a black suit and carrying his black leather sword case, opened the front door of his house in Neuilly and kissed Rachel, who looked ashen.

"I love you," he whispered. "For always and forever."

"And I love you," she whispered back, tears in her eyes. "And my prayers go with you, my darling."

He forced a tight little smile.

"When I come back," he said, "have a nice lunch ready."

He kissed her again, then went out to go to his carriage.

Fifteen minutes later, the carriage pulled up behind three other carriages at the Pré Catalan in the Bois de Boulogne, the enormous park to the west of Paris. It was a cool morning, with a light mist beginning to burn off. Johnny got out of his carriage and was joined by Dino and Edmond la Motte, a sandy-haired young man who was Cashier at the bank.

"The Marquis's over there under the copper beech," Dino said, quietly, indicating the gentleman in question who was talking to his two seconds, Comte Xavier de Ganay and Edouard Drumont, of *La Libre Parole*. "By the way, the grass is dewy. Be careful you don't slip."

"Yes, I will. So, what do we wear?" Johnny said. "I'm a little new at this game."

"You'll remove your jackets and roll up your sleeves. No gloves are allowed, or any other kind of protection."

Johnny opened his sword case and took out his épée, which was long and glistening. He handed it to Dino, then took off his coat, which he folded and gave to la Motte.

"My wallet's in the inside pocket," he said. "If something happens to me, would you get it to my wife?"

"Of course, Johnny. We'll take care of everything. And Johnny . . ."

"Yes?"

"May God go with you."

Johnny squeezed his arm a moment.

"All right," he said, "let's get this over with, one way or the other."

His seconds went over to talk with the Marquis's. Then Dino came back. "He's ready," he said. "Let's go."

The beautiful park seemed strangely silent and empty as the two duelists approached each other. De Ganay indicated the spot where they were to meet. The Marquis and Johnny faced each other, sword in hand. The Marquis smiled as he bowed. He said, "Good morning, monsieur. I hope you are ready for a little sport? It's a charming day for a duel."

"I have a question. Did you murder Kitty Kincaid?"

The Marquis's smile remained fixed as his eyes bored into Johnny's.

"As to that, monsieur," he said, "I'll answer that the moment before I kill you—or you kill me."

"Fair enough."

A coin had been flipped to judge which side should choose the President of the duel, and the Marquis had won, picking Comte de Ganay. Now the Comte stepped back as Johnny and the Marquis saluted each other by raising their swords.

Then de Ganay shouted, *"Allez, messieurs!"* And the duel to the death commenced.

The Marquis launched a fiercely aggressive attack, which Johnny had expected and was ready for, since Dino had told him the Marquis's strategy was to dispatch his opponent as quickly as possible, preferably in seconds. The Marquis had lunged from sixte, Johnny countered octave. The slender, lethally delicate blades clashed together, swirling swift and bright as lightnings, almost impossible to follow with the eye. Johnny realized within seconds that the Marquis was as fierce an opponent as his reputation, a man whom constant practice had given extraordinary speed and a technique as near-perfect as possible. However, Johnny also knew that no fencer is perfect, mistakes are always made. Johnny also was in top physical shape.

For the first few minutes, the battle raged on, Johnny counterattacking as often as he could, but so far, Dino and the others knew that it was the Marquis's game. Dino and Edmond la Motte, both of whom were genuinely fond of Johnny, began to despair.

And then, Johnny made a lucky hit, cutting the Marquis's upper left arm. As blood gushed onto his cambric shirt, which Johnny's sword had slit open, de Ganay called "time" and hurried up to the Marquis, tearing a handkerchief as a makeshift bandage.

"It's nothing," the Marquis sneered. "The American Jew-lover was lucky. This will be over in five minutes."

"Nevertheless," de Ganay said. Expertly, he tied the bandage around the Marquis's arm, then stepped back.

"*Continuez,*" he announced.

The two men were at each other again, their swords clanging. But Johnny now saw a ray of hope: the Marquis had lost blood. If he could hold him off long enough, he could tire him. A break in his superb swordplay must inevitably occur, and Johnny could hit him. Despite the cool weather, both men were soaked with sweat: the physical exertion was fiercely intense. And the Marquis was beginning to tire: Johnny could sense that his swordplay was not quite as fast. He was even making a few errors, enabling Johnny to assume the attack. The onlookers sensed that the duel was balancing out.

And then, Johnny, hopping back in an evasion, tripped over a tree root and fell on his back, dropping his sword. The

Marquis was on top of him instantly. He pressed the tip of his sword to Johnny's throat and smiled down at him.

"Well played, my friend," he whispered, panting heavily. "You're better than I thought. But, alas, you're not good enough. As I promised you, I will answer your question before sending you to God. Yes, I murdered Kitty Kincaid. The bitch—and your father—had cost me a fortune, and she deserved what she got. As, my dear Mr. Savage, do you . . ."

Johnny raised his right leg—the leg that had scored so many touchdowns at Harvard—and kicked the Marquis in the groin, hard. The man howled with pain, dropped his sword, and doubled over, holding his organs with both hands.

"Foul!" yelled de Ganay.

"Yes, I know," Johnny shouted, jumping to his feet and grabbing both his and the Marquis's swords off the grass. Panting, desperately out of breath, he waited until the Marquis had straightened before tossing him his épée.

"*En garde!*" he yelled, lunging at the Marquis with his fiercest attack yet. The Marquis parried and riposted, but the edge was definitely gone. A minute later, after fierce beating, Johnny scored a hit under his left arm, drawing blood a second time. As the Marquis staggered backward, he slipped on the wet grass and fell on his back.

Johnny was on top of him, his blade against his throat. The Marquis tried to kick him in the groin, but Johnny was prepared for this and was standing to one side, whereas the Marquis had been straddling him. The kick missed. The Marquis stared up at Johnny with defiant black eyes.

"Then kill me," he said. "Get it over with. I have led a good life."

"You've led a miserable life," Johnny said, hotly. "You're a murderer, a bully, and a bigot, and the world would be a helluva lot better off without anti-Semitic scum like you. But I'm not a murderer, and my honor is satisfied. So, keep on living. But just stay away from me and my family."

He removed his sword from the Marquis's throat and started back toward Dino and Edmond, wiping the sweat off his face with his sleeve.

"Johnny, watch out!" Dino yelled.

Johnny swiftly turned around to see the Marquis charging him with his sword, ready to stab him in the back. Johnny parried his thrust, then ran his sword through the Marquis's heart.

The Marquis grunted, staggered a moment, putting his hands to the sword as if trying to pull it out. Then he dropped to the ground, dead.

Silence for a moment as Johnny and the others stared at the Marquis's corpse. Then de Ganay came up to Johnny and extended his hand.

"Congratulations, monsieur," he said. "You did not exactly play by the rules, but neither did my former friend, the Marquis, when he tried to attack you from behind. If he had succeeded in killing you, I would never have spoken to him again. As it is, you have saved me the trouble. Good day, sir. I will arrange to have the Marquis's body removed."

A half hour later, an exhausted Johnny returned to his house, where he embraced an ecstatic Rachel in the doorway.

"Thank God, thank God!" she cried, kissing his face a dozen times. "Did you kill him?"

"Yes," Johnny said. "I wouldn't have, but he attacked me from behind. So, that's over, and I'm starving. What's for lunch?"

"I was so afraid, I forgot to tell Cook to make something."

"I can't believe it!"

"We'll go out," she said, kissing him again. "I'll take you to the Ritz. And this time, we don't have to worry about the mad Marquis interrupting our meal."

Eight days later, Justin arrived in Paris, enormously relieved to find his son alive. His first night in town, Johnny and Rachel entertained him at dinner in their house, after showing him the children. Justin was thrilled with Brook.

"What with Julie and Tim having children all over the place in Hong Kong," he said as he started his soup course, "and you two here in Paris, I'm becoming what you might call a professional grandfather."

"I can think of worse professions," Rachel said, with a smile.

"Since everything seems to be in good shape here in Paris," Justin went on, "maybe you and Rachel should start thinking about coming back to New York soon. I could certainly use you at the bank. It's your bank now—both of you. You're the future of this family."

"You're not thinking of retiring?" Johnny exclaimed.

"Not right away, but soon." He smiled, rather mischievously, his son thought. "I've put in my years being a solid citizen. Maybe it's time I became unrespectable again, like I was as a kid. Maybe it's time to start having some fun again."

"Why, my dear Mr. Savage," Rachel said, sounding purposely stuffy, like her mother. "I'm shocked! Whatever are you thinking of?"

"I think I'll go on to Rome in a few days and check out the bank there. And I'll pay a visit to your mother, Johnny. She writes me that she's feeling lonely." He smiled. "Maybe I'll go courting—at my age!" There was a twinkle in his eye.

Johnny looked thrilled.

"Oh Father, if we could only all get back together again! I'd be the happiest man in the world!"

"Yes, Johnny, so would I."

Look for the sequel to
The Young Savages

THE

NAKED

SAVAGES

Available in hardcover August 1999

PART ONE

THE PARTY
OF THE CENTURY

1. **"WELL, TOMORROW'S THE BIG DAY,"** RACHEL Savage said as her butler refilled her wineglass. "Or should I say the big night? With all the publicity this ball has gotten in the tabloids, I just hope it doesn't turn out to be a fiasco."

"Why should it?" Teddy Roosevelt said. He was sitting to Rachel's right in the dining room of the Savage's limestone mansion at Fifth Avenue and Fifty-fourth Street. Johnny Savage had bought the place from his parents when his father, Justin, moved to Rome to live once again with his wife, Fiammetta. "Personally, I think it will be a bully show."

"An expensive bully show," Rachel said, cutting into her lamb chops. "I can't believe the money the Bradley Martins are spending. It's rather vulgar, and after the depression this past winter, it seems particularly ill-timed."

"But darling," said Johnny Savage, who was sitting opposite his wife, "that's why Mrs. Bradley Martin is giving the ball. She told the newspapers she wants to give an 'impetus to trade,' and I quote her."

"An impetus to the wine trade," said Edith Roosevelt, Teddy's second wife, sitting to Johnny's left. "I read in the *Herald* that she's ordered sixty cases of 1884 Moët et Chandon. That's enough to float a small battleship. I agree with you, Rachel: it's all rather vulgar."

"Yes, Edith," said her husband in his high, squeaky voice, "but your nose would have been out of joint if we hadn't been invited."

Edith Roosevelt, who could be chilly and imperious on occasion, gave her husband a look that almost frosted his famous *pince nez*.

"Is it true, Teddy," Johnny said to his longtime friend and Harvard classmate, "that you're posting two hundred policemen and forty plainclothesmen on the streets around the

Waldorf-Astoria?" Teddy, had become the Commissioner of Police of the City of New York, and a rising star in the Republican Party.

"Yes, it's true."

"Then you must be expecting some trouble?"

"The Bradley Martins simply want to insure that there won't be traffic jams. After all, they've invited nine hundred people. That's a lot of carriages."

"Still," Rachel said, "two hundred policemen to handle traffic? If you ask me, the Bradley Martins must be a bit nervous."

"About some sort of Socialist or Nihilist demonstration?" Teddy said. "Well, yes, that's a possibility, I suppose. But I seriously doubt anything will happen. New Yorkers like a good show, the way Londoners like to watch a royal procession."

"Whom are you going as, Rachel?" Edith Roosevelt asked.

"Marie Antoinette, which I now think was probably a bad idea on my part. I can just hear someone say, 'I suppose Rachel Savage thinks we should all eat cake.' "

"Rachel, you're making too much out of all this," her husband said. "Personally, I think costume parties are silly, and so do most people. I know I'm going to feel silly in my costume."

"Which is what, Johnny?" Teddy asked.

"I'm going as Chief Crazy Horse."

Teddy Roosevelt guffawed, his laugh "an ungreased squeak" as once described by his mother. "A blond Indian?" he chuckled. "I say, Johnny, that's a bully idea."

"I'm wearing a wig."

"I thought Mrs. Bradley Martin specified costumes from European history?" Edith said.

"I hear J. P. Morgan's daughter is coming as Pocahontas, so why can't I be Chief Crazy Horse?"

"Well, you'd better wear a horse blanket, old man," Teddy said. "The weather says there may be a blizzard tomorrow night."

"Is your Marie Antoinette costume elaborate, Rachel?" Edith asked.

"Yes, I'm afraid it is. It's quite beautiful, actually. I had the final fitting this afternoon, they're shipping it to the Waldorf in a wooden crate that makes it look more like a piece of furniture than a dress."

The butler repassed the crystal decanter filled with 1886 Lafitte-Rothschild as the candlelight flickered off the magnificent vermeil candelabra. The candelabra had belonged to Rachel's first husband, the Englishman Felix Rothschild before he had been pushed off a cliff into the English Channel. His strange murder still remained officially unsolved.

However, everyone in New York who knew the story was certain who had committed the murder.

"Well," Teddy Roosevelt said, wiping his lips with his damask napkin, "they say it's going to be the party of the century. And since this century is about over, we might as well go out with a bang."

That evening, February 10, 1897, the beautiful eight-year-old boy stood at the window of his third-floor bedroom overlooking Fifth Avenue and watched through the whirling snow his mother, Rachel Savage, and his stepfather, Johnny, climb into their carriage on their way to the Bradley Martin ball. The boy's name was Cesare, pronounced *Chay-sar-ay*, in the Italian fashion, and he was the son of Rachel's second husband, the Italian-born Franco Fosco. How many times Cesare had been the butt of jokes and taunts by his classmates at school. How many fights he had initiated—and usually won—when boys would snicker and call his dead father "The Murdering Wop." For everyone knew—or at least, thought they knew—that Franco Fosco, a penniless but charming son of Fiammetta Savage's Roman lover, had insinuated himself into Rachel's graces—and then her heart—while she was still married to Felix Rothschild. And then, the story went, Franco had conveniently pushed Felix off a cliff so he could marry Rachel and get Felix's fabulous fortune, which he in fact did.

But Cesare knew it was a lie. He knew that his handsome father, whom he only dimly remembered, was not a murderer. Nor had he been involved in shady loansharking, as was also rumored. Even though Franco had been shot to death in Central Park by a young immigrant—the man called Fosco a "vampire" for charging exhorbitant "vigorish," or interest, on a five-hundred-dollar loan—Cesare was certain that was a lie, too.

His father was an honorable man, a gentleman. After all, their family was one of the oldest in Italy—a much better family than these nouveau riche Savages, whose money dated back only to the beginning of the century, when Justin Savage's father had founded a line of clipper ships trading with the Orient. And Justin—what was he? He'd been a pirate! All very exciting, perhaps, but hardly qualifying him as a gentleman.

Cesare had been adopted by Johnny Savage, but he didn't think of himself as a real Savage. He was an outsider. *But*, he thought, *I'll make it my own way. Someday.*

When his parents' carriage rattled off down Fifth Avenue toward the Waldorf-Astoria, he thought for a moment. Then, putting on his bathrobe and slippers, he let himself out of his bedroom, quietly closed the door, and started tiptoeing down the upstairs hall toward the stairs. His elder sister, Beatrice, and his half-sister and brother, Brook and Nick Savage, were all tucked in bed in their own rooms; Cesare had the house to himself, aside from the servants. He felt the knife in his bathrobe pocket, the knife he had "borrowed" from the kitchen that afternoon.

Reaching the stairs, he started down to the second floor. The house, built some twenty years earlier, had been modernized with electricity and telephones, and an electric sconce on the wall illuminated the stairs. When he reached the second floor, he walked down the broad hallway hung with gilt-framed paintings to his parents' master suite at the end. Letting himself in, he turned on the lights. His parents' bedroom, done quite beautifully in the style of Louis XVI, with paneled walls painted a delicate blue, was a thing of beauty which he loved—except for the fact that his mother, whom he adored, shared the big bed with Johnny, whom he loathed. He looked around a moment, listening. Hearing nothing, he crossed to the left where, he knew, a door led into his stepfather's dressing room.

He opened the door and turned on the light. The dressing room was long and narrow, with sliding mirrored doors for walls. He opened the door to the left, revealing a row of suits beneath which, on slanted wooden shelves, were neatly placed three dozen pairs of shoes, all with custom-made shoe trees fashioned from the same wood used for violins. Cesare knew that his stepfather was considered one of the best-dressed men in New York and was more than a little vain. He also knew that on the opposite side of the room were built-in drawers holding dozens of custom-made shirts, as well as racks of silk ties in bright array.

Pulling the knife from his bathrobe pocket, Cesare took the left sleeve of the first suit and cut it off with a savage slash. Then the right sleeve. Throwing them on the floor, he whispered:

"My father was not a murdering Wop!"

He moved on to the second suit and did the same thing.

"My father was not a loan shark!"

Then the third suit.

"My father was a fine gentleman, much better than you, Johnny Savage! My father was *better*!"

When he had destroyed six expensive suits, he looked at the pile of torn sleeves on the floor and burst into tears. Then, turning out the lights, he ran back up to his third-floor bedroom, locked the door, threw himself into bed and sobbed his heart out as, outside, the winter blizzard blanketed the great metropolis in snow.

"Have I told you lately that I'm madly in love with you?" Johnny asked as he twirled his wife around the ballroom floor of the Waldorf-Astoria Hotel at Fifth Avenue and Thirty-fourth Street.

"Not lately," Rachel said with a smile. "But I like to hear it."

They were waltzing to Victor Herbert's orchestra in the ballroom that had been decorated to re-create the Hall of Mirrors at Versailles. Six thousand mauve orchids and hundreds of feet of hanging asparagus vines were festooned around the cavernous room, though what mauve orchids and asparagus vines had to do with Versailles was anyone's guess. When Rachel and Johnny had arrived at the hotel in their carriage, the traffic was so jammed that it took them twenty minutes in line to get to the porte cochere. Then they were escorted upstairs to individual dressing rooms where hairdressers and fitters waited to help them into their elaborate costumes. In Rachel's case, the costume's designer had been there to help her into the extravagant eighteenth-century dress she had created, made of pink and white silk with a huge skirt adorned with seed pearls and blue silk bows. Rachel had put on a towering white wig, and she was wearing the diamond and emerald necklace and earrings her husband had given her for their fifth wedding anniversary. Then she joined Johnny, who had smeared his torso and face with brown stain and war paint and was wearing leather Indian pants and moccasins, as well as an impressive chief's headdress of eagle feathers. Together, this distinctly odd-looking, if handsome, couple went to the ballroom to wait in line yet again to be greeted by the hostess, who was dressed as Mary, Queen of Scots, presumably oblivious to that unfortunate lady's decapitated end, and her husband, dressed as Louis XV, seated thronelike before a Beauvais tapestry from one of their many homes, Mrs. Bradley Martin draped in French crown jewels formerly worn by Empresses Marie-Louise and Josephine.

Johnny, as he had remarked earlier, thought the whole thing was rather silly. But he couldn't help but be impressed by the thought that gathered in that ballroom on that snowy night were people whose total worth was probably well in excess of a billion dollars at a time when the average American family's annual income was less than five hundred dollars and the budget of the Federal Government was less than a hundred million dollars a year.

Johnny remembered what Mark Twain had written a quarter century earlier:

"What is the chief end of man?—to get rich. In what way?—dishonestly if we can, honestly if we must. Who is God, the one only and true? Money is God. Gold and Greenbacks and stock—father, son and the ghost of the same—three persons in one; these are the true and only God, mighty and supreme."

If Mark Twain was right—and he himself was caught up in the scramble for quick bucks—then God that night was at the Waldorf-Astoria Hotel.

But many of the poor New Yorkers shivering outside on the streets in the howling blizzard and watching this cavalcade of vast wealth, must have thought that the resident of the Waldorf-Astoria that night was not God, but rather the Devil himself. Steve Carson of the *Journal* watched the show from the sidewalks with Socialist disgust, then he went to a saloon to wash down his disdain with a beer.

The next morning, he looked at photographs of some of the guests that Mr. Hearst had printed in the rotogravure section of the *Journal*. He was amused by the picture of thirty-eight-year-old Johnny Savage in his Indian costume. Steve Carson knew that Johnny was blond, and a blond Indian was as phony as the entire Bradley Martin ball.

After changing out of their costumes and into their "regular" clothes, Johnny and Rachel drove home at four in the morning where they were admitted by a yawning footman.

"I guess it was a 'bully show,' as Teddy said," Rachel remarked as they climbed the stairs to the second floor, "but I'm glad it's over."

"And my feet are killing me."

She smiled and took his arm.

"But you're still the best dancer in New York. And the handsomest. By the way, you have a new admirer."

"Who's that?"

"The girl who designed my costume. She told me at the hotel as she was helping me in the dress that she thought you were extremely dashing."

"Ah well, what can I say? Women just fall all over me."

"But there's only one woman who owns your heart: me."

"Absolutely."

They reached the second floor and went down the hall, going into their bedroom and turning on the lights.

"Thank God tomorrow's Sunday," Johnny said, sitting on a chair to take off his shoes. "I can sleep in. I'm exhausted."

Taking off his tailcoat and pants, he went to his dressing room to hang them up. When he turned on the light, he looked at the floor.

"What the hell is this?" he almost yelled.

"What's wrong?"

"Look—someone cut the sleeves off a bunch of my suits! One, two, three . . . my God, six of my best suits! They're ruined! Who the hell . . . "

He stopped and turned to his wife who had just appeared behind him at the door and was staring at the torn sleeves.

"Cesare," he said, softly.

"Johnny, don't jump to conclusions . . . "

"Who the hell else would do such a crazy thing except that son of yours? By God, I'll spank the living daylights out of him. . . . "

"No!" He started past her, but she restrained him. "Not now, it's late and he's asleep. Wait till the morning, when we can talk to him. There must be some explanation . . . "

" 'Explanation'? It's no great secret he hates my guts!"

"It will only make it worse if you attack him! Let's talk with him, reason with him . . . Believe me, darling, that's the wiser course. I know Cesare has angry feelings toward you because of his father, but everything I've read in the most advanced medical journals say that physical punishment can be counterproductive . . . "

"Did you ever hear 'Spare the rod, spoil the child'?"

"Johnny, please . . . there must be a better way. You know how much I adore that child, who's been so wounded at school with his friends saying those terrible things about his father . . ."

"They happen to be true!"

"Nevertheless, we have to be extra careful with Cesare, because he's carrying this terrible burden about his father. Now please, darling. Come to bed and cool off. We'll talk to Cesare in the morning."

Johnny, who was fuming, began to cool down as Rachel kissed him tenderly on his mouth.

"Oh, all right," he finally grumbled, taking off his tie. "But that kid had better straighten up, or I'll know the reason why."

At ten the next morning, Rachel wearing a light green negligee, came into the bedroom from the hall and sat on the bed next to her sleeping husband, whom she gently shook. Johnny gave a half-snore of surprise, more like a snort, then opened his eyes.

"What time is it?" he asked.

"Ten. I just had a talk with Cesare, and he broke down in tears and sobbed. He said he's so full of hurt about his father that he almost didn't know what he was doing last night. You know, he's a very injured child, and we have to do everything we can to help him heal his wounds. He's so beautiful and intelligent. He's outside the door now, and he wants to apologize to you."

Johnny sat up and rubbed his eyes.

"Couldn't he wait till I had some coffee?" he grumped.

"He's on his way to Sunday School."

"Probably trying to pray that crooked father of his out of Hell."

"Shh! Johnny!" she whispered. "He's right outside the door."

"Sorry. Send him in."

Rachel went to the door and looked outside. Cesare, looking handsome in a dark jacket with matching knickers and well-shined black shoes, his shiny black hair carefully brushed, was standing in the hall staring at his mother with his intense violet eyes that were so much like her own.

"Darling," Rachel said, coming over and taking his hand, "your father will see you now."

"He's not my father," Cesare said in a loud voice. "And I'm not trying to pray my father out of Hell, because he's not there! He's in Heaven!"

Jerking his hand out of his mother's, he ran down the hall to the stairs as Rachel rolled her eyes and sighed. Going back into the bedroom, she said: "He heard you."

"Yes, I gather."

"Oh Johnny, you have to try harder. You have to be more careful with him. Please promise me you'll try."

Johnny, looking sulphurous, got out of bed and started toward the bathroom.

"The damnable thing about this," he said, "is that the kid cuts up my suits, and I come out looking like the villain!"

He went into the bathroom and slammed the door.